A NOVEL OF SPINE-TINGLING TERROR

A Story of a Family That Loved . . . Then Cried . . . Then Screamed in Horror as They Watched What Happened In—

The House Next Door

A HOUSE THAT KNEW EVERY EVIL— AND KNEW NO END.

"HAUNTING . . . EERIE!"
New York Post

The House Next Door

Anne Rivers Siddons

BALLANTINE BOOKS • NEW YORK

Library of Congress Catalog Card Number: 78-18431

ISBN 0-345-28172-1

This edition published by arrangement with Simon and Schuster

Manufactured in the United States of America

First Ballantine Books Edition: November 1979

For Annalee

Prologue

PEOPLE LIKE us don't appear in *People* Magazine. We are not rich or about-to-be rich enough; we are not young and lithe and up-and-coming, though we are not old and venerable and full of endearing foibles and crusts of pithy wisdom either. We have no particular talents except, I think, a small talent for living fairly serenely and well most of the time. We have neither of us ever written—nor will we write—a first novel that sold for $1.5 million in paperback rights and caught the fancy of Robert Redford, who thought it would make a fine movie. We have formed no national organizations for minority groups or children with rare and baffling diseases. We have no children. We do have some few friends who have been in *People* Magazine, fringe celebrities, people who do odd things, but none of the biggies, none of the ones who elicit two columns of letters to the editors. We have some friends who are fairly eminent in other ways too—in their professions, in their social standings (though not a great many of those), in the amounts of their personal fortunes (not so many of those either). But we are not eminent. We are appreciators. It seems to serve us well.

We have a good house, but not a grand one, in a better neighborhood than we can really afford, because the down payment was a wedding gift from my parents. We have two cars, which is all we need since there are only two of us. Walter has the obligatory tobacco-brown Mercedes sedan, and I have the obligatory compact station wagon, in which I can comfortably carry the things I like and collect—some antique pieces of the Georgia Federal period, which do not at all fit the mood of my old, square, two-story brick

1

house but which I love; many plants; stones picked up out by the river for the rock garden I'm slowly building. It accommodates the cats and their carrier very well, too, on their frequent trips to the vet. They are both neutered, but race memory is strong and they tackle with relish any marauding tom who comes through looking for a fight. They usually lose.

We have careers that we like—or rather, Walter has a career; he's president of a medium-sized, good advertising agency which he formed seven years ago with his friend and then co-worker at a large, exceedingly dull advertising agency. Charlie and Walter have done well, and they are under no illusions about the agency, either that it will set the world on fire and win Clios every year or that it will fold and leave them jobless at the mid-life crisis. Kennedy and Satterfield, Inc., is right for them. It will grow but not too much. It has kept us comfortable.

I do free-lance public relations for a few loyal and fairly prestigious accounts, people I've known since I came to the city fresh out of Vanderbilt with an English degree and a burning desire, not to write the Great American Novel, but to work in a public relations agency. I did, for eleven years, and became accomplished enough at it to have a title on the door and a Bigelow on the floor, as it were, and my own secretary, and when I left the agency I shamelessly took three or four of my favorite small accounts with me. I can handle them in about three days a week, and I have the rest of the time free to pursue my own interests. They are self-indulgent, leisurely interests, and I figure I've paid for my right to them. I would not be content if I didn't do some sort of work. Happily, I am good at what I do.

All this is by way of saying that we are fairly ordinary people, Walter and I. Not the norm, maybe; I think we add up to something quite graceful and special, something that both enriches and adorns the small world we live in. Our friends say so. But not, surely, the stuff of *People* Magazine.

And yet there we are, this week, Walter and I. Sitting on the white wrought-iron patio chairs, looking just like what we are—mildly affluent people in their

2

middle thirties, well and casually dressed, tanned from a summer of not-so-good tennis at the club, pleasant people who like their lives and appear to love each other. Two people leaning a bit forward, looking across a lawn that doesn't appear in the photograph to a house, a house built on a pretty, hilly, wooded lot next door, which doesn't appear in the photograph either. But the house is the reason we are there. The house next door is haunted, and I am the one responsible for all the publicity. I called the local *People* correspondent and told him my story, and I suppose he thought I was just nut enough to warrant checking out. After he did, he thought it was a good story. He thought his editors would like it. And he undoubtedly thought I was an aggressive, faintly mad, publicity-seeking, middle-aged housewife with nothing to do and a house next door that did, admittedly, have some pretty odd things going on in it.

It doesn't matter what he thinks or what other people think. Not any more. Our friends are going to think we have taken leave of our senses, and we are going to lose many of them. This is the sort of thing that engenders mild teasing or pleasurable gasps of not-quite-believing fear when it is kept within the bounds of the group. It is something else entirely now that we have spread it out for all the world to see. That isn't done in our set. It lacks taste, and though we don't use the word, class. Worst of all, we have believed the unbelievable and spoken the unspeakable. Yes, we will lose our friends. We cannot worry about that either.

For the Harralson house *is* haunted, and in quite a terrible way. And it is up for sale again. We're telling as much of the story as we feel is necessary—but by no means all of it—to warn people about it. We took this way because we know by now that no reputable straight news medium will give us air time or column space and we wanted to reach as many people as possible as fast as possible. We can document just enough of the story to intrigue *People;* we do not try to explain it. We have a theory of sorts, but that is beside the point now.

We know we run the risk of attracting people to the

house; there is a certain type of person who, God help him, will come in droves to see the house, will want to buy it perhaps. These people we will try to see and warn on an individual basis, as they come. We will keep watch. The agents will loathe us, of course, and will tell these people that we are crazy, but we will keep on. Perhaps someone will sue us—we are not sure who exactly, since the people who lived in the house until a month ago are dead now. We notice that a different realty firm is handling the house this time. That doesn't surprise us. It's been a different firm for each sale. Eventually, we hope, no reputable firm in town will touch the house and it will be quietly taken off the market.

But until that happens we will try to get to everyone who comes to see the house, and we will tell them whatever we need to tell them to drive them away. If the article in *People* leads to more publicity—and this sort of thing usually does—we will welcome it and use it, and we will tell again about the house. And again. Walter thinks it is probable that he will have to pull out of the agency, to sell his interest to Charlie. The agency will suffer from this if he does not. Thirty people's livelihoods will be in jeopardy. I know that I will lose my clients. Two have left messages with my answering service for me to call them since this morning. We have a few stocks, some savings, other investments. Charlie's offer will be generous. We can live quite comfortably for as long as it takes.

If we find that all our efforts have failed and someone buys the house, we shall set fire to it and burn it down. We will do this at night, before it is occupied. In another time they would have plowed the charred ground and sowed it with salt.

If it should come to that, I do not think we will be punished.

I do not think we will be alive long enough.

4

PART ONE

The Harralsons

Chapter One

CLAIRE SWANSON from two doors up was the first one to tell me about the Harralson house. She and Roger have lived in the yellow Dutch colonial for years, far longer than we've been in ours. Claire is square, sturdy, and somehow comfortingly basic-looking—low to the ground, as she says herself. Built for stamina, not speed. Those solid hips, impervious to her regular tennis matches and her clockwork morning jogging expeditions around the little park that divides our street, have cradled and spawned three boys. Nice kids they are, in their middle and late teens. The whole street enjoys them and employs them regularly for yard work and the kind of nasty, heavy work you can't get anybody to do for you anymore. They do it cheerfully, coming in with a twang-thud of screened door for Cokes and midday sandwiches and to use the telephone.

"Hi, Colquitt," they'll say to me, looming large and rank-sweating from a morning of wrestling our ill-tempered old power mower up and down our terraced front yard. "You look like you're painted into those Levi's."

Since I have known them through broken arms and acne and sullen excursions to dancing classes, and since the Levi's do look painted on me, and I am proud that I still have the long, flat thighs to wear them, I don't mind the familiarities. I would mind them, very much, from almost any other boys their age. I am not a formal person, but I am rather private.

Claire and Roger are old money in the city, and the boys don't have to do the work. Their parents insist on it, however. In this very New South city, Walter and I have noticed that the Old South element of it clings to the substantial virtues of work, lack of ostentation, and a nearness to the earth that survives even in their manicured city neighborhoods.

"I don't see the point in all this plain downhominess," a vivid, restless woman whose husband's nationally prominent corporation had just moved its headquarters here said to me once at a ballet guild meeting. She was in linear black linen and Elsa Peretti silver on a swimming August afternoon in Florence Pell's legendary back garden, a coutured raven in a field of sundresses and pants and espadrilles.

"I mean, what good does their money do them? I know they have it—my God, Carl says some of them could buy and sell Fairfield County. But I haven't seen live-in servants or a driver since I left New York. They keep going to *Europe,* for God's sake, if they go anywhere at all. They don't have boats. If they have summer places, they're down on that God-forsaken, potty little island you all are so insane over. I haven't seen one single piece of fantastic jewelry. They send their kids to *Emory;* can you name me one kid in this town who goes to Harvard or Yale or Vassar? They go to the grocery store. When they go out at night it's to that mausoleum of a club. Why have it if you don't have any fun with it?"

I suppose she felt free to say it to me because she knew Walter and I are not natives. And we certainly are not in the same financial league with some of our friends. But we are *of* them precisely because we understand the way they choose to live. It is our way too; we find grace and substance, a satisfying symmetry and a kind of roundness to it. We like our lives and our possessions to run smoothly. Chaos, violence, disorder, mindlessness all upset us. They do not frighten us, precisely, because we are aware of them. We watch the news, we are active in our own brand of rather liberal politics. We know we have built a shell for ourselves, but we have worked hard for the means to do it; we have chosen it. Surely we have the right to do that.

At any rate, Claire and Roger Swanson are a satisfying unit in our world, and have been good friends to us ever since we moved here. So when I stopped the car at the mailbox on my way home from work that afternoon a couple of years ago—I hadn't left the agency then—and Claire hailed me from midway down the street where she was walking Buzzy, their elderly Schnauzer, I didn't walk halfway to meet her, as I would have with some of the neighbors to whom we are not so close. I shouted, "Come on to the backyard and let's have a sundowner. Walter's working late. Bring Buzzy."

"I have some news you're just going to hate," she said when she had leashed Buzzy to the leg of the wrought-iron table on our patio and had taken a long, grateful gulp of the bull shot I'd brought her. "Mmmm, that's good. You make good drinks. Roger says you're the only woman in town whose drinks don't give him diarrhea the next morning."

"Walter made me learn before we got married. It was one of the conditions. Living well is the best revenge—old Spanish proverb or something. What am I going to hate? Don't tell me . . . Eloise is pregnant again."

Eloise Jennings, in the gray Cape Cod across from us and catty-cornered across from the Swansons, had four children under the age of eight, two in diapers, and a front yard full of Day-Glo-colored plastic tricycles and wading pools and swing sets. They were whining, unattractive children who terrorized neighborhood pets and were apt to materialize in your kitchen uninvited, fingers in noses, looking into your refrigerator. Walter and I are very fond of some children, but not across the board, not as a species. No one on the street was very fond of the Jennings children. Or, if the truth were known, of the Jenningses. The house was his family home; they had been substantial people who had died and left the house to Semmes Jennings before we came. He was a broker downtown, and a posturing bully. Eloise had been his secretary.

"Probably," Claire said, licking salt off her upper lip. "But that's not it. The McIntyre lot's been sold and they're going to build a house on it."

"Oh, *shit!*" I wailed. I don't say that often, not like some of our friends, to whom casual obscenity is a not-uncharming habit. It's not that I disapprove; I just don't say it much. But this warranted a hearty "shit."

"Isn't it awful? I knew you'd hate it worse than anybody." Claire did not look sympathetic; one of the things I find amusing about her is a totally un-malicious malice. Besides, the McIntyre lot was not next door to her. It separated our house from the Guthries' to the left, and I have always loved it.

It is a peculiar lot, shaped like a narrow wedge of pie, broadest in back and tapering to a point at the street. It has—or did have—a steep ridge running like a spine down its length, thick with hardwoods and honeysuckle and tall old wild rhododendron. It is a shallow lot, stopping about on a line with our back patio, and a creek runs through it parallel to the street, bisecting it neatly into two halves. The same creek winds through our front yard and dips under the street, through a culvert, to reemerge in the small park that divides the street. Because of its narrowness and lack of depth, because of the ridge and creek, we had always been sure that no one could figure out how to put a house on it. Indeed, it had been up for sale at the same time our house was, and we had not bought it primarily because everyone on the street assured us that architect after architect had surveyed the site and pronounced it impossible to fit a house onto comfortably.

It had remained unsold. In our midtown neighbor-hood it was an oasis of wild, dark greenness, luminous in the spring with white dogwood and honeysuckle and rhododendron blooms, giving one the feeling of being cloistered away in a mountain retreat even though our street is only a block off one of the city's main thoroughfares. Our bedroom windows overlooked it and so did the unused upstairs bedroom that I planned to make into a office when I left the agency. Down-stairs, the kitchen and breakfast room looked out into its lacy bulk through prized old French doors. Outside, our patio faced it. The places, in short, where we lived, where we spent most of our time. Though the Guthries were just on the other side of the ridge, I could and did move freely and without constraint in that end of the house in my nightclothes, or in nothing, if I chose.

I have a rather shameful penchant for that. I like the feeling of air on my body. I loved the sturdy chuckle of the creek, the nearness of the woods, the squirrels and birds and chipmunks and occasional possums and raccoons that skittered and shambled there. Virginia and Charles Guthrie loved the lot, I knew, for the same reasons we did. They are, as are most of us on this street, people who treasure space and greenness and privacy. The lot was a buffer, a grace note. Any house there, any house at all, no matter how well done, would stare directly into the core of our living. No matter how careful the architect, trees would have to go.

"Are you sure?" I asked. "There've been a million rumors about houses going up there since we've been here, and none of them came to anything. Everybody says it's just not possible to build on it. Martin Sawyer, he's that *very* good architect who's Walter's tennis partner, he said it couldn't be done. Who told you? There's not a realtor's sign. We heard old Mrs. McIntyre took it off the market when it didn't sell, back when we moved in."

"Old Mrs. McIntyre has gone to her reward, whatever grim thing that might be," Claire said. "Her daughter in Mobile put it on the market. In fact, daughter sold it directly to somebody she knows here. And I know about it because whoever handled it at the bank told Roger about it."

Roger will probably be the next president of the third-largest bank in the city; at forty-eight he's been executive vice-president for eight years. His grandfather was president. His uncle is chairman of the board. Roger would know.

"Well, that doesn't mean they'll be able to build on it. You know what the architects say."

"There's one that says otherwise. Roger didn't believe it either, so he checked it out, and he says there are plans, sketches, elevations, the whole schmeer, already done. He says it can be done; he's seen the plans. The architect is some young hotshot right out of one of those eastern architecture schools; he's out to put us all in *House Beautiful*. It's very contemporary, from what Roger can tell, really a pretty good-looking

11

house, if you like that kind of thing. I know you don't, but I've often thought that all that open space and light and stuff . . . Well, anyway, up it's going, and pretty soon too. The people are anxious to get into it."

"Oh, Claire, oh, damn. That's going to mean bull-dozers and chain saws and red dust and red mud and men all over the place—they'll have to doze it. They'll have to take down trees . . . Who are the people, do you know?"

"No. Except that they're a very young couple, and her daddy gave her the lot and house for a baby present. Yep. Pregnant and with a rich daddy. I do know that she calls him Buddy and he calls her Pie. Roger got that from whoever handled the closing."

"Sweet God. Buddy and Pie and bulldozers and baby makes three. You know, I'd almost think about moving. I really would."

"No." Claire's broad, tanned face was serious; the gentle malice was gone. "This house and this street is right for you and Walter, Colquitt. You fit here like you were meant to be here—from the very first you did. You . . . enhance it for us, for Roger and me especially. Hang some curtains and start wearing clothes . . . oh, yes, I know you run around naked as a jaybird in there. I'm not going to tell you how I know, either. I'd do it myself if I didn't have three adolescent sex maniacs and old man Birdsong next door and did have a body as good as yours. Hang some curtains and grit your teeth, and meanwhile give me another drink, and then I've got to go home. You might even like the house, and I suppose it's barely possible that you might like Buddy and Pie. *God!* But even if you don't, it's not worth moving. It's only a house."

AFTER SHE left I finished off the watery bull shot in the pitcher and went upstairs, a trifle giddy with vodka and dismay, and took a shower. The bathroom that connects our bedroom with the room destined to be my office is large and airy, and the woods from the McIntyre lot, together with the ferns I've hung in the bank of high old windows, give the room an undulating, greenish, underwater light that I've always loved. It makes me feel like a mermaid, wet and sinuous and

12

preening in her own element. There had never been curtains; we had never needed them. Those rooms looked straight into treetops. "I'll hate whatever curtains I put up," I thought, toweling myself. "No matter if they're Porthault and cost the earth, I'll hate them."

I put on white slacks and a tee shirt and went, barefoot, down to the kitchen and started a salad. We'd have it with the half of the crab quiche I'd made for Sunday brunch, which I'd frozen. I put a bottle of Chablis into the freezer, made a mental note to myself to take it out in half an hour, and then, on impulse, stuck a couple of glasses in the freezer and mixed a pitcher of martinis from the Russian vodka Walter had brought home—smooth, silky, lovely stuff. Why not. Why not, indeed? It's Friday. Weekend coming up. Long, lazy, golden weekend. We'll drink to that.

"We're drinkin', my friend, to the end . . ."

Aren't you the lugubrious one, though, Mrs. Colquitt Hastings Kennedy, sozzling martinis and weeping over a piece of ground that doesn't even belong to you, I told myself. But it does, I said back. It's more mine than it will ever be theirs, these dreadful, faceless Buddy and Pie people and their awful, faceless baby. I looked out the kitchen window at the piece of ground that did not belong to me, settling itself into the fast-deepening green darkness that seemed to well up from the very earth of it. My mini-mountain.

The headlights of the Mercedes swung across the kitchen and stopped, and went out. I heard the nice, solid *thunk* of its door closing and went out onto the back porch, cats eeling around my ankles, to meet Walter.

He would not yet have heard about the house next door.

Chapter Two

BUDDY AND PIE did not remain faceless long. We had
faces, last names, and nearly intact genealogies for
them both the very next day. It had been a perfect
summer Saturday, one of those blue, crystal-edged
days you occasionally get here in late August, when
the thick, wet heat lifts for a small space of time and
there is a portent of October in the air. We had drunk
the pitcher of martinis the night before, and another,
and ate the quiche quite late, sitting in the screened
part of the patio and listening to the crickets and the
ghostly nighttime dissonance of the katydids from the
woods behind our house and on the McIntyre lot. We
had talked about the house-to-be, and what it would
mean to us and the way we lived, and Walter had
made me feel a little better about it.

"We've always known it might happen one day,
Col," he'd said. "Don't prejudge it, or them. Maybe
there's a way to build in and around most of the trees,
and nobody in their right mind would take down those
rhododendrons at the edge there. They'll make a good
screen. Besides, they're much younger, they'll have
their own friends. A tiny baby can't be all that much
of a nuisance. And you're not home in the daytime.
You won't be bothered with the noise and mess."

Walter is the pragmatic one of us. He is my anchor;
I am, he says, his wings.

"I won't always be at the agency," I'd said
mulishly. "I want to try it on my own in a couple of
years. You know that. I've showed you what I want
to do with the upstairs bedroom for an office—it's going to look right smack down their throats, and I've
so looked forward to having all that green right out

14

my window when I'm working. Like a treehouse—oh, I *wish* we'd bought it when we bought this house!"

"Well, so do I. But we didn't have the cash for it then and it's too late now. Hang some curtains and you can still go naked from dawn till midnight. I'll have to divorce you if you give that up."

"That's what Claire said. But she's used to having people all over her. I just don't *want* to be knee-deep in people for the rest of my life."

"You're spoiled," he said.

"So are you."

"And we'll keep it that way. I promise. That's what we're all about."

The next morning, feeling pleasantly heavy-limbed and a bit frail from the vodka and wine, we skipped our regular tennis match and did the sort of groceries-dry cleaner-drugstore chores that I don't really mind. We do them together usually, and it's one of the small, adventurous rituals around which we have built our life together. We had a late lunch at one of the pretentious little patio-type places that have sprung up around town, where the consciously chic young gather in their flocks for Bloody Marys and brunch and lunch, to show off their new Saturday clothes and see and be seen and map out the remainder of their weekend. Unencumbered by small children, we are able to do that when we choose, and weekends are good times for us. We feel grateful not to be trapped in the rites of the very young, and are able to enjoy their sleek health and preenings without envy because we have what we want together. We are not out of place among them; neither are we of them.

After lunch we saw an Ingmar Bergman matinee, which we did not especially enjoy—we like his earlier films better—and came home about four. Walter laid my latest batch of river stones into the steep bank destined to be my rock garden, and I took shears and a Mexican straw basket and went to thin out the zinnias. After we had finished, Walter made gin and tonics and brought them to the patio, and I thrust the glowing armful of zinnias into a bucket of water and set them on the round table, admiring the rowdy extravagance of them against the green of the lawn and woods. Comfortably tired, we stretched our legs and sipped our drinks and listened to the pitter of the lawn sprinkler.

"Do we have to go to that thing of the Parsons?" Walter asked.

"Not really if you don't want to. It's going to be so big they'll never miss us. Would you rather stay home? Only I didn't thaw anything for dinner."

"What I'd really like to do is go out and get the sloppiest, biggest pizza in the world and bring it home and watch the late show. I've got a tennis match at eight o'clock in the morning. I really don't want to go stand around and drink all night."

"Consider it done," I said, and looked around as a gray Mercedes purred into the driveway.

"Who the hell is that?" Walter said, frowning.

Three people got out of the car and came toward the patio with the apologetic smiles of people who aren't sure of their reception. A tall, pretty blond girl in a pink linen pantsuit, her hair tied back with a hank of pink yarn. A slight, moon-faced young man in stiff new Levi's and a stiff new blue work shirt. And a tall young man, only slightly older, with brick-colored hair to his shoulders and a wiry bush of red beard. His denims were faded to milky blue, worn soft and thin. A faint bulge of pregnancy lifted the jacket of the girl's pantsuit, and she walked with the ancient backward tilt of a woman adjusting to an un-accustomed front weight.

"If I had to guess, I would say that is the famous Buddy and Pie. Our new neighbors. I have no idea who Vincent Van Gogh there is," I said, and we rose and went to meet them.

"This is really awful, isn't it? Just to drop in on you people this way. But I told Buddy you all really ought to know what you're going to have to put up with—and your house looked so pretty and peaceful, and I said, well, they've just got to be *super* people to live in a house like that, and so we just took a chance you wouldn't simply *hate* us for barging in on you like this . . ." The girl said it in a light, fluttering rush, coming toward me with her hands extended, smiling the smile of one who has never been rebuffed in her

16

life. There was a tangle of gold bracelets on her slender wrist and a startling, enormous diamond on her left hand along with a diamond wedding band.

"I'm Pie Harralson," she said, taking my hand in both of hers. "This is my husband, Buddy. We've bought that gorgeous, gorgeous lot next door, and this wild man behind me is the architect who is going to build the most fabulous house in the world for us. Kim Dougherty. I know you're the Kennedys because your mailbox says so." She stopped, tilted her head to one side, crinkled her nose, and waited for us to respond.

"Walter Kennedy," said Walter, shaking hands with the silent, grinning Buddy and towering Kim. "And this is my wife, Colquitt."

I nodded and smiled. There was a small, stretching silence. Rasputin, our orange tiger cat, appeared from the depths of the McIntyre lot and came to curl around the girl's ankle, and she swooped at him in an ecstasy of joy. Razz backed off and looked at her flatly.

"What a *darling* kitty," cried Pie Harralson. "And he's been playing on our lot, yes, he has, *hasn't* he? I love kitties, we're going to get one when we move in and the baby comes. What's your name, you pretty thing? Will you come to my house and play with my kitty?"

Razz is by no stretch of the imagination a darling kitty. He turned his back ostentatiously to the girl, sat down, and began to wash his face. Pie Harralson looked at us, smiling. Silence spun out again.

Oh, all right, I thought crossly.

"His name is Rasputin, but we call him Razz," I said. "He's not very friendly, I'm afraid, but he isn't mean. We just heard last night about the lot being sold, and it's good to get to know you so soon. Won't you come have a drink with us? We were just having a gin and tonic . . ."

"Oh, no, we were just passing and thought we— Pie thought—I know you folks probably have plans," said Buddy Harralson rather miserably. His voice was a surprising deep bass.

"Aren't you darling to ask us! I think that would be

17

just super, if you're sure we're not keeping you from anything," said Pie. Her blue glance took in my old gardening pants and zinnia-stained hands and Walter's paint-spotted dungarees. Not-going-anywhere clothes.

"Nothing at all," said Walter. "If you'll forgive us for looking like Tobacco Road, we've got plenty of gin and tonic. Come on back to the patio and tell us about your house. *Your* house too," he said to Kim Dougherty, who nodded but said nothing.

We sat late on the patio, Pie Harralson burbling and crinkling, gesturing with her long hands and looking lovingly at the McIntyre lot—the Harralson lot now—as she described the house. Buddy Harralson loosened up a bit as the gin and tonics were refilled, and put in an earnest, booming amendment now and then to Pie's skittering stream of enthusiasm. Kim Dougherty drank steadily and silently and regarded them both with faint amusement and a sort of unwilling tolerance, and he looked frequently at the lot next door too. It was a measuring, far-off look, with nothing in it of Pie's proprietary love. The look reminded me of the guarded, preternaturally alert look a dog gives another dog he has just encountered before he has ascertained whether there will be calm or danger. Later, as full darkness began to fall, he spoke a bit about the lot and what he hoped to create there. He had a soft, clipped voice. It was obvious that he was a good architect.

We learned in the course of the evening that Pie and Buddy Harralson had both been born in the same small city in South Georgia and had been sweethearts —Pie's word—since the eighth grade, had gone off to the state university together, where Buddy had been a Kappa Alpha (all the guys from home go KA) and had made the dean's list in prelaw with some regularity. Pie had been Chi Omega (all the girls from home are), Kappa Alpha Rose one year, Homecoming Queen her senior year, and had made abysmal grades in Elementary Education.

"Daddy was fit to be tied over my grades," she confided. "But everybody knew I'd never teach school anyhow. I knew I was going to marry Buddy and have

18

babies and a *super* house way before he knew it, so what difference did grades make? I do volunteer work with the League now, but I guess I'll have to stop that pretty soon—are you in the League?"

I shook my head no and smiled. "I do public relations work; I stay pretty busy," I said, and hated myself for saying it. It is a degrading small thing about myself that I dislike intensely—not being a Junior Leaguer and still caring just a little that I am not. I was annoyed with myself for explaining to this child.

"I just bet you're fabulous at it too," Pie said. "You look like a career woman. But I'm real disappointed that you won't be home in the daytime. I know I'm going to get bored with just the baby to talk to."

"Colquitt's planning to quit and work at home before too long," said Walter, and I glared at him in the darkness.

"Oh, well, that's all right then. I'm not the utter child that Mother and Daddy and Buddy think I am—and Buddy's mother, of *course*—but I *will* feel better with, you know, an older woman close by. Not that you're *old*—oh, Pie, really, your mouth!" She gurgled at herself. "Mother and Daddy will feel better too. *And* Buddy's mama, naturally. They all wanted us to live at home, at least until the baby was a year or two old, but that's just so tacky; *nobody* stays in that town anymore. I told Daddy that if he'd buy me—us, I mean—the lot and house, I'd make friends with all the women in the neighborhood, and that's just like having your own family around you. Not that I mean to hang all over you, but I'm a real extrovert, and I love people, and friends mean so much to me. Do you have any children?"

"No," I said. "It's just the two of us." Her silent "why" hung in the air, but I did not explain.

Buddy, it developed, was a brand-new member of a large, prestigious downtown law firm, and planned to specialize in tax law.

"It's steady, and with this firecracker here and a new bambino on the way, I figured I'd leave the glamour stuff to the hotshots."

It was obvious that he adored Pie and was awed and bursting with pride about the baby, and even more obvious that there was family money waiting in the wings on both sides. Brand-new lawyers do not drive a Mercedes or give their brides two-carat solitaires. Most brides are not dowered with four-bedroom contemporary homes in our neighborhood.

"Daddy died when I was nine," Buddy put in, answering the unspoken question. "Mama raised me by herself, but he left her pretty comfortable. She's been generous helping us get started." Pie snorted in the darkness, and I guessed that there was dissension there. The mother of this good, stolid boy might well have been reluctant to relinquish him into Pie Harralson's darting, butterfly hands. I thought, wearily, that I would probably be the recipient of not a few mother-in-law horror stories in days to come.

Just before they left, Pie darted out to the Mercedes and brought back the house plans, and we spread them out on the table in the screened room, turning on the yellow overhead light. The house-to-be lay in a pool of radiance, as if spotlit. I drew in my breath at it. It was magnificent. I do not as a rule care for contemporary architecture, finding it somehow sharp and intrusive and demanding, in spite of the obvious virtues of air and light and ease of maintenance, of functional living space. This house was different. It commanded you, somehow, yet soothed you. It grew out of the penciled earth like an elemental spirit that had lain, locked and yearning for the light, through endless deeps of time, waiting to be released. It soared into the trees and along the deep-breasted slope of the ridge as though it had uncoiled, not as though it would be built, layer by layer and stone by stone. I could hardly imagine the hands and machinery that would form it. I thought of something that had started with a seed, put down deep roots, grown in the sun and rains of many years into the upper air. In the sketches, at least, the woods pressed untouched around it like companions. The creek enfolded its mass and seemed to nourish its roots. It looked—inevitable.

I looked at Kim Dougherty, who lifted his head from the drawings, his face a sculpture, and looked full into my eyes.

"It's beautiful," I said. "It really is beautiful."

"Yes," he said.

"Isn't it just the most fabulous thing you ever *saw?* Don't you *love* it?" Pie squealed, feeling the force of my approval in the darkness. "Isn't that the cutest thing, the way that balcony wraps around and hangs over the creek? That's going to be the baby's room, right there over the little waterfall. He's going to go to sleep right there in the treetops every night!"

"Let's hope the bough doesn't break and the cradle fall," Walter said cheerfully. I could tell he liked the house too.

"Right! Or down would come baby, cradle and all!" chortled Pie Harralson. "Oh, that's terrible! Nothing like that is going to happen to my baby. Not in this adorable house. Oh, Daddy's just going to *hate* this house! We haven't shown him the plans, and I'm not going to either. Nobody from home is going to see it till it's finished. Daddy wanted us to have something with columns. But I said, Daddy, I want something so fantastic that cars stop in the street just to look at it. I said, when my house is built, you're going to see the real me, you're going to see a side of your baby you didn't even know existed. And this house *is* me, but definitely. Oh, he's going to be fit to be tied!"

In the darkness I felt rather than saw Kim Dougherty flinch.

They stayed for the space of another drink, and then Pie rolled up the drawings and Buddy shook hands solemnly all the way around, and Kim nodded and said thank-you-for-the-drinks-I'm-glad-you-liked-the-house, and they got into the Mercedes and drove away.

WALTER WENT out and got a fine, fat pizza crowded thickly with what he calls "all that good ginney shit," and we ate it in bed and watched a rerun of *Night of the Hunter*. It is eerie, beautiful, poetic, disturbing, and I have always loved it. We made the sort of slow, sweet, deep love that seems to belong to summer nights, different from the muscular, blanketed love of winter. It is always good, always rich, this thing we have together. I always think, when it is over and we lie ebbing in each other's arms, that there should be

21

something wrong between us, something basically abrasive and thin and sour. It is uncanny what we have built with each other, all the areas of accord and pleasure we have nurtured. Sometimes I feel that we are very selfish, very unsharing of the whole to which we add up. But from the very beginning we knew we did not want to dilute it. We have no children for that reason. We are sufficient. It often frightens me, and I sometimes feel guilty that we are really, basically, only involved with each other. I think we should give more to the world, somehow. Perhaps one day we will give more, perhaps we shall have to. I think so, soon now.

"What do you think?" Walter said, late into the night.

"I think the house is . . . really special. I think it's probably a great house. But I can't imagine those two simple-minded children wanting a house like that. I don't know about Buddy-boy, but Pie-baby has no idea in the world what she's got in that house. Just no idea."

"Of course not. She's trying to get a rise out of Daddy. Literally, probably. Oedipus and all that. It's as good a way as any to screw Daddy. That poor son-of-a-bitch husband of hers would obviously live in an igloo if she wanted it. And if Mama let him. Did I detect a subtle little nuance there?"

"Not so subtle," I said, watching the moon shadows stretch and dwindle and stretch again into our open windows. Razz and the gray tom Foster Grant were heavy, sleep-sodden mounds at our feet. "I like that architect too. I think he might be an authentic, working genius. Why on earth does he put up with them, do you suppose? He must know they don't understand that house."

"Where else is he going to get clients with the bread to build that kind of house? I don't think he gives a holy shit what they think of it. It's his house, not theirs. I bet he'd build it for KKK headquarters if they paid him for it. He just wants it up. Couldn't you tell?"

"I guess so. Darling, are you just going to hate having them for neighbors?"

"No, because I don't plan to see them except maybe once a year, at Christmas, like your mother. What do

22

you think, that we've got to have them for dinner once a week? She could be a problem for you, though. I'll bet she's already got you pegged as a baby-sitter-confidante-mama-figure. It's obvious she's going to be somebody's little girl till she's eighty, even if it ain't Daddy's. God, did you ever see such a classic cheerleader in your life? I'll bet she's still got a drawer full of angora sweaters and charm bracelets. And money. If you're smart, Col, you'll cut her off gently and firmly as soon as you can. You're not my idea of somebody's wise old mother."

"Thanks for small favors."

Much later I awoke and heard an owl in the woods on the lot next door. We don't get many of them in the city; I could not remember the last time I had heard one. It was, for some reason, a truly dreadful sound. I lay listening to it, something wild and heavy uncurling in my chest. And I reached down carefully, so as not to wake Walter, and I tied a knot in the corner of the top sheet.

He rolled over and looked at me, propped up on one elbow.

"What are you doing?"

"Nothing."

"Yes, you are."

"If you must know, I'm tying a knot in the corner of the sheet. I heard an owl in the McIntyre woods."

"He doesn't care for our sheets, he's saying?"

"No. It's just something my grandmother always did. You tie a knot in the bedsheet when you hear an owl. If you don't, it means somebody is going to die."

"That somebody is going to be me, at eight o'clock on the tennis court, if I don't get some sleep. Go to sleep, Col. It's going to be all right about the house."

I did, finally, with the lost call of the faraway owl still in my ears.

Chapter Three

THE HARRALSON house got under way the day after Labor Day, and all through the slow, burning, dry autumn, yellow insect machinery crawled back and forth across the ridge, buzzing and gnawing implacably at the curve of it. Trees did go down; my heart squeezed painfully at each new gap when I drove in from work every afternoon. A culvert went into the creek, which docilely accepted its new channel and flowed on through our yard, its cola-brown water stained blood-red. A driveway was carved out, and straggled over the culvert. The keen of chain saws rang on the street day after day as the fallen hardwoods were sectioned and chained and borne away. All that fall, pink dust lay over our lawn and patio and driveway, filming the cars and sifting into the windows and puffing from the cats' coats when I brushed them. Annoyed by the shrieking invasion of their foraging grounds, they gave the lot a wide berth and stayed close to our house or deep in our back woods all day. They did not hunt in the evenings either, as they always had. They slept close to us in the den while we watched television, and planted themselves stubbornly at our feet when we went to bed, refusing to be ousted. If we did put them out and close the bedroom door, they scratched patiently at it until we let them in again.

"Sissies," Walter said one evening, trying to nudge Foster out the back door onto the patio. "Or snobs, maybe. They're as big snobs as you are, Col. They want nothing to do with the outlanders or their house, only they make no bones about it."

"The noise and confusion scares them," I said,

24

scooping up Foster and returning him to the haven of the lighted kitchen.

"They're not scared of hell itself," Walter said. "They're pissed off. I don't blame them. From the looks of those sketches of Dougherty's, I didn't think so many trees would come down or so much of the ridge go. I'm glad neither of us is here during the day. You'd probably go berserk and axe-murder the entire crew."

The crew was almost always done when I arrived home in the evenings, well before Walter did, their equipment littered along the desolated ridge like the discarded carapaces of megalithic insects. The raw earth looked shocking, like bleeding flesh, but to be fair about it, Kim Dougherty had not marked so many trees for death as it appeared when they first began to come down. Grudgingly, I had to concede that when the house was up and the foundation planted with shrubbery, the lovely woman-curves of the land would not be so badly altered after all.

"You won't even remember how it looked before when it's all up and ground cover is planted and some landscaping's done," Claire said to me one evening early on when she and Roger had walked over with a market basket full of jeweled late tomatoes from the Farmers' Market.

"I'll remember. But I'm not going to hate it as much as you'd hoped," I said. "It really is a beautiful house, or will be. It's the teeny-weeny baby Harralsons I'm going to have a hard time with."

"I saw them yesterday," Claire said. "Out climbing around all over that dirt, looking down in the foundation like the Holy Grail was down there. She looks like Shirley Temple knocked up. And he looks like Andy Hardy. He had her by the arm like she was going to have the child right there—though I guess it isn't too bright to go climbing around construction sites when you're—what? Five months? Six? I don't see a whole lot of them, though, thank God. But that bearded wonder is over there every day, almost all day long."

"Well, it's probably his first house. I guess he wants it to be perfect. I would too—something that spectacular."

"Are you turning modern on us, Colquitt?" Roger Swanson asked. He has always teased me about being born a hundred years too late. He told Walter once, late into a rather boisterous evening party in the Guthries' beautiful back garden, that I always reminded him of the Lady of Shalott. "Only he pronounced it like the onion," Walter told me. "Very much of the earth, is Roger."

"No, you know I'm too reactionary for that," I said. I like Roger, like his comforting bluntness, his deep and abiding sense of responsibility toward his family and his world, and his clumsy, earnest attempts at gallantry. He has a rare sweetness to him, a perfect foil for Claire's earthy briskness. Duck, their oldest son, is a carbon of Roger. The other two boys are a very satisfactory blend of both of them.

"I think it's the architect Colquitt really has a letch for," Claire said. "Fresh young meat. I see him over here all the time before you get home from work, Walter. Colquitt feeds him and plies him with your best stuff. Duck saw the empties in your garbage can the other day when he was mowing your lawn."

"Duck talks too damned much," I said, kicking her lightly. "Walter knows all about Kim and me. He gives his full approval. We made a deal. I said he could take that set of walking boobs he calls a receptionist to lunch every day if he'd let me get Kim Dougherty drunk every afternoon. It's working out just fine."

Actually, Walter did know about the friendship that had sprung up between Kim and me. "If I ever find concrete dust in the bed, I'll kill him," he said, but I knew he liked Kim too, and he often joined Kim and me for the late-afternoon beer or gin and tonic that had, somehow, become a ritual with us that fall. It *was* a friendship, would never be anything more. I have what I want and do not need the adulation of very young men, even though, I modestly admit, there have been some around my agency who have offered it. Walter has always known that.

It would never be anything less than a friendship either, and that pleased me. I like my relationships to be full, open, and well defined, and I had found a genuine friend in this quiet young man so in love with the house he was building. I think it started, really, with my response to the plans Pie showed us that first evening on the terrace. With the instinctive and uncluttered perception you often find in really creative people, he had known at once that I felt, at least in part, some of what he did for the Harralson house. He accepted it as his due, and we went on from there, instant equals. It is a trait you don't often encounter in the very young.

He had come over one evening just after I had driven in, not long after construction had started. He was red all over, a skin of dust and stain of earth blending into the red of his hair and beard. Even his old denims were red, and his heavy boots. I laughed spontaneously.

"Eric the Red, I presume?"

"Speaking. Or sneezing, as the case may be," he said, fanning helplessly at the effluvia of red dust that hung over him. "And speaking of presuming, I wonder if you'd mind terribly making a phone call for me. I need to talk to my partner, and I can't go up to the shopping center and call because I've got a guy coming in with a load of sand. I wouldn't bother you with it, but I'm scared to ring the doorbell next door. That lady looks like somebody just ironed her, and she always looks at me like she's about to call the police and the sanitation department when I see her out in her yard. I hate to think what all this dust has done to it."

I laughed again. Virginia Guthrie is a lovely, gentle woman, a true lady, and as immaculate at every waking moment as a mannequin—which she was when she was younger—but she *does* look starched and ironed, and she did indeed hate what the dust was doing to her garden. It's an incredible garden, invariably included on the city's glossiest spring garden tours, and I couldn't really blame her. Still, I knew well the slight flaring of those elegant nostrils, the nearly imperceptible lift of the delicate eyebrows.

"She won't bite you," I said. "She's a nice person. But, sure, I'll be glad to make a call for you. Only why don't you come on in and make it yourself, in the den, where you can be private?"

"I really couldn't, Mrs. Kennedy. I'd wreck your house. I'm like Pigpen in 'Peanuts.'" He grinned, a startling flash of white in all the redness. It was a child's happy, free grin. He had not smiled at all, that I remembered, during the evening we had spent together. He had hardly spoken. I liked him very much indeed all of a sudden.

"Tell you what. You sloosh off some of that dust at the faucet there, by the side of the patio, and I'll make your call for you, and then we'll have a drink. Or a beer if you'd rather. You must think we do nothing but sit on our patio and drink, but I promise we're really very respectable people and not out to lure young geniuses into sloth and degradation. Go on, you look dry as a bone, and the dust can't hurt the patio. It's already got your calling card all over it."

He didn't demur or assume the deferential coyness of someone you know would like to accept an invitation but thinks it seemly to hedge a bit, and I liked that too. He said, "A beer would really do the trick," and disappeared around the side of the house toward the faucet, and I took the grimy slip of paper with the number he had given me and went to phone his partner and tell him Kim would be back in the office about eight, if he wanted to wait and go over the Douglas specs. I opened a cold beer for him and made myself a weak gin and tonic and took them both to the patio with a basket of pretzels. He was tumbled loosely in one of the white chairs, face and hands the color of skin again, droplets of water glistening in his beard. He was looking at the Harralson house with the same level, measuring look I had seen that night in August.

"Looks like hell, doesn't it?" he said, drinking deeply of the beer. "I didn't realize how bad it looked from over here. You must have really loved that lot when it was wild."

"Yes. I really did. And I thought I'd hate the house and the poor Harralsons, and I wasn't all that fond of you either when I first saw you. I considered you the murderer of my private mountain and all my privacy. But the house is a lovely, lovely thing. It's going to make me happy just to look at it. It looks so . . .

organic or something, at least in your sketches. You wouldn't *maintain* a house like that; you'd feed and water it. You'd need to give it nourishment and love to keep it alive and healthy. I think that house will bring out the best of whoever lives there—the fortunate young Harralsons, in this case. I hope they'll love it properly."

"I'm glad you like it," he said, not looking at me. "I could sort of tell you did when you saw the plans, and understood it too. I've always felt that way about design—that first you plant something. The site, the ground will tell you what to plant. You plant it, and you raise it, and the hell with what the clients say they want. The house should be its own boss, and they should live by its rules, not the other way around. It's up to them to . . . make it grow, as you say. This house *is* its own boss. It *does* ask the best of you. That's good. I like that. Those poor, stupid children, though . . ."

"I'd say you were probably precisely one year older than those children," I said, amused. "And they love it. You know they do. They're so proud—"

"They don't know what they got. I couldn't care less. I wish somebody like you could live in it, but I wouldn't really care if it was Adolf Hitler and Eva Braun."

"That's almost exactly what my husband said— that it was your first project, and you'd build it for the KKK just so you got the chance to build it."

He gave me a sidewise look out of long light-gray eyes. "It's my first house, but it's not my first project. I had a couple of others while I was still in school, but they were never finished. That's one reason I'm hell-bent on getting this one up. Does your husband like the house?"

"Yes, he does. Very much."

"That's good. It's got two friends in the neighborhood anyway."

"Indeed it has, and it'll have more. Just wait till it's up and all the dust has settled."

We sat quietly for a while, drinking and looking at the Harralson lot, and out into our woods, dusty and used-looking now in the early autumn heat. Foster

29

Grant and Razz joined us, sedately, as if by appointment. Foster draped his length along the brick wall of the patio, and Razz arched himself once or twice against Kim's boot, and then put his leg over his head and began to lick the base of his tail with the loving self-absorption that drives me wild. I poked him with my toe.

"Playing the cello," said Kim, and I laughed again, with a certain joy, because that's exactly what Walter and I call it. I thought we had always known each other, Kim Dougherty and I.

"Aren't you awfully young to have an office and a partner?" I asked. "I thought young genius architects were supposed to starve in a garret and refuse to accept commissions that weren't true to their art and suffer in big firms till they could go out on their own."

"And blow up their first big project when it's defiled by Philistines. I know, I read *The Fountainhead* when I was in first-year architecture. Howard Roark I'm not. He was a first-class schmuck. If I insisted on people worthy of my houses—house—I'd have to shoot the Bobbsey Twins over there and go around like that old Greek with the lamp, searching the world over. Present company excepted of course."

"Coy and modest you're not, Mr. Dougherty."

"No, I'm not." He looked a little startled, as if the thought had just occurred to him for the first time. "Do you think I should be?"

"No. I'd think *you* were a schmuck if you didn't know what a great house you'd done. I just wonder what's going to happen to you when you get rich and famous and start to mingle with high society."

"I am already, aren't I?" he said seriously. "This street, I mean. You all. The guy up the street there is some kind of honcho at a big bank, isn't he? And I heard the guy down the street owns half the town, and the Coca Cola bottling company to boot."

I wrinkled my nose at him. "If we represent high society, God help the writers on the women's pages. There's some money around, but none of it is Walter's and mine. And none of us are very exciting."

"Real money usually isn't," he said.

"Spoken like a true Boston Brahmin."

"I guess I am, sort of," he said.

I looked at him, red and loose-jointed and large-knuckled. He caught the look and laughed.

"I know. I look like I ought to be slogging in a peat bog or shoveling sheep manure in Oklahoma. And for all I know, I should be. I'm adopted, and I don't have the foggiest idea who my real folks were. But my old man's as dug-in, fifth-generation New England as you can get and richer than hell. Although the family bread comes from manufacturing, so I guess they really aren't strictly above the salt. I think my dad's grandfather was one of the great robber barons; the rumor is that he worked women and infants fourteen hours a day for two cents an hour, by candlelight, or some damn thing. But Dad is as straight-arrow and full of the milk of human kindness as any guy I've ever known. He really is. He passes out the dough like it was going out of style, as long as it's for underprivileged minority groups and stuff like that. He won't part with a cent of it for what he calls highbrow shit —excuse me, Mrs. Kennedy."

"Colquitt," I said.

"Colquitt, then. Yeah, his fondest ambition was to be a lawyer, and he'd probably have been one of those storefront, legal-aid-type cats who starves happily all his life and does no end of good. But his old man died early and there just wasn't anybody else to take over the mill."

"The mill?"

"Mills, rather. Seneca Mills, in Massachusetts."

"Good Lord," I said. "You weren't kidding about being rich, were you? You're on every floor in my house. Every house on this street, probably."

"Well, to get back to your original question, that's why I've got an office and a partner just out of school. Dad set me up. I guess it ought to embarrass me, but it doesn't. It just means I can start building that much earlier. Poor Dad, he was hell-bent on me being the lawyer he wasn't, but when he saw the handwriting on the wall he gave in and sent me to the best architecture school in the country and then shelled out for the office. Plus enough to carry me till the clients start coming in. The only thing he said about it was that he'd cut my balls off—God, excuse me again—if I ever designed an opera house or a culture center."

"And will you?"

"Probably not, though not because I think he'll cut my—he'll disapprove. Residential architecture is just my thing. It knocks me out. From the very beginning it's all I've wanted to do."

"It doesn't pay all that much, does it?" I asked.

"I don't have to worry about that right now. Don't look shocked; I'm not a mooch. I have no intention of living off Dad's money any longer than I have to. My houses are going to make me as much money as I need. And make him glad he drew me instead of some other homeless waif."

"I guess they will at that," I said. "Isn't that your load of sand coming in over there?"

"Yep. Thanks for the beer. And the talk. I'll come back tomorrow afternoon for more of the same if you'll have me," he said with the unself-consciousness of a child or an animal who has found a friendly house.

"I'll have you, though I don't know why. You're a cheeky young whippersnapper who doesn't know his place."

"Wrong. I know exactly where my place is. And I'm a genius, remember?"

He gave me a cheerful, wolfish leer and went shambling across the patio to meet the sand man.

Chapter Four

WE MET Pie Harralson's father when she lost her baby in November of that year, at the beginning of her seventh month.

We had not seen as much of the young Harralsons during the course of construction as I had feared. They were usually there on weekends, early on, heads together as they peered into the hole that would be the foundation or clambered gingerly around the framing after the flooring went in. They would wave at us, and Pie would call, "Come see how my nest is looking," and we'd walk over and admire the latest bit of structural alchemy the carpenters had wrought. Buddy would alternately beam at his emerging kingdom and mutter at Pie and catch at her arm as she chattered and scrambled among the piles of lumber and sheet rock or hung dizzily out over a level where the steps were yet to come. She seemed to need to be reminded of her pregnancy, though her expensive maternity tops jutted further out and she had lost much of her pep-squad bounce.

"I *hate* looking like a tacky old cow and waddling like a duck," she pouted once when Buddy had darted at her and jerked her back from the still-unrailed height of the third-floor balcony. The baby's treetop balcony. "I'll be so damned glad when it's born and I can dance again. I haven't been able to dance at any decent party all fall."

"Pie is a fabulous dancer," Buddy said fondly. "But I don't think she realizes that she's not going to be able to hit the dance floor two days after the baby comes. It's going to be hard to make a little mama out of her."

Walter grimaced showily at me in the deepening dusk, and I said hastily, "I bet she'll make a great mother," and was annoyed at myself again. These two had a way of wrenching hypocritical platitudes out of me which I would not countenance from anyone else.

"Oh, sure, I didn't mean she wouldn't. We want a bunch of kids, four at least," said Buddy, and Walter grimaced again. This time I said nothing.

"Well, I'll be a mother, but I sure won't be a prisoner," Pie said, putting out her pink underlip over her sharp baby teeth. "And for all you know, Buddy Harralson, I *will* be out on the dance floor two days after the baby comes, because I'm going to have a live-in nurse. Daddy's giving me one, Colquitt. Isn't that just the sweetest thing you ever heard of? He says it would be a shame for me to spend the best part of my girlhood tied down to a baby, and besides"

—she dimpled—"he says he wouldn't trust his first grandchild to me for all the tea in China. Buddy just hates the idea, though. And so does his Mama." She dimpled again, at her husband, who flushed deep red.

"She just doesn't think it looks right, is all she said," he mumbled. "I don't either. Nobody else at the firm has live-in nurses. It'll look like we're throwing money around, or something."

"He cares more about that silly firm than he does me," Pie said, mock-sulking. "It's all I ever hear about. And they're the *stuffiest* people you ever saw, Colquitt; you just ought to go to some of those firm parties. Everybody sits around talking about business, and all the women wear shoes that match their dresses and have blue hair and are older than God."

I grimaced at Walter this time; some of those older-than-God people were our good friends.

Buddy's face seemed to swell and tighten. "Those are senior partners, Pie," he said. "I for one am very grateful to be invited to their parties. Not many of the junior members are."

"You must be a real comer," said Walter, more to break the tautening wire of tension than to observe a fact. It did not seem likely that this earnest, round-faced, conventional youngster was a brilliant lawyer in the making. Later, though, we asked one of our older-than-God friends in the firm about Buddy, and he verified that, indeed, the boy did have a startling streak of brilliance in him. "Steady as a rock and a tiger for work too," our friend said. "We have real hopes for him."

At any rate, though we saw them on weekends, they seldom appeared at dusk when Kim ambled over and showered and settled in for his ritual hour before he went back to his office or wherever he went. He kept a change of clothes at our house by then and had unquestioned access to the guest-room shower, and I never felt intruded upon. I was surprised to find that Walter did, a bit.

"It'll be his shoes under the bed next," he said one evening after Kim had gone. I looked around to see what he was talking about and saw him picking up a damp, discarded work shirt Kim had left on the floor of the guest bathroom.

"What time does he get here in the afternoon, anyway?" he went on, his back to me.

"Oh, about two. We have hours and hours of mad, brutal sex before you get home. All architects are alike; remember *The Fountainhead?*"

"I'll have to start knocking off earlier," he said, and something in his voice made me walk around to look at his face. It was smiling, but only just.

"You're kidding," I said finally.

"I am. But he sure is here a lot, and he's a good-looking kid, and you're a dynamite lady, whether or not you realize it."

"I'm *your* dynamite lady, whether or not you realize it. Come on, Walter. This is me. He's not here that much."

And he wasn't. He did not come every night; he seemed to have a sort of radar about the evenings when we had plans or just wanted to be alone. And he never stayed for dinner, though we invited him. I'd asked him where he lived and if he had a crowd, friends, a girl friend, and he'd named an unfashionable but rather grand, fading old apartment house near his midtown office, and said that he had a few friends he drank beer with, and saw a little lady-type action every now and then. But he did not volunteer much about his private life, and we did not ask. He seemed realest, somehow, in proximity to his house.

The Harralsons he dismissed with an "Oh, well" or "Who gives a happy rat's ass?" We knew that he would not see them again after the house was done, and he said that he did not see much of them while he was on the site.

"Condition number one, before I even gave them an estimate," he said. "I'm an architect, not a baby-sitter."

"Are you going to be that high-handed with all your clients?" Walter asked. "How did these happen to find you, anyhow, if you've never done a house before?"

"It depends, to answer your first question. And to answer your second, they didn't find me. I found them. Frank—my partner—was at some party with them and came back and told me there was a little old rich gal whose daddy was going to build baby daughter any kind of house she wanted, and she was going on about how she wanted the most knocked-out, far-out, spit-in-your-eye—I believe those were her words—house in the city and maybe the world, and I got him to find out who she was and called her the next day. And then I went over there and came back with her in my pocket."

"What did you do, put Spanish fly in her pink lady?" Walter asked.

"Is that ethical?" I asked.

"Nope, to both. I showed her some sketches and working drawings from school, and told her I'd build her a house that would put daddy in his grave."

"You didn't!" I exclaimed.

"Sure I did. That's what she really wants to do, isn't it? That or marry him, and since her mama's already beat her to that, I guess she'll have to kill him."

"Well," I said, "whatever you said, they really are crazy about the house. We don't see much of them, though. Hardly ever at night when we're home."

"No doubt she's home in an apron over a hot stove whomping up a peanut butter sandwich for ol' Buddy-baby," Kim said. "He may act like a wet cornflake, but I bet he insists on wifey being there, with his slippers in front of the fire and the swill a-simmering on the hearth when he gets home from the jungle. A place for everything and everything in its place. I bet he's up to his ass in insurance policies and has the kid in Harvard already."

"Oh, God, no," Walter said. "The state U was good enough for her daddy and her, and it's good enough for whatever-Harralson the third."

"Have you ever met her father?" I asked Kim.

"Once. When he came up from South Wiregrass or wherever it is he lives to close the deal and dish out the bread. He looks just like ol' Miss Pie magnified about fifty times, if you can imagine. Little squinky blue eyes and a pug nose like hers, only bald as an egg. With a purple face. He's either got the bluest blood or the highest blood pressure south of the Mason-Dixon Line. Called her "Punkin-pie" and me "son" and that poor sonofabitch Buddy nothing at all. Laughs a lot and whacks you on the back and looks like he raises rattlesnakes for a living."

"What does he do?" I asked.

"I don't know. Clips coupons, I'd say. Raises some cows, *he* said. Has a little land, *he* said. Does a little contracting, *he* said. I heard he's been in the state legislature for about a thousand years. He's probably got state-built roads all over his land, which I hear takes in roughly the southern half of the state. Or awards all the contracting to himself. Isn't that the way the legislature does things here?"

We laughed, because it is sometimes.

"Well," said Walter, "I guess baby daughter meant it when she said she wasn't going to let him see the house till it was done, because we haven't seen hair nor hide of him, and I think she'd have told us if he'd been up. She seemed to derive considerable enjoyment from anticipating his reaction."

"Sure. Like I said, she wants to put him in his place once and for all. Like six feet under the green, green grass of home."

"I don't really think that's very funny," I said.

"I don't either," said Kim Dougherty.

On the seventeenth of November, when the shell was up and the interior finishing work begun, Pie fell down an unrailed flight of stairs leading into the basement of the house and miscarried. It was a Thursday, and Walter and I were at work. Claire Swanson came over with the news when she saw my car pull into the driveway. Her face was ashen, and she was holding her upper arms with both hands, as you do when you're cold.

"That poor little dimwit neighbor of ours has had an awful accident and lost her baby," she said. "Oh, God, please give me a drink, Colquitt. I can't stop shaking."

I made one and brought it to her in the den. She looked awful, stricken. I thought it was odd, because though Claire's own children are the core of her

37

heart, she is usually rather philosophic about birthings and dyings and what she calls, with her charming triteness, rites of passage. Besides, she hardly knew the Harralsons, and did not seem to wish to.

"How do you know?" I asked.

"Because I was there! I found her! Lord, Col, it was terrible. I was walking Buzzy by there, early today because we're going out—and he stopped and cocked his head and put his ears up like he does when he hears something, so I listened too, and I heard a sort of . . . high, mewing sound. I thought maybe a cat had gotten trapped in the house and couldn't get out, so I walked up in their yard to see if I could hear where it was coming from, and then I realized it wasn't a cat, it was too continuous for that. It literally made the hair stand up on my head. So I went in through that side door frame where they haven't hung the door yet, and I walked around calling out, and it got a little louder, and then I realized it was coming from the basement. So I went to the top of the steps and looked down there, and there she was, lying all hunched up on her side. Just blood all over. I never saw so much blood."

"Oh, my *God,* Claire!"

"Yes. And I just ran like a demon over to Virginia Guthrie's and almost knocked the poor maid down when she answered the door and called an ambulance and grabbed a comforter off Virginia's bed and ran back over there. By the time I got back she'd fainted, and I swear to God I thought she was dead. I really did. She was so damned *white,* and all that blood, and the baby—"

"Don't, Claire!"

"Oh, yes, the baby, you could see it was—oh, God!—just . . . mashed and lumpy . . . and bloody—"

She put her head down on her knees abruptly, and I got a wet dishcloth and put it on the back of her neck, and then rubbed it over my own face. In a moment she was better.

"So then the ambulance came and they got her on a stretcher and into the ambulance and started an intravenous something-or-other and packed her full of gauze. . . . I rode with her of course. They took her into emergency surgery like a shot, and I sat like a fool staring at the wall and trying to remember what firm her husband worked for. The desk nurse finally had to call him. He was there in less than ten minutes. I never saw a kid so devastated. He kept asking over and over, 'But what was she doing there? I told her never to go over there by herself. What was she *doing* there?' And then he cried and I cried, and finally we both stopped crying and just sat there staring at the wall until the doctor came out and said she'd be all right."

"Thank God for that. How bad was she, really?"

"Nearly dead, from what I could gather. She almost bled to death. Nobody has any idea how long she'd been there. If I hadn't— But he said she's young and healthy and will be okay."

"Did he say anything about other children?"

"Oh, yes, no problem. It was a 'good, clean miscarriage'—lovely phrase, isn't it? It was the blood loss that almost killed her. I stayed until one of the older men from the firm came to be with Buddy, then I came on home. I think I felt as sorry for him as I did for her. He was just in pieces. His first little boy . . ."

"How . . . how do you know it was a boy?"

"Because I went back over there when I got home and threw a load of sand over . . . everything," said Claire and began to cry. I went into the downstairs bathroom and vomited. I hardly ever do that, and I have never seen Claire cry. I suppose we both knew that the silly, elfin child that had been Pie Harralson had bled away with her baby and what was left would be something else entirely.

We were wrong, though. At least on the surface, Pie did not seem to have changed all that much. Walter and I went over to the hospital to see her after I had called and been told she had recovered sufficiently to have visitors. We did not want to go, but of course we had to—you just do. We knocked at the half-open door of her room, mercifully not on the maternity floor, and heard a deep masculine voice call "Come in," and tiptoed in, faces grave with the sheeplike lugubriousness hospitals paint on you. The room was throttled with flowers and baskets of fruit, and Pie lay propped up in her narrow hospital bed in a surge of yellow lace, surrounded by magazines and folded newspaper crossword puzzles. Her television was on—*Let's Make a Deal* was going on, insanely, with the sound off—and a big man rose from one of the chairs by the window and came toward us.

"Colquitt and Walter!" Pie yelped. Her voice was weak but nearly as breathless-bright as always. "Aren't you loves! Look at those *gorgeous* mums! Daddy, these are my super next-door neighbors, Colquitt and Walter Kennedy. This is my Daddy."

He shook hands with both of us and mumbled something about how nice we were to come see his baby. He retreated then to the chair and sat down heavily. Kim had been right. He did look like a grotesque parody of his daughter. But nothing else about him fitted Kim's description. The bluff heartiness, the posturing, the inflamed face, the badinage were missing. He was gray-white and his eyes were swollen and bloodshot. He looked older than I had imagined.

"Pie, I'm so terribly, terribly sorry," I said. "I'd give anything if I'd been home."

"Don't you worry a minute about it, Colquitt," she said. "That darling Mrs. Swanson was, and she saved my life—she really did, all the doctors say I'd have died—but I feel just fine now. Really. I'm eating like a horse and I'm not all that weak anymore. Just too thin, the doctor says . . ."

Her voice trailed off as though she had only then comprehended the reason for the thinness, and she looked quickly at her father. His mouth worked silently, then his face straightened. I slid a glance at Walter. I could not quite assess the girl in the bed. She seemed more like a child than ever, a very young child, to whom a visit to the hospital, the flurrying attention of doctors, the whispered urgency, were high adventure. Just that. She did not seem to realize she had lost a baby, nearly died herself.

As if she had read my thoughts, she said swiftly, "It's terrible about the baby, I know. I'm really heartbroken." You're not, I thought. "And Buddy and Daddy . . . but I keep telling them, look on the bright side, I'm young and healthy, that's the important thing. I'll have millions of babies, millions of grand-babies for Daddy. Really. I wish you'd take Daddy out and cheer him up, though. You'd think the world had come to an end."

"Of course, we'd love to. Wouldn't you like to come have some supper with us, Mr. Harralson?" I said hastily, and then realized that of course his name was not Harralson. That belonged to Buddy. I thought dimly that it might be the only thing that did now.

He smiled bleakly at my confusion. "It's Gladney. Matt Gladney. And you're mighty sweet to ask me, honey, but I think I'll stay around here with Punkin-pie for a little while, until her Mama can get back from the motel. Or Elliott, from the office. When he can spare the time, of course."

Elliott, I realized, must be Buddy. We had never heard his proper name. Nor Pie's, for that matter.

"Now, Daddy," Pie purred. She literally purred. It was a silky, oddly disturbing sound. "Buddy's been here lots of times. Be fair. Besides, you don't really mind being stuck with your silly baby for a little while longer, do you?"

Walter stared at her. Matt Gladney said nothing. I said, "Well, if you have some spare time on your hands and you need to get away for a little while, Mr. Gladney, please come by and see us. We want to get to know Pie's family; she's going to make us a nice neighbor." I knew I was babbling but could not stop the words. "You know where we are, the white brick next to Pie's house—or maybe you haven't seen the house yet?" Oh, God, stop me, I prayed.

"I've seen the house," he said. "But I wish to God I never had. I wish to God I'd taken a rag and a can of kerosene and a match and burned the goddamned thing right to the ground."

He made a small, choking sound and turned away. Pie gave us a helpless child's smile, and I hugged her and said, "We'll come back and see you in a day or two," and we fled before she could reply.

Chapter Five

"WHAT ON earth got into Eloise tonight?" Roger Swanson asked on an early December evening some weeks later. We always repair to our house or theirs after Eloise Jennings' annual Christmas party. The snickering fire behind the brass fender, the softly lit cedar, the Oxford College "Festival of Carols and Lights" on the stereo are soothing.

Kim had joined us about ten, though he had refused, politely, Eloise's invitation to her own affair. The house was taking shape and was generating a good bit of talk around the neighborhood, and he had become a reluctant minor celebrity. Eloise invariably referred to him as "that young architect of Colquitt's," which bothered no one who knew Eloise, Kim least of all.

"She's just pissed off because I'd rather hang around Colquitt's body than hers," he told us and the Swansons once after Eloise had come over, dropped her little appellation, and gone home. "Hers looks like it ought to be on Mount Rushmore."

"Competition is what got into Eloise," Claire said tartly. "Too much talk about Pie's losing her baby. Eloise can't stand the thought that somebody might upstage her from her Earth Mother role. If you can't be anything else, be a professional brood mare. She may be right about Pie, though. I got the impression she wasn't all that broken up about the baby, though her poor little husband and the famous Daddy sure are in shreds over it. You have, I presume, met Daddy? I don't think he left the room the entire time she was in the hospital. Something a little funny there—or am I a dirty, paranoid old lady?"

"You're a dirty, paranoid old lady," said Roger.

"What do you think, that he's got a thing for his baby daughter?"

"Not exactly, I just—"

"I think that may be exactly what it is," said Walter. "With no little encouragement from Lolita. When we were over there, she was out-and-out flirting with him. It was damned creepy."

"If you think daughter and Daddy are creepy, you ought to catch the sonny-and-Mama show," Kim said. "The mother of the groom was there when I went to see Pie, and she couldn't keep her hands off poor old Buddy. Smoothing his hair, and straightening his tie, and saying what a soldier he'd been about the whole thing, and not once even looking at the bereft little mama, who was glaring daggers at her. *She's* the soldier in the family; looks exactly like Douglas MacArthur. And he was practically peeing on the rug with gratitude. If you ask me, there's something Tennessee Williams about the whole tribe of 'em."

"I didn't know you'd been to see Pie," I said.

"Why not? I'm not a total ogre. You sound like you're surprised I didn't send her a congratulations card."

"I didn't mean that. It just—isn't like you, somehow."

"I have a lot of sterling characteristics you haven't run into yet, Col," he said. "For all my soaring genius and artistic crustiness, I'm still a pushover for a pretty lady, and Pie is that, if she's nothing else. You don't really think I come over here to listen to you talk about architecture, for that matter, do you? It's because I'm waiting for my chance to run off to Madagascar with you. No, the reason I went to see Miss Pie was because I was afraid she'd change her mind about the house, and I was going to get her to sign a check and then strangle her."

We all laughed, and fell silent. Walter got up and went into the kitchen and clinked some glasses around, and Claire looked gravely at Kim and then at me. The silence lengthened. What on earth is the matter with everybody? I thought. Surely nobody takes that prattle of Kim's about Madagascar seriously.

"What a pack of jackals we are," I said rather

loudly into the silence. "Pie's poor father is crazy about his daughter, and he's just lost his first grandchild. And almost lost Pie. And Buddy's mother is naturally concerned about him; he's her only child, she's literally raised him. It just shows you how little drama we have in our own lives if we have to invent Tennessee Williams goings-on about those poor, simple children and their parents."

"Well," said Claire, "all seems to be going smoothly now. I saw the Munchkins over on the site yesterday, looking pleased as punch, showing off the house to a guy from Buddy's firm. He's that tall, distinguished man who came to be with Buddy when Pie was in surgery; he looks just like Gregory Peck. Who would I be talking about, Walter? You know most of those people."

"I don't have the foggiest. Everybody I know down at Skinner, Franklin, Et cetera, Et cetera is ugly as seven miles of bad road. And, as Miss Pie points out, older than God."

It turned out that the man was a new senior partner at Buddy Harralson's firm, lured from a lucrative Connecticut practice by one of the partners who'd gone to Choate with him.

"A fine addition to the firm," rumbled the partner, who was a friend of Walter's. "We were extremely fortunate to be able to persuade him to join us."

"That's not what *I* heard," smirked Eloise Jennings when I told her who the man was, in response to her avid questions. She too had seen him on the site with the Harralsons.

"*I* heard there was something funny with a law clerk in his firm back in Connecticut, and he was only too happy to come down here. Don't ask me how I heard it either, because I'm not going to tell you."

"I wouldn't dream of asking you to disclose your sources, Eloise," I snapped. "Even though most of them seem to be safely hidden away in a septic tank somewhere." I watched her indignant back departing down our driveway with satisfaction. Unfounded malice is her specialty, and I have never been as quick to excuse it because of her obvious inferiority complex over her origins as, say, gentle Virginia Guthrie. She does a lot of damage with her tongue, and I cut her off whenever I can.

"He's a brilliant man," Buddy Harralson told us one Saturday in January after the attractive stranger had made a cursory tour of the nearly completed house with the young Harralsons and had driven away in his lustrous BMW Bavaria. "He's only been with the firm about six months and he's already completely reorganized the tax department. I'm working almost exclusively with him."

"Buddy's his protégé," bubbled Pie. "Luke told me he's got more promise than any young lawyer he's ever seen, at this stage."

She was looking radiant again, her rosy blondness glowing against a satiny nutria trench coat. "Daddy gave it to me for Christmas," she said when I complimented her on it. A little of the pink pleasure that had bloomed in Buddy's face at her words about his promise ebbed. Or perhaps I imagined it.

"Luke?" I said. The man I'd seen with them had seemed impeccably dignified and somehow unreachable, even in a faintly shabby camel's hair coat and tweed hat. He did not look as though he would have a nickname, or share it with a junior lawyer if he did. He did indeed remind me of Gregory Peck, though. He was, from a distance, a strikingly handsome man.

"Lucas Abbott. *Schuyler* Lucas Abbott, please," Pie said, dimpling. "Isn't he gorgeous? He's going to make my sweet husband into a star. He's teaching him all about tax law"—she crinkled her nose—"and he's going to get us into the club—they have a reciprocal with his club in Connecticut, it's some famous, fancy old thing—and he's going to get his daughter to play tennis with me when his family moves down here. He's looking for a house now. He says if he'd seen the plans for mine he'd have put a gun to Kim's head until he agreed to build it for them and not us. He just loves it."

"Well, it's a beauty," Walter said, looking up at the bulk of the house, darkening against the grape-colored sky.

It was. The exterior was done now, and the roof on, and the windows in. Against the delicate crosshatching of the winter trees it looked more alive and sweetly grown than ever, waiting. I thought with pleasure of yellow lights in those windows, smoke curling up from the chimneys like the breath of the house. It needed life now, like a heart to beat.

As January melted into February and the soft gray thaws of soon-to-be spring came, the interior finishing of the house went on and Buddy and Pie appeared more often on their Saturday and Sunday excursions, she laden under swatches of carpeting and books of wallpaper, he gravely poring over chips of paint samples. Forsythia that I thought had been dozed into oblivion sprang up and misted the foundations with the lemon icing I yearn for all winter. Wild violets and a few crocuses pushed up through the mud. It was a warm, wet spring, and Kim Dougherty's boots were left, by unspoken agreement, on the patio when he came for his Scotch and water.

"I switch in April," he said. "Vodka touches not my lips until after I've given the IRS its pound of flesh."

I thought he seemed quieter that early spring, pre-occupied, though his skirling banter never flagged. But it seemed forced, desultory talk to mask the fact that his mind was far away.

"Are things going badly with the house?" I asked him finally.

"No. I never saw a house go up so smoothly —though I haven't seen many houses go up," he said. "Why?"

"You've seemed a million miles away lately. Like something was bothering you. I thought maybe you were running into snags over there."

"Not over there. That baby is a jewel of a house. I'm running into snags at the office, though."

Walter and I waited; we had never pressed Kim. It was a major bone in our friendship. He would tell us or not.

"The fact is, I don't seem to be able to design worth shit," he said finally, looking into the depths of his glass. "I'm a good month behind on the Douglas plans, and that should be a piece of cake. It's a fantastic site—it just seems to be sitting there telling me

46

what to do on it, just shouting out sometimes, and it's like I can't understand what it's saying. When I first saw it I knew just what ought to go up there, I just had it whole in my mind. Like, as you say, Col, it just grew right up out of the ground. Christ, I could see it. And now I can't. I can't even get a pencil going. What I've done so far is garbage; I'd have flunked out of first-year architecture if I'd submitted what I'm doing now. I can't show the Douglases what I've got. They've been over there and looked at the Harralson house, and they think I'm God Almighty. And I sit there doing tic-tac-toe on a brand-new tracing pad."

"Everybody gets stale," I said, distressed. He seemed, suddenly, as fragile and vulnerable as a child. "You've been pushing awfully hard on this one. Maybe you ought to ease up for a little while and just rest your head. Can't Frank take over?"

"He's going to have to. But it's a crummy deal for the Douglases. He's damned good, but he's not as good as I am——or was. It was me they wanted."

"Maybe this one has just plain demanded too much of you," Walter said. "That happens to me sometimes. I get a campaign going that I really love, and just can't seem to put it away. It obsesses me, and I'm no good at all till it's sort of finished itself in my mind."

"No," Kim said. "It's never been like that with me before. When a design's done, it's done. I'm not tired or obsessed or any of that temperamental shit. I just can't design. Something's gone. It's like some ear inside me that used to be able to listen to a site isn't there any more. I'm beginning to think I'm a one-house architect, than which there is nothing sorrier. Maybe I *should* have been a lawyer like the old man wanted me to be. Or gone into the business, God help me. Sell carpets."

It was a heavy, painful joke, and no one laughed. He had another Scotch and stared a while at the dying fire, and then went home. I listened to his old VW chugging off down the street. My heart hurt, physically. I wondered if it was the way I would have felt about the children I would never have. For the first time, regret for them washed over me.

47

Walter came and stood beside me, one arm around my shoulder.

"What do you think?" I said.

"You mean, do I think he's shot his wad with this house? No. I think he's young and he's done one fantastic house and he's practically scared himself to death with it. I mean, what do you do for an encore? He knows he's got a hard act to follow and he's choked up on it. I also think he's feeling more than a little sorry for himself. Christ, everybody who's creative goes through the same thing, but there's no telling a novice that. Kim is a fine architect, but he's got to learn to run on a mud track sometimes. Every house he does just can't be as spectacular as that one."

"I think it can or he won't do any more. I don't think he'd settle for being just good. I almost think he *would* go sell carpets rather than not be able to do this again. Oh, Walter, I can't stand it if this is his only house. It would kill him. And I don't think he's feeling sorry for himself at all. Kim doesn't do that."

"It won't be his only house, and it won't kill him. And I think he *is* feeling sorry for himself. You spoil him to death, Col; you've gotten almost obsessed with him. I don't understand it. It isn't like you."

I stared at him and then out the den window. Walter had never talked like this before about any of the young men who had, over the years, become friends of mine. Many had. I'd always thought it was because I was able to offer rapport and easiness without the tiny, crackling undercurrent of sexuality that runs through most of the friendships women have with men. Nor did I think I was devoid of attraction for them. You can tell when that's there, and I had always been able to transcend it, make the relationships both more than that and less. Any of my emotions that went past friendship went to Walter. I thought he took that as much for granted as I did.

I looked deeper into myself, and back at the relationship with Kim. Was there anything in it of obsession? Anything of the delicate electricity I always banished from my other relationships with men? Anything at all that I might be concealing from myself? No. I knew there was not. I looked up at Walter.

"Are you saying that you think there's something *between* Kim and me?" I asked. "Because there isn't. I shouldn't even have to tell you that there isn't. This isn't like *you*, Walter. I really love Kim, but I thought you understood *how* I did. I thought you were fond of him too."

He sighed. "I do understand. I am fond of him. I really am. I don't even know why I said that. I just don't like to see you worrying so about him. You're not his mother. You're my middle-aged sex bomb. Come here and give me a big smooch, and we'll go on from there." I did. "Nobody says smooch anymore," I said. "Nobody says sex bomb anymore."

"So my mind stopped in 1958. There's nothing wrong with my pecker."

"Nobody says that anymore either."

LATER, WHEN I opened the back door to let Razz and Foster in, I saw a light bobbing in the darkness next door. It was a round disc of white light, and it swayed and skipped erratically over the ground, now playing across a swath of bare foundation, now plucking a piece of cypress siding out of the blackness, now dancing insanely over the red-rutted driveway. I stood very still and watched it. It disappeared, and then I saw it flickering like swamp fire through the black windows. I stared, uncomprehending and beginning to be frightened, and then I heard the front door slam and the unmistakable rumble of Buddy Harralson's voice saying, "I don't know where in the hell it could be. I'll come over first thing in the morning and go over every inch of it. Jesus, I'm sorry."

There was an indistinguishable answering rumble, and I called out, "Anything wrong?"

Buddy shone the flashlight toward me. "Colquitt? No. Luke's missing his watch and thought it might have slipped off when we were over here this afternoon. But I can't find it. Sorry if we scared you."

"Just for a minute," I yelled back, beginning to be cold. "I thought you were a ha'nt."

"No ha'nts, Mrs. Kennedy," and I heard Lucas Abbott's voice for the first time. It was like the rest of him, mellow and modulated and cultivated. "Just a

49

starving lawyer looking for his watch so he can pawn it." He laughed. I liked his laugh. "I'm looking forward to meeting you people sometime soon," he added across the black driveway.

"Us too," I called back. "Come on over for a drink next time the Harralsons drag you over to admire their house." I thought that probably sounded sour and unneighborly, so I added hastily, "It's a beautiful house."

"Isn't it?" he said.

"What was all that about?" Walter yelled down the stairs.

"Just a starving lawyer looking for a watch to pawn," I yelled back. "Do you want some of this Rocky Road here?"

Chapter Six

THE NEXT weekend March came in like the lion February had deluded us into thinking was sleeping. A black, killing frost stole in from some Canadian peak and blasted my camellias. The ground froze hard, turning the rutted driveway at the Harralsons' into corrugated iron, and a high banshee wind sang in the treetops. We forewent our round of Saturday errands and I made a pot of split-pea soup and we ate it in the den, where Walter had lit a fire and turned on the TV to watch the Celtics and the Lakers. It was like being at sea, a wild sea, in the snug, warm cabin of a ship.

Around midafternoon there was a rap on our back door and I uncoiled from beneath the sofa afghan and went to answer it. We were halfway expecting Kim Dougherty, but it was Pie and Buddy Harralson and Lucas Abbott who stood there, necks curled into

shoulders against the freezing wind. They came gratefully into the kitchen, and a red tumble of puppy
came with them on the end of a green leather leash,
his nails skittering across the waxed tile.

"Buddy said you invited us this time," said Pie, giving me her ingenue's smile. "When you saw him and
Luke the other night, looking for Luke's watch. I
wanted him to meet the world's best neighbors, and
I wanted you to meet Casey. Isn't he adorable?"

I sighed inwardly, cursing my late-night, back-door
chattiness, and led them into the den. The puppy pre-
ceded us, capering and sniffing and bounding, and
when we entered the room he was sitting on Walter's
lap licking his face in an abandonment of ecstasy.

"Company," I said brightly, and Walter fondled the
silky red ears and said, "We've just met. Hi, Harralsons." He gave Lucas Abbott a questioning smile.

"This is our friend and Buddy's boss, Lucas Abbott," said Pie, prodding him a little forward. "Call
him Luke. Luke is a combination daddy-mentor to
Buddy, and we just think he's the greatest thing on
earth. Colquitt and Walter Kennedy, Luke."

Lucas Abbott and Walter exchanged "What can
you say?" grins over Pie's bright head and Buddy
turned his accustomed dark red.

"Mentor hardly, and daddy I fervently hope not,"
said Lucas Abbott in a deep Eastern drawl that
spoke of prep schools and an Ivy League college.
"He's going to be a *very* good lawyer one of these
days, and I'm pleased to have him in my bailiwick at
the office. It's good to meet you people. Pie talks of
little else."

He was wearing a bronze tweed jacket over a
rough turtleneck sweater, and I thought again how
good-looking he was. There were brushes of pure
silver in his thick chestnut hair, and he had a carved,
high-planed face and gray eyes that reminded me of
Kim's. It was like being in the room with a celebrity
or a personage of some sort; you've seen them in pho-
tographs and on film, but nothing prepares you for the
sheer physical perfection. You can't look away. In
Lucas Abbott the impact was softened by his affable
matter-of-factness and easy humor, and I decided

that I liked him very much. He had the innate, unself-conscious dignity of a fine animal.

"Who's your friend?" Walter said to Pie, setting the puppy down on the rug and scratching under his chin. The puppy crouched and wriggled, and I knew I would have to get out the can of rug cleaner and erase the spot when they had gone.

"This is Casey," she said, gathering the puppy up in her arms, where he wriggled and whimpered against her newly flat stomach. "Luke gave him to us for Christmas. Daddy always had setters, and I guess I went on so about them that he thought . . . I mean, it was just after the baby and all. . . ."

There was a small, thick silence. Buddy's face tight-ened and Lucas Abbott looked distressed and re-mote. "What a lovely thing to do," I said quickly. "He's a love, isn't he? I don't know anything about setters, but he looks like a good one."

"He's going to be a champion," Pie squealed. "He's got papers and all that stuff and bloodlines back to Adam and Eve practically. I could show him if I wanted to, Luke says, but I just hate the idea of all that training and making him do things he doesn't want to do and having people stare at him in show rings. He's just going to be my friend and stay with me while Buddy's at work. Which is practically all the time." She wrinkled her nose at Lucas Abbott, who smiled at her.

"They need discipline," he said. "You won't be do-ing him a favor if you let him run wild. Setters are high-strung dogs. He'll be the terror of the neighbor-hood if you don't teach him some manners, and Mr. and Mrs. Kennedy will heap curses on my head daily."

"Hardly. I can't answer for our cats, though," I said. "Razz and Foster are already the terror of the neigh-borhood. I've seen them chase the Swanson's schnau-zer down the driveway in a full rout more than once. I don't think you'll have to worry about Casey, though. The street is crawling with dogs, and they all seem to coexist pretty well together."

I made a pot of coffee and brought out the cheese Danish left over from breakfast. The puppy fell into an abrupt, tumbled puppy sleep in front of the fire, where he twitched and whimpered occasionally. Lucas Abbott talked about his family back in Darien, of the sort of house he was trying to find for them. There was, in addition to his wife Anne, a married son and a daughter in her last year at Wellesley.

"So I really have until summer to find something," he said. "Anne will stay in Darien until she sells the house and Marty finishes school. I have specific instructions to look for something big and roomy and older, on a street just like this one. So far, nothing."

"Houses in close-in old neighborhoods like this one aren't that easy to find," I told him. "You generally have to wait until somebody dies. That sounds ghoulish, but I think people here check the obituaries before they look at the real estate section. I know some good agents I could put you in touch with, though."

"Thanks, I have all faith in the energetic young lady the firm found for me. I'm driving her bananas, but she's unfailingly polite. You know, I've never liked contemporary stuff before, but since I've seen the Harralsons' house, I'm almost tempted to rent something and get this young Dougherty of theirs to do one for us. In fact, I've talked to him about it."

"Oh?" Walter said noncommittally. Kim had not mentioned it.

"He didn't seem very interested. I don't know if he disapproves of Yankees or what. He was polite, but that was about it."

"Oh, it couldn't be that, Luke," Pie put in. "He's a Yankee himself. Massachusetts or somewhere. I'll talk to him; I'm sure he'd—"

"Do you get back home very often?" I asked Lucas Abbott, to divert her.

"No," he said. "I'm afraid I haven't as much as I'd hoped, this winter. Christmas, of course, but the office is keeping me hopping. I'm in there almost every Saturday and Sunday."

"Don't I know it," Pie pouted. "I might as well be a divorcée for all I see Buddy. But I guess that's the price I have to pay for having a successful husband. Luke has dinner with us almost every Saturday and Sunday night, though. This beautiful man, Colquitt,

53

he even swears he likes my cooking. Can you imagine?"

I couldn't. Why would this cultivated man, so much older and obviously so far out of their league, want to spend his weekends with the utterly conventional young Harralsons? Pie's chatter must drive him mad. Oh, well, I decided. He hasn't had time to make many friends yet, and he must miss his family. They're probably like his own children to him. I made a mental note to have a small dinner party soon and invite him. Minus the Harralsons. I thought he would like our friends. There was the same air of quiet and solidarity and substance there.

"Come over to the house with us and see the wallpaper I picked out for our bedroom," said Pie when they rose to leave. "Or rather, Luke picked it out. He says he didn't, but we were over at the wallpaper place and he found this one book and said this pattern was something he'd like to wake up looking at, and when Buddy saw it, that was it. I was outvoted. And you know, it's perfect."

I looked at Lucas Abbott. Wallpaper? He looked back at me and gave me a faint shrug and a half smile. "What can you say?" hung in the air again.

We got coats and scarves and walked across the driveway and up the bank to the house. The puppy, unsnapped from his leash, bounded up into the yard and disappeared around the house. From somewhere out of sight he set up a frantic yipping, and then a dismal puppy howl. Buddy went around the corner of the house to see.

In a moment he was back, the puppy in his arms. His face was rather white.

"Don't go around there Pie, Colquitt," he said. "There's a mother possum and her babies that have just been . . . torn apart. God! I never saw anything like that. There are just . . . pieces left. It looks like somebody took a chain saw—"

Pie gave a small scream and clapped her hands to her mouth, and I stayed with her while the men went around to see. It upsets me to find dead things. Mashed squirrels and possums in the road give me unreasoning grief, as though I were responsible. I hate the intruding automobiles, the roads that my species has carved through their territory, ribbons of death. I even have brief moments of hating my own cats when they bring me maimed and bleeding chipmunks and birds. I know it is instinctive with them, but I hate it. Could Razz or Foster . . . ? No. Their limit was chipmunks. And they did not tear or savage.

The men came back looking disturbed and sickened. Walter got a shovel from our basement and buried the possums at the edge of the woods, deeply, so that dogs would not be attracted. We walked the Harralsons and Lucas Abbott to the gray Mercedes, subdued and upset.

"Could a dog do a thing like that?" Buddy Harralson asked. "I never saw such a mess. God, I hope for Casey's sake that there aren't any dogs around who would—"

"No," Walter said. "I know all the dogs in this neighborhood and none of them would do anything like that. I doubt if any dog could. Certainly not a cat. I suppose there could be a wild pack around in the woods somewhere, but we've never had any trouble with wild dogs before. I'll keep a lookout, though. Col, we'd better keep Razz and Foster inside for a day or two until we can tell if there's anything around."

SOMETHING WAS, even though we never saw it. The next week Kim found a nest of very young birds tumbled from one of the trees and slaughtered. The pulped body of the mother lay nearby.

"I couldn't even tell what kind of birds they were," he told us that evening. "I'd suspect one of your fuzzy friends here, except they looked like something heavy had just . . . smeared them. One of the painters told me he's found chipmunks or something in the same condition two or three times, laid on the back steps like something had drug them there. Little ones, babies. Have you ever seen any really wild things back in those woods? Something—oh, bigger than a racoon, even. Heavy."

"God, no," Walter said. "Those woods are dense, but they only go over to the next street. There couldn't be anything savage back in there, not this close to town. And I've been looking out for roving dogs, and I haven't seen any at all that I don't know as well as their owners. Forget Razz and Foster. They won't go near the house or the lot."

"It just makes me sick," I said. "That beautiful house, and all those little things that live in those woods. I hate the idea that something is . . . stalking around over there. It's not natural, somehow. And I'm afraid it's going to spoil the house for Pie and Buddy. You too."

"It's already spoiled for me," Kim said flatly. "It looks like it was my swan song. That doesn't exactly make me love it."

"Things still going badly?" I asked. He had not been over in the evenings for the past week or two, though a couple of times I had seen him standing in the yard gazing up at the Harralson house, in the twilight, when the workmen had gone. Just standing, hands in the pockets of his old windbreaker, and looking. As if he were memorizing the house, stone by stone and board by board. I'd thought that he would come on over to our house and had not called out to him, but when he did not appear and I looked again, he was gone. I had hoped his absence meant that the dam had burst and he was working again.

"Things could not be worse, Colquitt," he said. "I've turned the Douglas house and the rest of the design work over to Frank. Not that there's that much of it. He's brought in a couple of new things, but nothing he can't handle. I'm going to finish up on the Douglas site—I can still supervise a crew even if I can't design—and then I think I might split for a while."

"Oh, Kim, no!" I stared at him. He was thinner, and his eyes were shadowed underneath. He looked gnawed at, eroded. My heart turned over with helpless pain and love. I wondered why I had not noticed before—but, then, we had not seen him for a while.

"Where would you go?" Walter did not protest. I wondered with a brief flare of anger if he might be glad, and then decided that perhaps he understood Kim better than I. He had always brushed my sympathy aside.

"Nowhere for a while. I've got a good six months on the Douglas site. But, you know, I've never been to Europe? Can you imagine, in this day and age? I always had summer construction jobs—the old man insisted on it. Said if I was going to be an architect, I better know how to build better than hell. And I do —I can flat build. Maybe when I'm done with the Douglases I'll take a few months off and do the grand tour. I can sell out to Frank. My half the business isn't worth crap anyway. It would be enough for a cracking good fall abroad. Or, hell, the old man would spring for it. Though I'm not going to ask him. How about it, Col? Paris in the winter, when it drizzles?"

Unreasoning anger surged through me; unreasoning tears flooded the back of my throat with salt.

"I certainly never figured you for a quitter, Kim," I said fiercely.

"Blessed is he who knows when to quit," he said.

"I think you're feeling sorry for yourself. I think you're acting like a child. I think you don't have any right to just throw away what you have and go play around Europe like some . . . spoiled rich kid."

He looked at me, hurt and anger in his eyes. And something else. Betrayal? Pain sang in my ears.

"And I think you don't know what you're talking about," he flared. "Besides, that's what I am, isn't it? A spoiled rich kid. Who got hooked on his Lincoln Logs and thought he could be an architect."

The evening was broken, and soon he went away. We went to bed, heavily. Walter was silent, and soon turned off his reading lamp and turned over on his side, his back to me. I did not know if he was asleep or not. I lay still in the darkness, in pain and sorrow. The depth of it surprised me.

That Sunday Pie came over alone just as I was starting dinner. Walter was playing a last set of tennis at the club with Martin Sawyer, and the sun was setting behind our woods. I offered a drink, which she refused.

"I just came over to unlock the door for the carpet people," she said. "And I thought I'd come tell you about my party. Buddy and Luke are coming back from the office for supper, so I can't stay long. Is it all

57

right if I fasten Casey's leash to the patio table? He's all over mud."

"Sure," I said. "Do you think it's wise to leave the door unlocked all night, though? And what party?"

"There's nothing in the house that isn't nailed down," she said. "And I can't get here in the morning as early as the carpet people are coming. And the party—I think I'm going to have the biggest house-warming party in the world, Colquitt, as soon as we're in and settled. Do you think the people on the street would think I was presumptuous? I want to get to know everybody over here, and I want to have the people from the firm, and Mother and Daddy of course, and anybody else who'll come. I'm going to ask Kim Dougherty too; I thought he'd like to see his house all shined up for a party. Will you and Walter come?"

"I think it's a lovely idea, and of course we'll come. Nobody will think you're presumptuous. We all love parties, and everybody will want to see the house. Nobody talks about anything else. I want to meet Buddy's partners too."

"Not partners yet," she said, dimpling. "But soon. That's a secret, Colquitt, but Luke says he's doing so well he wouldn't be surprised if he was made a junior partner by fall. That's just unheard of at Buddy's age. And it's all because of Luke. I just can't believe that darling man is being so nice to us."

"He certainly is a nice guy, isn't he?" I said. "Buddy's lucky to have his guidance and you're both lucky to have him for a friend. He'll be there of course."

"Oh, sure. His wife and daughter may be down for it. He's got a couple of houses he wants them to look at, and if we time it right, it should be about the time of his daughter's spring break. He's even offered to bartend or get a bartender from the club. I think that would be fancier, sort of, don't you?"

"By all means."

"Who's bartending? Can he spare an aging athlete a little booze?" said Walter, coming in damp and flushed from the kitchen, a soggy club towel around his neck.

"I didn't hear you come in," I said.

"Too busy girl-talking," he said smugly, knowing I hate that term.

We sat in the darkness, fully dropped by now, and Pie told him all about her party and Buddy's impending partnership, and then rose to leave. We went out onto the patio with her. The green leash was still affixed to the patio table, but the puppy was gone.

"Oh, my God," Pie yelped in distress. "I'll never find him in this dark. Oh, Buddy will kill me! He thinks the sun rises and sets in that dog. Oh, please, will you help me look for him?"

"Of course," Walter said. "I doubt if he's gotten far. Let me get the flashlight, and we'll scout around."

Casey wasn't in our backyard, and he did not come in from the woods when we called and whistled. He wasn't around the gray Mercedes either, or in the front yard.

"Maybe he's strayed over to your house," Walter said, and we picked our way up the bank and into Pie's yard. Pie darted ahead, whistling and calling, her voice high and childish with fright. Walter followed, swinging the flashlight back and forth methodically, sweeping orderly sections of the yard.

In the end it was I who found the puppy. I stepped on him in the darkness—or on what was left of him. Hearing my soft grunt, Walter swung the light over to me, shining it on my feet so I could see what I had stumbled over. If I had not known the color of his fur, I would not have known what it was. The puppy was literally destroyed.

Claire Swanson told me later she could hear Pie screaming all the way into her den, where she and Roger were watching television.

WE LOOKED into it, of course. We called the animal-control division of the Humane Society the next morning, and the police. There was something killing ruthlessly in our woods and we could not ignore it. A car with two large young officers came, and the men prowled the woods all that morning, guns drawn, looking out of place and somehow frightening in our quiet morning neighborhood. A team of young men from animal control came too, in a caged truck, and for the better part of the day we could see them among the near-naked trees and hear them calling out to one another, beating systematically through the woods behind our house and all the houses on the street. They went as far as the houses on the next street over, and in the afternoon they went from house to house asking if anyone had noticed anything unusual, seen any strange and large unknown dogs, any unknown animals at all. No one had.

Whatever it had been was never found. Kim Dougherty and his crew discovered no more small murders at the Harralson house. It was as though the murderer, having made some small point to the Harralsons, had moved on.

Chapter Seven

THE DAY of Pie's housewarming was as perfect a day as late April can produce here. There had been a small chiming rain in the night, but it had stopped before dawn, and when I let the cats out the back door that morning the pure sweetness and greenness of the day washed over me like a wave on a summer sea. Sunlight dappled the lawn with that gold-green light that is always gone by May, birds were ruffling and caroling in the trees and around the bird feeder, chipmunks and squirrels were whisking busily and prissily about their morning chores.

"It looks like Disney World," said Walter over my shoulder, standing with a cup of coffee and breathing the day.

"Or 'The Peaceable Kingdom,' " I said, watching Razz and Foster pad, high-hipped, across the yard and into the woods, ignoring the birds and squirrels and chipmunks, who ignored them in return.

"What's on for today? You got tennis, or shall we go out and dig up some more rocks for the rock garden?"

"Whatever. We've got the Harralsons' party tonight."

"Ah, yes. The social event of the season. What shall I wear, the gold lamé jumpsuit? My old school tie?"

We were in and out all that day, but between trips we caught glimpses of the city's most favored caterer's truck disgorging men with round white plastic trays swathed in foil, cases of red and white wine, cardboard boxes. None of them bore the institutional silver trays and chafing dishes that most of us have come to know as well as our own over the years. Pie had a formidable array of wedding-present silver, I knew, and had spent a full week polishing it. She'd only borrowed a couple of trays from me and two dozen highball glasses.

That afternoon, as we were returning home from our last jaunt, Buddy and Lucas Abbott appeared, laboring under cases of liquor. The Harralson driveway and front walk had been swept to skeletal bareness, the newly green front yard raked and mowed, the creek banks raked. With the hardwoods full and blooming green and the fledgling shrubs around the foundations glistening from a recent hosing, the house looked dressed and combed. A debutante, a bride on the threshold of the aisle.

"You've got enough booze there to keep the entire north side of town in bed till noon tomorrow," Walter called from our driveway. "Need some help?"

He went over to help them wrestle the last two cases into the kitchen, and I carried my bags of groceries into our house and came back out. They were standing at the edge of the pristine driveway and Pie had joined them. She was breathless and a little pale in faded Levi's and a sweat shirt with her sorority's Greek letters on it.

"How's it going?" I asked. "Need any help at all?"

"No, this is the last thing until the bartender comes," Pie said. "I'm just scared to death, Colquitt. Mother and Daddy are driving up, but they won't get here until about six—they're going to spend the night with us—and I'm just terrified that nobody's going to come and the ones who do are going to hate it. What am I going to say to the first people who get here?"

"Why don't Walter and I come over early and be there when they do?" I said. "We know everybody on the street, of course, and some of the people at Buddy's firm. Would that make you feel better?"

"*Loads* better! Would you?"

"Of course," I said to her, and to Lucas Abbott, "Your family must think you've deserted them. Why don't you go on and let Walter and me help with the last-minute details? Did they have a good trip, by the way?"

"A fine trip," he said. "They got in at noon, and I dropped them at the hotel and left them in a pile of underclothes and stockings and shampoo. I don't think they've missed me yet. They'll be here a few days more, so we'll have plenty of time to get reacquainted. I'm going to take them out tomorrow and show them the house I picked out, and I plan to take a couple of days off and show them the sights."

"They'll be here tonight, won't they?" Walter asked.

"Oh, yes. Wouldn't miss it. I imagine they're fussing about what to wear right now."

"Well, we look forward to meeting them," I said.

We were there by a quarter to five. James, a magisterial bartender from our club, permitted himself a small smile at the sight of us and made us drinks from behind his white-clothed bastion. The bar had been set up at the end of the living room in front of the sheer expanse of glass that let in a wall-sized panorama of woods, creek, and the first-level balcony. The room looked born of air and green light, wild and glorious in the slanting sunlight. Flowers glowed everywhere and candles shimmered.

"It looks gorgeous," I told Pie. "Everything does. You've done a sensational job. Your table looks like something right out of a Cunard ad, and you look like something out of *Vogue*." She was in silky pyjamas of apple-green crepe de chine and did look beautiful, fragile and very young. One long strand of creamy pearls, unmistakably real, was her only jewelry.

"Thanks. Do you really like the pyjamas? They're not exactly my kind of thing, but Buddy bought them for me just for tonight. Only I'll bet Luke picked them out. Buddy likes full skirts and waists."

"They're great, and Luke knew just what he was doing, if indeed he's responsible for them," Walter said. "You're a lucky gal to have your own resident Pygmalion."

"Who?"

"Just an old Greek who had a thing for statues," Walter said, draining his drink and not looking at me. "Pay no attention to me. James is out to get me drunk tonight."

James tittered and the doorbell rang and Buddy came down the stairs, resplendent in a correct light-weight blue blazer and with damp comb tracks in his hair, and Pie went to greet the first of her guests.

It started out well enough. People on our street trickled in first, knowing instinctively that their early presence would please and reassure the young Harralsons. None of them except us, the Swansons, and Charles and Virginia Guthrie to their left had seen the inside of the house, and with the white sorcery of the candlelight and the fading sunset and the splendid table and James's alchemy at the bar, the house took on an almost enchanted air, like Morgan Le Fay's Castle Chariot in its fairy aspect. I could hear soft gasps of pleasure and admiration from the knots of people at the bar and around the buffet table, and murmured compliments. In the face of our capitulation, in the first flush of her success, Pie's little-girl party manners gave way to happy chatter and small flirtings and exuberant gestures. Buddy alternately beamed and frowned with suppressed pride, and kept glasses refilled, and agreed, yes, it was a pretty good house if he did say so himself. Pie took platoons of women up the stairs to see the top two levels, and raised a radiant face to me as the bell rang more and more frequently, and once made me a small, gay circle with her thumb and forefinger. Okay. Going well.

A few of the people from the law firm came, and then more. Between us, all the people from the street seemed to know all of them, and the young Harralsons

63

wove and bobbed and smiled among the groups that formed and broke and reformed around the table, all talking of comfortable small things and half-forgotten sillinesses, as people will who have known each other for a long time. Before the downstairs became too crowded and clotted with smoke, in that lovely, golden time when a good party is trembling on the verge of becoming whatever it will become and expectation seems to thrill in the air like a fine silver wire, I looked around and wished that Kim Dougherty were here. It seemed to me then that the house at this moment might somehow have healed him, restored him. But he hadn't come yet.

Pie's mother and father came then, and I watched Pie's evening swell and crown and burst into joy. She ran to the door with small squeals of pure delight, and ushered them into her beautiful, ringing house, an arm around each one of them. Her head tossed as if plumes were affixed to it. Her skin glowed like her incandescent pearls. Look, Mama and Daddy. Look what I did. Look what I have. Look what I *am*. Her mother, a tiny, plump woman in harlequin glasses and shoes dyed to match her teal-blue silk, beamed back and breathed in this overwhelming aura of daughter, audibly. Pie clung to Matt Gladney's arm, giving it small, quick pressures, dimpling up at him. His face was florid once more, and the small blue eyes twinkled, and he smiled broadly, but I felt a small finger of unease watching him. Somehow, I thought, he disliked this moment. He shook hands firmly with Buddy, but his gaze was already beyond the boy, measuring the house and the room and the guests like an inchworm. A duller, deeper flush crept up his broad neck into his face.

"Ain't no white columns here tonight," Walter murmured to me, and I saw that he too had been watching Matt Gladney. "I think he hates baby's castle—what do you think?"

"Well, it doesn't have very good associations for him," I said, thinking of those basement stairs that had bled his grandchild away. "And if he's a stickler for columns and Chippendale, all this would hardly enchant him. This white and chrome and leather *is*

64

pretty overwhelming. He'll come around, since she's so proud of it."

Pie herded them up to the bar, and Buddy introduced them, correctly and gravely, to a knot of the firm's senior members who stood around it. Many of them seemed to know Matt Gladney—the legislature, I remembered. Their wives moved in to encircle Pie's mother, welcoming and assessing at the same time. I saw Virginia Guthrie break away from a group of neighborhood women and join the women around Mrs. Gladney. She looked stunning and imperial in the gunmetal silk that almost precisely matched her prematurely gray hair. Charles's emeralds, the twenty-fifth-anniversary present she so treasured, caught a last shaft of sunlight and sprang into fire. She smiled and held out her hand to Mrs. Gladney, and I thought once again what a beautiful woman Virginia is, even though she's closer to fifty than any of us really know, and has raised and sent out into the world three children. Not just handsome, or beautiful for her age, but really beautiful, period. Virginia ought to soften up that shark's grin on Daddy, I thought. Virginia plus those emeralds. He's got to approve of all that, even if the rest of us leave him colder than a mackerel. I thought we probably did. His neck had grown redder and his voice louder, even though his voice was hearty and his feral smile never wavered.

"What the hell is Big Daddy so mad about?" Claire Swanson asked me as we stood at the buffet table. "He looks like his face is going to explode. You can feel the mad like a cloud of smoke. There's just no reason for it that I can see. I think Pie's doing very well tonight."

"Too well, I'd say." Walter appeared beside us wearing the half-satanic, half-cherubic smirk he gets when he's had just a trifle too much to drink. "She did the whole schmeer all by herself, without Daddy and with just old Buddy-baby. Can't have that. It smacks of treachery and insurrection. I bet he'd just love to see his cherished son-in-law with his fly open, or wearing a lampshade on his head, or going berserk and pouring a drink down Eloise's utterly astounding cleavage."

Claire and I looked over at Eloise Jennings, whose

65

sun-speckled breasts were in imminent danger of spilling out of her deep-V'd black caftan. We snickered.

"Save the whales," said Walter, pleased with himself.

"Go eat something," I said. "Go have some of that top grade sirloin steak tartare. You're a disgrace."

Lucas Abbott and his family came in last, along with Kim Dougherty. The party was throbbing by then, showing no signs of abating. You knew that it probably would soon, that someone—an older couple —would drift away, murmuring thanks and compliments, and then another, and others would follow. The alchemy of a party is a strange and individual thing, though; you learn early to read them. This one would lose a considerable number of guests before long but none of its momentum. A hard core of neighborhood people and younger guests would stay and drink late into the night. People would remember this party as a good one.

Pie brought Lucas Abbott and his family up to meet us, maneuvering them like a giddy sheep dog. Kim sauntered behind them. He looked older and thinner in a well-cut summer suit, the only one I had ever seen him wear. His eyes were still smudged with shadows, though he did not look as hangdog as he had when we had seen him last. He looked around at the glowing house as though he had not seen it before, a faint, puzzled frown between his red eyebrows. He cocked his head to one side, as though listening for something, then shook it slightly, as though he did not hear what he was expecting. Someone had given him a drink, and he hugged me and gave Walter a soft jab on the arm, and stood with an arm across both our shoulders, but he said nothing except, "Hi, Kennedys."

"I found this guy standing out on the lawn admiring his handiwork," Lucas Abbott said. "I thought he was rooted to the ground. We had to drag him in, practically; for a minute there I thought he was going to bolt. I didn't know architects got opening-night nerves."

Spots of color burned on Luke's polished cheekbones, as though he had been too long in the sun. In the candlelight he looked spectacular.

"Meet my wife Anne and my daughter Marty. Colquitt and Walter Kennedy, the Harralsons' next-door neighbors on the right. I heartily approve, and so will you two," he said, turning to the tall, slender woman and the girl at his side.

We exchanged greetings and pleasantries. I watched as Pie led Kim into the body of the party, where people pressed close around him, clamoring praise for the house. His face was closed and still, and he nodded and mouthed words I could not hear. Once or twice he looked around almost desperately over their heads, as if seeking the nearest exit. I was disturbed and unhappy for him. Perhaps, after all, it would have been better if he had not come.

"We've grown very fond of your husband," I said to Anne Abbott. "He's been wonderful to Buddy and Pie, and we see a good bit of him. I hope it will be far more now that you're moving here."

"Luke has told us about you too," Anne Abbott said. She had a soft, even Bryn Mawr voice. "And about the Harralsons, of course, and their house. It really is lovely, isn't it?"

"It is. And from what I know of your husband's taste, yours will be just as lovely. I think he's saved the Harralsons from some near-suicidal decisions about wallpaper and such, and if the party is a success, they have him to thank. I know he's a wonderful family man because he's been so generous to them."

"Luke is a generous man," she said flatly. There was nothing in her voice of the small, social lilt that you usually hear in the voices of people you have just met. There was a silence.

Lucas Abbott said, "Let's go sample some of that excellent stock Walter here helped us lug in today. I am as arid as the Gobi Desert." He placed a hand lightly on each slim, tanned arm and bore his two women away toward the bar, Buddy following in their wake like a sturdy tugboat. I saw that Lucas Abbott was staggering, almost imperceptibly.

"I think Lucas Abbott is drunk," I whispered to Walter, shocked. I don't know why I was. Most of us were slightly tipsy by now. But I had never seen him waver, never heard him slur, and it was as alien to his cool dignity as a shrill scream would have been. He seldom drank at all, that I knew.

"Depths and depths," Walter said owlishly. "I think he is too. A little tiff with the Girl of the Golden East there, do you think?"

"Maybe. She was sort of . . . brusque with him there for a minute, I thought. Maybe she felt ignored, with him spending most of their first day here off with Buddy and Pie. What do you think of the ladies Abbott?"

"Pretty neat. Prime goods. Good-looking women, both of them, in that Eastern way those women all have. The tans and the streaked hair and the little-bitty voices. They look like they just won a regatta. The three of them look like a matched set of Gucci luggage."

"You've got a Gucci attaché and I don't hear you complaining," I said absently. Something in the brief exchange with the Abbotts had set my interior antenna pinging uneasily.

Roger Swanson motioned to Walter, and he crossed the room and joined him. They put their heads together and then threw them back and laughed, and I knew Roger had told one of his heavy-handed, stunningly obscene, endearing jokes. The smoke around the buffet table was palpable, lying in still blue strata in the air. My eyes prickled and my head ached suddenly. I slipped away from the table and walked through the kitchen and out onto the back deck. The darkness was fresh and fragrant and I took a deep, grateful breath, and then noticed that a figure was leaning against the deck rail at the far end, head in hands. I started to slip back into the kitchen so as not to intrude, and then recognized the long, rangy body. Kim.

"Don't you feel well?" I said, going to his side. He raised his head and looked at me in the faint light from the kitchen.

"There's something wrong with this house, Col," he said bleakly. His voice was low and ragged.

"Oh, Kim, no! There isn't! It's even more beautiful than before, it's just breathtaking like this, all shined up for its first party. It's like it was born for this, for this night. Everybody's talking about what a great house it is; a million people have told me they think so. And they have you too, you know they have."

I put my hand on his arm, and he covered it with his own, as blindly as a child reaching out for solace. He shook his head, almost angrily.

"I don't mean the way it looks. Christ, do you think I don't know how it looks? It's a goddamn perfect house as far as looks go, and how do you think I feel, seeing it and knowing I can't do it again? I've been over here a thousand times, just looking at it, wondering how I did it, what I thought and felt while I was designing it—and I just can't remember. But there's something else wrong; there's something in this house I didn't put here. I can feel it, I can hear it talking to me, but I can't understand what it's saying. If I could, I think I'd know what was wrong with me. . . . Colquitt, it's just all gone. I'm not going to get it back."

His voice broke and he stopped. Tears welled in my own eyes. I put my arms around him and held him silently, and he stood quietly in their circle for a moment, fighting to control his breathing. Then he stepped back and passed a hand over his eyes, and ruffled my hair.

"Tantrum's over," he said. "Let's go get another drink. I either need two less than I've already had or four more. Thanks for putting up with me, Col. You've done too much of that lately, you and Walter both."

We walked back into the kitchen arm in arm. Walter and Claire Swanson stood there, at the sink, watching us as we came in. They said nothing. Walter's face was mild and still, Claire's pink with embarrassment or indignation or both. They had seen the small tableaux on the deck, then. Sudden irritation made my own face warm. I did not attempt to explain, and knew I would not. Both of them knew me far too well to suspect that I felt anything for Kim except what I did, and Walter should have known Kim well enough by now. Let it go and be damned to them.

"Walter spilled clam dip on his coat, and since we couldn't find you, I did the honors," Claire said, brandishing a damp dishcloth.

"Thanks," I said drily. "What are friends for if not to help out when they're needed?"

"What, indeed," she said. We all returned to the roiling living room.

Something seemed to creep into the evening about then. Afterward we could not isolate what it was. "It just went sour," Claire said. "Everything got . . . too much." That was about as close as any of us ever came to it until much, much later. In a way I am glad that other people noticed it. It gives a small shred of validity to what we think now, Walter and I.

It started, for me at least, with a flurry of raised voices at the end of the room where the bar was. Just a small flurry, like you get sometimes when someone brings up local politics at a party where everyone has had too much to drink. I could hear Matt Gladney's voice above the others. It roughened as I listened, went flatter, more nasal, more wire-grass South. Pie's voice skimmed into the middle of the babble, high and artificial, but I could not hear what she said. Someone stepped back then, and I could see that Matt Gladney and Buddy Harralson were standing very still, facing each other. Buddy looked whitened and miserable and furious, as he had when they had come back from burying the puppy. He said nothing. Matt Gladney's face was inflamed, incandescent, purple, the savage smile ludicrous in all the compacted anger. A record dropped on the stereo then, drowning the sounds, so we could not hear what Matt Gladney was saying. I saw Lucas Abbott put his hand on Buddy's arm and pull him gently away from the group. They disappeared toward the kitchen. Matt Gladney stood still, looking after them. On the other side of the room, by the buffet table, I saw Kim Dougherty standing with Anne Abbott and the daughter. They were looking toward the group at the bar but did not move toward it. In a moment Kim said something close to Anne Abbott's ear, and she smiled, stiffly, and they turned back to the plates they were filling. The music spun up and out and people began to move up to the bar again, and Matt Gladney turned away in response to something Pie's mother said. The moment broke and the party bowled on.

"I'd just as soon go home," I said to Walter. He was looking thoughtfully at the crowd around the bar, apparently having decided to dismiss the incident with Kim for what it was. "I don't like the looks of that. Everybody's had too much to drink, and if that awful father of Pie's is going to jump on poor stupid Buddy and ruin this party, I don't want to be here for it."

"I don't think he is," Walter said. "I don't see him anywhere. Though he could be out in the kitchen beating the hell out of Buddy and Abbott. I don't see them either. I hope Abbott's somewhere cooling the kid off. He looked like he'd like to kill the old man. Okay. Let me finish this drink and I'll see if the Swansons want to come over for a nightcap and hash over this glittering affair. I think I'll ask Kim too. He looks lower than I've ever seen him."

"He is," I said, hugging his arm in love and gratitude. "Thank you for seeing that. Walter, what you saw out there—that was all—"

"I know it was, baby. I may get an occasional bee in my bonnet about Dougherty, but that's all it is. Just a very small bee. I know what we're all about. Kim's my friend too, remember? Now let me go see if I can find the Swansons."

I wish we had left then. I wish it more than anything in the world. Perhaps it would have broken the chain if we had not seen. Perhaps by not seeing we could have escaped the strings and webs, the net that has reached out and caught us up. I doubt it, but perhaps it might have been possible, there at the beginning, to get free. Walter doesn't think so. He thinks we had to see it. We had, after all, been a part of the house, of Buddy and Pie Harralson's life, from the very beginning. Present at the creation, as it were. He thinks we were woven into it then, at the start.

There was a terrible, high scream, Pie's, unmistakably. I had heard it once before. I don't remember getting from the living room to the downstairs bedroom, where the scream came from. I was aware only later that I stood there, in the doorway, and that a few late-lingering senior members from Buddy's firm were behind me. And Walter and Kim Dougherty and Anne and Marty Abbott.

Pie stood just inside the room screaming thinly and senselessly, over and over and over. Matt Gladney lay on his back at her feet, the magenta draining rapidly and finally out of his face. The blue eyes were open, but we knew even then that they saw nothing, and would not again. His face was insanely contorted to one side, mouth dragged down to his chin.

Across the room, beside the neatly made guest bed, Lucas Abbott and Buddy Harralson stood, locked together in each other's arms, frozen and staring at us as stilly as wild animals pinned in the headlights of an oncoming car. They were naked. I thought idiotically that Buddy's legs were almost as smooth as those of a young girl, while Lucas Abbott's were corded like the trunk of a tree. In the chaste gloom of the bedroom their white flesh was as shocking as blood on the face of a child. Their clothes were flung across the comforter on the bed beside the strewn handbags of the women who had not yet left the party.

Chapter Eight

THE HOUSE went up for sale almost immediately, handled by the sedate old firm that has always marketed properties in our part of town. The agent was a friend of most of us on the street—a small, funny girl who had gone to school with Claire Swanson and is a member of most of our clubs and committees. She had not been at the party.

"It was a terrible tragedy, and a scandal, of course," she said to Walter and me a week or so later when she came to oversee the setting up of the "For Sale" sign. "But it's no worse than others we've had in town. You remember that awful thing over on Blackthorn a couple of years ago, and the Fairchild affair. Those houses sold in less than a week. We're not going to have a bit of trouble with this one. I'm just sorry it had to happen here, in front of all of you. But it's not as though they were *us*—I mean, you all didn't really know anything about them or their people, did you? It just goes to show, doesn't it? You never know about people."

"You never do," said Walter.

We were sickened and devastated. Everybody on the street was. Shocked and stunned by the ugliness, the sheer dreadfulness of that ghastly, frozen moment in the Harralsons' downstairs bedroom. Torn with pity and horror. Helpless and outraged in the face of the appalling waste of lives and youth and promise. I had turned on my heel and fled like an animal after that first instant in the doorway, back to my own lighted kitchen. Walter found me there a little later pacing the floor and crying, clutching a squirming Foster against my face.

"I can't go back over there," I said finally. "I can't. I know we have to—that poor child, her poor mother —there are things that will have to be done, somebody's going to have to call an ambulance or something—God, Walter, and Luke's wife and daughter down here not knowing anybody—and Buddy—Walter, I cannot do it."

"They don't want anybody, Col," he said. "She slammed the bedroom door and ran upstairs and her mother went with her. Claire and Virginia went up and knocked, and her mother told them to go away. Everybody's gone by now. They were leaving when I left. They're not going to want to see any of us, not after we saw . . . that."

"But what will happen to them? All of them?"

"What more can?" he said.

I hovered, hiccoughing and whimpering, at the kitchen window, vacillating with the need to help and the greater need to know no more, for two or three hours. Walter made coffee and we drank it, but we did not talk much. I halfway expected Claire and Roger to call or come over, or Kim, perhaps, but none of them did. The house next door was darkened except for a light on the lawn that must have come from Pie and Buddy's upstairs bedroom. I could not make my mind examine what must be going on in the house. I felt confused and displaced and fragmented, the way I have been told you do after a terrible accident.

Late that night—into the morning, really—an ambulance came silently into the Harralsons' driveway and two white-coated men got out. When they went around to the back and opened the door and began to unfold a shapeless wheeled thing, I let the curtains drop and turned away. We went to bed, but we did not sleep and we did not speak. I heard the ambulance drive away after a bit, and another car. Much later a third car started up and ghosted out of the driveway. The rest of the night was silent.

In the morning the house was deserted. No cars were parked in the driveway. When Walter and I finally mustered our courage and went over and knocked, no one answered. The knock had the sound of echoing into a house that had not been lived in for a long time.

We talked about it on the street, of course. But it was subdued talk. I did not have to guess what would happen at Buddy's firm. There would be two quiet resignations, one fewer dynamic Eastern senior partner and one fewer promising partner-to-be. The firm would go on. I did not know what would happen to Buddy and Lucas Abbott after that. I still do not know about Lucas, though we heard later that summer that Buddy and Pie were divorced and he had left the small southern city where they had grown up and gone somewhere in the Southwest. Virginia Guthrie heard that Pie was living with her mother. We did not see her again. A woman from the real estate firm came and supervised the moving van that took the new chrome and leather furnishings away. We were at work and did not see it. I have always been grateful for that.

We did not see Kim again after that night for almost a month. I knew he would come and talk about that night when he was ready to, if he would ever be able to do it. He did not call either, and I did not have the heart to call his office. When he did appear, one evening at his usual time, I was surprised to see that he looked fit and, if not happy, at least amiable and quiet in his skin. The skin was burned almost walnut-brown from the sun, and he looked hard and honed, if still too thin.

I hugged him, and Walter's smile was spontaneous. "Where have you been?" I asked. "We've been worried to death about you. I thought you really had cut and run for Europe, or Madagascar, or wherever."

"To lose myself and blot out my haunting memories? Not yet. There's too much I've got to figure out still. Besides, the Douglas house is coming down to the wire, and I've been on the site from dawn till midnight every day, practically. It's going good." He accepted the drink I gave him and scooped up Razz, who came bounding and prancing around his feet as he always used to do, purring loudly.

"He's missed you," I said. "We have too. I'm glad things are going so well with the Douglas house. Does that mean you're designing again?"

"Nope. Not a line. Not a curlicue. But I've been thinking, and I think now I can beat it. There's a reason for it somewhere, an answer. I think it's in that house." He jerked a thumb over toward the Harralson house, standing silent and lovely in the late sunlight.

"What do you mean?" said Walter, looking at him.

"I'm not really sure what I mean. It's just a feeling. I had it the night of that Christ-awful party. You remember, Col, I told you—and it's been getting stronger and stronger. If I can lick that house, I'll get the juice back. That simple. It sounds crazy as hell, but I think that's it."

We were silent, and then Walter said, "Kim, it's just a house. Just a pile of boards and stone. You know that. You built it. What's to lick about it? You sound like you've declared war on it."

"I have. I'm going to break it. It's not going to break me, not like it did those poor, miserable kids and her daddy. Not like it did Abbott. Uh-uh. No way."

We stared at him.

"Kim," I said, "You can't ascribe that—that awful business over there to the *house*. That's just . . . lunacy. People have strokes all the time. You know what her father was like; you know that eerie, funny little thing she had going with her daddy; you know he never liked poor Buddy. And some of the most unlikely people in the world turn out to be homosexual; it's not all that unusual, tragic as it turned out for them. We might have seen that coming—I mean, it wasn't exactly a healthy relationship he had with his mother, and his father dying so young. God knows what Luke Abbott represented to him. He wouldn't even have been aware of it until he was so mad and desperate, and he'd been drinking—and Luke. Now that I remember, Eloise Jennings told me when he first came down here that she'd heard there'd been something funny with a law clerk back in Connecticut. I thought she was just being Eloise, and I assumed she meant a girl when I thought about it, which wasn't much, but law clerks are usually young men, aren't they? It was just horrible, just awful, but at least you can sort of understand."

"I'll bet you a million dollars those guys weren't gay," Kim said. "I'd stake my life on it. I'm absolutely certain nothing like that had ever happened to those guys before that night. Did you see their faces? They didn't even know where they were."

"They'd both been drinking."

"No."

"You upset me badly when you talk like this, Kim," I said, my voice trembling. "It isn't you. It's all been horrible enough without this kind of stuff. Please, please, let's don't talk about it anymore. You're going to . . . make yourself sick. I can't listen to any more of this."

He studied my face, and then Walter's.

"I'm sorry, both of you," he said heavily. "I *have* let it get to me. I didn't realize how much until I heard myself talking. Christ, I sound practically certifiable. Forget it, if you can. I really ought to knock off at the Douglas site for a few days and go somewhere—the beach or the mountains or something. I really am tireder than hell."

The talk turned to other things, and presently he heaved himself up off his chair and walked out to his car. Walter walked with him. I carried our glasses back into the kitchen and started a salad, tearing up lettuce and slicing tomatoes blindly and mechanically. Walter came back into the kitchen.

"Walter, I'm worried sick about him," I said. "He sounds obsessed. Almost not normal. Not at all like himself. I almost wish he *had* gone to Europe back when he first started talking about it. I'd miss him, but it would be better than seeing him doing this to himself."

"He'll be all right, Col," he said, leaning his chin on the top of my head. "He's just lost his perspective. And he's probably right about working too hard. I think a few days out of town will fix him up. Want to offer him the beach house?"

"No," I said slowly. "I think he'd rather find a place on his own. I don't want to seem like I'm hovering over him. You know how he hates that."

"Well, you know the gentleman better than I," he said matter-of-factly. "We'll let him be and see what happens. If he's determined to engage in some sort of spiritual wrestling match with that pile of rocks over there, he's going to do it whether or not we think he's nuttier than a fruitcake. Personally, I think he just may be enjoying the drama of the whole thing a tiny trifle."

"Whatever it is, he's not enjoying it," I began, but I could see from his face that he did not want to talk about Kim Dougherty anymore, and so I dropped it.

A week later the "For Sale" sign came down and Buck and Anita Sheehan moved into the house next door.

PART TWO

The Sheehans

Chapter Nine

THE FIRST thing we noticed about Anita Sheehan was a nervous, vivid luminosity, a hectic radiance that seemed to flicker like a candle in the wind. The second thing was her shyness. It was painful, almost palpable, so that you hated to intrude upon it with even a smile or a wave. I had never seen anyone so eager to go unnoticed. There was nothing in it of unfriendliness or unnatural modesty or exclusivity. It was the pure, shining agony of a lonely and unlovely child.

But Anita Sheehan was not unlovely. She was beautiful, almost as beautiful as Virginia Guthrie in an exotic, strangely Eurasian way—high cheekbones, too sharply shadowing her face, as though she had been ill recently; long winglike brows repeating the arch of her cheekbones over dark, lash-shuttered eyes; a tremulous child's mouth and small pointed chin. Her hair was a heavy mass of pure black, without luster but also without the hard chalkiness that spoke of dye. Her tall body was fragile and far too thin. You could almost see through the white skin of her hands.

Yet for all her physical magnificence—"My God, it's Tondelayo," Walter said reverently when we first saw the Sheehans from the window of the den the morning the moving van arrived—there was something bleached, faded, scrimmed, as though with gauze, about her. I thought then that she probably had been very ill.

"She looks like a Persian cat," Walter said. "One that somebody's starved and beaten. She looks like she'd bolt if you clapped your hands. Christ, I wonder if they know about what happened over there."

"I doubt it," I said, looking at the well-cut slacks and shirt that hung too loosely on the woman's slender figure but still said money. "Margaret Matthieson said she didn't tell them when they bought the house. They'd looked for so long, he said, and she apparently just fell in love with the house when she saw it and seemed so grateful to find it and so anxious to move in. Margaret said she just didn't have the heart. Besides, she said some sixth sense told her not to. She says there are some people you can tell about any trouble there's been in a house and they won't turn a hair, and there are some you can't. Apparently she's one of the can'ts. Margaret said she seemed very frail and nervous, and he was terribly protective and solicitous toward her, so she figured she'd been sick or something."

"Sheehan, you said," Walter said.

"Yes. Buck and Anita Sheehan. From somewhere in New Jersey. He's taken over the Computer Tech branch, but that's all I know about them. Margaret said he saw the house last week and bought it the next day, and she came down yesterday, and that's it. I don't think they know a soul in town, so they probably wouldn't have heard. I hope nobody finds it necessary to blurt it out. She does look like a breeze would blow her away, doesn't she? Well, what do you think? Shall we go over and introduce ourselves?"

"I guess so," Walter said without enthusiasm. I knew what he was thinking. The Sheehans seemed, from our window, at least, attractive people, but somehow I did not yet want to get close to the people who would live in that house. Some portent of pain and madness lay around the frail woman's shoulders like smoke. There was a small, leaden clot of dread deep behind my ribs, too, whenever I looked across at the Harralson house. Too soon, it was too soon.

But we did go, late that afternoon, after the moving van had ground and lumbered out of the driveway and down the street. I do not lean to popping in on new neighbors with casseroles and hearty smiles; indeed, the Harralsons had been my first experience with new neighbors, and Pie's gregariousness had solved that problem for us early on. But soon after we had moved into our own house Claire and Roger had walked over just to say hello and welcome to the neighborhood, and Charles and Virginia Guthrie had stopped in briefly the next day, and it was simply what one did on our street. Now it was our turn, and we could not, of course, ignore the Sheehans. I knew they had seen us; Buck Sheehan had given us a cheerful grin as we'd left for work that morning, and we'd waved back, and Anita had come face to face with Walter when he drove in from work that afternoon, her arms piled high with books, and had given him a startled, frozen little smile, and averted her face and hurried into the house.

So I cut a hasty armful of purple iris and we walked across the driveway and up the bank to the house next door, following the natural pathway that broke through the towering rhododendrons that marked our property line. My feet seemed reluctant to climb the small rise that I had climbed so often before when the Harralsons had lived there. I had not been over to the house since that terrible last night, had not even looked often at the house, waiting quiet and empty and beautiful among the still trees in the pure, early summer sun. Razz went with us as far as the edge of our driveway, then stopped and sat down and watched us out of sight through the foliage. At the place in the side yard where I had stumbled over the puppy Walter took my hand, and I squeezed his gratefully but said nothing. For some reason my heart was pounding and my mouth was dry.

Anita Sheehan answered the doorbell. For a moment she stared out at us blindly, as though the sun were shining in her eyes, though it was setting behind the trees across the street now, and the front door lay in green shadow. Seen closely, her face was years older than I had thought when I first saw her from our window. The translucent white skin was webbed about the eyes and mouth with fine lines, like cobwebs. Deeper lines bracketed her child's vulnerable mouth and cut across her high forehead. Her eyes were wide and had an unfocused look. At first I thought her gaze was riveted in dread at something over our heads, but then I realized that we had taken her by surprise and she was frightened. I did not know what to say and so said nothing, feeling for a long moment large and awkward and deeply embarrassed.

Then her eyes seemed to register us, and the wide whiteness in them dwindled, and she smiled a convulsive little smile. "Hello. I'm Colquitt Kennedy from next door" and "You must be Mrs. Kennedy from next door" we said together, in a rush, and then stopped. I laughed, and she did too, and her face was younger and sweeter and almost gay for a moment. Then it closed again.

"Let's start over," I said. "I'm Colquitt Kennedy from next door, and this is my husband, Walter, and we just wanted to give you these and say welcome to the neighborhood."

She reached out with thin arms and took the iris, looking down at them as if she had never seen iris before, and back at me. Her smile trembled.

"I'm Anita Sheehan," she said, "This is really lovely of you, they're perfectly beautiful—the house is such a mess, I—let me go put them in some water, and then—you must meet my husband, Buck—" She was gone from the doorway before either of us could speak. We stood in the open door uncertain whether she intended us to come in, to wait, or to go away. I wanted desperately to slip back across the driveway, not to intrude on her any longer, not to feel the physical force of her terror—if that's what it was—under my impaling gaze. I could not move.

Beside me, Walter started to say something, and then a man's large bulk filled the doorway, and a man's voice, genial and overbright, swam out to meet us. I got a confused impression of enormous hands, furred on their backs with dark hair, and a heavy, tanned face starred with startlingly beautiful black-lashed blue eyes. The man's voice was distinctly southern New Jersey, but his face, as the cliché goes, was the very map of Ireland. His dark hair was thick and rough and would have curled if it had been longer, and his jaw was square and only slightly slackened underneath with age and weight, and his smile was wide and white and sweet. You knew instantly that it was as genuine as it was ingenuous. He wore faded running trunks and a tee shirt with the ubiquitous Lacoste alligator on the breast, and his feet were bare.

84

"Hi, neighbors," he boomed, but somehow it was not an offensive, intruding boom. "I'm Buck Sheehan. I've been looking forward to meeting you. We've been enjoying your garden all day, and those sure are pretty flowers you brought. Anita's putting them in water now." He came out onto the doorstep and pulled the door closed behind him gently.

"Walter Kennedy," said Walter. "And this is my wife, Colquitt."

I put out my hand, and he pressed it warmly. "We're happy that you're here," I said. "I know how it is on the first day in a new house, and we're certainly not going to keep you. I just thought you might need something, or maybe want to use our telephone, or something . . ."

"Thanks. Ours is in and working," he said. "It's just a matter of raking through the debris now. I didn't realize how much you can accumulate in twenty years in the same place. This house is a good bit bigger than our old one, but somehow we've managed to clutter up every corner of it, and one reason we liked it was all the space. Well. It'll just take a few days. I'd ask you in, but I'm afraid Anita's pretty whipped. I didn't give her much notice when I made this move, and she's worked herself almost to death. Please forgive her if she doesn't come out. Anita's the kind of woman who wants everything just so before anybody sees it. And she hasn't been very well . . ."

He looked at us anxiously, as if silently imploring us to understand something that he could not or would not put into words. I realized that he did not want us to think him unfriendly or his wife's behavior odd. I liked him suddenly and finally, in a way I seldom do people I have just met. The way I had liked Kim Dougherty. I knew Walter liked him too, because he settled himself loosely and comfortably against the porch railing and began to tell Buck about the day we had moved into our house.

It had been a typical harried suburban moving day, complete with a moving van gone astray, burst cartons leaking excelsior and canned goods, and Walter and I, hideously begrimed, trapped like animals in our barren burrow by the gloved, hatted and calling-carded Misses Fortenberry from down the street. By the time Walter was through the story Buck was laughing aloud, a great tasting, relishing laugh, and Walter and I were grinning with pleasure at his enjoyment. "They'll undoubtedly call on you too, along with everybody else," I said.

His face sobered and closed; he looked alert and nearly alarmed.

"But not for a while, not until you get settled in," I added quickly.

"I don't think Anita will be ready for company for a little while," he said apologetically but quite definitely. And somehow I knew that I was meant to spread the word quietly on the street: Let the Sheehans be for now. Well, I thought, I'll warn off Claire and Virginia, but I'm not going up and down the street to plead for Anita Sheehan's precious privacy. If she wants to be alone she should have picked a house in the country with no neighbors on either side for ten miles. I was obscurely annoyed at having to assume any responsibility at all for yet another woman in that house. But then my sense of fairness raised its head; I treasure my privacy too. But I manage to insure my own, somehow. Walter does not run interference for me. Buck Sheehan obviously did for Anita.

As though he sensed my slight drawing away, he turned to face us, and his face was very quiet and somehow pleading and tender at the same time.

"Anita has been sick," he said. "She was in the hospital for more than eight months. She's only been out three weeks. We thought—the doctors said—they said that a complete change would be good for her. This new job came up about a month ago, and since the timing was right and we've never been anywhere near the South, I took it almost on the spur of the moment. And so far it *has* been good for her. She likes the slower pace and the peace—we had a pretty hectic life in Jersey. I traveled a lot. She was by herself too much. I won't be traveling much now, and this seems to be a quiet neighborhood, and she truly loves the house. She'll like you too. She's a friendly, sweet gal when she isn't . . . before she got sick. She's just got to take it very, very easy and slow. She's going to be completely fine. But I hope you'll forgive her if she seems nervous. It's hard to get back in the world when you've been out of it so long."

He stopped. He looked down at his big hands.

"Well, of course," I said. "I'm sorry she's been sick, but I'm glad she's going to be okay. You tell her for me that I understand perfectly, and so will everybody on the street. Tell her to take her time, and by all means call or come over if she needs anything at all. I'll give you all about a week, and then I'll have you to supper with the Swansons up the street and the Guthries on your left, maybe. Just quiet, and slacks or shorts and hamburgers or something. And meanwhile you come over for a drink whenever you like. We get home from work around six, and we're in and out on weekends."

"Thank you, Mrs. Kennedy," said Buck Sheehan. "Thank you very much. We'd like to have dinner with you. She'll be settled in and rested by then. It'll be just the thing for her. She's just overdone it for today."

We said goodbye and turned to go. He did not go back into the house. We half-paused, the way you do when you know someone is looking at your back, as if there were something unfinished hanging in the air.

"Oh, by the way," he said. We turned.

"Have you folks got any children?"

It was not so much a peculiar question as a peculiar time to ask it. These small ritual sniffings—the finding of slots and niches for each other—are usually accomplished in the first few moments of conversation, pontoons laid down, one by one, in the bridge that will lead to friendship, or away from it. The lapse of time and space around his question gave it an odd portent. Did the Sheehans have children, then, and hope for suitable companions for them? I had not noticed, in the subliminal summing-up sweep I had made of the Sheehans and their worldly goods during the day, any evidence of children. Or did they dislike children, hope that there would be none near?

"No, we don't," said Walter. "Do you?"

"No."

He didn't say anything more for a moment, and then he said, "I haven't seen many kids on the street. Is everybody old middle-aged folks like us? Not that you two are middle-aged, but . . ." His voice trailed off, and the strangeness of the moment grew. I knew without knowing how I knew that he did not want to seem to query us closely on the matter of children, but was for some reason impelled to it.

Walter answered, his voice neutral and guarded, and I knew that some of the easy liking he had felt for Buck Sheehan was being held in abeyance.

"There aren't many, as a matter of fact," he said. "The Guthries, on your left there, with the garden, have three, but they're married and live out of town. The Jenningses over there have about a million, mostly in diapers, and they're such pains in the behind that standard operating procedure is to tell them you'll break their arms if they set foot in your house, so they shouldn't be too much of a problem. The Swansons up the street have three teenagers. And that's about it."

"Teenagers. That's nice. Are they boys or girls?"

"Boys," I said. "The youngest is thirteen and the oldest is seventeen. They're good kids. They're no problem as far as noise or anything. Most of us use them for chores and yard work, and I'm sure they'd be happy to do some for you. But they certainly won't bother you otherwise."

I hadn't meant to sound abrupt, but the strangeness was stretching out uncomfortably. Buck Sheehan said, "It isn't that. I just wondered if there were any." His smile was miserable and thinned with the effort to be ingratiating, and I felt again the vapor of strangeness around the man and woman in the Harralson house and a real pity for this nice man's discomfiture.

"Well," said Walter. "Back to the rock garden for me, and the digging out for you. Glad you all are here. Col will call about that dinner, and meanwhile, you certainly will know where we live."

"Thanks for coming over," he replied. "And thanks for the flowers. We'll be looking forward to the evening."

"I'll call," I said, and we scuffed back down the path through the rhododendrons to our patio. I looked back once, and he had gone into the house. The doorstep was empty and the door closed. The lovely lines of the house seemed, in the settling shadows, to have shrugged more closely into the earth and trees, as if with a sigh of contentment. Warm light shone softly from the windows once again. A wood thrush, author of that most beautiful and liquid of all sounds, began his splashing song in the Harralsons' woods—the Sheehans' woods now—just as the lucid strains of Handel's *Water Music* sprang to life in one of the Sheehans' downstairs rooms. The unease and alienness of the past few minutes washed out of my mind at the twin sounds twining and soaring in the dusk, but then I saw Buck Sheehan come into the lighted kitchen and lean against the refrigerator and drop his face into his hands, and it came flooding back.

When we got home we did not talk about the Sheehans. I knew that we would eventually of course. But I felt tired and tumescent with a sort of gnawing disquiet that I could put no name to, and out of sorts because I could not identify the sensation and resented having it. Such feelings make me very lonely and a little frightened, because I am never more terribly, finally and irrevocably alone than when I cannot share my infrequent, fey sadnesses and neck prickles and intuitions with Walter. It is not that he laughs at them or fails to understand that I am uncomfortable. It is just that his is a sturdier and more sunlit nature than mine, and when I get twitches of what he calls The Sight, he is more apt to comfort and cajole and perhaps tease than to try and share them. It is one of the few areas in our natures that do not dovetail, and when I am in the grip of a nameless prickling that does not prickle him too, I know the shape of my final and inevitable aloneness on the earth. Walter is sensitive. I am, he says, a sensitive. Not in any silly, conventional psychic way; we have both always laughed at that. But in the fact that I feel currents and whorls and eddies keenly, even when, perhaps, they are not there.

So I did what I always do when my own ultimate aloneness stalks me. I wanted him quickly and silently and totally, to blot and blur and dissolve me into himself. I was nearly whimpering with the wanting. I drew him into the downstairs guest bedroom and urged him with my hands and with small sounds and cries, and, knowing and answering, he took me on top of the rowdy, faded old quilt that had been my grandmother's, fast and driving and absolute in his determination to scourge and ream the fright and alienation out of me. He did. He always does. He knows. Walter has saved my life and perhaps my soul for me in countless ways, without having to search for the proper one, for all of our life together. It is the sum of what we are, he and I. When he can no longer do so, he will die with me.

"DOXY," HE said, lying on his back and staring at the ceiling. His breath still tore at his throat. "You didn't even take off your shirt."

"That word is right out of Thackeray or somebody," I said comfortably, twining my leg over his and scratching his instep with my toe. I felt drained and eased and back in my skin again, and somehow into his too. "You need to learn some new words. Neither did you take off yours. Which is just as well, because you'd be scratched to pieces, and then what would you tell the boys in the locker room?"

"Tell 'em I had me a high-class 'ho on the side. My stock would rise no end."

"Did you ever wish you did?" I said lazily, knowing that he didn't.

"I do, don't I?"

After a small space of time he said, "Do you feel better now?"

"Yes," I said. "You know I do. But I don't want to talk about the Sheehans right now, Walter."

"I know you don't. I wasn't going to."

My eyes flooded with sudden salt and my nose and throat ached. I rolled into his shoulder and buried my face in the hollow of his neck. He pulled me closer and stroked my hair, still damp with sweat.

"I love you more than anything in the world," I said fiercely. "Anything."

"And I love you, my darling," he said. "It will be all right."

Chapter Ten

I DID have the promised dinner party for the Sheehans on the next Saturday evening. It was a soft twilight edging into night when they came through the rhododendrons and around onto the patio. Roger and Claire had walked over early and were stretched out lazily, clinking ice in their first drinks, Claire on the chaise and Roger making a comfortable, rump-sprung bundle in our big Pawley's Island hammock. Kim had come by earlier in the afternoon, and we'd asked him to stay, and he did. He didn't, normally, when we were expecting other guests, but I thought he was probably curious about the new people who would live in the house. Charles and Virginia Guthrie had just arrived and were in the kitchen making themselves the chaste vermouth on the rocks that they prefer. Neither of the Guthries drinks very much.

I had called Anita Sheehan the Wednesday before, and the phone had rung a long time before she answered it.

"Hello?" Even on the telephone, she sounded apprehensive.

"Anita? This is Colquitt Kennedy, from next door. I hope I'm not disturbing you."

"Oh, Colquitt. Yes. How are you? No, of course you're not." Her voice changed, became lighter, quicker, more assured. "I'm sorry I was so long answering," she said. "I was wrestling with some curtains in the upstairs bedroom and didn't hear the phone for a minute."

"Well, I won't keep you," I said, knowing with absolute certainty that she had heard the phone and hadn't wanted to answer it. What is this stupid prescience I've suddenly developed toward the silly Sheehans? I thought in annoyance. I'm not having any more of this. "I just hoped that you all would come have hamburgers with us and some friends on Saturday night," I said. "Nothing fancy at all."

There was stillness, and then she gathered her voice together and said, "We'd love to come Saturday night. We haven't gone out much lately, and it's high time we did. You're kind to ask, and Buck will be so pleased. What time, and can I bring something?"

"About seven," I said. "And nothing at all except yourselves and a big appetite. Walter cherishes the belief that he's the Toscanini of the charcoal grill. And please be comfortable. We'll all have on slacks or shorts. Just come on through the shrubbery and around the back to the patio. You can see it from the edge of the driveway."

"Thank you, Colquitt. We'll see you at seven on Saturday."

We had been filling in Kim and the Swansons on what we knew of the Sheehans. Charles and Virginia came out of the kitchen and sat down on the edge of the brick wall to listen. Somehow, after the pain and horror of the young Harralsons, neighborhood curiosity did not run as high about the new owners of the house as it usually does when, infrequently, a house on our street changes hands. I think we were all still shocked and hurt and obscurely afraid to open ourselves to new involvements. But there they were; by their very proximity, we would be involved with the Sheehans.

"He's branch manager at Computer Tech," Walter said, judiciously poking at his whitening coals. "I get the idea he was a real hotshot in computers, and for some reason I think he must have been in sales. He's got the personality for it—genial and outgoing, though he doesn't clap you on the back or smoke cigars, thank God. He's a nice guy. There's some money around somewhere—you can smell it. I'd say the Sheehans are about as lace-curtain as they come. He seemed really anxious to be friends."

Claire and Virginia looked at me, waiting for me to perform my part of the ritual and tell them about Anita. Claire was rumpled and solid in shorts and a sleeveless shirt, perspiration dewing her short upper lip and brown snub nose. Virginia was in white linen pants and a striped jersey and managed to look like a duchess opening a cattle fair. I looked back at them; I did not know why I was reluctant to talk about Anita Sheehan.

"Well, for God's sake, Col, what about her?" Claire said impatiently. "Does she weigh three hundred pounds and have a mustache? Is she red-headed and freckle-faced, does she go around saying, 'Wurra, wurra?' Is she a midget? What?"

"She's haunted," I said mindlessly, and then looked helplessly at Walter. I did not know why I had said that. It was not a word for this twilit suburban backyard. It should not have been said. It hung there, swelling in the evening and absorbing the very air. Kim Dougherty raised his head and looked at me, his gray eyes darkened and still.

Virginia murmured wordlessly in distress, a gentle reprimand. Claire snorted. "Bullshit. What's got into you, Col?" Charles Guthrie looked apprehensively at Walter and then at me, and Roger Swanson just stared at me. Walter did too for a moment, and then he said, "Colquitt's being fey again. Cut her off the vodka, Roger. There's nothing in the world wrong with Anita Sheehan except that she's the shyest woman I ever met in my life. One of the most spectacular too. A great addition to the neighborhood. Charles, you lucky devil, their upstairs bathroom must look right down into your backyard. I give you about two weeks before you get yourself a pair of binoculars and take up bird-watching."

"I already have a pair," Charles Guthrie said seriously, and we all laughed. Charles is dignified and cultivated and literate, and possessed of not one shred of the bantering humor that Walter and Roger exchange. Somehow it has not marred the friendship between them. They complement each other, and Charles and Virginia are almost ludicrously well matched. For all her elegance and coolness of demeanor, Virginia is a warm, strong, supportive woman. A born nurturer. Though they are not demonstrative toward each other in public, I have seen Virginia take her husband's arm and give it a small, affectionate squeeze—it is the only intimacy I have ever seen between them—and when she does, he looks at her with a sort of awe and wonder that is as touching and revealing as it is totally unconscious. He cherishes her. She keeps his carefully wrought world spinning smoothly in its orbit.

The laughter broke the strangeness, and I said, embarrassed, "She *is* shy. That's all I meant. And she's sort of nervous. Buck said she'd been very ill and in the hospital for a long time; she's just out. You know how strange and frail people are when they're getting over a long illness. But apparently she's going to be okay."

"This illness of Anita Sheehan's, Colquitt—what sort was it?" said Virginia Guthrie. The concern in her voice was genuine. Without being a professional do-gooder, Virginia is the one we all count on when there is illness and trouble. Quietly and efficiently, she is there, soothing fright and taking phone calls and doing the marketing and sitting long hours with bored, uncomfortable convalescents. She has never alluded to it, but I know that when old Mr. Fortenberry was dying, it was Virginia and not the cowed and hysterical Misses Adelaide and Jimmie who sat beside his bed in the long, hot, pain-wracked afternoons and read aloud to him from Macaulay and Toynbee.

"I don't know," I said. "Just that it must have been pretty bad. She's awfully thin, and he's terribly protective of her. Really very sweet."

The rhododendrons parted, and we heard Buck Sheehan's voice calling, "I heard there was a party over here someplace." Everyone straightened up and looked toward the driveway, and Walter went to meet them.

Anita Sheehan was valiant that night. I never saw such strength of pure will. She was whip-slim and upright in yellow slacks and a vivid yellow-and-orange-print silk shirt that lit her thin, lovely face with color. Her lightless black hair was pulled back and tied with a silk kerchief, and only when you were very close to her did you notice the almost imperceptible tremor that played around her mouth and thrilled through her hands. Her face glowed with perfectly applied makeup, and she wore brilliant red lipstick like a banner. Her smile was nearly steady and her eyes met ours without the spectral ring of white, without sliding away, and her voice was light and gay and said the proper meeting-people things. I wondered if I was the only one who sensed the little winds of fear and strangeness that seemed to whip around her, but then I caught a warmer, softer note in Claire's voice as she introduced herself, and saw Virginia reach out gently and take her arm and draw her to the chaise that lies partly in the shadows of an overhanging dogwood at the edge of our patio, away from the yellow lights, and I knew that I was not. Kim sensed the slight skew in normalcy too. He said little during the evening, but he watched her steadily and gravely, and there was a gentleness on his saturnine face that I had not often seen. Gentleness, and something else I could not put a name to.

Walter and Roger and Charles were marvelous, enfolding Buck Sheehan in the circle of their friendship as though he had been a part of it for years. They are not usually so quick to do that with strangers. Favorite anecdotes were brought out for his approval, and he did approve, laughing in his deep, delighted child's way and offering his own in return. He shook his head at Walter's offer of a drink and drank Tab all evening, saying only that he was determined to get fifteen pounds of flab off if it killed him, and no one pressed him.

He talked of his business as men do when they meet and listened to their talk of theirs. It turned out that Walter was right; he had been a top-notch salesman, with what Walter told me later was a truly astounding record with his computer company in New Jersey. It did not seem strange to us then, knowing what we did about Anita's illness, that he would leave such a position and the life it must have bought him to come to a strange city so far away, to take charge of a company that was so much smaller than his old one.

Walter said later that he'd just assumed Buck had gotten a tremendous deal out of the move, probably a big piece of the company and a salary handsome enough to compensate for the dazzling commissions.

He talked little of the life they had left and almost not at all about their personal history, but that too we put down to a natural reluctance to talk about the time of his wife's illness. He seemed buoyant and truly excited about the future he hoped to build in the city, and about the peace and serenity of the neighborhood and the beauty and rightness of the house. He paid fervent and extravagant compliments to Kim Dougherty when he learned who he was, and Kim accepted them with a clipped brevity that might have passed for modesty. Buck entered into the evening fully and openly and naturally, but he did not leave his wife's side.

The evening was going well, I thought. Anita Sheehan sipped at a glass of Chablis and responded to our chatter with an effort that was, at first, near-heroic, and I suppose we all liked and admired her for it. Courage must be given its due, no matter what it masks. Gradually, during the evening, she began to relax, very, very slowly. After an hour or so she left her rigid perch on the edge of the chaise and slipped back to rest her head against its cushions and put her feet up, and by the time Walter got around to the hamburgers she was laughing, tentatively and with a rusty, unused little sound, but laughing, at some foolishness between Claire and Roger.

It was obvious that she loved her house. She was shy with Kim, but her words of appreciation to him rang real, and the only spontaneous animation I saw in her face all evening was when Virginia Guthrie told her she thought it was probably the most beautiful house she had ever seen. That was simply more of Virginia's sweetness talking, I knew. She had gradually come to admire the unmistakable artistry of Kim's design, but she still did not like the house. But Anita's face bloomed, and I was glad I could warmly and truly say, "I do too. I really do. I didn't think I was going to like anything contemporary there, and if the truth be known, I thought I was going to hate anything at all, because the lot is so close to ours. I wasn't so wild about my redheaded friend here either, because he designed it. But now I have to admit that it's probably the greatest house I've ever seen."

Kim shot me a shallow gray look, but the face Anita Sheehan turned to me was rapt with gratitude, and I thought guiltily, well, whatever happened over there, it doesn't change how the house looks. I can still say that honestly.

In the darkness I could feel Claire's eyes on me too. She knew that I, of all of us, had felt grieved and torn and sickened by the Harralsons' tragedy, and Lucas Abbott's, and by the unhappiness and loss and disturbing obsession the house had brought to Kim. She knew that I had loved the grace and beauty of it, and that now my pleasure in its beauty was diminished and its nearness oppressive to me. I thought for a moment that she was, in her blunt manner, going to chide me openly for the half-lie, but she said nothing.

"I felt that way too," said Anita Sheehan. "I never thought I'd be comfortable in anything so contemporary—we had a very traditional house at home. . . ." Her voice fell but climbed again. "But when Buck brought me to see it for the first time and I opened the door and went in, it was just as if it had been waiting for me to come home. You might have built it just for me." She smiled at Kim, who nodded stiffly.

"It's a pity the young couple who lived there moved back to their home town after such a short time. But lucky for us. Why on earth did they, do you know?"

Kim opened his mouth, and then closed it. No one said anything. Buck Sheehan was on his feet in an eye blink, taking Anita's glass to be refilled and asking Walter about the rocks in our rock garden.

"River rocks, unless I miss my guess," he said loudly. "Too smooth and flat for anything else. I'd love to build one like it for Anita, right back there where the ground rises at the edge of the woods."

I thought of the terrible little cemetery that lay there now. The small animals. The puppy. I knew Walter did too. As I turned toward Anita Sheehan I heard him say, "If I were you, I'd put it around on the other side there, where the ridge runs along the side of the Guthries' garden. I think there's solid rock at the edge of those woods."

"There is," Kim said.

Anita was still looking around at us questioningly, but there was nothing more than ordinary curiosity about the former occupants of her house in her face. The strain and fine-edged fear were almost gone.

"They were having marital troubles," I said. "But they did love the house, and so will you. For a million years at least, I hope."

She gave me a smile of tentative happiness, a quick one that flickered away again, but I could see what a stunningly lovely woman she had been before she was ill, and might be again when she recovered. Let it be all right for them, I breathed to whoever might control such things, and said, before any more talk of the Harralsons could come up again, "I have a strictly-from-scratch strawberry shortcake here that is guaranteed to put fifteen pounds on everybody on this patio, and I'll be furious if anybody refuses it. That means you too, Buck."

"I never say no to a lady," he said, and laughed, but it was the same thinned, ersatz sound we had heard that evening on his doorstep, so I hurried into the kitchen to get the cake. Claire followed.

"She doesn't know about the Harralsons, then," she said. "And he does. And is damned if anybody's going to tell her. What's *wrong* with her, Colquitt? I see what you meant by haunted, sort of. Do you think it was mental?"

"I don't know. I just know I'll murder you if you ever so much as breathe a word to her about it."

"Well, of course I wouldn't," she said indignantly. "What do you think I am? But she's bound to find out sometime."

"Well, by the time she does, maybe she'll be stronger and more settled. I don't know, Claire—I have a bad feeling about her. She's just barely holding herself together, or was at first. I think she's unwinding a little now. What do you think of them?"

"I like them, I think. She may be funny and he may be overprotective, but she has real class, and he's really sweet, isn't he? Don't worry. I'll curb my mouth and be an angel, and you all won't know me. Do they have any children, by the way?"

They were almost the exact words that Buck Sheehan had called after us that first evening. Natural words now, in this context, not stilted and ringing with portent as they had been before. But the queer wing-brush of uneasiness touched me again. I had meant to warn the Swansons and the Guthries and Kim not to mention the children, but I had forgotten. It had not come up so far, but it would, almost inevitably.

"No. And there's something funny about that too. He asked about the kids on the street in a strange sort of way, as though he hoped there weren't any, or that they wouldn't see much of them. I meant to tell you all to hold off on that until we know them better."

"Well, God, I'll shut up about the Harralsons, and I'll shut up about Lucas Abbott and all those dead animals, and Pie's baby, and I'll try to be gentle and kind and all that to her, but I can't very well hide Duck and Tommy and Rog in the basement. You think she lost a baby or something?"

"I don't have any idea. I'd say a little too old for that. But there's something there. See if you can pass the word to Virginia on the QT when you go back out there. I don't think any of the guys will bring it up if we don't."

Apparently she was able to alert Virginia, because the talk for the rest of the evening was quiet and comfortable and drifted gradually into sources for shopping, dentists, doctors, maids and yard men—the armatures around which, in our set, satisfying lives are sculpted. I thought, as the night grew older and the moon higher and the katydids louder, how ordinary, how ordered, how worldly and yet in a way how fragile our lives all were. That richness and substance should rest on such mortal bones. I felt the way, suddenly, that I had the night almost a year ago when the owl had begun his calling deep in the woods behind the house next door. I remembered precisely the sour taste of fear. It would take so little, so little . . . I reached across the little gulf of space that separated Walter's chair from mine, and I took his hand, and I squeezed it.

Out at the edge of the driveway, where the street-light threw a pool of white light over the curb and a small slice of our lawn, a voice called out.

"Ma? Hey, Ma? You over there? I need to talk to you about something."

Turning my head, I saw a stocky, solid figure, limned at the edges in light, diffused radiance spilling around it, coming slowly down our driveway. You could not see the features or clothing, only the shape, moving steadily toward us where we sat on the patio. I could not hear the footsteps either, but I knew it was Duck Swanson, padding silently toward us in ancient Adidas.

"Ma? I need you for a minute."

Claire turned, grumbling a little. "Excuse me a minute. Ten to one he's lost his key again." She half rose to go and meet her son, coming on and on down the driveway toward us.

A violent motion from Buck Sheehan caught our eyes. We turned to him. He sat staring at the figure in the darkness, his face as still as if it were settled forever into death. Then he turned to Anita, and we looked too. In the half-light that bathed the chaise she sat with her feet up and her hands folded loosely in her lap, so still that she might have been carved from marble. Her face was absolutely white and pure and mild, and her eyes looked unblinkingly into middle distance. Not at Duck Swanson, but over his head into nothing. A thin stream of Chablis began to trickle from the overturned glass in her lap, and ran down her leg and dripped from the chaise onto the patio flagstones. She did not move, and there was something in her stillness so far removed from ordinary quietude that my heart gave a sick leap and began to race. Then, very slowly, she began to rock, back and forth, back and forth, bending from the waist and straightening up again, the precise same distance each time. Like a machine, she rocked in her marble quiet, like a metronome. Her eyes did not blink. Duck came on down the driveway into the light.

Buck Sheehan moved fast to his wife on the chaise, and gathered her into his arms, and tried to force her sightless face against his shoulder. The muscles of his arms tightened and flexed, but they could not stop the rocking. We were very still. I simply sat beside Walter and Charles Guthrie thinking nothing at all. The night rang with shock. Virginia rose hastily and crouched down beside Anita on the other side of the chaise and put her arms around her, covering Buck's arms with her own. She made soft, quiet noises. Duck Swanson stopped uncertainly, and Claire ran to him, and Roger followed.

Buck Sheehan and Virginia managed to raise Anita Sheehan from the chaise and start with her toward the Sheehans' house. She walked stiffly, with even steps, eyes open and straight ahead. Buck stopped and she stopped with him, standing straight and still in the circle of his arm. He looked at us out of the ruin of a face.

"Our son was killed in Vietnam," he said. "He was our only child. The boy looked very like him for a minute there, with the light behind him . . . she thought . . . I almost did too . . . It was the way he walked, I think. The walk was very like . . . forgive us. Forgive her. I'll need to take her home now. I hope you'll understand."

We stood silently as Virginia and Buck Sheehan took Anita Sheehan back across the driveway and up the bank and into the house next door. Off in the darkness of the driveway I heard Duck Swanson say, "Mama, I'm sorry. Mama, I didn't mean to scare anybody—I just forgot my key."

"It's all right, baby," I heard Claire say. "I know. It's all right."

But of course it wasn't.

Chapter Eleven

THE NEXT day, sometime after noon, I saw the Guthries' car stop on the street in front of the Sheehans' house and Buck Sheehan, in a dark summer suit and a tie, get out and smile and say something to Charles Guthrie and go into his house. I knew that Charles and Virginia had been to church; they hardly ever miss the services at the Episcopal cathedral. Could Buck Sheehan, after the dreadful ending of the night before, have left his wife alone to go to church with them? It had been a terrible scene; we were wrung with pity for Anita and Buck, and I had been certain that whatever frail hold she had gained on health and stability was shattered now. Somehow I had expected cars, doctors, lights during the night, some ghastly echo of that other night in April. The pain and terror, the dead, stony calm, had seemed so deep. But Buck Sheehan's step this morning had been firm as he walked down the driveway to his house, and his smile had seemed sunny and normal.

The night before, after the Sheehans and Virginia had disappeared into the darkness of the rhododendrons, we had moved silently and by tacit agreement into our den and sat down to await some summing up, some period to the wreck of the evening. We waited for Virginia to come back with some sort of epilogue, or for Buck Sheehan to call with some word that things were better or that he needed help. Claire had come back to sit with us, though Roger stayed with Duck and the younger boys. We had made ourselves nightcaps, rather strong ones, and even Charles Guthrie had poured himself a sturdy shot of brandy. Only Kim had refused a drink. He sat quietly for a little while, his long body slouched into the corner of the sofa, deep in some private reverie of his own, saying nothing. Soon he murmured his thanks and good-nights and went away. The rest of us looked at each other helplessly but said little. There is little to say in the face of such agony.

Claire said finally, "It *was* mental, then. It must have been. God, that poor woman, that poor guy. And poor old Duck. He just feels awful—responsible, somehow. You know how Duck is; he tries to be responsible for the whole world. But we can't just banish all the kids in the neighborhood. They must know there will be children—teenaged boys—wherever they go. I wish they'd let us know. I could have at least warned off the boys. Ten to one she's back to square one now. I never saw such . . . walking death."

"I think it might have been different if she'd been able to get used to the kids gradually," said Walter. "Poor old Duck did look ghostly as hell padding down that driveway, with the light behind him, not making any noise. If he really does look like their kid, you can sort of understand. Christ, what rotten luck for her."

"It didn't do Duck a whole lot of good either," Claire said fiercely. "He's really upset. How was he to know we had an arrested psycho over here? This was a pretty good place to live until Happy House went up over there."

It was so nearly what I was thinking that I snapped at Claire. "I'm glad Kim wasn't here to hear that. How do you think he feels? Our trouble is that we haven't *had* any trouble," I said. "Not real trouble, not the kind that the Harralsons had, or Luke Abbott, or the poor Sheehans. We're so insulated and fat and happy over here that we've forgotten that there's real pain and trouble in the world. Oh, yes, Claire, even among 'nice' people. Don't blame the house. That's just absurd."

"You blame it."

"I damned well do not, Claire! That's *crazy!* I hate what happened to the Harralsons, and my heart breaks for the Sheehans, and for once in my life I'm close to tragedy instead of reading about it in the paper or hearing about it at the club, and I'm going to do what I can to help, and you're a very callous woman if you don't do the same."

Claire stared at me in hurt, and my face flamed with shame. She had not been callous. Claire lashes out when she is troubled and threatened. I retreat and brood. She allows me my reactions in silence and tolerance, and I have always allowed her hers in the same vein. I had broken faith. I went to her and hugged her and said, "I'm truly sorry. I really am. I talk a good game, but I don't handle trouble very well. Forgive?"

She hugged back. "Of course. Neither do I. You're right, what you said. We *have* been lucky, all of us. And fools to think there would never be real trouble among us. I'll help Anita, of course I'll help her, if somebody will just tell me how I can. We all will, you know that. Virginia is helping right now."

"Well," said Walter, "let's wait and see what Virginia has to say when she comes back over. She'll know what they need."

We sat waiting for a long time, but Virginia did not come back, and finally Charles Guthrie rose and said, "She's probably going to stay the night with them. She does that sometimes. She's good at getting people to talk things out, and that's probably what they need more than anything. I'll go on home and wait for her, and she'll be in touch. Thanks for dinner, Col. Our turn next time."

Claire left just after he did, and Walter and I went to bed, for once leaving dirty dishes and glasses piled in the sink. Simple exhaustion gave us both quick, dreamless sleep.

I don't know quite what I had expected the next morning, but not the quiet banality of the Guthries' dropping Buck Sheehan off after church. Walter and I went to the club that afternoon, and I played a dispirited set of tennis with Margaret Matthieson, and cut her off rather brusquely when she asked me how I liked the new neighbors she'd sent us. Walter sat in the sun by the pool and read *The New York Times,* and we had a salad from the cold buffet line, and then came home about dusk. The curtains were drawn over at the Sheehans', but both cars were there, and the house had the look only of a somnolent Sunday in

June. The phone was ringing as we came into the kitchen.

It was Virginia Guthrie and she said briefly, "Could you and Walter drop over for a little while about nine? I'd like to tell you a bit about last night. The Swansons are coming."

"Is Anita okay?" I asked.

"I think so, or will be. Tell you when you get here."

Virginia's house is very like Virginia, cool and elegant and yet somehow warming and soothing. The light, graceful Hepplewhite furniture is unmarred by the scratches and dents that three children should have left. No one knows how Virginia managed that, because the children are sound and whole and unscarred by excessive fussing and discipline, if slightly humorless and otherworldly, like Charles. Virginia let her live-in maid go when they married and moved away, but she has daily help, and her house speaks of it. I had thought, on this hot evening, that we would sit in the beautiful gazebo in her garden, as we usually do, but she said, "We're in the library. Come on back." When we did, Claire and Roger were already there. They sat straight in their chairs, hands in laps, as if in a waiting room. We all knew we had been summoned. The Guthries don't go in for spur-of-the-moment get-togethers.

Virginia sat down in a wing chair facing us. She said, "There are some things I need to tell you that I wouldn't ordinarily. Buck asked me to do it. He thinks you should know. He was very definite about it; he wants you to hear all of it. Anita doesn't know that I'm telling you, so I don't need to say that I hope it won't go any further. I don't like doing this, but he felt it would be less . . . embarrassing for you if it came from me. He is a remarkable man."

Her face lit gently and then straightened into severe lines of distress. Virginia feels actual pain at disclosing what she feels are the private hells of other people.

"Anita's illness was emotional, as you've probably guessed," she said. "There was a long time when they didn't think they'd ever reach her again. She was in deep catatonia. She was hospitalized for a very long time. It almost wiped out everything they had. When she began to pull out of it, the doctors told Buck quite simply that it was as near a miracle as they'd ever seen.

"It was triggered by the son, but it didn't start there. Anita's mother died when she was very small, and she was more or less raised by her father and her older brother. The father was a GP in Montana, where they lived, and was away a lot of the time, so she formed a very special closeness to the brother. I gather there was more money than just what a country GP would make, because her father had his own small plane and a private airfield. He'd fly anywhere they needed him, and he often took the boy along. Anita never went. She was afraid of planes. She stayed with the house-keeper."

I looked at Walter, sensing where this was going. He was grim-faced and quiet. Virginia went on.

"They were flying up to Billings one day, the father and the boy, and she came down to the field with them to see them off, like she always did. The plane took off and her father circled and waved, like always, and then the plane just . . . fell out of the sky. Crashed and burned, practically at her feet. They never did find out why; there wasn't anything left. She was knocked down by the explosion and burned slightly herself, and she just lay there on the ground, not able to get up, and she heard them screaming until they . . . died. After that she lost consciousness, and when she woke up in the hospital she didn't talk or move again for almost five months. Some of her mother's people came out from the East and took her back with them and got her into a good clinic, but it was still that long be-fore she could move or talk. Pure, classic catatonia. They kept her alive with IV's. She was nine years old when it happened. Her brother was barely eighteen."

Claire gave a small whimper of pain, and Virginia looked at her. "Yes," she said.

"Well, they got her over that finally, and she seemed to do all right with her mother's people. She went to school in Philadelphia, and on to Swarthmore, and it was while she was there that she met Buck. He's a good bit older than she is; he was already starting to make a success in computer sales, and he thinks she must have seen something of her father in him. The brother too. She often told him how much he reminded her of both of them.

"I gather they had a very good marriage. They didn't have children for a long time, and she'd travel with him when he went out of town, and had quite a good career as an interior decorator. She always depended on him a lot, but he enjoyed that. Then the son was born, and he was simply Anita's world. Buck's too, but a man usually has other things. Buck had his work; he loves it. Anita gave up her business to take care of the boy. He must have been a really exceptional boy. He'd had every honor and office he could hold at Lawrenceville, and he'd been accepted at Princeton. He joined the army against Anita's wishes, but Buck was proud of him. He's basically a pretty simple man, I think. He was proud that his boy felt an obligation to his country when so many others were burning their draft cards and running off to Canada. Anyway, the boy—Toby, they called him—went to flight school and got to be a helicopter pilot. Anita was frantic of course, but the boy loved flying, and he was a good pilot. He'd flown sixty-something sorties. He was set to come back to the States in a week or so to be an instructor. He called them from Taiwan to tell them. And the next day the officer was at the door to tell them that he hadn't . . . come back from his last one. Buck was out of town—he traveled almost constantly then—and Anita was alone. It was the next morning before they could reach him. He said she was just literally almost destroyed."

She paused, and that long-ago pain in a New Jersey living room coiled into the room almost palpably. Claire closed her eyes. I knew she was thinking about her three sturdy sons and a knock on her door in the middle of a sunny morning.

Virginia went on in a voice formal and level against the pain. "The doctors kept her pretty well sedated for a while, but then she just . . . withdrew. After the first day she never cried again, Buck said. She didn't talk much, and she wouldn't let him dispose of any of the boy's things. She wouldn't let his room be touched. She sat in it for hours, rocking in an old rocking chair

107

there, and he just couldn't seem to reach her. He was terrified that she was going to slip back into the catatonia. The boy had been just the age her brother was when he died. Just about Duck's age. The two things were so alike, you see.

"Buck is an outgoing man. He needs to be around people. He needed somebody he could talk to about his son. He really *needed* that, but he couldn't, to her, and he didn't dare leave her alone for long. He was just isolated, and it wasn't fair to him." She said it fiercely, looking around at us as if she dared us to contradict her. None of us did, of course. No one spoke.

"Well, she didn't go into the catatonia, quite," said Virginia. "But she moved through the house like a robot, they stopped talking almost entirely, they stopped . . . having marital relations. He begged her to let him apply for a new territory, to get out of that town and that house, to make a new life somewhere where there weren't so many memories. She refused. She would not leave that house. He said it was the only real emotion she showed the whole time. He said he should have seen where she was headed, but in a funny kind of way she seemed almost contented there, and quiet. She functioned, in a not-there kind of way. He thought she'd work through it in time. One weekend he came home all full of plans to take her on a long cruise to the Caribbean or to Europe or somewhere, and she looked at him and said, 'What do you think you could buy me that will replace what you gave away that was mine?,' and he realized then that she blamed him for encouraging the boy to join the army, or at least for not discouraging him. It almost killed him."

Tears were running silently down Claire's face and stinging behind my nose. Walter and Roger and Charles were not looking at each other. These terrible words should not be spinning out into this dim, polished, peaceful room. These words brought unimaginable enormity too close. Virginia went on in the same level voice, but her hands were clamped to the arms of her chair, and her knuckles were white.

"You can probably guess what happened after that.

A man like Buck isn't used to bottling up pain. Men like that need other people. But men like that often don't know how to ask for help from friends or acquaintances. He didn't have anybody. Anita didn't seem to need him at home any more. So he started going out on the road more and more often, working incredible hours so he could sleep at night, bringing in more and more business. He said it was sort of funny, really, that at the time money meant the least to him he was making more than he'd ever thought he'd make in his life. He just couldn't seem to do anything wrong. In that five or six months after Toby died he almost doubled his commissions, and they'd already been the best in his company.

"But then he started drinking, *really* drinking, for the first time in his life, and in the end it just . . . did him in. There was a woman too, in one of the cities he usually visited, and a lot of the time he was with her when he was supposed to be somewhere else. He said he still loved Anita with all his heart, but it was something he just couldn't seem to help, and Anita never gave any indication at all that she suspected he had somebody else. She was spending most of her time in that awful room by that time. But his firm knew about the woman. A lot of people did.

"It caught up with him eventually. He started getting ugly with some of the company's best customers, and of course the word got back to the home office, and after a while they really didn't have any choice but to fire him. He said he'd have done the same thing himself. He was with the woman in—Dayton, I think—when they made the decision to fire him, so they sent him a wire there and told him not to come back. He left the girl's apartment, but he stayed in Dayton for another week, at a hotel. He doesn't remember any of it. But he woke up one morning and he said he absolutely knew that if he had one more drink he would be dead. He would just die. So he went home to Anita, and he was going to straighten things out between them no matter what it took. He was going to get her a good doctor and start at AA himself. When he got home she was sitting in the chair in the boy's room and she didn't even see him.

She must have been there for a day or two, he said, because she . . . she had soiled herself and her clothes. There was a letter on the floor beside her from the woman in Dayton. It had been sent to Buck's office, but they had sent it to his house with his last check and his other things. Anita had read it of course. There couldn't have been any doubt in her mind about what had been going on. And that's when she went back into the catatonia. She just didn't move again. He got her into the best private hospital he could find, but she didn't move or talk again for almost seven months after that."

Tears had started from Virginia's eyes by now, running into the corners of her mouth. I thought I could not bear any more of this and made a movement toward her to stop her. She held up her hand. She licked away the tears.

"Wait, Colquitt, I'm almost finished. They had some savings and a summer place on the Jersey shore. He sold that, and he sold the house. He took an apartment near the hospital. He started at AA. He said that he knew by then that loss and pain couldn't kill you, but guilt could, and when the doctors first told him there was very little hope of reaching Anita, he went into a church—the first one he came to walking along the street from the hospital—and he promised God that if He would make Anita well, he would devote the rest of his life to taking care of her and being the best person he could be. He said that in that moment he believed absolutely and totally in God, and in Christ, and all the rest, everything that went with it, because there simply wasn't anything else in the world he could do. He asked for a miracle. And within a month he got it. She began to respond. And he found this job, and the house, and he brought her here. There was just enough left to make the move. And of course he got a very good deal at Computer Tech because he's very, very good at what he does, and he hasn't had a drink in more than a year."

Her hands dropped into her lap and she smiled, a misty, soft Virginia smile. We waited.

"That's it," she said. "That's the whole thing. He gave Anita one of her tablets last night, and after she

110

went to sleep we talked for most of the night. I didn't want him to feel he had to tell me any of that, but he insisted. He thinks the only way she's going to get completely well is for all of us to know all of it, so there are no secrets and no whisperings and no . . . undercurrents that can touch her. He hoped it would help you understand Anita better."

We were silent again. This sort of shattering disclosure makes most of us almost unbearably uncomfortable. It is harder to live with than almost anything I know. Our set shrinks from it. In distance there is decency.

"I think it was the bravest thing I ever heard," said fastidious Virginia Guthrie, whose own private distresses will go forever unaired.

"But if it matters to any of you, don't feel badly about not seeing them. He doesn't care about that. He has his wife back. He has what he wants and needs. He'd like to have our friendship, but it has to be openly and freely and honestly given. Those are his terms. There will be setbacks, almost certainly, like last night with poor Duck. But they will work them out. There's a lot we six can do to help, and one thing is either to know all this and accept them openly or not to see them at all. Nothing else will do.

"He has my friendship for as long as he wants it," she added. "They both do."

We all pledged it then, and meant it. I did, from the bottom of my heart, and I knew Walter did. Claire snuffled a little and Roger cleared his throat, and Charles Guthrie looked at his wife with the luminous wonder I have seen a few times before. I knew he had cast his lot with Virginia sometime in the hours before dawn, when she had come back to their house to tell him this. I had never felt closer to the other five people in that room than in that moment, with all veneers and varnishes and glosses gone. I never have again.

Virginia served us coffee and one of her spindrift angel food cakes then, and we talked a little longer about the Sheehans, with no constraints or small cool reserves between us. Just before we left, Claire said, "The whole thing reminds me of that story by—who was it? Graham Greene? Where the woman promised

God she would give up her lover and follow Him always if He'd just let him be alive. It was in England during the war, and there had been a direct hit on the house they were having a rendezvous in, and she knew with absolute certainty that he was dead. And she got down on her knees and prayed for a miracle, and he came walking through the door. Not even hurt. This reminds me of that."

"The End of the Affair," I said. "But that had a pretty miserable ending. The woman died. Buck has his miracle, it seems to me. His happy ending. At least, I hope he still does."

"Knock on wood," Claire said.

"Heathen," said Roger Swanson fondly and slapped her on the rump, and they went home. Walter and I followed in silence. The house next door was dark and quiet and seemed to breathe sweetly in sleep.

Chapter Twelve

THE WEEK after that evening at the Guthries' we went down to the island just off the coast that we have both loved since we came to this city. It is one of the Sea Islands, but not one of the glossier ones. It is a sleepy, gently shabby little island, with a sprinkling of chic new condominium resorts and one newly restored grand old hotel, and a flock of rambling old clapboard cottages facing the ocean, owned mainly by the second and third generations of the families who built them. A great many people in our city vacation and summer there, and when Walter left the agency he worked for to start his own with Charlie Satterfield, part of the deal they worked out was half ownership of the cottage Charlie's father had built on the island in 1925 —just before the Depression put beach houses out of reach for most Southerners for decades. Charlie takes his brood of four down for the entire month of August, and since Walter and I are more flexible, we like to use the house a few days or a week or two at a time throughout the year. There's never been any wrangling about who wanted the cottage when.

We fell in love with it when we first drove off the beach road and down its rutted, sandy, burr-matted lane. It is as forthright and solid and square as a well-born dowager, gray-shingled and green-shuttered, and skirted on three sides by a screened porch that looks straight into the tired, flaccid surf of that warm ocean. No trees grow near it, but a flag snaps smartly in the freshening wind at the turn of the incoming tide, and two outsized hammocks and an old-fashioned glider, as well as a porch swing, sag and creak and groan comfortably on the porch. The porch is where most of our living is done. We eat there, and entertain there, and on hot nights we have slept there, in the hammocks, waking up early with the already hot morning sun red on our lids and rope-square imprints on our bare behinds. We once made love in one of the hammocks, or tried to, but it wasn't what it's cracked up to be, and I really think Walter insisted only because he thought it madcap and adventurous and a trifle kinky. We ended up tangled together on the porch floor in weak, hysterical laughter, with rope burns.

These were two good weeks. Walter loves the sea, and I need it in some elemental way that I cannot even come close to verbalizing. I become dim and shriveled, somehow, at my very core if I am away from the sea too long. When I return to it I seem to fill up and overflow with it, soaking in the vast, sighing wetness of it like a parched vine in a long, soft spring rain. Our times at the cottage are more than refreshment and rest for us. They are a sort of renaissance, a reaffirmation, a statement of policy and condition of our life together. We know most of the summer colony, and we play a little tennis on the lone, weedy old clay court, and have a few people for lazy drinks now and then, or go to some other surf-singing screened porch for drinks and cold suppers. But mostly we are alone with each other and the sun and wind and water.

Our weeks on the island are as far removed from our life in the city as if we had been to New Zealand. When we get home it takes me a day or two to get my bearings again, to find my footing in the back-home world that is only half familiar to me. So when Claire called the night we got back and said, "Guess what? Anita's joined the garden club and is having a dinner party for twenty people—y'all will be invited—and played golf with Buck and Roger and me yesterday," I thought stupidly, Anita who? And then I remembered. Anita Sheehan, next door. And then it all came flooding back through the lingering sea-strangeness, and I said, "Well, I think that's fantastic, Claire! Bless her heart. She's making a superhuman effort, isn't she? Is it an awful strain being around her?"

"Not in the least. None of it seems to be an effort for her at all. If you didn't know—all that stuff— you'd think she didn't have a care in the world and had never been sick a day in her life. I never saw such a change in anybody. She's not exactly outgoing of course, but she's sweet and funny, and looks like she must have gained at least ten pounds, and can drive a golf ball a country mile, and actually said 'damn' when she three-putted the last hole. I don't know what happened to her. I never would have believed anybody could come back so fast after that scene at your house."

"All that in two weeks? Buck really must be the happiest man in America."

"He just beams. All the time. Just walks around grinning from ear to ear. Col, you'll just have to see her to believe it."

I did see her, the next morning, on my way out to the car to go to work. She was bringing the newspaper down their driveway from the mailbox, wearing shorts and a jersey, and she looked like a different woman. Literally. Her beautiful skull had a modeling of sweetly fitting flesh now, and the fabulous cheekbones wore a stain of sun and natural color. Her eyes crinkled at the sight of me; her hair shone and bounced on her shoulders, and her body wore a becoming five or ten new pounds. She looked spectacular. I simply stared at her.

"Well, hi, Colquitt," she said, smiling. "Welcome home—only it's not so much fun coming home after a vacation, is it? Virginia told me you two had gone down to the beach. You look great, all tanned and rested."

"You're the one who looks like you've been on vacation," I said. "You look just wonderful, you really do. I never saw such a—" I had been going to say "change," and then winced inside myself for the insensitivity of it. The fragility and madness and fear, the dreadful moment on our patio, the whole terrible chain of events that had led to that moment, all those would be inherent in that one word, "change." I stopped. She smiled.

"I know. 'Such a change in anybody.' Don't be embarrassed. I'm delighted with it myself, and I'm glad you noticed. It *has* been an incredible change, hasn't it? Colquitt, I'm not going to apologize to you for that inexcusable scene at your house the other night, because I know that you know all about us now, and you understand."

"Anita . . . ," I began.

"No. Buck told me that he told Virginia all of it. All of it. And he told me he'd asked her to tell you. I'm glad. There mustn't be any more . . . distance . . . between Buck and me, and I hope there won't be any between us and all of you. I've learned that I'm tougher than I thought I was; I can take almost anything except aloneness. I *have* taken almost everything. It was the aloneness that I created for myself that almost killed me. And it almost killed Buck too. It was one of the worst moments of my life, seeing the poor Swanson boy . . . for a minute I literally thought it was Toby . . . but somehow it made me really face, for the first time, the fact that he's dead. I had to do that before I could really start to get well. I haven't the depth of faith that Buck has, but somehow he gives me some of his; I can live without Toby now. Not without an awful hole in my heart, but I can live. What I couldn't live with was the awful feeling of somehow *waiting* for him. I had to *know*. And I do. Ever since that night, I've known, and the . . . the healing began then. And I have Buck back, one hundred and ten percent. I know I always will. The one thing, the *only* thing that could get to me now would be to lose Buck, and I'm not going to do that. I'm a lucky woman, and I'm ashamed of myself for hiding in sickness like that for so long."

I hugged her impulsively, across a waist-high holly bush, and she hugged me back and laughed a little as we both jumped back from the holly's prickly leaves.

"Well. Welcome to the neighborhood once again, Anita Sheehan," I said. "Because you're a whole new lady and one I like immensely, and I hope you're going to be very, very happy here."

"I am going to be," she said. "And you and Walter and the Swansons and the Guthries are part of the reason I am. Virginia is—I just don't have any words good enough for Virginia. She's been over every day since that night—just for a little while, no big deal— and I've talked her poor head off. All this stuff that comes spilling out—and she just listens. She *really* listens. I think she's probably responsible for the way I've been getting well. She and Buck and this beautiful house."

"I'm glad you still feel that way about it," I said.

"I didn't know I could love anything inanimate as much as I love my house," Anita Sheehan said. "I feel like it . . . needs me, sort of, to be at its best. When I walk in from shopping or somewhere, I feel like it almost preens itself, because it knows it's prettier with me in it. I give it something. That's a nice feeling to have about a house. Usually a house gives *you* something—status, security, identity, or whatever. My house needs *me* to give *it* identity. It's a flattering feeling."

She stopped and looked at me and laughed, a little embarrassed. "It's not the crazies cropping out again, I promise. I sound a perfect fool, prattling about my house."

"Well," I said, looking up at the house, "it's a hard house to be impersonal about. You'd never be able to take it or leave it alone."

"No. Well, I mustn't keep you. You'll be getting an invitation, but I want to have a few people on the street in for a buffet in a couple of weeks, and I really hope you and Walter can come. It's sort of a house-warming for us, only you absolutely must *not* bring presents."

I thought of that other housewarming, in that luminous green April twilight, and I almost told her then. She seemed strong enough to handle it; it seemed to me imperative that she know about that other ghastly party. But then I thought, Maybe it's just what we all need. To go, and have the party be a smashing success, and flush out those old horrors and memories and replace them with good ones. To lay those ghosts once and for all. We can't go through the rest of our lives averting our eyes from the Harralson house.

So I did not tell her.

I will always wonder if it might have made a difference. But I really don't think so. Not by then.

The thing that waited for Anita was already spreading its shadows across her shoulders.

THE EVENT that triggered the first frail beginning of the terrible, blooming awareness was the housewarming that Anita Sheehan never had.

All through the week following our return from the beach we had caught glimpses of Anita and Buck working in their blossoming yard in the still-hot dusks, coming in and out with armfuls of groceries, leaving early for golf on Saturday morning and church on Sunday.

Once they came over in the late afternoon and sat with us on the patio, Anita turning a glass of white wine around in her hands and Buck drinking iced tea. We talked of the settling in at the Sheehans' house that was going so satisfactorily, and Buck's work at Computer Tech, and I told them about my work at the agency, and how I planned, if things went well during the coming fall and winter, to leave the agency and establish my office at home. I had already put out some tentative feelers to three of my favorite clients, and all had seemed receptive. I took Anita upstairs and showed her the unused bedroom that I planned to convert into an office. It was a long, narrow room with dormer windows and a feeling of snugness and charm, even though the space was troublesome and difficult to plan around. She showed a real flair for working with space and form and color and an instant grasp of what I wanted to do with the room. She made some hesitant suggestions for building in desk and bookcase units that had not occurred to me but would be perfect for the room.

"You really ought to consider getting back into the business, Anita," I said. "I know several decorators who'd be glad to talk to you."

"I'm better, Col, but I'm not ready for that much involvement yet. I still get a little panicky when I'm out in a crowd of strangers, and I'm a long way from being able to waltz into somebody's house and tell them to throw out the ancestral fumed oak and get some light and color in there. One step at a time. Right now this party's got me in a dither. You'd think I'd never had a party before in my life, and we used to entertain constantly."

"Well, you know I'll help, and Claire, and Virginia. Just say the word."

"Thanks, but this is a party *for* you all, not *by* you. It's just opening-night nerves. I want to get everybody over the notion that they've got to walk on eggshells around me because I did time in the funny farm. I want to be your equal, not your problem child."

I laughed, because she did seem so equal then, so sound and matter-of-fact and funny about her illness, and she looked so beautiful. There were deeps of sadness in her eyes, sadness that would look out at the world as long as the eyes did. But the same sadness looks out of many eyes, and they are still able to dance and spark with anger and quicken with love and tenderness. Anita's eyes could do all of those things, and would. Were, already.

"It's all yours, then," I said, and we went back downstairs.

"You think she's up to the party?" Walter said when the Sheehans had gone home and we sat down to tuna fish salad. Razz and Foster sat at our feet like temple cats, imperious and stiff with their ignoring of the tuna fish. I put dollops of salad on two napkins and put them down on the flagstones, and after a minute or two they arched and stretched and seemed to discover the booty. In great surprise they sniffed, and then began to nibble daintily and with vast ennui at the fish.

"Yes," I said, "I think she can handle it with no trouble at all. And I think it's going to be just what we all need, and her too. She's a gallant lady, and I hope it's the first of a thousand great parties in that house. I hope she gets to be a hostess of legend in this town of legendary hostesses."

"And I hope you're right," he said. "They're really good people, aren't they?"

"Among the best, my friend."

The next week, on Tuesday, Buck Sheehan called and said, "I've got to go out of town for a day or two, and I just wanted to tell you so you could sort of keep an eye on Anita, you and Virginia."

"Of course," I said.

That was on Tuesday. On Friday morning, before I left for work, Virginia Guthrie knocked softly at the kitchen door. I stared at her in surprise through the glass. She was in a severely tailored, belted housecoat, and her hair was a wild cloud framing her face. Virginia never popped in, in the morning or at any other time, and I had literally never seen her in her night-clothes or with her hair and makeup less than perfect. Alarm stabbed at me. I opened the door.

"What is it? Is somebody sick?"

"No. Well, I'm not sure. May I come in? It's Anita."

She came into the kitchen and leaned against the counter, as distraught as I have ever seen Virginia. I poured her a cup of coffee and steered her into the den. We sat on the sofa. I could see that her eyes were sunken with fatigue; she looked as though she had not slept for the entire night.

My mouth was stiff with dread. "What's happened to Anita?" I said.

"It was—just terrible, Colquitt. Just terrible. Charles and I were sitting watching TV last night, pretty late —the Carson show—and we heard this—this—kind of measured, slow hammering at the back door. Perfectly spaced, slow, hard knocking, like something mechanical. Charles ran to the door, and there was Anita, in just her nightgown. She was . . . staring again. Just looking right through Charles, staring, not

119

blinking, no expression at all on her face. Just like the other night. Even when Charles opened the door and pulled her into the kitchen, she just stood there staring past us, making that knocking motion with her fist, in the air. She was white as death. I thought somebody had tried to break into their house, or she'd had bad news about Buck, or something. It was worse than the first time."

"For God's sake, Virginia, what *was* it?"

"It took us almost two hours to find out. I sat her down on the sofa—she was like a dummy you could move around any way you wanted to—and I brought her some brandy, but she wouldn't hold it or look at it, and when I held it up to her mouth she spilled most of it. I told Charles to go call Mark Florence. I know he's a GYN, but I couldn't think of anybody else, but before he could pick up the phone she made this tremendous effort—you could see her whole body shake with it—and she said, 'No doctor. No doctor. No doctor.' Over and over, kind of a chant. I thought she would just go out of her head. I held her, and we asked her over and over, was there somebody in the house? Was Buck all right? Was she in pain? She just sat stiff as a board and shook her head, no. No."

"Oh, God—" I breathed.

"I left her with Charles, and I went over for her pills—I knew from the other night where she kept them. The door was wide open, and the lights in their den were on, and the TV was going. I brought the pills back and got one down her finally, and after about half an hour she relaxed that awful stiffness a little, and her eyes kind of focused, and she began to try to talk. She kept saying, 'No doctors, no doctors. Don't call Buck. I won't go back to the hospital. I won't go back.' So I promised her we wouldn't call anybody, and then finally she was able to tell me what had happened."

I was breathless with dread and said nothing. Virginia looked at me oddly and went on.

"Apparently it was something she saw on television," she said. "She said she fell asleep on the couch about ten, and when she woke up, there was this movie on. She woke up in the middle of it. You know how strange and disoriented you feel when you do that—and she said it was about a boy—"

"A boy?"

"A boy—who was killed. In the war. In Vietnam. She said she woke up just as his helicopter was going down, and she could see him in the cockpit, and there was fire all around him, and he was screaming—"

"Oh, my dear Jesus, Virginia," I cried softly, in pain. "How terrible! How ghastly, to wake up to something like that—even a helicopter. What a rotten, awful coincidence, and with Buck out of town. Oh, God, what will happen to her now? Should we try to get hold of Buck? I don't even know where he went."

"She was able to tell us finally, and Charles called him. He'll be in this morning. I don't know what will happen to her, Colquitt. After she told us about the movie she went back into that horrible stillness and quiet, just like somebody snapping off a light, and Charles and I literally pushed and carried her up to our bedroom and laid her down on the bed. She didn't move again, so about four I turned off the lights and left her alone. I don't know if she's asleep, or what. She hasn't moved this morning. Fanny's there, or I wouldn't have left her. I just wanted to tell you so you could call everybody and cancel the party. I thought maybe Claire would help you. I just . . . can't."

"Of course," I said automatically. "Of course."

She didn't move to go, and my heart squeezed tighter with premonitory terror. I knew she was going to say something else, and I knew that it would be something irrevocable and unspeakable. I waited.

"Colquitt, after I left her upstairs, Charles and I got the *TV Guide*, just to find out, you know, what the movie was. We thought maybe we could talk it out with her after she woke up, or something."

"What was it?"

"Colquitt, there wasn't any movie about Vietnam on last night. Not on any of the channels we can possibly get here. Not even any kind of war movie. Charles called all three stations this morning just to make sure. There was nothing even remotely like that. The Carson show, and a movie about moonshine runners or something, and an old Alice Faye movie on

121

the network channels, and—I don't know, some panel thing or something on the ETV station. But nothing like what she saw."

"Well, of course she dreamed it, then, Virginia. She thought she was awake, but you know how you do sometimes, you think you're wide awake but you're still in the middle of a nightmare. I've done that. It was a perfectly awful thing to dream, but you can see why she would have—"

"No." Virginia dropped her face into her hands. She sat like that, still and stricken, and then she raised her face. It was ravaged and runneled with fright.

"She wasn't dreaming. Because when I went back over there to turn off the lights and lock her door, I looked in at the TV."

"Don't tell me this, Virginia," I said.

"It *was* a war movie. It was just ending. There was a shot of a helicopter burning in a jungle at night. And then it switched to this bombed city, and a man's voice said, 'Saigon, 1967,' and 'The End' flashed on the screen."

"How DO you explain it, then?" I said to Walter that evening after dinner. "If there's got to be an explanation, what is it? Virginia *saw* it, Walter. They checked the *TV Guide,* they called all the stations."

"I *don't* explain it, Colquitt," he said very firmly. I could tell he was afraid I was losing control. He wasn't far from wrong.

"I just said there has to *be* a logical explanation. The most obvious is that she dreamed it."

"Walter, Virginia stood right there in that den and *saw* it."

"Virginia saw what she was expecting to see. I'll admit she doesn't seem the type for hallucinations or whatever, but suggestion is a very powerful thing, and she must have been shocked out of her wits to see Anita like that again, so soon after the other thing, after she'd been doing so well. Virginia was naturally hyperreceptive in a state like that. Or it could be that the movie really was on, and somehow it didn't get printed in the *TV Guide*. These stupid-ass local stations are always substituting old movies for something you'd much rather see, at the last minute and without any notice."

"But they called the stations."

"Well, there are cretins in TV stations just like anywhere else. Ten to one some idiot didn't want to be bothered going to look at the log and just flipped through the *TV Guide* and read out what was there. You almost sound as though you don't want there to be a logical explanation, Col."

"I do!" I cried. "I do, more than anything in the world! Do you think I'm a total fool? Do you think I believe the Sheehans have got a haunted television set? It's just so . . . bizarre and cruel. Of all things for that particular woman to see on that particular night, with her husband out of town. Even right down to the burning helicopter. It's almost as though there were some kind of . . . malign intelligence behind it. Oh, I don't know what I think. It's just that she had finally buried the boy, Walter, let him go. She was coming back so well."

"And will again. You wait and see. Buck said, he told Virginia, you heard her say it, that he expected setbacks. The doctor in New Jersey said there would be setbacks. Okay, so she's had one. She'll work out of it. Christ, Col, she was one sick lady. Don't minimize all those months in that place. You wouldn't just get up one day and walk out and start laughing and picking flowers. You come out of a thing like that in stages and by sheer, painful will, and it takes a long, long time. I always did think she'd pulled out of that last one too fast."

"First Duck, and now this," I said bitterly. "What's next, I wonder? Do you think Buck will run off with Mary Wells Lawrence or get himself creamed on the freeway? That ought to fix her once and for all."

"You aren't making any sense, Colquitt," he said severely and rose and got me a glass of neat Scotch. "One hysteric and maybe two, if you count Virginia, is about all I can take. I don't want to hear any more about Anita Sheehan for at least twenty-four hours. I want you to drink this, and then I want you to go to bed. I'm going into the den and read the *Wall*

Street Journal, and I just may take the television set out in the backyard and shoot it."

I knew he was upset, as much about my state of mind as the frightful thing that had happened the night before. Perhaps because I needed to so badly, I believed what he had said about dreams and the power of suggestion and human error in television stations. Maybe, I thought, settling into bed with Razz and Foster and the latest *New York* Magazine, maybe they were right in the old days. Maybe madness *is* as close as we'll ever come to the paranormal. Poltergeists are supposed to be caused by disturbed adolescents, aren't they? Why shouldn't a woman whose mental health was shaky see something that wasn't on a television screen at all but only in her anguished mind? And persuade a perfectly sane, balanced woman that she too had seen it? In the old days they'd have said that Anita Sheehan was possessed, and they'd get some exorcist or something to cast out the spirit. Maybe the abnormal has always been the normal, or vice versa.

It wasn't the most soothing train of thought I'd ever pursued, but there was some comfort in it, and I was asleep long before Walter came to bed.

We walked over the next morning, the Saturday morning of the party that would not be, to see if we could do anything for the Sheehans.

Buck answered the bell, and this time he asked us in. The house was quiet in the green, tree-filtered morning light. The dishwasher was gurgling sunnily in the kitchen, and a lingering smell of coffee spoke of normal mornings. There were silver trays and serving pieces set out on the dining room table, where Anita had placed them after polishing them for the party, but the quiet downstairs showed no other sign of disarray, no sign of illness and havoc and terror.

He was obviously tired, bone-tired, death-tired, but his smile was serene.

"Thanks for coming," he said. "She's upstairs sleeping. She's slept for almost twenty-four hours straight, and it's the best thing for her. I never should have left her alone. I never should have. But I called her doctor in New Jersey and told him everything she remembers about the night—the television program, and all that—and he said it wasn't such a strange thing to happen, all told. He thinks she probably overdid it with the moving and the party, and the thing with the Swanson boy was a worse shock than we thought. He says she really must just rest for a couple of weeks. He thinks it was probably some sort of hysterical hallucination, or very possibly a vivid dream, and she agrees now that it probably was. There's a good local man he wants her to get started with after she's had a couple of weeks of total quiet."

I did not say anything. Was it possible that Virginia Guthrie had not told him that she too had seen the movie? Shouldn't he know? If he were to help his wife, shouldn't he know everything, all the cruel, bizarre, baffling details?

"I know about all of it, Colquitt," he said, catching my thoughts. "I don't have any explanations, except that it's entirely possible that there was some kind of auto-suggestion working with Virginia. I only know that she'll be all right, because I am going to make her all right, with God's help."

He said it naturally and unself-consciously, and I said only, "I believe you will."

"I have a great idea," Walter said. "Why don't you take her down to the beach for a couple of weeks? Stay in our cottage, if you don't mind roughing it. It's right on the water, and you couldn't get any quieter than the island this time of year. Just soak up the sun and eat and sleep and don't think about anything. It always puts Col and me back together, and you couldn't be more welcome to it."

I loved him achingly in that moment. Of course. The beach house. We had, I thought, been very selfish with it.

"I think that's the best idea I ever heard," I said. "There are linens and pots and pans, everything you could possibly need, and nobody will be using it for at least another month. Do it, Buck. It's not a bad drive. It's the perfect place to rest and invite your soul."

His tired face lit with something like a child's expectation, in July, that Christmas might really come again.

"You know, that really might do it. It really might. She loves the ocean; she loved our beach place. That's incredibly generous of you people. Only I'd want to rent it."

"Absolutely not. I'm going to be very offended if you even mention that again," I said. "I mean that, Buck."

"Well, then, let me talk to her about it, and if she'd like to do it, I'll give you a call tonight or tomorrow."

As we left he called after us, "God bless you."

The Sheehans left early the next Monday morning for our house on the island, and the house next door was empty and quiet again, and the summer spun on.

Chapter Thirteen

FOR A little while, then, there was a gentle time, the time in any summer that seems suspended in a sort of still, green hiatus, swung between two seasons, swaying almost imperceptibly in the languorous currents of heat and indolence. It is the time in our summers when children and animals abandon their first summer-struck frenzies of activity and motion and explorations and mischief; they drift in shoals through backyards in the cool of mornings and the honey-suckle-smelling twilights. Middays are given over to swim teams and tennis lessons and day camps for the younger children, and for long, heat-deadened sleeps beneath shrubbery and automobiles for animals. Among adults, the ruffled rush of spring cocktail parties and poolside galas slides into lazy weekends at the club or hastily thrown together suppers for a few friends on screened porches and patios. The late-spring debutante marathon slows into the desultory entertainments of the "little season"; weary teenagers abandon their froths of white and twelve-button gloves for swimsuits and cut-off jeans. People leave for vacations, and the neighborhood is subdued and not unpleasantly diminished.

On our street about a third of the old houses were empty for a time, and more were minus children, most of whom were in mountain camps or on exchange programs abroad. Duck Swanson was visiting the North Carolina cousin with whom he would room at Yale in the fall, and Claire's two younger boys were working in OEO-sponsored youth programs in the city's blistering, blighted southwest section. They still came, willing but leaden-footed, to do the minimal summer yardwork that our lawn requires. I had told Claire that it wasn't necessary; let them have their summer weekends. But she insisted.

"I can't stand them underfoot on Saturdays," she said. "They sleep till noon and get up expecting twelve-course breakfasts, and mope around the club pool all afternoon mooning over that little Carruthers tramp with the bathing suit that vanishes right up the cleft of her dewy little butt, and then they stay out till all hours on Saturday night and Roger is furious with them Sunday morning. Thank God, Duck's not at home; I'd have him *and* Libby Fleming billing and cooing all over the house ad nauseum. As it is, I'll bet he's called her fourteen times a day for the past two weeks and charged it to us, and Roger will kill him. I almost wish they'd go ahead and get married. It would be a lot cheaper and less nerve-wracking for everybody. Oh, no. Tommy and Rog can do their playing on Sundays. This summer is for old Mom, here. Since Tommy got his driver's license I haven't driven a car pool all summer, and with Duck away, Roger's been getting his own breakfast, and there was one decadent, go-to-hell morning that I slept until nine-thirty. Not only that, but I have a Bloody Mary with lunch every day, and take a nap after that. I'm going straight to hell in a handbasket this summer, and I love it."

"You sound like something out of a Somerset Maugham novel," I said. "If you don't watch it, you'll take to tottering around in a muumuu and drinking sloe gin straight out of the bottle. But it is a quiet, nice summer, isn't it?"

"It is since the poor Sheehans went to the island, anyway. Have you heard from them? God, I hope it's doing her some good."

"Just one call, to tell me where their spare key is and ask if I'd go over and water their plants. I haven't done it yet, but I will tomorrow or the next day. I think it will do her good if anything will. You know, I'm terribly fond of both of them, and my heart breaks for them, but I have a sneaking, nasty little sense of relief—as long as they're down there, there won't be any more of the upsets and the night horrors. Isn't that selfish of me? But it's really been an upsetting time for everybody since they came."

"Since the Harralsons came, you mean," said Claire. "I know. I truly am fond of Buck and Anita, but I'm beginning to feel like we've paid our dues with trouble for a while. If it was an old house, I'd almost think it was haunted, but who ever heard of a haunted contemporary less than a year old? Maybe there was an Indian graveyard on the property once, and the natives are restless."

"That kind of garbage really makes me uncomfortable, Claire."

"Oh, come on, Col. Where's your famous sense of humor? You know I'm kidding. Virginia told me about the movie on TV, and I told her she was either going through the change or she and Charles had been smoking pot over there and wouldn't admit it."

"You don't believe her, then?"

"It's not that I don't believe her. I just think Anita upset her so badly she didn't know what she was seeing. Christ, *you* don't believe it, do you?"

"I guess not," I said. "Walter certainly doesn't. But Virginia seemed so *sure.*"

"Well, she's not all that sure anymore. She as much as admitted to me later that she could have been mistaken, and then she changed the subject. I haven't said any more to her about it because it's so obvious that she's embarrassed and doesn't want to talk about it."

It was true that Virginia Guthrie did not want to talk about that evening. She simply refused to do so. When I told her, early in the week the Sheehans left for the island, that Walter and I had been thinking about the incident and he had had some ideas that might make her feel better about the whole thing, she said, "I shouldn't have disturbed you with all that, Colquitt. As far as I'm concerned, it was a case of the sillies on my part, and the subject is closed." I respected her feelings, but I wondered if it really was embarrassment that lay behind them. Somehow, I did not think it was. Virginia is not in the habit of doing things that will cause embarrassment, to other people or to herself.

Friday evening of that week Kim Dougherty came by at dusk. Walter had a meeting with a client, and I had worked longer than usual, so the late-slanting light was thickening and greening with shadows when I pulled into the driveway. I saw his dusty old VW first, and then, rounding the corner of the house to the patio, I saw Kim. He was slouched in his usual chair, drinking a beer and regarding the Sheehans' house solemnly and fixedly over the rim of the can. Foster was curled lumpishly in his lap. We had not seen him since the incident with Anita and the television set, and I wondered if he had heard about it. I hoped not. I did not plan to tell him.

"Your favorite mendicant is back with his empty stein," he said, brandishing the beer can at me. "I helped myself. Was that okay?"

"I wish my favorite mendicant had brought his bowl too," I said, looking critically at his long figure and his face. Both were thinner than ever, tautened down to bone and tendon. There was something—a coiled intensity, an interior smoldering—that disturbed me. "Have you been eating at all? You look like something right out of Bergen-Belsen."

"Sure I've been eating. I've been working like a field hand over on the Douglas site is all. Damned bricklayers walked out on me and I've been laying brick like—who was that stonemason in that book everybody had to read in high school? Jude the Obscure? It's better than Weight Watchers to get you in shape."

"Work going okay?" I asked casually. I didn't think it was. Not the design work, anyway. The interior cauldron was obviously consuming him.

"In a word, the work is shit, if you mean the designing, and you do. Jude the Obscure wasn't a bad analogy. Kim the Obscure has picked up the torch that cat dropped. I'm going to get it back, though."

"I know you are."

"No, I mean really. I left it over there, and that's where I'll find it again." He gestured at the Sheehans' house with his empty beer can, and I studied his face uneasily. He had said that before. There was a crystal raptness shining just under the calm mask of Kim-shaped bones and features. The obsession that had upset me before had not lessened; it was growing, eating.

He turned his face back to me. "Where are the Sheehans?" he said. "I've driven by here several times this week and their cars haven't been here. No lights either."

"They went down to our place on the island for a couple of weeks," I said neutrally. "She had a little . . . setback, and we thought the beach house would be a good place for them to unwind."

"What kind of setback?" Through the fast settling darkness I could feel his eyes steadily on my face.

"Just a movie on television that upset her."

"What movie?"

"I never did get it quite straight," I lied. "It wasn't much of anything. I guess it wouldn't take much, as fragile as she still is. I've talked to them since they've been down there and they seem fine."

He was quiet for a time, and then he said, "You're a rotten liar, Colquitt." I did not answer.

Presently I said, "They called to ask me to go over and water the plants, and I've been putting it off. Come walk over with me while I do it, and then I'll fix us a sandwich or something. Walter's not going to be here for dinner and I'd like some company."

"I'll wait for you here," he said.

"Oh, come on, Kim," I said crossly, tired suddenly

of levels and sublevels, portent and obsession. I was irritated at myself too. I realized that I did not want to go into the Sheehans' house alone in the thick stillness.

He grunted and stood up loosely, and we walked through the rhododendrons and up the bank and into the Sheehans' yard.

Anita had left the key under a flower pot on the back deck. I fished it out, jerking my hand back when it came in contact with something fat and damp that wriggled away from my fingers.

"Ugh. This particular key-hiding ploy wouldn't fool a retarded first-grader," I said, and unlocked the back door and walked into the kitchen. Kim followed. I groped for the light switch and could not find it. He reached around me with a long arm and plucked it out of the darkness, and the kitchen bloomed with white light.

"Are you a clairvoyant too?" I asked brightly. There was a swelling in the air, a charged tightening that I could feel on the skin of my arms and face and neck. It felt like a small, hot wind drying wet flesh, so that the small hairs stood up stickily. I moved away from Kim's arm quickly.

"I'm the one who put that fixture there, remember?" he said. His voice sounded as though there was not much breath behind it. The room was bright and white and still and silent, but soundless sound roared and howled in it.

I found a plastic pitcher under the sink, and filled it with tap water, and watered the hanging plants in the kitchen windows and the African violets that stood on the wide windowsills. I chattered steadily about nothing that I can remember now to Kim Dougherty, who leaned against the kitchen counter in silence, his face lifted as into a freshening wind. He did not reply. He did not move from the counter when I refilled the pitcher and walked into the dark living room. There was just enough light from outside so that I could see the showering shapes of the plants that hung in the windows there, some nearly brushing the floor. I felt along the wall for the living room light switch but found nothing. I did not want to call out to Kim for help through the roaring silence, and set the pitcher down on the floor to free both hands, but I still couldn't find the switch, and finally I called out, hating the ersatz jollity in my voice, "Where the hell is your living room switch?"

"It works off a rheostat thing by the door into the dining room," he called back. "It's that round thing. Just push it in and turn it." But he did not come into the living room.

I stumbled in the darkness to the wall by the dining room door, taking great, silent gulps of the dense air. It was hard to breathe. I wanted desperately to be done and out of this swelling, prickling house and back in my own kitchen. I wanted Kim to be gone. I wanted Walter. I could not find the rheostat.

"I give up," I called. "You'll have to come and turn it on for me."

I heard his steps come slowly through the kitchen and into the room, and turned and saw the bulk of him, thicker darkness in the dark, beside me, and he reached out past me for the switch, and then closed his arms around me. I stood stiffly in Kim Dougherty's arms, feeling nothing but the violent wrenching of his heart, hearing his grating breath and the deep singing of the silence. It rose and bloomed into a keening that filled my ears and blood and blinded my eyes, and I put my arms around him and pulled his mouth down to mine. Even as his arms dragged me into his bending body, even as his mouth devoured mine and my own opened to his, a thin thread of pure consciousness that was all that was left of me, of Colquitt Kennedy, crouched in a corner of my head and whimpered, high and childishly, "I don't like this. I want to go home now. I don't want this to happen anymore."

Light blazed. Kim lifted his head and pushed me back, and I stumbled against the back of the sofa and caught myself with my hands, head hanging, breath choking in my throat. The very air of the house seemed to be filled with stinging, buzzing things like bees. I saw dimly, as if through smoke. Kim's face was white and blind. Walter stood in the door from the kitchen, and his eyes were as sightless as Kim's, though they were fastened on me. He stood very still

132

and straight. In his hand, dangling against his leg, was Anita Sheehan's French boning knife. No one moved or spoke. Then Walter moved toward us into the room.

The deadness lifted and I drew in my breath in mindless, ineffectual terror. His blind face was a wolf's honed smile, a jackal's killing rictus, a whipping, snaking death. The silent air howled with blood and inevitability. Enormity sang and screamed, a limitless gulf seemed to open in the floor that rotted under my feet. I saw murder in the face I had loved for so many years, saw my own end there, and Kim's, and Walter's. I lifted both hands weakly, but could not move my feet. Kim did not move either, but looked at Walter as he advanced slowly toward us, looked at him with a desperate puzzlement, an anguished incomprehension. And then he moved, fast and violently, and shoved me ahead of him into the living room toward the French doors that opened onto the front deck. Dimly, as my feet stumbled toward the front door, I heard him shouting, "Get out of this house! Get out, Colquitt! Walter, get out of the house now! Now!" He reached the glass door as I did and shattered it as easily as if it had been plastic wrap, with his shoulder, and when I was aware of anything again the three of us were standing in the cool blackness of the Sheehans' driveway, and the air was only the air of a summer night again, and the sounds were only the sounds of a summer night.

Another sound broke the night then. Walter. Walter was crying. He sank to the driveway like a child whose tired legs will not support him any longer, and sat on the asphalt and put his face into his hands and cried. He cried great wrenching, silent sobs. He was saying something, but it was a long moment before I could understand what it was, and then I could.

"I would have killed you," he sobbed. "I would have killed you both. My God, I don't understand what has happened."

I was crying too, and went to him and crouched down beside him and held him in my arms.

"I didn't mean it," I wept hopelessly. "Darling,

133

Walter, baby, what you saw—I didn't mean that! I don't know why—I don't understand—"

He shook his head back and forth in his hands, tears running through his tanned fingers.

"I would have killed you, Colquitt, and then I couldn't have lived!"

Kim said nothing, looking at us. His face was dead. His voice, when he spoke, was formal and precise.

"I know what happened," he said. "I know about all of it. I understand it now. Colquitt, help me get him back to your house. I can help you both. Please come now."

I got up obediently. Kim and I raised Walter to his feet. He walked with us, quietly, back through the rhododendron hedge and across our driveway and into the den. We sat down on the sofa, and Kim brought the brandy bottle from the pantry and took a long pull of it and passed it to us. We drank in turn from the bottle and looked at him expectantly and blankly, like children waiting to have something enormous, incredible, made credible. I remember feeling almost peaceful, ebbed and emptied, waiting. Walter said later that he did too.

"First," he said, looking at Walter, "do you really think there's anything going on between me and Colquitt? Forget what you saw over there. Do you really think we've been having an affair, shacking up, running around behind your back? Do you really think she would ever do that to you, with me or any other guy?"

Walter looked at him, and then at me. "No," he said. "I don't think that. I know what I saw, but I don't believe that."

Kim looked at me. "Why were you kissing me?" he said. "Do you remember what you felt? Do you know why?"

I shook my head. I felt nothing but a gentle, vague confusion mingled with a faraway, sleepy, simple relief and the dreaming sense that things were not, perhaps, broken between Walter and me. None of it seemed real or seemed to matter a great deal.

Kim said, "I can't ask you to believe this if you don't, Walter, but I am not in love with Colquitt, I do not lust after her, I had no intention of touching her when we went over there tonight, and I don't remember why I did it. I don't even remember how I felt."

Walter shook his head slowly. "I don't remember picking up that knife either," he said. "I don't remember thinking that I would kill you both, but I know that I would have. I would have done that. If I hadn't left there I would have done it."

Kim's face wore the rapt, luminous sheen I had seen earlier that night when we'd first talked on the patio. "It's that damned house," he said. "It *is* damned, that house. It's a greedy house. It takes. You said once, Col, that it would bring out the best in whoever lived there. You were wrong. It takes the best. It took that miserable Pie's kid, and her marriage, and her daddy. It took that poor sonofabitch Buddy's whole future. It took that Abbott guy's future. It's taking Anita Sheehan's sanity—I know damned well there was more to her little 'setback' than you told me, Col —and it took my talent. And tonight it almost took you and Walter away from each other for good. Don't you see that? Don't either of you see that?"

I felt normalcy flood back into me like a freezing current, and watched it fill the husk that was Walter. Pain and shame and self-loathing at the dreadful scene in the Sheehans' living room came roiling over me too, but the queer, flattened, childlike suspension was gone. Kim's obsession had slid over into something approaching madness, and the fright and sickness of that restored me.

"Kim," I said. "Kim, listen. I cannot forgive myself for what happened tonight. I never will. I will spend the rest of my life making it up to Walter, if he will let me, and to you too. I don't know how or why it happened, and I am ashamed and sick about it, but it's not your fault, and it's *nothing in that house*. Things like that don't happen. It was something in me, something . . . sick and awful that I didn't know I had. I will accept the responsibility for it. But I will not listen to you talking like this anymore. You've let this—this dry spell you're having make you sick. You need to get some help from somewhere, you need to go away for a while, go home, go to a doctor—"

Walter broke in. "Col's right, Kim. Christ, I owe you both an apology; it must have looked like something out of a Ken Russell film there for a minute. Look, I've smooched up a neighbor lady in the kitchen myself, and felt like an ass about it for the next month, and it hasn't changed things between me and Colquitt. Neither will this. You've been under a godawful strain lately, and you've gone off the deep end about the house, and I agree—I think you *do* need to get away from here for a while. Maybe a session or two with a shrink wouldn't be a bad idea, and it's certainly nothing you need to be ashamed of. And Col's been under a strain, with Anita and all, and I have—hell, the whole street has, for that matter. I think we can all three forget this . . . this thing tonight. Just not speak of it again. It's not going to change things between the three of us."

Kim looked silently from me to Walter, and then rose. He came to me and hugged me, and then went to Walter and gave him a brief, hard hug around the shoulders.

"I love you both," he said. "I really do. I'm sorry."

And he was gone.

Walter and I looked at each other, and then we went upstairs and got into bed and held each other, long and hard and quietly, and we did not speak of the evening. It was a long time before we did again.

KIM WENT away three days after that, away to Europe. He left us no forwarding address.

When Walter and I got up the morning after that hideous night, the day was overcast and freighted with a heavy ordinariness that reminded me of a mild hangover. We were both tired, and moved slowly and quietly, and were gentle with each other. There was no constraint between us, and no flinching, hurtful shying away from the previous night in either of our minds. I am sure of that. Both of us had, sometime during the dreamless night, locked the thing away and sealed it and walked away from it.

The following Monday there was a note from Kim in the mailbox when I drove in from work. It sounded like Kim, like Kim a year ago, bantering and dry and flippant.

"To Europe," it read in part. "Starting with Paris and going on from there. With a backpack and the whole thing. I can just hear you now, Col, fussing about how I'm going to live. Don't worry. I've got enough money for half a year if I'm careful, and my old man's got a million contacts all over Europe, so I'll get a good dinner and a fancy bed and introductions to whoever in every city from Norway to Spain, if I want them. I may even end up in the jet set. You'll read about me lolling around on some fat old Greek's yacht in Antibes, or water-skiing with Jackie Onassis. I'll be the toast of the Continent. I'll write you later and let you know what's happening. Please take very good care of yourselves."

He signed it, "Love, Kim."

I cried a little when I showed it to Walter that night, but not much. They were the foolish, simple tears of missing someone you're fond of. We had been, both of us, very fond of Kim Dougherty.

The next Sunday evening the Sheehans returned from the island, and Buck called to thank us and to say that the trip had done Anita a lot of good and that he really thought she was much better.

"We'll drop over tomorrow night and bring the key and tell you about it," he said. "Things okay here while we were gone?"

"I'm so glad it helped," I said. "Do come on over tomorrow night; we'd love to hear. Yes. Things here were fine."

Chapter Fourteen

BUCK SHEEHAN did come over the next evening to return the key to the beach house, but he was alone. He was deeply tanned and peeling across the bridge of his nose and looked rested, but there was a faint abstraction to his voice and in his eyes. He looked frequently across at his house, its lights glowing once again in the dusk.

"Anita asked me to make her excuses," he said. "She's sleeping. She slept for twelve straight hours last night and took a long nap this afternoon and dropped off again after dinner on the sofa. I think it's probably good for her. She slept like there was no tomorrow the whole time we were on the island."

"It does that to you," Walter said.

"I know," said Buck Sheehan. "I never slept so much or ate so much or turned into such a bone-lazy slob in my life, and Anita just soaked it up. I couldn't keep her out of the water when she wasn't in the hammock or in bed. And ate enough fresh shrimp to sink the Sixth Fleet. We really loved it; it was everything you said it was. It's the funniest, greatest little old island I ever saw. I don't know how we're ever going to thank you. I really don't."

"If it helped Anita, that's all the thanks I need," I said.

"It did. There's no doubt of that. She was . . . almost the way she was before, down there. You know, I was wondering if, later on, after things are more settled at the office, you might tell us where to start looking for a piece of property down there, or maybe an old house like yours. I wouldn't even know where to start. But it would make a great place to . . . retreat to."

I looked at him; the choice of words was, somehow, unsettling.

"There are probably some around," I said. "Most everybody wants to buy or build over on Sea Island or one of the fancier islands down there. There's not all that much demand for houses on St. Agnes. If you looked around, you could probably find something pretty cheap, if you wouldn't mind a lot of fix-up work."

"That's right up Anita's alley," he said. "It might be just the thing. Speaking of fixing up, I meant to ask you. I found some broken glass on the front deck, and I wondered if either of you might have noticed anything . . ."

We were silent for a moment, and then I said, "I

have to confess. I—we—went over to water your plants the other night and I couldn't find the light switch in the living room and blundered into that pane and broke it. We got it fixed of course, and I hoped you wouldn't notice. It was hardly a neighborly thing to do."

"God, don't give it another thought. You weren't hurt, were you?"

"No."

"Well, don't even think about paying for it. Send me the bill. I should have told you where that rheostat is; you'd never find it unless you knew exactly where it was. It's a small price to pay for the two weeks you gave us."

"It's paid, and that's that. You are not going to reimburse me for my consummate clumsiness. End of subject. Now. Why don't you two come over and have some supper with us one night this week? Just us, after Anita's good and rested. I want to hear what she thought about it."

He hesitated, and looked again toward his house. "She's . . . maybe not quite so strong as I thought she was when we were at the beach. Can I call and let you know when?"

"Of course," I said. "Let her rest."

I saw Anita the next morning hosing off the shrubbery around her front door. Her dark hair was pulled back under a red bandanna and her eyes were shielded by outsized sunglasses. She wore white slacks and a checked shirt knotted across her tanned, polished midriff and looked like a fashion sketch in *W,* attenuated and careless and elegant. I smiled and waved, and she laid the hose down and came to the edge of the driveway, smiling in return.

"Welcome home," I said. "We missed you."

"Missed you too, and thank you four million times," she said. "I love your cottage and I love your island and I love you both for letting us have those two weeks. They were . . . something I'll never forget."

She took off her sunglasses. The fine lines were back around her eyes, and there was a look of immense distance in them, but a peaceful sort of distance. I knew the feeling; part of her was still lost in the depths of the sea she had just left behind her. I'm the same way when I come back from the island. She didn't look as taut-skinned and vivid and glowing as she had when I'd first seen her on our return from vacation, but neither was she the same frail, tight-pulled, half-mad woman we'd first met. Well, I thought, two steps back, one forward. Maybe Walter's right and this *is* the way she'll come out of it. Slowly.

"I want to have you and Walter over for dinner sometime soon," she said. "I'd planned to do it this week, but I just can't seem to get my act together. I sleep all the time; are there tsetse flies on your island? But I want you to know that I'm not planning to turn into a recluse."

"Don't even think of it," I said. "You're supposed to be resting this summer. Let us feed you all for a while. We'll make you feed us fifty times over this fall and winter when you're up to it."

"No. I mean it, Colquitt. I'm starting with this new man down here tomorrow, and if he says the word, I'm going to start pulling my weight around this neighborhood. You all mustn't worry about me, Colquitt, any more than you can help worrying when I go around throwing fits as regularly as clockwork. I was tired from getting ready for the big party; that was a mistake, so soon. And I had a rotten dream, or hallucination, or something, and I wigged out again for a little while, and I'm sorry for the hell it put you all through, but my doctor back home told Buck that it was probably just the way it was going to be for a while—and if so, so be it. It was a momentary wigout, not a permanent one. I'm going to get myself straightened out eventually. I took it too hard and fast is all."

Buck had not told her about Virginia Guthrie's terrible moment in front of their television set, then. Or about Charles and Virginia's checking of the *TV Guide* and the television stations. Of course, he wouldn't have.

"Well, whenever you're up to it, then, but not one moment before," I said, starting for my car.

"Soon," she said. As I got into the car she was coiling up the hose and yawning, a vast, deep, stretching yawn, and when I drove away she had gone into her house and closed the door.

WE DID not hear from the Sheehans during that week, and except for a couple of times when Claire Swanson saw Buck drive up to the house during the day and pick up Anita and bring her home an hour or so later, nobody saw her at all. I supposed, when Claire told me about seeing them, that he was taking her to the therapist the New Jersey doctor had recommended, and that the man had, perhaps, advised her to curtail any sort of social activity. I was rather grateful for the moratorium. We were in the middle of a new business presentation at the office, and I had been working late all week. I hadn't really liked the idea of an evening with the Sheehans so soon after their two weeks at the beach. I didn't want to talk about their problems for a while or have them feel they must thank us over and over. I did not want to hear any more hopeful allusions to recovery and wholeness and eventual health. I simply wanted it to happen, quietly and without incident. I was tired of pain and fear and strangeness. Anita's and Buck's. Kim's. Walter's and mine.

Midway during the next week I ran into Virginia Guthrie on the street downtown outside my office building just as I was coming back from a hasty trip to soothe a client whose press kits had arrived forty-five minutes after the press had departed. She was trundling along toward the multilevel parking garage at the end of the street, department-store boxes piled chin-high in her arms.

"You look like you're ready to spit nails," she said.

"I am. And you look like you're about to collapse in the street. Let's go blow two hours on lunch at Rinaldi's. With Bloody Marys. I'll treat. If I go back to the office right now I'll probably bash my dim-witted secretary's head in with a zip-code directory. Or ruin her manicure, which would be an even greater disaster."

She seemed reluctant for a moment, and then she said, "Oh, why not? I don't have to be anywhere until four. And I'll take you up on that Bloody Mary. I may even have three."

"Bad day on the barricades?" I said. Virginia does not like to shop.

"Bad week, sort of. I guess. I don't really know. It will be good to talk to somebody about it."

"Anita," I said, looking at her closely in the white noon light.

"Anita," she said.

We walked across the street and went into Rinaldi's, and Vito, the maître d' who had professed a courtly and florid letch for me for all the years I'd been at the agency, found us a quiet table in a sunny bay overlooking the milling human traffic on the street outside. The contrast between the teeming street and the subdued noon restaurant bustle was soothing. We ordered the Bloody Marys and they came immediately, rich and thick and sprinkled with snips of fresh dillweed, in outsized frosted goblets.

"What's happened?" I said when the silence had spun out between us. "Has there been anything else about the boy?"

"Well, not directly. I'm not really sure anything *has* happened. It's just that she isn't snapping back like Buck seems to think she should; she sleeps an awful lot. Late in the mornings, and long naps in the afternoon, and at night, in front of the television set. Of course she's on some kind of medication this man down here is giving her, and that could account for the drowsiness."

"I'm sure it could," I said. "Didn't her other doctor, the one in New Jersey, say she *would* sleep a lot?"

"Yes, but it's not just that. She watches television from the time she gets up to the time Buck puts her to bed. That's where she naps in the afternoons, in front of the set."

"I guess a lot of women do that, especially when they have to stay inside and rest and can't go out."

She looked past me at a robust, startlingly proportioned mural of the Bay of Naples. "Buck thinks she's waiting to see . . . something else about the boy. She doesn't say so of course, and he wouldn't mention it, but she gets very querulous, very peevish, when he tries to turn the set off. He says she never cared for television before."

142

"Don't you think Buck might be overreacting?" I said. I was annoyed, but I did not know why. "Reading things into what she's doing because he's so afraid there *will* be something?"

"It's possible. I suggested that, and he admits that he could be. But she says there have been some phone calls too."

Dread brushed my heart. "Phone calls? From whom?"

"From nobody. I mean, she says the phone rings, and when she answers there's nobody on the line."

"Probably our friendly corner burglar trying to find out what her in-and-out patterns are. That happens to most of us sometimes, Virginia."

"Well, she insists that these are long-distance."

"How can she tell if there's nobody on the line?"

"She says there's that sort of faraway rushing sound, like you hear when a long distance call comes in, before anybody speaks."

"Has Buck taken any of them?"

"She says they come during the day, when he's at work. I don't think there have been many of them, but they seem to upset her—out of all proportion."

"I guess maybe they would, if you were sick and jumpy like she is."

"She . . . Colquitt, she thinks it's that woman."

"What woman?" I said stupidly.

"That woman that Buck—you know, when he was drinking so, and she read that letter the woman had written him, and he found her there in that rocking chair—"

"Oh, *God!*" I moaned. "What did she say? Anita, I mean? Did she *say* she thought it was the woman?"

"No. She never did, directly. But Buck came in last week, one night late, and found her sitting in that rocking chair, the one that was in the boy's room where he found her before. It's that bentwood by the fireplace. She was just rocking, and rocking. And staring straight in front of her. The phone was on her lap; she was rocking it in her lap."

"Ah, dear God, Virginia, she *didn't* go off into another one of those awful things—"

"No, no, she didn't. Nothing like that. He thought

she had when he first came in, but she looked up quite matter-of-factly and said that there had been another of those long-distance phone calls where nobody was on the line."

"That's all she said about it?"

"That's all."

"Then why should either of you assume she thinks it's the woman calling?"

"Well, it was so like that other time, the time that put her in the hospital, you see. The same chair. The rocking, the staring. And she'd just found out about the woman then." Virginia frowned. "I know it sounds like a huge assumption, but when you hear Buck describe it, it sounds . . . plausible, somehow."

"When *did* you hear him describe it?" I asked.

"He called me when it happened. I went over." She finished her drink and looked around for the waiter. He appeared, and we ordered another Bloody Mary apiece.

"And what was she like? What was going on?"

"Nothing much was going on. She was still in the chair, but she was pleasant to me, just a little detached. She said she was sleepy and wanted to go to bed, and Buck took her upstairs. She did say one thing that just about broke my heart. She stopped on the bottom step and looked back at me, and said, 'Can you ever really fix things that have been broken once? I thought you could, but I was crazy for a long time, you know.' "

"Oh, poor, poor thing! Poor Buck. Poor you, for that matter."

"Well, it's mainly Buck I'm worried about right now. He came back downstairs and talked to me for a long time—that's when he told me about the TV watching and the phone calls—and I did tell him I thought he might be reading in things that simply weren't there. But he was so worried that I finally insisted that he call her doctor."

"And?"

"And the doctor said he didn't much like the sound of it. He said at first he thought she might be better off hospitalized for a week or two, so they could do some really intensive therapy and keep her away from televisions and telephones, but Buck didn't want to do that, and the doctor said she could stay home *if* there was somebody with her during the day, when Buck's at work. He's also seeing her every day now, and he's got her on some stronger medication. Stelazine, or Thorazine, or something—one of the really strong tranquilizers. She's been very calm since then of course, with all that gunk in her, and a little—distant. She doesn't talk much. But she's beginning to perk up some. She isn't sleeping so much. She's been reading a good bit for the last two days, and yesterday she washed her hair and let me set it. There haven't been any more phone calls. The doctor said there was a good possibility that there never were any. I thought that too. She's eating all right."

"You've been over there with her all day every day?" I asked.

"Well, not *all* day. Buck goes in late, and comes home for lunch every day, and he gets home early every evening."

"Virginia, it's too much on you. You really should have let us know. I could have taken some time off. Claire would have been glad to come and spell you. This is just above and beyond the call."

"She didn't want any of you to know, not quite yet. Not until she's better. She's embarrassed and angry at herself and so anxious not to be a burden to anybody that it's pitiful to watch. She's really trying *so* hard to pull out of this thing, Colquitt. I never saw anybody fight so hard to be strong and well. She's had such rotten bad luck since they came—"

"I know," I said. "It's almost macabre, the things that have been happening to her. Scary. It almost seems as if there's some intelligence, or force, or something, that knows just what would hurt her most." Faces swam before my eyes, flickered, and were gone: Walter's, blind and alien, in a white light; Kim's, rapt and incandescent. I took a long swallow of my drink.

Virginia looked at me severely. "You mustn't let Anita's illness get to you, Colquitt," she said. "You've never been around mental illness before, have you? I have. My mother was hospitalized for years, off and on, with awful bouts of depression, only they didn't know what to call it then, or how to treat it, really. It started after my brother was born. I know how it can affect you if you're close to it. You lose your own perspective if you're not careful. You have to keep telling yourself that it isn't in the air, or due to some kind of force, or something—that it's a concrete illness and it's in them. Not in you. I got through mother's, and I really think I'm a stronger person for it. I don't mind staying with Anita, because I've been down that road before and I can keep my own wits and help her better than somebody who's had no experience with this kind of thing. Like I said, we talk. I think she really does trust me. She's just going to have to go through these ups and downs, and even if the things that have happened to her do seem particularly cruel, they're *natural*, they're explainable, in the light of her particular illness. They all could have happened to her anywhere, and probably would have."

"You think that thing with the television set is explainable, then? You didn't that morning." Distress and the flickering image-faces of two men, quickly banished, made me harsher with Virginia than I have ever been.

"I was upset myself," she said levelly. "I jumped to a conclusion that wasn't logical; I saw something I was expecting to see. I don't like to think it of myself, but I guess I can go just as temporarily bananas as the next person when the circumstances are right. Which they were that night, in spades. I want that thing forgotten; it isn't important. What is is that Anita does seem to be pulling out of it again, slowly, and that we all help her and support her in every way we can. Him too. It may be quite a long haul for her yet, and getting the willies over it ourselves is not what either of them needs."

"You're right," I said. "You always are. I'm ashamed of myself. What can we do right now that will help? You can't just devote your whole summer to baby-sitting with poor Anita Sheehan. Let some of us take a turn now."

"No, really. Tomorrow's my last day of duty, and I've had all of today off until four. Fanny went over today. Her cousin, the one whose family took her in after the accident, is coming down day after tomorrow to stay with her for a week or so, and by that time she may be able to stay alone. Or she may go home with her cousin for a little while. Buck doesn't want her to do that; her doctor thinks she ought not to break treatment. But we'll see how it goes. She told me that she didn't mind if I told you and Claire about these past few days. She wanted me to, in fact, eventually. She wanted you both to know she's not just ignoring you. But she really isn't up to seeing you yet."

I was obscurely and guiltily glad. We finished the drinks and ordered lunch and talked of other things. Eloise did indeed think she might be pregnant again, and we groaned and laughed a little over that.

"Somebody ought to tell Semmes what's causing it," Virginia said, and I laughed again, because it was as close to bawdiness as I have ever heard Virginia Guthrie come. She flushed a little and laughed with me.

"See what two drinks does to me?" she said. She looked incandescently beautiful and young in the plant-dappled sunlight of that restaurant window, with the shaded silver-gray strands of her hair loosened and curling around her face like dandelion fluff and the twin flags of liquor and laughter burning in her cheeks. Her image in that precise moment, in that particular noon, burned into my brain and has shimmered there ever since. I am terribly, terribly glad.

A LETTER came from Kim Dougherty that week. It was postmarked Rome. He didn't say a great deal, and what he did say sounded determinedly cheerful and having-a-good-time-wish-you-were-here. But there was a restlessness to it too. He loved Italy, he said, and had been staying with friends of his parents in cities all through the country, and they had been kind and had shown him a royal good time. He had met a contessa, he said, who had a face like Rocky Marciano and wanted him to come and spend two or three months at her villa in Calabria to oversee some renovations, but he had, he said, a pretty good idea what she wanted to renovate and he didn't think even an architect could help her there.

Walter and I laughed at that; it was a glimmer—just a glimmer—of the old Kim.

He said that he'd had about enough of the high life

and that he thought he'd take off pretty soon on his own, with his backpack, or maybe by train or bus, and work his way up through Switzerland and into France, and stay a while in Paris.

"I'll come back to Italy after that," he wrote, "and catch up on some of the things I've been avoiding on purpose this time around. Everywhere you look here the architecture and the art just yell out to you. All those centuries, all those minds and hands. I can't ignore it forever, even if I can't do it anymore. I hope to spend a lot of time in Florence this fall and winter. I ought to be ready for it by then."

"I miss you both," he finished. "I hope things are better there now."

I folded the letter and set it aside. I knew that I had been expecting to hear that his travels had restored to him what had vanished into the red earth of the next-door lot. But it was not here in these scribbled, banal words, not on this grimy, flimsy paper. And I knew that it was not in him. Not yet. I had not thought about Kim much since he left, but I missed him suddenly and achingly, missed the gray eyes crinkling out of the brick tangle of beard and eyebrows, the tall, shambling figure, the sudden boy's grin, the big, deft hands. My eyes prickled, then cleared.

"I hope things are better there now," he had written.

I was glad, for the first time, that he was not here to see how things were.

Chapter Fifteen

ANITA SHEEHAN'S cousin was a larger, older, paler echo of Anita, with Anita's graceful bones and sculpted face lying under drifts of excess flesh as if under snow.

"She looks like Anita melted," Walter said when Buck had brought the cousin over to meet us shortly after she arrived and they had gone back to the house next door, where Anita lay dozing in her Stelazine peace.

"She seems like a thoroughly nice woman to me," I said. "Brisk and warm and no nonsense about her. I get the idea she's been a trifle annoyed with baby cousin all along for letting anything so trivial as catatonia, or whatever it was, get to her. I don't mean that she's unsympathetic; she of all people knows what Anita's been through, right from the beginning, with her father and brother. But I think she may be just what Anita needs now. Maybe you're right and everybody *has* been a little too indulgent with her. It's hard not to be when you're so close to the situation."

"Buck seems relieved, at any rate."

"Well, he's been having an awful time too, don't forget. There's just a limit to what anybody can take. I'm sure he's grateful to have somebody else besides poor Virginia worrying about Anita, at least during the daytime. He does have a business to run."

"It's always interested me," Walter said, "the people who crack and the people who don't. The exact same things have happened to him that have happened to her, except for the thing with her father and brother. He lost his only child too. But he didn't end up in the funny farm. Granted, he had a bad time with the booze and the girl there for a while, but he pulled himself out of that. He got himself straightened out and her out of the hospital, and he got himself another job and found her a house down here and set her up in it, and he's hanging in there. Seeing Duck Swanson that night must have been as bad for him as it was for her, and all this other stuff that's set her off must have almost been worse for him, really, because he couldn't prevent it. But he's not back on the booze. He hasn't run off with his secretary. I've often wondered if some people are just born weaker than others, flawed somehow."

"Are you forgetting about that television movie and those phone calls?" I said. "Those things happened to her, not to him. There's no telling how that horrible

149

thing on television might have affected him if he'd seen it. Everybody has a last straw, Walter."

"If there was a movie at all, Colquitt. That thing was part of her flaw, her weakness, don't you see? Buck doesn't see movies or get phone calls that aren't there, because there's something in him that's going to hold together no matter what."

"Or maybe it just isn't his turn yet."

"What do you mean?" he said, frowning.

"I mean that maybe whatever it is is going to get her first before it goes to work on him." I had not known what I meant and was shocked and frightened at my own words.

He came over to where I was standing, in front of the mirror over my dressing table. He put his arms around me and rested his chin on the top of my head. In the mirror I could see his face above mine. His eyes were closed and there was fatigue and distress in the lines around his mouth and eyes. My heart squeezed with love and remorse. Those lines had not been nearly so deep the last time I had really looked at Walter. When, in the past dizzying spring and summer, had they deepened? What betrayals, what self-indulgent dreads and fancies of mine had helped etch them there?

"Colquitt, when you talk like that I get the worst feeling in the pit of my stomach. I feel like I'm losing you to something I can't fight or even see. I feel like you're going away someplace where I can't follow and leaving me alone. Please don't do this to me. Please don't talk like that anymore. That isn't you talking. I want you back, baby. That's all in the world I do want."

"You almost lost me for good one night not so long ago," I said, unable to stop the spiraling fright. "We almost lost each other for good. Don't you remember that? Don't you remember where it happened?"

His face twisted with pain and a terrible, lost grief.

"Oh, darling, I'm so sorry," I said, and began to cry with shame and love. "I've been so terribly damned selfish, with all this stupid apprehension and these childish things I've been thinking. I know you didn't—I know you wouldn't have—please, please forgive me. I just let myself go and rattle on and on and never stop to think how you must feel when I do. I *won't* talk about it anymore. I won't do it ever again. I won't even think about it. You're not losing me; there's nothing in the world that could make that happen."

In the cool, summer-night sweetness of the tangled bed we forgot it all for a time, and I remember thinking, just before I fell asleep in the lightly sweated curve of Walter's arm, that this was what we were all about, this was the sum of us, and as long as there was this, nothing else mattered in any basic, bone-deep way. I slid into sleep on a tide of lightness and peace.

Marguerite Condon, Anita's cousin, lived up to our first impression of her. She turned the house inside out in a flurry of cleaning and polishing and waxing. Virginia Guthrie lent her cleaning woman for the first three days of Marguerite's stay, and the hum of the vacuum cleaner and the cheerful chuckle of the washing machine in the basement sang through the heat-heavy air in the mornings, even before I left for work.

In the afternoons, toward the last week of her initial stay in the house, she would get Anita up and dressed, and they would walk together in the backyard or as far as the mailbox and back again. Anita looked to me, the first time I saw her walking with her cousin, like a placid animal docilely following at the end of a leash. She was cave-pale, and her tan had faded, and her hair was awkwardly grown out but neatly caught at the back of her neck with a scarf, and her slacks and shirt were immaculate. She smiled at me and said, "Hello, Colquitt, how have you been?" and I said, "Just fine. It's good to see you out again."

Marguerite Condon said, "Nita's doing just fine too, aren't you, Nita? We're going Monday and get her hair done, and then we're going some place nice and expensive for lunch. It's time she got out of the house for a little while."

She squeezed Anita's arm fondly, and Anita smiled again, peacefully and agreeably. But she said no more, and I didn't either. It was as if she were suspended in air and time, unmarked by anything that had happened to her before, unsurprised by the present she

151

found herself in. It seemed the unsullied peace of the very young, not that of a mature woman who had wrenched and wrestled peace for herself out of an overpowering world. I knew too it was a peace born of drugs. She seemed caught in an aspic of drug-quietness. And it lasted four more days.

On a Tuesday in the third blistering week of July I was on my hands and knees in the upstairs bedroom that would become my office snaking a steel measuring tape along the wall. I was at home because the whole office had worked through the weekend and until near midnight the night before on a crash campaign for a new urban complex that had just netted and boated its first major tenant, a multimillion-dollar Eastern cosmetics firm, and wished to tell the breath-holding world about it as soon as possible. I had directed the team that put the campaign together, and gave my tired flock the next day off. I was thinking, at the moment when Anita Sheehan came stumbling and pounding onto the patio, how lovely and peaceful it was going to be, working in my new office in the treetops, mapping out my proposals and programs judiciously and at my own leisure. Razz slept in a square of sunlight under one of the dormers, and Foster lay on his side at the other end of the tape, giving it a desultory, heavy-footed swat when I moved it and it whipped past him. When Anita's voice tore into the afternoon, both cats started up violently, and fluidly reassembled themselves into the ancient, classic crouch of cats in danger, ears skinned back to skulls, tails swelling. I stayed where I was for a moment, my nails digging into the carpet, my heart stopping for a sickening interval and then jolting on crazily. And then I scrambled to my feet and half ran, half fell down the stairs and through the kitchen to the patio door.

She stood against the door, head hanging down, breath whistling in her throat, still knocking, knocking. I fumbled at the lock and threw open the door. She fell into my arms, crying and laughing, laughing with a tear-strangled, bubbling sound that I still hear when I cannot sleep at night. A drowning laugh. We stumbled together backward into the kitchen, and I held her away from me so I could see her face. It was radiant, blurred with a wild and almost mystic joy.

"He's alive!" she cried, her head thrown back, tears flooding from beneath her closed lids. "He's alive! Toby is alive, he's alive, he's going to come home, he's alive! He's all right!"

"Anita—Anita. What are you saying?"

"I'm saying that my son is alive! I'm saying that it was somebody else we buried; it was all an awful, awful horrible mistake! He's alive! Oh, my dearest God in heaven, my son is coming home!"

She collapsed into my arms again, sobbing terribly and laughing. Mindlessly I pulled her into the den and dropped her onto the sofa. How many women have I done this for now, I remember thinking mildly in the middle of the whirling nothing-numbness that fogged my mind and stopped my speech and dragged at my limbs. What must I do for this one? What is this she is telling me?

The kitchen door slammed again and Marguerite Condon was in the room, struggling for breath, her face stark and old with terror. We looked at each other.

"Get on the phone and call her doctor," she gasped. "Quick. And call Buck."

She went to the woman on the sofa and sat down beside her and put her arms around her. She held her close.

"Baby, baby, baby," she crooned, tears starting in her own eyes. "Honey, baby, please, *please* try and get hold of yourself. You imagined it, darling, you imagined it—don't do this to yourself. Don't start thinking he's coming back. Sweetheart, Toby died, Toby is dead. He's *dead*. We buried him, you remember—Nita, you're going to destroy yourself with this."

Anita Sheehan shook her head against her cousin's shoulder, no, no. She struggled to free herself from the older woman's arms. She got her head free and looked at me, frantic with the effort to talk through the tears and laughter. I stood rooted with the sheer hideousness of the moment, the pain of her joy. She is quite mad, I thought, mildly and clearly again. Finally and forever mad, now.

"Colquitt, I *talked* to him! I talked to him on the telephone! Not five minutes ago! It rang, and I picked it up, and it made that sound, you know, like when it's coming from far away—that same sound it's been making. That's what it's been all along, only he hasn't been able to get through until now—and of course, it *was* coming from far away, because it's overseas, you see. And I said, 'Hello?' and Toby said, 'Ma?' He always calls me Ma, and he said, 'Ma, I need you, Ma, I want to come home—' And then we got cut off, there wasn't any more, but, oh, don't you see? I *talked* to him, it *was* Toby, and if I talked to him, then of course he's all right, and it's all been a horrible mistake. He's been missing in action, of course, a prisoner somewhere, and he's escaped, and if he's somewhere there's a phone, then we can find him! I've got the operator tracing the call. We'll find out where he is and go and get him. Buck will know what to do."

"Make those calls!" Marguerite hissed at me, and I fled into the kitchen and fumbled at the telephone. Buck Sheehan's number at work had been written on the pad that hung beside the wall phone ever since the night of the television movie incident. It was written in Virginia Guthrie's house too, and in Claire Swanson's. I dialed, blank with fright. A girl's voice told me that Mr. Sheehan was in a meeting but would call me back when he got out.

"Get him," I said in a thin, silly voice, and in a moment he answered.

"Buck? It's Colquitt Kennedy. Buck, you'd better come home. Come to my house. There's been . . . something else with Anita. Can you call her doctor and get him here? Or I will if you'll give me his number—"

"I'll call him," he said. "I'm coming. I'm coming."

He did not ask me what was wrong.

I have never been able to fully reconstruct the next half hour. I simply do not remember much of it. There are flashes—Marguerite with her head drooping over the dark head of her cousin as Anita talked and laughed and wept and talked again. Me in a dream-like sprint next door, up the stairs of Anita's house to her bathroom to snatch the vial of blue tablets from the medicine chest, where Marguerite said they would be, and pounding back down the stairs. This bathroom looks like a sea cave, I remember thinking dreamily. Like Merlin's crystal cave. It celebrates water. Clever Kim.

I have a clear and endless moment caught in my mind of standing over the two women on the sofa while the older, whimpering in anguish and concentration, tried to force the younger to swallow the pill. She must have done it, though Anita kept pushing the glass away, showering water over both of them, saying over and over in that high keen of joy, "No, I have to be clear for when the operator calls back. No, we have to go back to my house now. She said she'd call me back. No, Maggie, no."

But the pill had obviously found its mark, because when Buck came running into the den and my mind clicked into gear again, Anita was huddled in her cousin's arms, sobbing peacefully and quietly, hiccuping a little like a tired child, her face misty with joy. Marguerite Condon held her and cried silently.

The doctor was with Buck. They must have met in our driveway. I saw the two cars there a little later, angled crazily, doors still open. He was a short, wiry, sandy-haired man—a very young man, I thought dimly, to wade into battle against this enormity. He went straight to Anita Sheehan, looked at her for a moment, and then said to Buck, "Let's get her upstairs." To me he said, "May we?," and I nodded wordlessly. They raised her from the sofa, and I could hear her on the stairs, supported between them, beginning her terrible catechism about the phone call, about her son's voice. They made soothing sounds back, but I could not make out the words. A door closed, and there were no more sounds. I looked at Marguerite Condon.

"Can you tell me about it?" I said. "Would you like a cup of coffee or something?"

"No. No, thank you. No, I can't tell you anything, except that I heard the telephone ring, and before I could get to it I heard her make this shrill, awful noise, and I ran upstairs and she was sitting beside the phone staring up at me, and then she told me that she

155

had just talked to Toby and he was alive. I just—I couldn't do anything for a minute, and then she picked up the phone and very coolly dialed the operator and asked her if she could trace the overseas call that had just come in to that number. And then she put the phone down and stared at me for a minute—her face was just transformed, just shining with this awful intensity—and before I could even move she was out of the room and down the stairs and on her way over here. Apparently she is convinced that she has talked to Toby and that he is alive. I don't know what will happen to her now."

"Mrs. Condon," I said thickly and carefully. "Marguerite. There isn't any possibility at all—I mean, you don't think she possibly could have—"

"Oh, my God, no, of course not. Of course not! Toby is dead. Toby is in a grave in Morristown, New Jersey. Don't you think we'd *know* if there had been any . . . mistake? The army checks, they had—dental charts. They—he has been dead for three years now. He is dead, and Anita is out of her mind."

"But there *was* a phone call?"

"Oh, yes, there was a phone call. But it could have been anybody, Mrs. Kennedy. It could have been the —the—man calling to say the power mower is ready to be picked up. God forgive me, I never thought it was this bad. Not even after all that time she didn't talk, I never thought it was like this. She really did seem to be getting better, very slowly, but better."

"Buck will have to check that telephone call," I said. "I don't know how you go about it, but surely somewhere there's a record of calls, somewhere in some office. Because, don't you see, if there *was* a call —a long-distance call—if somebody was playing some kind of ghastly *joke* or something, that person must be found and punished. This is . . . not to be borne."

"They won't find anything. There was no joke; who would do a thing like that to Anita? Anita never hurt anybody in her life. There wasn't anything except some perfectly normal local telephone call, and somewhere some perfectly normal, nice local person is sitting and wondering if Anita Sheehan is crazy. And she is. She is!"

She began to cry again, the ugly, heartbreaking sobs of someone unused to crying, and I went and sat beside her on the sofa and put my arms around her. After a while she was quiet, and we did not speak. There did not seem to be anything else to say.

They brought Anita Sheehan back down my stairs then, Buck and the doctor. She must have had an injection of some sort, because she was nearly unconscious, and they were supporting her between them, her feet just brushing the floor.

"We're going to take her to the hospital now, Colquitt," Buck said. "Pacewood. I don't think it's far from here. Would you and Marguerite pack some things for her and bring them?"

His face was still and dead. Just that. Lifeless, like a mask.

"Bucky, do you have to? Isn't there any way I could take care of her at home? Couldn't she stay in her own house?" Marguerite Condon's face was corrugated with agony.

"No!" I almost shouted, the words coming from somewhere apart from my mind. "She can*not* stay in that house!" I stopped, aghast.

"It's out of the question," the young doctor said briefly. "She's got to be hospitalized. Later we'll see. Let's go, Mr. Sheehan. I didn't want to give her much of that stuff until we've examined her. I don't know how long she'll stay calm."

Buck gave me a look with something stirring behind it, a brief look that passed over his dead face like wind over water and was gone. They took Anita out of the kitchen, and I heard a car door slam, and then another, and one of the cars drove away. Marguerite Condon wiped her eyes on the tissue I'd given her, and we went across the driveway to pack some things for Anita. Buck's car still stood in our driveway, its door ajar, the radio purring out a little silver Mozart quartet. I reached in and turned off the radio and closed the door. It was very still and hot and seemed to be no time at all.

Chapter Sixteen

THE FINAL destruction of Anita Sheehan was in motion then, and so the next three weeks were, for all of us, borrowed time. But we did not know that, and with the frail, mindless buoyancy of the human animal, we burrowed gratefully back into our own lives and went about our own summer-slowed daily rituals. Marguerite Condon went back to Philadelphia. Walter and I had a party on the patio for Walter's office staff. The Swansons left for a month on Sea Island, and the Jenningses and their brood departed, Okie-like, for an educational pilgrimage to Washington, Appomattox and Valley Forge. It is an exquisite form of torture that I knew Semmes and the Jennings children hated, but Eloise is adamant about Our Nation's Heritage, and so they do it every year.

"She doesn't really give a shit about those eerie little gnomes absorbing heritage and tradition," Walter said. "What she's doing is getting this year's Christmas card sewed up. Just wait, it'll be all four million of 'em standing in front of Abraham Lincoln picking their noses."

We saw little of Buck Sheehan during the time Anita was hospitalized. He left early each morning to go by the hospital, I knew, and went straight there from his office in the afternoons. Anita was allowed no visitors except Buck, so no one had seen her, and when we called him, he said only, "She's coming along all right, I guess. She's on pretty powerful medication, and she sleeps a lot, and she's in therapy a couple of hours a day. Thanks for calling. When there's any real change I'll let you know."

He obviously did not want to talk, so we did not press it. I thought he must be spending a lot of time with Charles and Virginia Guthrie after he got home from the hospital, because the light from their den that seeps through the woods between our three houses shone later into many evenings than it usually does. I was glad. If anyone could help Buck now it would be Virginia.

We saw Charles and Virginia at the club one Sunday evening, and we all sat together on the terrace drinking Pimm's Cups and watching brown children churning in the pool and shrieking like starlings from the diving board. I asked about Anita and Buck.

"She's so heavily medicated that it's really hard to tell how she's doing," Virginia said. "The doctor thinks the best way to deal with this delusional thing is just to erase it for a while, let her rest. When she's stronger they'll start the serious digging and reduce the medication. She's going to have to be in intense therapy for a long time. She never really had any of that the other time, and probably should have. But it's possible that most of it can be done on an outpatient basis. The doctor thinks she may be able to come home in a week or two."

I shook my head, no, involuntarily, and Walter asked quickly, "What's the long-range prognosis?"

"Nobody can say, really. One good thing is that her condition is acute, a concrete reaction to a specific event or a series of them. It's not chronic. She's only been this way after very bad traumas, not continuously. Buck says this doctor thinks those other 'recoveries' were too quick, too pat. He thinks there was almost bound to be trouble of this kind."

Walter shot a "See there?" look at me, but I said only, "How is Buck?"

"Well, tired to death of course. Discouraged and let down. Too quiet and too wound up, too tight under the quiet. The other times there was a kind of . . . hope working there, but I don't see that in him now. I think he feels horribly guilty that he couldn't prevent all this, but of course that's foolish, and I've told him so. If he could just let some of it out—but he won't. He's strong, though. If she can just begin to show a *little* improvement, a *little* response, I think he'll be all right. He hasn't said, but I know he's terrified she's

159

going to slip back into that horrible catatonia, and never come out of it."

"Can that be prevented, do they think?"

"They think so, with a lot of care," Virginia said, "but there's just no telling what could trigger her."

The words gave me a dreadful, inexplicable wrench, and I said to Walter, "Let's go home. I'm uncomfortable in this wet suit."

Anita came home two weeks later with the practical nurse the doctor had found for her, and the house next door was quiet. Buck called to say that except for the daily visits for therapy at the hospital, she was not to see anyone, and he hoped we'd understand if they turned into recluses for a while. She was familiar with the nurse, he said, and it was she who drove Anita to the hospital every day. Aside from those visits, she slept most of the time.

"I know you're concerned, Colquitt," he said. "I can't ever thank any of you enough. When she's better I'll let you know, and maybe you can run over for a minute. We've been trouble enough for all of you. The rest will do you as much good as it will her."

So I saw virtually nothing of Buck and Anita Sheehan. Until the swimming August afternoon that smashed Buck and sent Anita spinning into her final silence, and wrenched the first major block from under our lives—Walter's and mine, Charles and Virginia's.

I stopped at the mailbox, as I always did, when I drove in from work that day. There was the usual welter of bills and circulars advertising lawn and tree services, and three or four letters, and a small, brown-wrapped package. My car's air conditioner was lackadaisical and ineffective in the swaddling heat, and I had a bag of groceries in the trunk, the frozen food going mushy, and so I did not look at the mail. I thrust it into the grocery bag when I opened the trunk, and took the bag into the kitchen, and put the food into the freezer. I went upstairs and got into shorts and a loose tee shirt, and tied my hair off my neck with a strand of yarn. I went downstairs and turned the air conditioner down to 65 and got myself a glass of Tab, and took the mail into the den to sort it. Razz lifted his head from the cool fireplace tiles and gave me his silent meow, and yawned, and went back to sleep. Foster switched his tail from atop the television set, but did not struggle up out of his twitching cat dreams.

The package was not for us. It was addressed to Mr. Buford A. Sheehan, and the return address was that of a medical supply house in New Jersey. I shook it. It rattled faintly, like pills. Oh, damn, I thought. I don't want to bother the Sheehans, but if this is medicine she's getting wholesale, she may need it right away. I never knew Buck's name was Buford.

I finished my Tab and then went grumpily upstairs, slid my feet into sandals, and walked across the driveway to the Sheehans' house. It was still and quiet in the afternoon heat. The nurse's yellow Rambler was gone, but Buck's car was parked in the driveway. I hesitated on the back deck. If Buck was with Anita, I really did hate to disturb them. But I remembered that Virginia had said that the nurse gave Anita a pill just before she left and that she slept soundly for three or four hours after that. Buck was probably spelling the nurse because she'd had to leave early. So I walked up to the back door and raised my hand to knock softly.

The back of the house that Kim built is all glass; sliding doors open onto the deck, and the glass lets in the entire sweep of deep woods behind, soaring up the remnant of the ridge that once ran along the lot. It is a lovely sight, looking out from inside. Even on that terrible, humming, unreal night it had been a lovely sight. I had never looked in from outside during the daylight hours. You got a glimpse of the kitchen to the left, all warm, waxed birch and white Italian tile bricks, and a full view of the den and living room beyond the kitchen, and the bottom of the stairs that wound up into the top two floors from the living room. Blinded with the glare from the glass and perspiration running into my eyes, I could see nothing at first.

I heard the sounds, though, and I stayed my knock, puzzled for an instant by the half-familiar, half-disturbing noise. A rhythmic sort of muffled thumping. Soft keening, a kind of strangled, rhythmic grunting.

Then a liquid crashing, as if from broken glass. Alarmed, I pressed closer to the sliding door.

The man and the woman were on the sofa in the living room. They lay in full view. They were naked, thrashing, pumping, deep in the embrace. Their heads were at the far end of the sofa facing me, their legs entwined and frantic and uncontrolled. The keening rose, the grunts soared into guttural cries. Profoundly shocked and embarrassed, I stood frozen for a moment, fist raised, heart pounding. I whipped my head around, preparing to flee as quickly and quietly as possible from my unwitting intrusion into this ultimate intimacy and communion between Buck and Anita Sheehan. A blur of red caught my eyes as I turned my head, an intrusive, jarring banner that was so dreadfully, terribly wrong in the room that it tore my eyes back, frantic as I was to be away from there and gone.

Anita Sheehan sat on the bottom step, facing the sofa. Her long robe, scarlet as running blood, was flung away from her tumbled legs. Her skin was the pale white-green of an underwater swimmer in the green-washed light slanting in through the trees. Her hands were clasped loosely in her lap, palms up, like those of a child receiving instructions. She rocked her body slowly back and forth, moving only from the waist up. Her face was turned to the sofa, but her eyes looked beyond it into the trees outside, and beyond those into nowhere. Into nowhere, nowhere-never, finally and forever. Her face was absolutely still and quiet.

I looked in blank, vibrating shock back into the living room. There was a white-frosted Gilbey's gin bottle on the floor beside the sofa and a glass on the coffee table and a sprinkling of crystal litter on the polished wood of the floor directly beneath the woman's foot. Buck Sheehan gave a great cry and heaved in spasm, and I raised my eyes slowly to the woman's face. It was contorted in a silent rictus, the mouth open and square like that of a child crying. Virginia Guthrie's face in passion was no longer beautiful.

THIS TIME I did not pace my kitchen floor in hiccuping shock and horror, as I had done after the terrible denouement to Pie Harralson's party. I ran straight back, across my driveway and into my kitchen, still clutching the packet of medicine, and I called Pacewood Hospital and asked for the doctor who was treating Mrs. Anita Sheehan. My own voice sounded faintly amazing to me, ringing coldly and precisely through the dome of humming distance that had settled over me.

"Carl Hunnicutt," said the dry voice I remembered, presently.

"Get over to Mrs. Sheehan's house," I said. "Right now. Mrs. Anita Sheehan. Something terrible has happened."

And I hung up before he could answer.

I called Walter at the agency and asked him to come home. I hung up again, before he could say anything. The phone began to ring, and I did not answer it. I went upstairs and sat down on the side of our bed and picked up from my bedside table the book I had been reading the night before, and I read steadily until I heard a car shriek into the driveway next door. Then I rose and pulled the drapes. By the time Walter came thudding up the stairs into the bedroom the smart blue Pacewood limousine had come ghosting into the Sheehans' driveway and had gone away again. I saw it from the window that faces the street, but I did not see who was in it. The doctor's automobile followed it out into the street, and I saw that too, but then I pulled all the drapes, so that the entire room was dim and shut away from the house next door.

Chapter Seventeen

PART OF the ultimate agony of the whole thing and, perhaps, part of the cause of it, is that we never told anyone. Not about the still horror of that hot afternoon living room. Not about our own personal, ringing horror earlier, in that night house. I think now that if we had, if I had told Claire about those two things, told even the other neighbors, at least about that afternoon, that some of the spiraling horror might have been avoided, some anguish mitigated. At least the finished tapestry might have been different, if no less terrible. I do not believe the whole cloth of the thing could have been destroyed, but perhaps some of the threads might have been broken. We might have gained some credence, Walter and I, if we had told. We might have been believed to a greater extent when we began to talk of what we thought. But to speak of either seemed unimaginable, impossible, and we did not tell.

I still do not know who knows about that last thing, that final thing that sent Anita Sheehan back into her New Jersey hospital and into unbroken quiet and, I pray, some final peace. The doctor, probably, but I have not seen him again. We did not see Buck again either, although Claire Swanson called Anita's cousin in Philadelphia when they returned from the island to find the Sheehans gone and Charles and Virginia Guthrie preparing for the around-the-world cruise they had been saving for Charles's retirement.

Marguerite Condon told Claire only that Anita had sunk back into catatonia and had been institutionalized again, and that it seemed unlikely that she would pull out of it. Buck, she said, was drinking again, but had agreed to start at AA once more, and they would just have to see how that went.

"She was very cold and distant to me on the phone, Col," Claire said one evening a few days after they'd gotten home. It was the first time we'd seen them. Walter had been taking our calls and telling my callers that I had a rotten summer cold. But of course that couldn't go on very long, and so the last time Claire called I'd motioned to him to tell them to come on over.

"She was polite, but she acted as though it were all our fault somehow," Claire went on plaintively. "And she can hardly talk about Buck. What in God's name happened, do you think? There must have been *something*. Didn't you see or hear anything at all?"

"No," I said. "I was at work. They just . . . weren't there that night when I got home."

"Didn't you call to see if anything was wrong?"

"Who's there to call in an empty house? I didn't see any cars, so I thought they must have gone out or something."

"Gone *out?* With her so zonked out on pills she can't walk?"

"I just didn't think about that, I guess."

"There's something funny, something not right about all this," Claire said.

"There's nothing right about any of it, Claire, for God's sake. It's tragic," said Roger Swanson, looking at the bulk of the Sheehans' house, dark against the evening sky. Still. We sat in the den. I would not go out onto the patio.

"No, I mean there's *something* that somebody isn't talking about, or something. Everybody is acting so queer. You, Colquitt, you look ten years older—well, I'm sorry, but you do—and you don't talk, and Walter acts like he thinks somebody's following him, and Virginia is acting just odder than hell. What's with this cruise, anyway? They've been talking about it for a million years, but it was for when Charles retired. How on earth can he just take off now? How can they get ready to leave day after tomorrow? Why right now? Virginia won't even talk to me. The maid answers the phone and says she's out. She answered the door when I went over there the other day and said Mrs. Guthrie was out, but she wasn't, because her car was there and I saw her pull the curtains aside up in her bedroom. Why on earth didn't Buck let anybody know where they were, that they were going back to New Jersey? He must have been around *some* of the time before they transferred Anita back, he must have come home to sleep. What are they going to do about the house? Anita's cousin didn't know."

"Anita must have been sent back almost immediately, Claire," I said, trying to control my breath. "I guess he stayed at a motel nearer the hospital, or something. Obviously, he didn't let me know what had happened because I wasn't home when it—when she got sick again, and I guess he didn't have time later. Or didn't think of it if he was drinking again."

"Virginia must not have been home when it happened either, or Charles would have known something about it," said Claire, frowning. "He only said he understood Anita was back in the hospital and Buck was staying with her. He didn't even know they'd gone back to New Jersey. He said neither he nor Virginia knew any more about it than that, and if I'd excuse him, they had a lot of packing and arrangements to tend to. That's when he told me about the cruise. He sounded so funny that I didn't want to pursue it. So that's when I called her cousin. I'm surprised you didn't think to do that."

"I . . . don't know why I didn't. I was just so sorry to hear she'd been taken back to the hospital, and I guess I thought they'd call when they needed us."

"Well, how *did* you know about it? I mean, if nobody saw them go . . ."

"Charles told me," I lied.

"But Charles said he heard about it from you!"

"Well, Charles is mistaken, and I don't know anything about any of it, and I just don't want to talk about it any more, okay?" I said, close to tears. I have never had any secrets from Claire aside from the very personal and private textures of Walter's and my life together, and I did not know how to evade her natural distress and curiosity. But it was unthinkable that that awful thing be spoken of, or the other. They were, in the strictest sense of the word, unspeakable.

Walter started to say something, something to serve as a decoy for Claire's puzzled, troubled probing, but she rose to her feet and looked at him, and then at me.

"It's time we were getting home, Roger," she said quietly. "Colquitt, I am certainly not going to pry and dig at you. I think something is terribly wrong and it's near to killing you, and I think that whatever it is, it has happened to Charles and Virginia too, and I am desperately sorry. When you feel you can talk about it I hope you'll come to me. I only meant to help."

"I know," I said, beginning to cry silently in the unlit den. "I know."

166

"We'll see you, then," she said, and they let themselves out the kitchen door.

We sat silently in the darkened den for a space of time. I stopped the weak, hopeless crying after a while, feeling only the currents of our silence and the ache of grief that Claire's hurt, stiff little speech had left. I don't think I'm going to be able to fix that, I thought. Something is broken with Claire and me now.

Presently I said, "Walter."

"Yes."

"We have to talk about this now. I know what I promised you. I know I said I wouldn't talk about it anymore. But that was before this. We can't pretend this didn't happen. It wasn't even any good trying to pretend that night over there with Kim . . . didn't happen. If we don't talk about it we're not ever going to be able to talk about anything again. We've hardly said a word to each other since that afternoon. Something horrible is happening to all of us. If I don't have you with me I don't think I can stand it."

He was quiet for a moment, and then he said, "All right, Colquitt, I guess we do have to talk about it. Tell me what you think."

"I think . . . what Kim did. I think that there's . . . something . . . in that house that is destroying everybody who lives in it. I think it's something that can somehow *isolate* what's the essence of you, the things you absolutely need most to keep on existing, the *you*-ness of you. I think it takes your life force, your vitality, and sucks it out of you. I think it needs the core of your life in order to live itself. I think it gets what it needs by working on your hurts and weaknesses, or something like that. We thought Kim was obsessed with it, almost crazy, but he sensed it first."

"Do you have any idea how you sound?" Walter said to me across the darkened den. He had not moved from his reclining lounger, where he'd been sitting when the Swansons came in. He reached over and switched on the lamp on the table beside the chair, and light came leaping into the room.

"Crazy, probably. As crazy as Kim. I don't care.

Do I sound any crazier than what's been happening over there?"

"Well, not to me maybe. But how do you think you'd sound to anybody else? Look at what we've got over there: two families who moved into a new house and who had tragedies in their lives. It may look hideously coincidental, but that's just how it does look. Coincidental. This can't possibly be the only time in history that two successive families have had ... bad experiences, bad luck, in the same house."

"But it's the things that happened to them! Not just bad luck, Walter, not just tragedies. The very precise things that those particular people couldn't withstand. The precise things that, out of all the things in the world, would destroy them. Why not other things? Look at Pie and Buddy—what mattered most to her? Her perfect, careful little world, all made up of puppies and babies and her husband's job and her *position* in the world. Her daddy. Gone, just like that. Those exact things.

"And Buddy, what mattered most to him? Her. His baby. His job. His future. Gone. Poof. And Lucas Abbott, Walter, with that wonderful reputation and social standing, that marvelous position in the firm, his beautiful wife and daughter, his *dignity*. And Kim. My God, what about Kim? What mattered most in the world to Kim? His talent, his architecture. Where's that now? Why not—oh, a bad sickness, or her *mother*, not her father, or why not something else that they could have stood? Why those things?"

"Colquitt, those things that happened to the Harralsons weren't all that unique. They were awful, but they weren't . . . specialized. If that's what you're implying. A miscarriage. A stroke. Two nice, upstanding, solid guys who turned out to be gay. Bad business, but every one of those things happens every day of the world to somebody, somewhere."

"But to the same people in such a short period of time? To the same two people, all that, when nothing else had ever happened to them until they built a house and moved into it? And happened in front of the very people they'd most want not to see them? His senior firm members? His wife? Lucas Abbott's wife and daughter, his business partners? I agree with Kim, Walter, I absolutely *know* Buddy Harralson and Luke Abbott weren't homosexual. It was something the—the house put in them at that particular time, when all those people were there to see it."

"If you're going to take that tack, Col, your reasoning is all wrong," Walter said. "If it goes after people who live in it, what about Abbott? He didn't live in that house. Matt Gladney didn't. Kim Dougherty didn't."

"But they were all *involved* with it, don't you see? They came close. Close enough so it could smell out what their best things were, and their weaknesses, and go after the good things by using the weaknesses."

"Colquitt—"

"Virginia Guthrie didn't live there either, did she, Walter? But she was close to it. She was involved in it. She stayed too long, she stayed long enough so it would know what mattered most to her too—her *dignity,* her *control,* her genuine caring for other people and her ability to help them. The life she's built with Charles. Do you think she's going to be able to live very easily with herself after what she and Buck did to Anita? Or with what she did to herself, to Charles? *God,* don't tell me you think Virginia Guthrie and Buck Sheehan have been having an affair all this time and just happened to get caught in the act by the wronged wife! The house did it, the house *made* them do it!"

" 'The devil made me do it!' Colquitt, honey, this just can't go on. You're making yourself sick. Badly sick."

"No, wait, Walter, let me finish. Okay, so the Sheehans move in, and what happens? She's lost her father and brother, and her son, and almost her husband, and her mind for a long time. He's almost lost her, and almost lost his whole profession, and he *has* lost his son. But they're putting it all together again. All right, does she fall and break her back? Does he have a wreck, or lose his job and go on unemployment, do other members of their family die? No. It starts on her with the son. You want to try to explain that movie on TV and those phone calls? You

169

really want to try to trace them? You wouldn't find anything, because they didn't come from anywhere. Not even out of Anita's head. They came from the house. So what does she have then? What's left? A bare hold, just the barest hold on her sanity. And him. As long as she has him she can make it somehow. But then one day she comes downstairs and sees that she doesn't have him anymore. He's drunk on the sofa screwing the one woman she trusted more than anybody except him. And him, what did he lose? What mattered most to him? *Her*. He lost her, for good and all, and he lost his control, his sobriety. Don't sit there and tell me there's nothing wrong with that house. Just don't you tell me that."

"Colquitt, you sit here and you ask me to believe that the house next door is . . . *haunted* or something. Don't you see that I can believe anything but that? Anything—bad luck, flaky neighbors, magnetic fields, noxious vapors, whatever godawful accident of natural laws and physical phenomena that might explain some of that stuff over there—yes, I can swallow any of that crap if I have to. But not that there is a malignant *intelligence* working in a house that's less than a year old, on *this* street, in *this* neighborhood. Colquitt, if I believed that, then I could not function in this world anymore. Nothing would mean anything anymore, nothing would make any sense. There just wouldn't be any core to my life or the world. I'd just have to go to bed and stay there the rest of my life, because I couldn't trust the world anymore. I won't buy it. I will not buy that."

I whirled on him. "Have you forgotten that I betrayed you in that house with Kim Dougherty? Betrayed you, when the only thing in this world that matters to me is you and the life we have? Have you forgotten that you came within an inch of *killing* us both? What did it almost take from us, Walter? Only each other. You know what it can do, you know what it *did* do, you know what it *will* do if we . . . mess with it. How can you sit there and say you won't buy it, for God's sake? What more is it going to take?"

He was silent. His body was heavy and his face was old, old. Finally he said, "I don't know what I think any more, Colquitt. All I know is that I will not let you destroy yourself over it. If we have to, we'll sell this house and move somewhere else."

"Then aren't you as good as admitting that there *is* something wrong over there?" I said, hating my own probing voice.

"All right, yes, then, goddammit, Colquitt. I think there *is* something funny over there. But I also think there's *some* sort of natural, physical explanation for it, because I will not believe that—that other thing. I cannot believe it and continue to exist. Coincidence is a natural law too, and right now I'm content to leave it at that. What could we do, anyway? What on earth do you think we could do about it, aside from moving? Do you really want to move?"

"No, I—no. I don't want to move. I just don't want anything more to happen to anybody over there. I want everything to be like it was. We could warn people, Walter. We could tell people what we think —what I think, if you don't want to be involved in it. Your position could be, 'Well, Colquitt has got this bee in her bonnet, and I'm just going along with her till she gets her head straight. Please do me a favor and humor her.'"

"Honey, what on earth good do you think it will do, if people think you're off your tree?"

"At least they'd *know*. They could make up their own minds then. At least, they'd have heard—"

"Whom do you propose to warn? Everybody on the street and in town, probably, knows pretty much what's gone on over there. You wouldn't be telling anybody anything they didn't know already, except . . . that last thing with Virginia and Buck. And what happened to us. Do you want to tell people that?"

"No, of course not. You know we couldn't do that. But we could warn the people who didn't know, anybody else who might want to move in there," I said.

He sighed, his brow furrowed with frustration. "Colquitt, you can't stop people from living where they want to. You can't go telling people who come looking at that house that it's haunted. They'd think you were crazier than a loon. It wouldn't stop anything. What are you going to do, greet everybody who comes to look at it and snatch them over here and tell them all about the haunted house? Besides the fact that the realtors or somebody could probably take legal action against you, nobody would believe you. When you spell it out, it sounds like two sets of very bad luck. Just that. Besides, how do you know the Sheehans will sell it? Maybe she'll be better, maybe they'll come back."

"Do you really think so, Walter?"

"I guess I don't," he said.

"What do you think we ought to do, then?"

"I think we ought to sit tight and hope it never goes on the market again. I think we ought to try and forget it. All of it. Okay, just for the sake of the argument, say you're right and something supernatural is going on over there, there's something *feeding* on people—maybe, if it's empty long enough, if it doesn't get the . . . the nourishment it needs, then whatever it is will just die. I don't know what's the matter with the damned house. I just know that if you go on this way about it much longer you're going to be ill. You're a strong woman, Colquitt. You've got judgment and strength of will—you're going to have to use them now. Use them or get some professional help in dealing with this."

"You think I really am losing my mind, then."

"Not in the slightest. It might give you some perspective on this to talk it out with somebody besides me or the neighbors. Somebody qualified. That's all I meant. I just want you to be yourself again, honey. That's all I want."

"It isn't in me, Walter. What if somebody *does* buy it and things start happening again?"

"We'll worry about that when it happens. *If* it happens."

"You know, Walter," I said, "we've never stuck our necks out. We've never put ourselves or anything we really value on the line. We've taken the best life has to give—and it's been good, it's been very good—and we really haven't given anything back. I wonder if this isn't the one crack we're going to have at it? The one chance we're going to have to . . . repay life, somehow."

"I don't think I'm afraid to put myself on the line, Col," he said. "I'd hate to think I was. But when I do, I want it to be for something more profound than a pile of rocks and boards and masonite. Pretty as it is."

"The pretty is part of it of course," I said. "That's its draw. That's the bait."

"Well, blame Kim Dougherty for that. I guess you'll be telling me next he's touring Europe on a broom."

We said nothing. I guess I had known we wouldn't. All that late summer and into September the house lay quiet. Weeds spiked up around its foundation; the yard went brown and burned in the dry heat. Once Margaret Matthieson, who'd handled the sale of the house to the Sheehans, came over to ask if we'd heard what they planned to do about it. I said I didn't know.

"It looks like God's Little Acre," Margaret said, "but we haven't gotten any instructions about keeping it up or anything. If they're going to sell, I wish they'd let us know. Of course they could be handling it through another firm, but you'd think—and I'd have heard, anyway. Funny."

"Yes," I said.

There was a good bit of talk in the neighborhood this time. At parties, at the club, at the various auxiliary meetings I went to, heads invariably leaned together and the Sheehans and the house were discussed. So was the Guthries' sudden cruise. Eyes would go to me, waiting for some comment, some explanation. You were there, the eyes said. You must know something. When I offered no comment the eyes would slide away. People on the street did not seem quite so open to me as they had been, but perhaps I was imagining that. The small coolness between me and Claire *was* still there, buried under chattings and droppings-in at each other's houses. There were not so many of those now. I was heavy with the sorrow of it, and the loss, but remained silent. Once, at the end of an evening down the street at the Parsons', when we'd all stayed too late and drunk too much, Claire had suddenly stretched out her hand to me, with tears in her brown eyes, "Col. Col." I almost took her aside then and told her about Kim and Walter and me, about Buck and Virginia Guthrie, about what I thought, the whole thing. But then I only hugged her.

So the distance remained.

Early that October Marguerite Condon came down and supervised the loading of the Sheehans' furniture into a van, and was gone again by the time I got home from work. Claire told me she'd seen her and the van, but had not gone over, and Marguerite had not called or come by her house.

Later that month I quit my job and moved my files into the upstairs office I'd been readying all that fall and began my work at home. I had, as Anita Sheehan had suggested, angled my desk in front of the dormer windows, facing away from them, and I did not often look into the blazing foliage that half shielded, half framed the house next door. I was absorbed and busy with my new clients and charmed with the novelty of working at home and the weekday ambience of the house and street. It was a microcosmic world that had spun around my house all along while I had been away downtown, and I had never tasted it. It was a little strange, but exhilarating too.

At the end of October a "For Sale" sign went up in the yard of the house next door. A different realty firm this time.

A card came from Kim Dougherty, from Florence. He was immersed in study at the Uffizi, he said, spending long hours every day there in that rich old dimness. He'd begun to help a little, in a very unofficial capacity, with restoration work. He was enjoying it, he said.

PART
THREE

The
Greenes

Chapter Eighteen

NOT so many prospective buyers came to see the house this time. I know, because all during the early days of November I was working in my upstairs office, my coffee pot hissing cheerfully, the classical FM station on my radio weaving a soft shroud of serenity and grace and symmetry around the warm, bright room. I was in and out of the house a lot during those first weeks at home too, dashing to radio and TV stations, dropping off press releases, meeting with clients and prospects at their offices. I'd have noticed if many people came to see the house. But there weren't many —several very young couples, wistful and careful-faced with the wanting of the house—lookers only, I knew. There was not the aura of money about them that had clung to Pie and Buddy.

At Thanksgiving the rotten cold I had lied about back in the summer, when I was hiding from our neighbors after that last ghastly incident in the house, struck me in earnest. It hung on and on, lodging finally and firmly in my lungs, and I coughed and rasped and rattled and ran a low-grade fever, and lost sleep and weight. I finished up the last of the outstanding work I had to do on my new accounts before Christmas, and since I knew that things would be slow until after the first of the year, and Walter's agency had drifted into its annual holiday hiatus, we called the young man who feeds the cats and waters the plants and brings in the mail while we're away, and we packed up and went down to the old white inn in Ocho Rios, where we'd spent our honeymoon.

I am a Christmas addict, a confirmed tradition buff, and I have always hated the idea of the holidays spent in some lush, vivid place of tropical feverishness.

We'd never been away from home at Christmas since our parents died. But this year it was right, it was healing. We were so totally away. The white sun and the incredible blue-green-purple water and the insistent soft trade winds washed the misery out of my chest and the heavy, lingering dread out of my heart.

We ate fish and seafood and chowder at lunch, and stodgy, stomach-boggling British dinners of roast beef and lamb and Yorkshire pudding and potatoes. I gained five pounds and lost the haunted, shadowed look around my eyes, and the lines around Walter's mouth and on his forehead smoothed out under the new tan. We both slept enormously in the still, hot afternoons, in the sudden, thick, total tropical darkness. We laughed and capered and made love and played like clumsy puppies at Dunn's River Falls, and moved politely but blindly among the young, determinedly worldly honeymooners and the elderly couples from Canada and the Midwest, who flocked to meals on the veranda or lounge chairs on the beach or around the bar before dinner. Among them we regained some of that special, secret sense of *us-ness* that we had always had among strangers. It lay between us on the air like a cat's cradle of invisible cords. We did not, this time, look up any of the acquaintances we had on the island.

Once, when we were dressing for dinner in the graying light of the abrupt tropical dusk, Walter called in from the balcony, where he was watching the sinking sun turn the sea to dull-silver foil, "Right now, at this very moment, the first people are trudging into Eloise's Christmas party. Semmes is bellowing, "Yule, y'all!' to Roger, and Claire is heading for the bar, and the littlest angel has just dropped a dog turd into the eggnog. Or one of his own."

"Yuck," I said, scratching at a patch of peeling sunburn on my collarbone and noting with satisfaction that the ridge of bone did not stand away in such stark, lunar relief now.

"Has it really been that long since the last one? It seems like just last week."

I remembered then that we had been talking about Pie Harralson's miscarriage at precisely this time last year, and that all the trouble had been yet to come. I wanted, suddenly and bleakly and desperately, to be back at that year-ago party, at the point in time and space before it had happened, to take different routes and choose different paths, to escape our own recent pasts. I remembered that after my father died I would wake up in the mornings and I would not remember for a moment that we had lost him, and then when I did, it was not so much anguish that I felt as a simple child's desire to be back in the time before he died. I felt like that then, in that Jamaican twilight.

"I don't want to go home," I said desolately. "I don't want to go home."

Walter came and put his arms around me and rested his chin on the top of my head. The familiar gesture started a sting of tears in my nose. I turned my face away so I would not get mascara on his jacket.

"I thought you were feeling better," he said.

"I was. So much better, and then it all came back. Maybe we were wrong to come down here. It's just going to be worse when we get home."

"It doesn't have to be," he said. "Not if we can keep this perspective we've gotten. That's what we have to do, Col. Remember how unimportant and sort of ludicrous it all seemed while we were here, away from it. Just not give in to it anymore. If we can lose it like this when we're away from it, don't you think that means it was mostly in our own heads? We can handle our own heads."

"I guess so. You can yours, anyway. I'm not sure about mine. But I'll try. Maybe you're right, and it won't sell."

But when we got back to our house a week later, shivering with the strangeness of remembered summer in the cold, wet wind, the "For Sale" sign was gone and there were two cars in the driveway, and a child's blue bicycle, and lights burned once again from the replenished windows of the house next door.

WE WERE spared the travesty of the welcome-to-the-neighborhood visit to Susan and Norman Greene by

Claire, who brought them by the afternoon after we got back. I was taking the last of the summer clothes out of the dryer in the utility room off the kitchen when there was laughter and the stamping of feet on the back porch and a sharp rapping of knuckles on glass. I let them in, feeling no curiosity, only dull fatigue and a sullen resentment at having to welcome new people into my kitchen and my life again. Walter had been right; the house and its terrible short history seemed to have lost its hold on me. I had indeed left the terror and the heavy tumor of foreboding in the vivid sea of that summer island. But what was left was not the lightness I had yearned for, only this stale, tired emptiness.

Claire thrust the three newcomers into the kitchen, a man, a woman, and a little girl of about eight, then hugged me briefly and turned to them.

"This is Susan and Norman Greene, and Melissa," she said. "And this is Colquitt Kennedy, who has been frying her considerable body in Jamaica for two weeks while the rest of us were freezing our behinds and cursing Santa Claus. Not really, honey," she appended, looking at Melissa Greene, who looked back at her gravely and acceptingly. We laughed, or rather Susan Greene and I did, because it was such a Claire thing to say. The man did not.

"Hello, Susan, Norman and Melissa," I said. "It's good to meet you. How long have you been in?"

"Hello," said Susan Greene. "Precisely one week. And it's still the biggest mess you ever saw. I just can't seem to get hold of it."

She was younger than Claire or me, about twenty-eight or -nine, I thought, but except for the discrepancy in their ages, she was almost a replica of Claire. Her crop of curls was sandy and wiry and her eyes were blue, but there was the same sturdy squareness, direct grin, snub nose, neat waist and short, muscular legs. The same air of earthiness, faint irreverence, and general competence. And yet there was something fragile and tentative there. Her small daughter, who had gone quietly into the den and was regarding a wary Foster Grant with polite interest, had the same air of fragility.

"Susan is a gal after my own heart," said Claire, giving Susan Greene's shoulder her characteristic little hug. "I've been in my house precisely sixteen years and it's still the biggest mess you ever saw. I think this is the beginning of a beautiful friendship."

Looking at the two women standing together in the warm light of my kitchen, with sleet ticking ominously at the French doors and the wind rising outside, I thought it probably was the beginning of a friendship. A real friendship, one of Claire's few deep and abiding and totally open friendships. They seemed so alike. They seemed already close and easy and comfortably offhand, as you do well into a good friendship. I felt a jolt of coldness somewhere deep in my stomach, which crept toward my heart. The dread I had thought I had left in Jamaica came flooding back, mature and heavy. Presentiment hung thick and almost palpable in my kitchen once again. I thought swiftly and clearly: This is dangerous. This woman is dangerous to Claire. This friendship must not bloom. This alliance must be broken.

And then I thought, just as clearly and vividly: I believe I am jealous of this friendship. That's all. Just plain, low-down jealous. That's awful, but I can deal with jealousy. That's not in that house. That's in my own head. And I smiled at Susan Greene and said, "I don't even have to tell you about the mess my house has been in all these years, because you're standing in the middle of it, and not for the last time either."

I turned to the man, who stood straight and silent, looking methodically around the kitchen as if memorizing it. He had odd gray eyes, pale and opaque and almost silver, like dull coins. He was tall and slender and had brown hair cut so short that it was startling; bone-clean white scalp showed through. I thought he might be a military man.

"Come on into the den," I said, "and I'll fix you a drink, or some coffee, if you like. Walter—my husband—will be home in a few minutes and I know he'd like to meet you. And it's such a ghastly, rotten night."

"That would be nice, for just a minute," said Susan

181

Greene. "I haven't sat down all day, literally. I meant it when I said I couldn't seem to get hold of things somehow. I don't know why, except that Lissa hasn't been feeling very well, but that's no excuse really. It seemed such an easy house to keep too when we first looked at it. So functional. But it's as bad today as it was five minutes after the movers left. It's driving Norm wild."

She smiled up at her tall, straight husband, who did not smile back at her. There was adoration in the smile and something else—apprehension? Eagerness to please? She is afraid of him, I thought roundly and suddenly.

"Mama," called the child Melissa from the den in a sudden, clear treble. "Mama, I have to go to the bathroom."

"It's right through that door by the fireplace, honey," I called back and started for the den to show her. "Come on and settle in by the fire, you all," I added over my shoulder.

"No. Not tonight," said Norman Greene, and we turned. He had not moved from his spot in the middle of the kitchen. "Thank you, Mrs. Kennedy, but Susan really does have a great deal of work to do on the house yet. A rain check, maybe?"

"For goodness' sake, Norm, at least let Melissa go to the bathroom—" Susan Greene began.

"Melissa can wait until we get home. And I'm not going to sleep in that bedroom until it's straight." He raised his voice and called, "Melissa. Get your coat on. We're going home now."

"Daddy," her clear small voice called back, "Daddy, I really have to go right *now!*"

"Melissa." He did not raise his voice, but it rang as if through a long stillness.

"Daddy, it *hurts!*" It was a cry of distress, not petulance. Susan Greene brushed by her husband and went into the den to her child.

"You can wait one minute, Norman," she said. "You know she's been upset ever since we moved. Is it all right, Mrs. Kennedy?"

"Well, of course it is," I said, not looking at Claire or at Norman Greene. Susan Greene took the child into the bathroom and closed the door. Norman Greene stood still. He said nothing, but his face seemed to fill, to swell somehow, though his expression did not change.

"I'm sorry she isn't feeling well," I said lamely to fill the prickling silence. "Moving can be upsetting to children, I know."

"There isn't anything wrong with Melissa," he said. "Susan spoils her. I find bids for attention unbecoming in children."

Claire and I looked at him. He seemed to gather his face together, and produced a rigid smile. "I look forward to meeting your husband, Mrs. Kennedy," he said. "Perhaps you'll come and have that drink at our house when things are a little more organized. I hope you had a fine time in Jamaica. We have several good friends there, very substantial old island families. White, of course. Next time you and your husband go down I'll write you some letters of introduction. It's always more pleasant when you know the right people, I think."

"Yes, it is," I said faintly. "That would be nice. I'm sorry you can't stay for a minute, but I do understand how it is when you've just moved. You'll let me know if there's anything at all you need?" This to Susan Greene, who had brought the child, pale and large-eyed, back into the kitchen and was buttoning her into her coat. She looked, oddly, as though she were about to cry. Then she rallied her grin.

"Of course I will. Although Claire here has practically given me every pot and pan and stick of furniture in her house, and has spent the last week driving us around and getting us acquainted with the city. She's even given me the name of her doctor and her dentist and her hairdresser, and she's fed us twice. So there's nothing in the world I need, except maybe a genie or a few slaves or something." She laughed, a stiff, social little laugh, aimed up at her husband. "Goodnight, then," she said helplessly when he did not respond to the laugh, and they turned to go.

"Goodnight," I said, and Claire said, "I think I'll stay and hear about Col's trip, Susan. Call you in the morning."

The Greenes went out of the kitchen into the roaring night. Claire and I looked at each other.

"Is he real?" I said. " '*Susan* has a great deal of work to do yet.' 'I'm not going to sleep in that bedroom until it's straight.' 'Very substantial old island families. White, of course.' And not letting that poor child go to the bathroom because it 'spoils' her! God! I'll bet he burns books and Jews."

Claire laughed mirthlessly. "That's one of his problems. He *is* a Jew. Half one, anyway. Greene with an *e?* Besides, Susan told me he was. But he's trying to pass for Episcopalian, I think. Isn't he a creep? And she's such a doll. I just can't figure it, the way she adores him. But she does. And he just walks all over her. Yells at her like a damned drill sergeant, or rather, hisses commands at her in that nasty, flat, cold, snaky voice of his, and she jumps out of her skin to do his bidding. That child is scared to death of him too. With good reason, I might add. He talks to her as if he absolutely loathes her sometimes—when he bothers to talk to her at all."

"Oh, Lord. Life with Little Hitler. Tell me about them. Where are they from?"

"Boston, or somewhere around there. He teaches at City; just took some position there and will start winter quarter. Math or something. I know he went to Harvard, because he told me so two minutes after I met him and has not ceased telling me since. He's one of those Ivy League Jews who never got over the fact that he couldn't join Hasty Pudding or whatever, and would sell his soul to the devil if his name could be Lowell or Cabot or Lodge. So he makes up for it by dropping names he barely knows and bullying his wife and trying to make that poor kid into Little Miss Perfect. I guess he'd never have bothered having one if it wasn't the proper thing to do. They just got her into Chase Preschool, or rather, I did. And, of course, buying six-hundred-dollar suits and big cars."

"On a teacher's salary?"

"I'm coming to that. He keeps missing, though; the suits are silk and the cars are Cadillacs and the furniture is reproduction French whorehouse, though I'm sure it did cost the earth, because he told me what he paid for most of it. And he's got Buffet paintings in there, can you imagine? What's so sad is that she used to be a painter, a pretty promising one, had shown a few times in New York, and she gave it up when she married him. She told me about it the other day when I took her shopping. She said he hadn't thought it looked right for the wife of a professor to be a painter —too Bohemian. Those were his words, not hers. She said it with absolutely no . . . rancor; I don't think it's ever occurred to her that he's a tight-assed, bullying, pretentious prick. She loves the asshole."

"Claire! Such language! Surely he can't be all that bad."

"He sure *can* be all that bad. You think he's kidding about making her clean up that bedroom before he'll sleep in it? I was over there Saturday, and they were in the basement—he was standing while she was on her hands and knees rearranging the food in the freezer. He was telling her where he wanted everything to go. The beans here, and the corn over there, and stack the meat by shape and weight and cut, and then by consecutive dates. He had a legal pad and was reading it off to her, in order, and when I said I'd pitch in and help so we could get some Christmas shopping done, he said no, she wasn't going shopping today, because she'd forgotten what he told her about the freezer and was just going to have to get it right. He was smiling, but you could tell he was furious. And then Melissa came downstairs looking for her mother, and he told her to go back upstairs and stay in her room until everything was in its place. I could have slapped him. The kid just turned around and flew back upstairs, and Susan looked like she was going to cry."

"How perfectly stinking. I wonder, if he's such an awful snob and perfectionist and all that, why he married her? I mean, I think she's charming, but if she's a disorganized housekeeper and a Bohemian to boot— I think I last heard *that* word in 1956—why on earth did he pick her in the first place?"

"That's what I was going to tell you. Her money. She's got a wad. And a lot of social position around Boston, though I think her parents are dead now. Apparently they were terribly Back Bay and all that, and really hated the idea of her being an artist. I guess they were glad to get her married to anybody at all. She's not at all bitter about it or secretive. She talks about it openly, with no self-consciousness or false modesty. She says she never cared very much about the money, except that he seemed to enjoy the things it bought them so much that she was glad she had it. She said he grew up very poor and went through Harvard on a scholarship and worked nights and weekends. The whole Horatio Alger bit. She seems to feel that the money is his due; she seems *grateful* to him somehow. She bought the house and is paying Melissa's tuition and all that. I don't know what the arrangement is, but apparently she's turned every cent over to him, and he spends it like he wants to. She's a plain person. She doesn't care a lot about clothes and parties and jewelry and stuff like that, but she buys them and wears them, and she entertains because he wants to. I simply cannot figure it. I think she's a fantastic person, and I think she's fifty times too good for him."

"Well," I said, "there really isn't any accounting for taste. I guess he's her blind spot. If she's stuck with him, I'm glad she's so crazy about him. Wouldn't it be awful if she wasn't? But it *is* hard to understand; she's so very personable and likeable. I've always been drawn to that kind of cheerful, disorganized, warm-hearted woman."

"You know," Claire said, "she isn't really. Disorganized, I mean. She was treasurer of her Junior League chapter for years. She says she ran a six-bedroom house plus a shore cottage with no trouble at all before they moved, and did a lot of volunteer stuff, and gave parties—everything he wanted her to do. She says she just can't seem to get things together here. I think she's worried about Melissa, and distracted, like you *would* be if you'd just moved and your kid wasn't feeling well, and he's jealous and resentful of the time she's spending with her. I think that's all it is. Why else would he be so *mean* to both of them? I mean, my God, so he wants a perfect house, but she's his child too. But he's driving Susan batty. She said the other day that if she didn't absolutely know she was hopelessly sane and doomed to stay that way, she'd think there was really something wrong with her. She can thank him for that."

I moved jerkily, inadvertently, and winced. Claire looked at me.

"Oh, no, nothing like Anita. She was kidding, really. There's not a saner woman in America. She's absolutely unflappable, except when it comes to pleasing him, and then she gets that kind of hunted look, like she's afraid he's going to—I don't know what. Hit her, or something. Or . . . take it out on the child."

"Do they know . . . about the house?" I asked.

"I don't know. She hasn't said anything about it. Somehow I don't think so, because I believe she'd have mentioned it. She says whatever she thinks the minute she thinks it. I don't think it would bother her; she's too balanced and down-to-earth for that. But it sure would him, so I don't think they know. I doubt if he'd have bought it if he did."

"He didn't strike me as the type who'd worry about that sort of thing," I said. "I wouldn't think he'd have the imagination."

"Oh, he doesn't. It isn't that he's superstitious or anything. He'd just find that kind of reputation in a house of his socially unacceptable. Gays carrying on in *his* house? A crazy woman in *his* house? A miscarriage, a sloppy stroke? Wouldn't do, wouldn't do at all."

And a sex scandal between a married guy and the married lady next door, I thought bleakly. And a near-double murder, a near-suicide. The image of those thrashing white bodies intertwined on the sofa snapped into my mind with the clarity of a slide snapping onto a screen. I heard Buck's hoarse cry of release and saw Virginia's contorted, gaping face. I saw Anita's face, emptied out and frozen. I saw Walter's face, and Kim's, and the death that was written on both of them.

"Claire," I heard myself saying before the words registered on my consciousness, "don't get too involved with her. Don't go over there. Let her come to your house if you just have to see her, but don't spend much time in that house. Better still, just don't see any more of her than you have to—" I stopped. Claire looked at me.

"What the hell is the matter with you, Colquitt?" she said in angry disbelief. "Susan is already my friend. I *like* her. I like her very much. She's warm, and real, and absolutely open—which is more than you've been with me lately. Are you jealous of Susan Greene, Colquitt? Because if you are, then you're really a spoiler. You don't want to be my friend, not like you were, but you don't want anybody else to be either, is that it? Well, I'll tell you, if that *is* it, you can take your fine friendship and all the neat little conditions you put on it and you can—"

"Claire, my *God!*" I cried. "I'm not jealous of you and Susan Greene! I'm afraid for you! I'm afraid of what that house can do to you—look at what it did to the Harralsons and the Sheehans—look at Pie's father, look at Luke Abbott, look at Kim, look at Virginia—" I stopped, but not in time.

"What about Virginia, Colquitt?" Claire said softly and levelly. "What did the house do to Virginia?"

I began to cry. I could not help myself. I was endlessly tired, endlessly sad. Fear and foreboding sat chokingly on my chest like twin succubi.

"I don't know anything about Virginia," I said through my tears, through my fingers. "I didn't mean to say Virginia. I'm just afraid for you, Claire. I love you, and I'm afraid that house is going to do something terrible to you."

She was quiet for so long that I thought perhaps she had tiptoed out of the den, and I raised my head to look. She was staring at me with a terrible concern, a sort of straining incomprehension on her face, like a bright, good dog who is trying with all its wits to understand an obscure, unfamiliar command. There was fear and worry and love in her face, but there was exasperation, too, and Claire's characteristic mulishness.

"I'm afraid for *you*, Colquitt," she said. "I'm afraid for your mind. You sound like somebody I never even knew before. You have, ever since Anita and Buck left. Since Charles and Virginia left. What are you saying about that house? Are you saying that the house is *haunted* or something? Colquitt, either you've taken leave of your senses or you're trying to hide something from me with all this garbage about the house, and either way, I'm not buying it. I know that something awful happened over there, and I know it happened to Virginia Guthrie, and I know you know what it is. If you're seriously trying to warn me about something —the house, or whatever it is—then you're going to have to tell me *why*. God, Colquitt, give me some credit for *some* sensitivity and discretion and understanding. Do you think I'd go blabbing whatever it is all over town? I want to help you too, Col, but I can't unless I know what it is that's scared you so."

"I can't tell you."

"You were my best friend in this world!" It was a wail of anguish.

"I can't, Claire."

"Colquitt, you—you *dishonor* me. Your lack of trust *dishonors* me."

"I can't!"

"All right. All right, then. We'll say no more about it. For Walter and Roger's sake, I guess we should keep seeing each other. But just don't give me any more manure about haunted houses and danger and not seeing Susan Greene, not when you can't or won't even make the effort to keep me for a friend. *She* makes the effort."

"You don't understand," I said dully.

"No. I don't understand. I want more than anything in the world to understand, but you won't help me. All I *do* understand is that you could help me and you won't. Do it, Col. Please. Please tell me. I want my friend back."

"I can't," I whispered.

"Then sit over here and go bananas on your own." She was crying too. "Just wig on out. Oh, don't worry, I'm not going to cut you dead in the street or turn my back on you at the Parsons' party. I guess I don't have any pride in me, Colquitt, but if you ever change your mind and want your old fat friend back, just whistle. I'll come running. I always did. But don't do it until you can do it with no reservations. I can't be half a friend to you. I don't want half of you."

She got up and walked rapidly through the den and kitchen and out the back door, not stopping to put on her coat. I saw her for a moment, limned against the flying black sky by the back porch light, struggling into the coat, gesturing and flapping like a dear, awkward bird. Then the night swallowed her and pure, mindless hurt flooded and drowned me, and I stretched out on the sofa by the fire and wept until Walter came home and found me.

Chapter Nineteen

WHEN I look back on that Christmas I remember the time when my father was dying of cancer and we all moved through the fragile structure of our lives as if submerged under heavy, scummed, brackish water. We clung to the small rituals of life as it had been before with a tenacity that often astounded me. On every side the grief and pain and dread, the heavy immutability of the death spinning toward him like a star pressed and gnawed and nibbled. The rites of life kept them at bay, but they were there, and you knew that a time would come when they would catch you with your guard down and would sweep over you and desolate you.

That Christmas was like that.

I did not see Claire again until the Parsons' splendid annual party on the twenty-third. Everyone in the neighborhood looked forward to Gwen and Carey Parsons' gala. It was just that; I always thought of the words "gala" and "fête" when I entered their shining foyer at Christmastime. Their house is one of the city's real showplaces, built in the closing days of the last century by an architect of great local renown who had spent much time abroad and favored the Italians. Gwen and Carey had made something wonderful of the old white stucco villa, set far back on a sweep of lawn and reached by a circular drive. Twin stone urns spilled glossy greenery on either side of the great door, vivid and perfect even in the ice-black of December.

Inside there were rich, faded old tapestries and great chandeliers and sconces and massive black Mediterranean pieces about, but Gwen had lightened and balanced them with pools of color and sweeps of space, scattering hectic Indian rugs on the old tiles and hanging brilliant, explosive contemporary paintings on the vast white walls. The drawing room had a few handsome, heavy pieces of glass and chrome and steel, and books swelled and spilled from floor-to-ceiling bookcases in many of the downstairs rooms. They weren't all old and leather-bound and matched, either. Rowdy paperbacks and contemporary fiction shouldered in among the dour Russians and Mr. Bulwer-Lytton. It shouldn't have worked at all, but somehow it did.

I had not wanted to go to the party, knowing that Claire and Roger would be there. I shrank from seeing her, as I knew she would from me. But Walter insisted. He had been deeply angry at Claire when I'd told him about the dreadful words that were said in our den that evening before he got home. He was angry and troubled and nearly as hurt as I had been. He was also, I knew, a little annoyed at me.

"She behaved like a spoiled kid," he said. "What kind of friend is that? But you had no business blurting out that stuff about the house, Col. Didn't I tell you what people would think if you did that? Besides thinking you've gone around the bend, that kind of stuff disturbs people. Nobody wants to listen to that. Maybe you thought you were doing her a favor, but you upset her, and she was already half-miffed with you, and she just blew up at you. Anybody would. I'm not excusing her. I think she acted like a real shit to you. I didn't think Claire had that in her. But it's what you're going to get from anybody you mention it to. Now, we damned well *are* going to that party. You're going in with your head up and a big smile on, with all your flags flying, and you're going to be nicer than hell to Claire, and we're going to straighten things out between you two. Why don't you get a new dress?"

I smiled dimly. "You sound like Rhett Butler telling Scarlett to wear that slutty thing to Melanie's party after those old biddies caught her necking with Ashley. Are you saying you want me to apologize to Claire?"

"No, of course not. If anybody apologizes, it ought to be her. I just want you to show her she hasn't gotten your goat and that you're willing to forget that business if she is. You all have been friends too long to let a stupid house come between you."

"Can't you see that that's probably its next move? Aside from whatever charming thing it has in store for the Greenes. Claire and I are just a sideline. There's plenty of time to take care of the Greenes and work on Claire and me too."

"I'd put Captain Queeg over there up against that house any day of the world," Walter said. "He doesn't have enough creativity to recognize a first-class ha'nt if one came out of the woodwork and bit him. And from what you tell me, she doesn't sound exactly fey and ethereal. You're jumping the gun. Nothing's going to happen over there this time. If it was, it would have started already. The Harralsons' troubles started before they even moved in. The Sheehans' started in less than a week. They've been in three and not a peep from nary a spook."

I knew that he had decided that brisk jocularity was the order of the day. He responded with gentle jibes whenever my fears about the house spilled over into words. I disliked the well-meaning banter even more than I did his reluctant understanding or his infrequent exasperation, and so I did not often mention the house. Except for the anguish of the quarrel with Claire, it was a waiting time, a suspended place in the dying days of the year.

So we did go to the party, me in a shockingly expensive new dress with a rictus of high spirits pinned to my mouth, Walter in the formal evening wear he purports to loathe but looks elegant and saturnine in on the two or three occasions during the year he puts it on.

Claire stood in the foyer with Roger and Norman and Susan Greene, waiting while gentle, elderly black

Henry took their wraps. Roger looked like a rumpled parody of George Raft, as he always does in evening clothes, and Norman Greene looked magisterial and perfect in his white tie. Newness puffed from him like a cloud of smoke. I thought he should have a scarlet military sash, medals, a saber, orders of some splendid martial fraternity pinned about him. Claire and Susan looked as though they had bought their floor-length silk sheaths at the same discreet designer salon of the city's most glittering emporium. Claire's had chaste beading around the hem and neckline and was blue. Susan's had fox fur on the cuffs and was green. That was the only noticeable difference, although Susan wore a simple choker of startling emeralds and kept moving her neck as though they were uncomfortable against her throat. I had seen few other emerald necklaces besides Virginia Guthrie's, but these looked to be flawless.

"Hello, fellow voyagers. Merry Christmas," Walter said, determined cheer puddling in his voice.

"Hi, everybody," I said, looking only at Claire.

She hesitated for a moment and then came and gave me her little hug. Her cheek was very cold against mine.

"Hi, Col," she said. "Hi, Walter baby. You know the Greenes of course."

"Yes," I said, and "Not yet," Walter said, and there was a flurry of introductions, and we walked into the drawing room to greet Gwen and Carey. It is the only room I have seen in the city that can properly be called a drawing room. Anything else would be ludicrous.

We went on into the great paneled library, where the bar had been set up and a giant spruce glowed against a bay of windows overlooking the blackened garden. Gwen—or the servants—had festooned it with exquisite carved wooden ornaments and madonnas and cherubs made from painted papier-mâché. It had an exotic, old-world air about it; the whole house did. I thought of *The Garden of the Finzi-Continis,* as I always did in Gwen and Carey Parsons' house. We got drinks from the young man behind the bar and took them over to a low oak table in front of the baronial fireplace, where a great apple-log fire hissed and snapped on the hearth. We dropped onto the facing sofas on either side of the fireplace. It was early yet, and there were no other people in the room.

"I always expect to see a whole steer sizzling away in there, or a boar," Walter said, gesturing with his martini at the fire.

"It's a beautiful house, isn't it?" Susan Greene said with nothing in her voice but pure pleasure. The Parsons' house brings out the latent covetousness in most of us, and we all do a lot of muttering about white elephants and drafty old barns after their parties. We all love the house.

"If you like this sort of thing," said Norman Greene. It was such a pointedly uncharitable remark that we all looked at him, not knowing how to respond.

"I'm a simpler person myself," he added.

I thought about the Buffet paintings and the reproduction French whorehouse furniture Claire had told me about and shot her a tentative look across the table. She twinkled back at me fleetingly and then leaned over to Susan Greene, who was looking unhappily into the fire, and said, "Yours is a thousand times more livable. Your house has been the envy of the neighborhood ever since it went up. You're seeing this one at its all-time company best. Gwen says herself she'd sell it in a minute if they could get their money out of it."

"How much are they asking?" said Norman Greene.

Claire shot him a positive glare. "I don't think they'd really sell it," she said. "It was Carey's family's house. She just meant that it was big and old and hard to take care of. I don't have any idea how much they'd want for it."

"I'm not interested in it, of course," he said. "Just thought it might give me some idea of what the neighborhood is worth in general. I'd like to think that little place of ours would appreciate over the years."

"I don't think you have to worry, Greene," said Roger in a dryer voice than he normally uses. "The street's not Park Avenue, but it's not Tobacco Road, either."

"Who's with Melissa tonight, Susan?" I said hastily. "And how's she feeling now?"

"Duck's pretty girl friend—Libby Fleming, isn't it, Claire?" she said. "Lissa's some better, I think, or at least she has been for a week or so. She's not so hot tonight. It was really awfully sweet of Libby to come and sit with her on such short notice. I haven't had time to line up baby-sitters yet."

"I hope you don't think it was a mere favor to a new neighbor," Claire said ruefully. "Duck was undoubtedly over there before the front door closed on you. I haven't seen much of him since he got home from school, but I'm sure the poor Flemings have seen far too much of him. God, I'm glad he's not in school down here, or she's not in New Haven. He'd flunk out before the first quarter was up."

"How's he liking Yale?" Walter said.

"Who knows?" Claire replied. "I don't get letters. I just get collect phone calls saying he's out of money or could use a couple of new shirts, or wants to spend Thanksgiving in New York with some person named Animal." Pride shone softly out of her eyes; Duck's full scholarship to Yale was one of the great things in Claire and Roger's life. He wanted to be a research biologist; I thought, with his gentle hands and leaping mind and Roger's endless, sweet patience and uncommon sense of responsibility, that he would be a good one.

Norman Greene frowned. "I hope those kids will behave themselves," he said. "I didn't know Duck was coming over. The girl's father is on the board of trustees for City, isn't he? I don't need him down on me."

"We've known Libby's father longer than we have Duck," Claire said tartly to Norman Greene, "and almost as well. And Libby too. She and Duck have gone together longer than anybody can remember. Ford Fleming has been stricter with her than a convent school. He seems to approve of Duck. I don't think you have to worry about either of the children. Both of them were raised pretty well."

"I didn't mean to imply that anything out of the way was going on," he said quickly. "He seems a fine boy and she's a nice little girl. Susan has been fussing over Melissa far too much lately, and she needs to be quiet is all."

"Duck and Libby won't bother her," Claire said briefly. She turned to Susan. "Still the same business with Lissa's stomach?"

Susan wrinkled her nose, but I thought her blue eyes clouded a little. "Off and on. I don't think it's anything much, but if it isn't better after Christmas I'm going to take her to your doctor, Claire. It's probably only the excitement of Christmas and moving. Stomachache, some diarrhea——"

"That's hardly appetizing cocktail talk, is it, Susan?" Norman Greene smiled thinly. "Melissa is overindulged. That's all. Come on. I see Dr. Holderbein from City over at the bar. He wanted to meet you. He's the president, you know."

Susan Greene gave us a little girl's rueful smile all around. "Excuse us for a minute?"

"Certainly," I said. They rose and walked away toward the bar. Norman Greene was talking into his wife's ear, emphatic words we could not hear, punctuated by little jerks of his cropped head. She ran her finger inside the emerald choker as though it were too tight.

"Turd," said Claire clearly as the Greenes joined the crowd around the bar.

"In spades," Walter said. "No redeeming social value at all, that I can see. What's a nice girl like her, et cetera? I wonder what *he* calls diarrhea? Poo-poo, like Eloise does?"

"Gastroenteritis, probably," said Claire. "The more I see of that Nazi, the less I like it. She came over the other afternoon almost in tears, wanting to borrow some cleaning fluid. He'd come home the night before and found some stains on his clothes in the big closet —you know, that cedar closet the Harralsons had built in? Well, that's for *his* clothes—and just jerked them all off the hangers and dumped them on the floor in their bedroom and said he was going to sleep in the guest room until she got the stains out. On the *floor,* please."

"What kind of stains?" I said.

"*I* don't know. Something that must have gotten on them at the cleaners in Boston before they moved, because they were still in the plastic hangers. But of course it was *her* fault. I sent her up to that place in the shopping center we use. She just hadn't had time to find a dry cleaner yet. And then there were the bedroom curtains."

"What happened to the bedroom curtains?" Walter said. I could tell that he was enthralled.

"That's really pitiful. Melissa was pulling on them and they fell, and before Susan could get them up again he came home and found them in a pile on the floor, and he was so angry Susan was afraid to tell him how it happened, so she said she didn't know why they fell. He told her that if she couldn't hang curtains properly to get someone to come in and do it professionally. Know any professional curtain hangers?"

"No, but I've got a good connection for a professional hit man," said Walter. "Maybe that's what she needs."

"I'd be glad to do it myself, should the need arise, which it already has as far as I'm concerned," said Claire. "I didn't appreciate that little insinuation about Duck and Libby one bit. They're so chaste they almost scare me. And imagine, *punishing* Susan because his clothes got dirty! By saying he was going to sleep in the guest room! I should think that would be a treat instead of punishment. God, all I can see is years ahead of trying to be her friend and dodging him at the same time. What a ghastly and endless prospect."

I felt the unwelcome, sick wrench in my stomach again and said, "Let's go get some of those hors d'oeuvres before the locusts come."

We got up and drifted toward the dining room, where the buffet glowed, jewellike, on Gwen Parsons' hundred-year-old damask. The painful estrangement between Claire and me had not vanished, but it had slunk away into a dark corner of the cave under the onslaught of our indignation at Norman Greene.

In the library, as we left it, someone sat down at the piano in a dim corner of the dark old room and began to pick out "Adeste Fideles."

Chapter Twenty

THE WEEK after Christmas an ornate, gold-scrolled invitation came from Susan and Norman Greene. "Join us for a Twelfth Night celebration," the message said in curly black script.

Walter ran a thumbnail over the letters. "Engraved," he said. "Twelfth Night. Jesus, it sounds like Shakespeare. What the hell is Twelfth Night?"

"Epiphany, you heathen. When was the last time you went to church?"

"Never, if you mean C of E," he said. "Good God, when he climbs he goes all the way to the top, doesn't he? When's the last time you got an engraved invitation to a neighborhood party?"

"Maybe it's more than neighborhood. There are bound to be some college people there. The president and the board of regents, no doubt. Lord, that poor woman."

"Shall we go?" he said.

"Of course we'll go. We can't not go. It would break her heart. I'm sure the engraved invitations and the Twelfth Night business were his doing, not hers. She must be embarrassed practically to tears. Besides, I'm dying to see the inside of the house. Claire said it looked like a French bordello. I guess you'll have to dress, though it doesn't say so. But with an engraved invitation . . ."

"Shit," said Walter.

We had a quiet New Year's Eve with Charlie Satterfield and his wife, eating turkey chow mein in front of their fireplace. At midnight Charlie opened a bottle of champagne and we toasted the coming year.

"To a good year for all of us," said Charlie, lifting his glass.

"I'll drink to that," said Walter.

I said nothing. We exchanged comfortable midnight kisses, and went home early. The next day we walked over to Claire and Roger's to their small traditional brunch-and-Bowl-games affair. The aroma of black-eyed peas curled into the foyer. Claire met us at the door and gave Walter an exaggerated smack on the cheek, leaving a coral lip print.

"I asked you early just so the first person over my doorstep on New Year's Day would be a dark-haired man," she said. "I'm going to have a lucky year."

It wasn't an unpleasant afternoon. Claire and I avoided being alone with each other by tacit agreement, but we bantered determinedly and good-naturedly with each other, as we had always done, and if there was a tension, a fine-nerved edge in the air between us, no one else seemed to notice. The Greenes were not there. Claire said they had gone to a reception at the home of the City College chancellor but were coming by for an early supper.

"Melissa was supposed to start Chase day after tomorrow, but she's still a little under the weather. The doctor couldn't find anything much wrong, but I think Susan's going to keep her home the rest of the week," Claire said.

We refused her invitation to stay for supper. I did not want to spend much time with Susan Greene and felt small and guilty that I did not. Part of me liked her enormously; part of me shrank from becoming intimate with her. I felt no compunction about my growing dislike of Norman Greene. Once, during the week after Christmas, I had heard him shouting in their backyard and had leaned back to look out my office window to see what was going on. It was dusk, and cold. He was standing at the wooden enclosure that housed their garbage cans, throwing something that I could not identify into the cans. Melissa, in a long nightgown, stood on the back deck watching him, shrinking back against the railing.

"If you can't take care of them, you don't deserve to have them," he was shouting. "You haven't had them three days and they're absolutely ruined."

"I didn't break them, Daddy," the child sobbed. "I promise it wasn't me. I didn't break them!"

"Don't lie to me, Melissa," he roared. "Now stop that whining and go on in the house. I want you to go straight up to your room and think about little girls who tear up presents their parents work hard all year to give them."

He slammed the lid on the garbage cans and took the child by the shoulder and pushed her through the back door. It shut with a glass-rattling bang and I could hear no more.

My stomach worked with anger and dislike. "Damned tyrant," I muttered aloud and turned back to the work I was doing. I made a mental note to stay at the Greenes' Twelfth Night party only as long as decency decreed.

We were late getting to their house on the night of the party, and it was in full swing when we walked into the living room. Norman Greene met us at the door. He wore the first and only burgundy velvet smoking jacket I have ever seen and had a sprig of holly in his lapel. His dark hair was even shorter, new-mown, and his scalp looked like polished ivory. His eyes glittered blankly, reflecting light, and his mouth was stretched into a caricature of good cheer.

"Welcome to our humble abode," he said. "Come have some of your grandmother's eggnog you were so kind to tell us about. I made it myself and it's first-rate, if I do say so. Those old Southern aristocrats really knew how to live, didn't they?"

Walter gave him an exaggerated leer and said, "Oh, to be sure. Col's grandmother was known far and wide for her eighteen-inch waist and her family silver and her eggnog. She made a batch every day for forty years until they locked her in the attic for good. For medicinal purposes of course."

Norman Greene looked at him closely, decided he was joking, and gave him a startling, conspiratorial wink. He led us into the living room, where Susan Greene, in a long velvet skirt and a white satin shirt, stood with her daughter. Melissa was enchanting, dressed in a long blue taffeta dress with a starched white pinafore over it. Her chestnut hair curled round her small pointed face, and her smile was quick and sweet, a carbon of her mother's. She had clear, lambent green eyes sheltered under feathering lashes, so lovely and startling and unlike her father's silver-gray ones or Susan's dancing blue that I wondered how I had failed to notice them before. There were tender mauve shadows under them. I thought she looked like a Kate Greenaway miniature and said so to Susan.

"She does have a funny, old-fashioned look about her, doesn't she?" Susan said. "She really likes dresses and ruffles and frills. I have a hard time getting her into blue jeans. Lissa, honey, show Mrs. Kennedy where to put her coat. Norm will take yours, Walter."

I followed the child into the downstairs bedroom. I had not seen it since the night I had stood in its doorway stricken to stone, seeing Buddy Harralson and Lucas Abbott frozen like statues beside the bed and Matt Gladney on the floor. The bed had been piled with purses then too and light spring wraps. I forced myself to look long around the room, to superimpose normalcy over that awful remembered image.

An enormous white-and-gilt bed teeming with cherubs and rosebuds and swags and garlands dominated the room. Lavender taffeta shrouded the bed and made a canopy. Lavender taffeta hung in carved folds at the windows and covered the padded cornices. Lavender petit point covered the vanity bench, which was white and gilt too, and there were lavender velvet pillows on a chaise longue in a corner of the room. A white-and-gilt escritoire against one wall had a crystal inkwell and a quill with a curling white plume. A silver seal, with an elaborate G cut into it, stood on the escritoire beside a stick of red sealing wax. An open door showed wallpaper with pink and purple shepherdesses, purple bath carpet, pink and lavender and purple towels. I'll bet it has gold fixtures, I thought, and peered around the door. It did.

Kim Dougherty's house was astounding. There was hardly an inch of floor space that did not house a piece of carved, polished, satined, damasked and gilded French furniture. Mirrors and paintings covered the white walls. The long expanses of glass were draped and tied and swagged with satin. The polished wooden floor lay under thick, pale-blue carpeting. A great log roared in the fireplace, and flowers, mostly white, stood spikily, formally erect on tables and mantelpiece. White candles blazed everywhere. In the dining room dour faces in frames of heavy gilt glared down on the buffet table. A lovely, heavy cut-crystal punch bowl held my grandmother's eggnog, and an ornate old silver ladle bobbed gently in the bowl. Ham glistened pinkly, and roast beef glistened redly, and enormous platters of sandwiches, crudités, canapés and cheeses covered the white lace tablecloth. It was a stunning array of food, enough to feed a battalion.

Claire stood at the table with Semmes and Eloise Jennings, looking down at it bemusedly. She held a cup of eggnog, and there was a creamy mustache on her upper lip. I moved up beside her and greeted her and the Jenningses.

"Quite a spread, isn't it?" I said. Walter handed me a cup of eggnog and I tasted it. It *was* good, thick and pungent with cream and rum.

"Think of the starving Biafrans," Claire said. "I'd sell my soul for a good stiff Scotch, but no dice there. Well, what do you think? Was I right or was I right?"

"You were right," I said. "Buffet paintings and all."

"Right about what?" demanded Eloise Jennings truculently. She was looking around the dining room and living room discontentedly, as though they were a personal affront to her.

"I told Colquitt it looked like a French whorehouse," Claire said, and I could tell by her voice that she and Roger had had a fortifying snort of something before they came.

"Well, I think it's sensational," Eloise said. "I never did care for that stark stuff the Harralsons had in here. And I never saw what the Sheehans did with it. Funny people, weren't they? I never did think she was all there in the head, and I hear I was right. That's a pretty little girl of the Greenes' too, but it's so sad when people dress children up like little adults. I've always thought so. Children should be free to express themselves. I'd never dream of putting an outfit like that on any of mine. She's showing the strain too. Look at her eyes. Peaky. She's getting something, mark my words."

"Not all children have that certain joie de vivre yours have, Eloise," drawled Walter.

Eloise's face reddened and puffed, but before she could reply, Susan Greene appeared at our sides with Norman and a short, squat, froggy man in heavy bifocals.

"I'd like you all to meet Dr. Holderbein," she said. "You probably already know him, he's president of City. Colquitt and Walter Kennedy, Dr. Holderbein, our next-door neighbors, and this is Claire Swanson, from up the street, and Eloise and Semmes Jennings."

"Indeed I do know most of these people, Mrs. Greene," said the little man in a piping treble. "Roger Swanson is a great friend of mine, and Mrs. Kennedy here did a superb job for City last year when we had our Centennial. Are you still with your firm, Mrs. Kennedy?"

"No, I'm on my own now," I said. "I have an office at home, and I handle three or four small accounts. It's good to see you again, sir."

Norman Greene swelled visibly with pride. "Fine neighbors, aren't they, sir?" he said. "Susan wasn't at all sure about the house when I first showed it to her —she liked an old one over in Druidwater, but you could tell the neighborhood was going—but now she's glad I talked her into this one. I think we're going to be very happy on this street. Solid people, everybody here. Very like our friends at home."

Dr. Holderbein smiled at Norman Greene and, charmingly, at Susan. "Fine neighbors indeed," he said. "And you could not be more correct about the Druidwater section being in a state of, shall we say, genteel decay, Greene. I've lived there myself for many years, and it really isn't what it used to be. May I trouble you for a cup of that splendid eggnog, Mrs. Greene?"

There was a painful silence, in which Norman Greene looked at one of us, and then another, and then Susan said, "Claire, would you get Dr. Holderbein some eggnog? Norm, I need you to help me start

203

another batch in the kitchen." She drew her husband toward the kitchen door. At that moment the lights flickered, then swelled, then flickered again, and died slowly out. We stood in the candlelight.

"What the hell is the matter with those lights?" I heard Norman Greene hiss, and Susan Greene said, "I don't know, Norm. Why don't you go check the fuse box? It doesn't matter, we have plenty of candle-light. Nothing needs to be heated. I'll mix this next batch by hand."

"No, it needs the blender," he said sharply. "Christ, Susan, I told you when they were acting up the other day to get somebody out here to check that fuse box; it shouldn't be doing this in a new house. Did you even think to call? I guess it's too much to ask that you remembered . . ."

His voice trailed off down the basement stairs, and a flashlight bobbed briefly in the darkness before he shut the door. Claire and I went into the kitchen to help Susan.

She had taken a candle into the kitchen with her, and Claire picked up another from a side table. The kitchen leaped with shadows. Susan Greene was rum-maging in her dark refrigerator for cream and eggs, setting them out on the counter. Her mobile face was fragile and miserable.

"I really meant to call," she said. "It was that day Melissa was worse again, and I called and canceled our lunch so I could take her back to the doctor, re-member, Claire? But I just forgot, and since it had only happened that once, I didn't think anymore about it. Now he's going to be furious with me again, and I really don't have an excuse, except that Lissa— I don't know what's the matter with me. I used to be so damned *efficient*."

"Don't worry about it," Claire said. "You've got plenty of light from the candles; they look pretty in the living room and dining room. Everybody can see. Nobody's bothering about it. They're eating and drinking and laughing up a storm. It's probably an accident with a power pole somewhere around here. They'll be back on in a minute."

They began putting eggnog ingredients into the

blender bowl, and I went to look out the back door. There were lights up and down the street; ours were still burning, and the street lights and other houses were lit.

Norman Greene came stamping back into the kitchen, cursing under his breath. "There's nothing wrong with the circuit breakers that I can see," he said. "Susan, go call the power company and see what's going on."

"Norm, I'm trying to get this eggnog done," she said. "Don't worry about it, we have plenty of candlelight. Go on out and mingle. I'll bring this in a minute."

"No, I'll do it. You'll just screw it up. Go on and call."

"Honey—"

"Go on!"

She turned and went out of the kitchen, and Claire and I went back into the living room. With the firelight and the flickering candles in the dining and living rooms, the house was only slightly darker than it had been before. People were still laughing and talking in groups and clustering around the buffet table. We joined a group in front of the fireplace, where Walter and Roger and some of the City people were laughing at some piece of Chick Herren's acid foolishness. He is the editor of our morning daily, and a great friend of Walter's and mine. Walter reached out and draped his arm around my shoulders.

"What's with the lights?" he said into my ear.

"I don't know. Nothing that anybody can find. Susan's calling the power company. It really doesn't matter, we don't need them. But he's just having a fit. Blaming her for ruining his precious social triumph. I think he thinks she's cut the main wires or something."

"I hope she has," he said. "Didn't you love it when Holderbein said that about living in Druidwater? Herr Goering isn't going to get over that little gaffe for a while. God, there's a real case of being your own enemy."

What happened next was distressing enough to all of us at the time, but terrifying, I think, only to me then. It was Norman Greene's reaction to it that set people to murmuring after the party. The lights came surging back. They swelled and bloomed and brightened, shimmering into a superintensity of brightness. The stereo began to purr forth music again, and a clattering, banging whine came from the kitchen, followed by a hoarse cry from Norman Greene and a high, shrill cry, as from a child. Then the lights died again, and we stood once more in candlelight. In the living room and dining room people were still and silent, faces turned toward the kitchen. Walter and I snatched up candelabra from the dining room table, and Dr. Holderbein and Chick Herren got candles from tables in the living room. We burst into the kitchen. The bulk of the party crowded behind us.

Norman Greene stood in the middle of the kitchen, his hands held out before him, fingers stretched stiffly apart. He was covered with eggnog. It masked his contorted face, clotted his hair, dripped slowly down the front of the velvet jacket. He was blinded with it. The runaway blender, untended when the lights had come surging back on, had spread it all over the walls, the ceiling, the counters, the floor.

In a corner of the room, beside the refrigerator, Melissa Greene crouched. She was drawn into a fetal position, head on chest, arms crossed over her stomach. She was whimpering and grunting with spasms of pain, and her taffeta skirt was drawn up around her waist. Excrement smeared her clothing and pooled on the floor around her. While we stood in mute horror in the doorway, another spasm wracked her, and another loose flood of feces splattered onto the floor, and she fell over onto the white Italian tiles and lay there, full length, crying monotonously, as though she would never stop.

Chapter Twenty-One

THE NEXT weekend, on a Saturday afternoon, Walter went to Norman Greene and told him what we thought about the house.

He had not wanted to. Despite the fear that had gripped and shaken me like a demented terrier during the days after the party, despite the murmurings that swept the street, despite Norman Greene's half-mad fury and humiliation and Susan's bewildered anguish, I do not think he would have spoken if it had not been for the child. And, of course, for me. But when Claire called late the following week and said that they had had Melissa in the hospital for intensive tests and found that she was suffering from regional ileitis and was very ill, he had reluctantly agreed.

"All right, Colquitt," he said when he had put the phone back in its cradle. He raised his hands, then dropped them helplessly in his lap. "All right. You win. They're going to think we're crazier than hell, but I'm going to talk to them. I still think you're wrong, but maybe they shouldn't stay there. Not if there's the child involved. Maybe they should know about that other stuff."

"You *still* think I'm wrong after that awful scene, after Melissa? You saw it, Walter, you saw every bit of it. Remember what I said about the house going after the precise things that you value most? Well, what do you think that poor, awful fool cares most about? His image, his social standing, his perfect, orderly house, his perfect little pseudo-Wasp parties, his perfect, competent wife and perfect, storybook child, his whole perfect, clockwork life.

"And her, what's her best thing? Him, God help her—his good graces, his opinion of her to run his perfect, stupid house and his perfect, stupid life—and her child. God, that adorable, immaculate little girl, in her ruffled pinafore— So what happened? All at once, in one night, in front of the people he wanted most in the world to impress, standing there dripping eggnog and looking like an utter ass. And his child lying there emptying her bowels in front of all of us. And it wasn't just an accident with her, a one-shot thing—she's sick! She'll be awfully, horribly, *messily* sick for a long, long time! She wasn't sick before they came here. Don't you see, the house isn't even being subtle anymore! It's not taking things one at a time, it's moving too fast, it's not going to give them the *time* it gave the Harralsons or the Sheehans, the child could *die*—" I was nearly incoherent with urgency.

"Colquitt, all I'm saying is, look at how it's going to *sound.* An electrical malfunction, a child with a serious disease—there's nothing *unnatural* about those, taken by themselves."

"They can't be taken by themselves," I said tiredly, "because they didn't happen that way. You said yourself there was *something* wrong over there, you agreed with me—you said we'd wait and see, and if anything else happened to anybody else over there, we'd do something about it."

"I *said* I'd talk to them," he snapped. "And no, you can't go, because the state you're in, they'd laugh you out of the house. Christ, I don't even *pretend* to understand this thing anymore. I'll go, and I'll tell them everything that's happened over there except about us, and Buck and Virginia, and I'll tell them why you— why *we* think it's dangerous for them to stay there. And they're not going to believe a word of it. But at least we'll have done something."

We had not seen the Greenes since that night. Susan Greene had appeared in the kitchen immediately after we had all gotten to the kitchen door, and had cried out in distress and pain at the sight of her pitiful, soiled child. I don't think she even saw her white-sodden husband. She had scooped Melissa up into her arms and run with her up the stairs, and Claire had followed, carrying a candelabrum. Most of the guests had crowded into the kitchen, exclaiming in helpless sympathy and embarrassment, and among us all we had soothed and reassured Norman Greene back into a cracked kind of mobility. Walter and Roger Swanson had taken him into the downstairs bathroom, and Gwen Parsons and I had gotten paper towels and tackled the worst of the eggnog. Dr. Holderbein, bless his dear, froggy heart, had rummaged in the kitchen cabinets and found bottles of Scotch and vodka and had set up a perfunctory bar in the living room, and Semmes Jennings had brought melting ice from the dead refrigerator, and Chick Herren had marshaled everyone back into the living room and handed out drinks. By the time Norman Greene had reappeared, washed and combed and clad in a lustrous ultrasuede jacket, the party was struggling lamely along in a ghastly parody of normalcy and niceness.

Norman Greene was white-faced and coldly furious, and when Chick put a drink in his hand, he tossed it down without seeming to know what he was doing. He set the glass down and faced us. The stilted chatting stopped and everyone looked at him in silence.

"I apologize to you all for my wife," he said in a loud, flattened voice. "She'll apologize to you herself, I'm sure, when she's seen to Melissa. I have asked her to have the wiring taken care of, but apparently she has forgotten. I wouldn't have dreamed of subjecting any of you to this if I had known it had not been repaired."

I gasped, my face burning at the sheer treachery of it. A babel of voices rose around him assuring him that it was nothing, he mustn't worry about it, things like that happened to everybody, the only important thing was the child. Several people began to tell rambling, disjointed stories of malfunctions and embarrassments in their own homes, and a grandly disheveled old doyenne bellowed, "My dear Professor Greene, I was at a pink tea in one of the city's finest old homes, and the toilets backed up. This was *nothing* to that, believe me."

We all collapsed into the helpless laughter of release, and Norman Greene managed a slitted, wounded shark's smile. But the evening was broken, of course, and guests began to glance at watches and murmur about the time and retrieve their coats from the downstairs bedroom. Norman Greene stood in the middle of his emptying living room saying helplessly, "No, it's early, please wait for a minute. Susan will want to say goodnight," but they murmured politely, "Please don't trouble her, we'll let ourselves out," and "Please don't worry, we had a marvelous time," and "We'll have to get together at our house in a week or two." The living room emptied quickly of everyone but Walter and me and Roger Swanson.

Claire and Susan Greene came down the stairs then. Susan had changed into an emerald silk caftan, and though her face was pale and her blue eyes large with strain and worry, managed to look self-possessed and nearly normal. Claire followed her, tight-mouthed.

"I apologize," Susan began on the landing. "I don't know what on *earth*—" She looked into the empty living room and stopped. She looked at her husband. "Where is everybody?" she said.

"They went home of course," said Norman Greene loudly, his back to her. "What did you expect them to do? Stay and play in the eggnog and the—the manure? You haven't been able to keep the clothes clean or the curtains hung since we moved in here, so I don't know why I expected you to be able to give a simple party in relative peace. I guess you realize that this has probably ruined me at the college."

"Norm," she said tentatively.

He wheeled around, his face blind and silver-eyed and terrible. "I *told* you to call an electrician," he roared. "I told you last week. I *told* you to take Melissa to a babysitter tonight, you *knew* she was having that . . . trouble . . ."

"Norman, that's *why* I didn't want to take her out tonight," cried Susan Greene. "I knew she didn't feel well—I'm not going to farm her out when she's sick. I didn't realize it was this bad; it hasn't *been* this bad; she's been better lately. You know that. But we're going to have to get her to a doctor tomorrow. I just wanted to let her tell people where to put their coats and then put her to bed. You know how she's been looking forward to that. I'm sorry about the lights, but I didn't think—"

"That's right!" It was a howl of rage, primal and out of control. "You didn't think! You didn't think nine years ago when you— You haven't been thinking ever since we moved in here—"

"Shut up, Norman," Claire hissed. "Just shut up. You're making an utter ass of yourself, and I'm not going to listen to you bully Susan anymore."

She stood, breathing heavily, for a moment, looking up into his face. He said nothing.

"I'm sorry, Susan," Claire said. "I have an awful mouth. I'll call you in the morning to check on Melissa. You ought to get back to her now. I think we should go home."

She went into the bedroom and returned with their coats. She and Roger walked to the door. Susan and Norman Greene looked after them.

"See you folks later," sweet Roger Swanson mumbled.

"I'm sorry, Norman," Claire said briefly, and they went out.

"We'd better go too," I said, looking desperately at Walter. His face was remote, and I knew that he had simply gone away to some private place inside his head, as he does when he is angry and upset and does not want to show it.

We went home. We did not talk about it that night.

At two o'clock the following Saturday afternoon Walter looked out to see if both the Greenes' cars were there, and then shrugged on his sheepskin jacket and slogged reluctantly across the sodden driveway and up the rhododendron bank to their house. I looked after him, watching while he rang the doorbell, thinking how alone he looked with the house towering around him, and the wet, green-black winter trees. Dwarfed. I was suddenly and terribly, childishly frightened for him and wanted to call him back. Let the stupid, intrusive Greenes wrestle it out by themselves. I hadn't wanted them there. Norman Greene was an impossible bully, a mean-spirited, rigid tyrant, a voracious climber. Susan Greene was a spineless jellyfish to take his abuse, and take it, and take it. I thought of the subterranean estrangement between Claire and me and flushed with anger. And then I saw again the embarrassed love, the hurting incomprehension in Susan's plain, pleasant face, and I thought of the child. No. We were right. They had to know.

I went into the kitchen and made a batch of red clam sauce for spaghetti, and riffled through the record albums and found the florid, familiar Chopin etudes that have soothed me through more than one crisis, and settled down on the den sofa with *The New Yorker*. Razz and Foster curled up in an elaborately ignoring heap at my feet on the afghan, and we all fell asleep. When Walter let himself back into the house it was close to five o'clock and dark was falling down through a rising wind.

His face was burned red with wind and cold, but there were vertical white furrows on each side of his mouth. He passed through the den without a word and went to hang up his coat. I heard him back in the kitchen getting a glass out of the cupboard, and ice clinked and a cork thunked.

"Bring me one," I said in sleep-distorted dread. He came into the den carrying two Scotches.

"Well? What happened?"

"He showed me the door is what happened. Ordered me out of his house. Said never to darken his door again. Said he'd call the police if he ever caught me with so much as a foot on his property. *Fini*. End of song."

"Walter, oh, baby, not really!"

"Oh, yes, really. I don't know as I blame him, to tell you the truth. I mean, it was a bad overreaction, but I could hear my own voice going on and on for almost three damned hours, and I sounded . . . crazy. Just crazy. Worse than I thought I would. I knew how I sounded, I knew I was screwing it all up. There's no way you can get across the—the *horror* of the stuff that's happened over there unless you've lived in the middle of it from the beginning. I could hear how I sounded to them. I should have just apologized and cut it short and come home."

"Oh, honey, I'm so sorry! I should have gone; it's me who really thinks all that stuff, not you! I wouldn't have cared how I sounded."

"Yes, you would, because you'd have sounded just

as flat-out insane, as I did. Those people had no idea what's happened over there, and then somebody comes in out of nowhere and starts telling them about miscarriages, and strokes, and dead puppies, and fags, and dead kids in Vietnam, and television programs that weren't on, and dead kids on telephones, and then says that there might be something unnatural in the house and they ought to move out immediately. You try saying that to people who don't know anything about that house, who haven't lived through some of this, and see what kind of reaction you get. Jesus H. Christ on a crutch, Colquitt, even Claire wouldn't listen to you, and she *knows* about that stuff!"

"Not about the last thing—not about Buck and Virginia! Not about . . . us. She'd believe that."

"Tell her, then! Tell the Greenes if you want to. We probably *should* have told somebody about them in the very beginning. Do you think the Greenes would believe me if I went running back over there now and said, 'Oh, by the way, the capper is that I caught my wife kissing the architect in your kitchen and almost killed them both with a knife, and my wife found the last guy who lived here screwing the lady next door, and it put *his* wife in the funny farm forever more?' Do you think that would change anything now?"

"But they didn't *know* Virginia, they didn't *know* Buck, they couldn't know how . . . impossible it would be for them to do that! They didn't know Kim, and they don't know us, not really."

"Claire did. Claire does. You want to tell Claire?"

"No," I moaned. "I can't tell anybody, ever. You know we can't do that."

"I know." He slumped back against the sofa cushions and rubbed his eyes tiredly. My heart strained.

"But, Walter, why did he get so mad? I mean, even if he thought you were a stark, raving lunatic, he must have seen that you were serious, that you were terribly concerned for their welfare. I mean, he could have just—thanked you, and not believed you—"

"Colquitt, he chose to think that I came over and told him that because we couldn't stand him and wanted to scare him out of the neighborhood. He got hysterical. Just went bananas. He was screaming stuff about anti-Semitism, and all of us thinking we were better than he was, and that he had, by God, worked all his life to live well, in a house like that, to get a teaching position at a college with some prestige, and no rich, effeminate Wasp was going to scare him off with lies and shit about haunting. He said he didn't give a damn if the whole town wanted to ride him out on a rail, he wasn't moving out. He said his little Wasp wife might toady up to all her Wasp buddies, but he was goddamned if he would. I'm surprised somebody didn't call the police, he was making so much noise."

"Oh, God," I whispered, "I never thought of that. Of course that's *just* how he'd take it. Poor damned fool. He'll never leave now. They're just . . . doomed. They're gone."

"Well, right now I couldn't care less," Walter said bitterly. "About him, anyway. I haven't exactly been thrown out of many houses in my lifetime, whatever else I may have accomplished. It's quite uniquely humiliating."

"What about her? Was she there?" I asked in dread and pain. "What about Melissa?"

"Melissa is in the hospital, and will be for quite a while, I gather. But, oh, yes, she was there. For almost the first time since they took Melissa to the hospital, getting some rest. She was there, all right. I made a clean sweep of it. She was absolutely scared to death. I think she'd have snatched the kid out of the hospital and left that house and this town that minute when I finished telling them about it if he hadn't turned it all around on her. He said it was all her fault, that she was such a slob nobody wanted to be around them, nobody could stand being in her house. He said she had herself to thank if his whole career went down the tube and her child grew up without any friends and none of us ever spoke to them again. He was very eloquent."

"Oh, my God, what have I done?" I cried. "I never meant to let such horrible, awful things loose."

"It's not your fault, Col," he said bleakly, pulling me close and spilling my Scotch. "I agreed with you.

214

I may have blown it, but I guess we had to try. I think I'd do it again if I had to. Whatever his reaction, they deserved to know what's happened over there."

"Maybe I could go talk to her . . ."

"No. Let her alone. I've scared her to death, and he's torn her practically to pieces. I started to defend her when he jumped on her, and that's when he threw me out. They're not going to want to see either one of us again. I'd almost hope whatever it is over there jerks a knot in his stupid Nazi neck, if she wasn't there."

"But she is," I said, beginning to sob with weariness and hopelessness. "She is."

Late that night Claire called. "Susan Greene has just left," she said. "She told me what you'd sent Walter over there to say. I know it was your doing. I just called to say that you've succeeded in practically destroying her, if that's what you set out to do. You couldn't have picked a better way to do it. He's been as brutal to her as it's humanly possible to be, and Walter has scared her within an inch of her life, and her child is desperately ill, and you can chalk up a good day's work. I don't want to see you again, Colquitt, and I don't care who knows what you've done this time. I'm going to tell everybody I know that you're a jealous, vindictive, *crazy* woman. People ought to be *warned* about you."

Her voice broke and she hung up before I could answer. I felt nothing. For days after that I walked in a void of stillness and emptiness.

SHE WAS as good as her word. The next weekend we went to the club for lunch. Walter made me go. He said it was still our world and we had to live in it. I knew he was right, but I shrank from entering the dining room. Claire and Roger often lunched there on Sundays. But they were not in the room. Martin Sawyer, Walter's warm-weather tennis partner, was, though, with his wife and some people I did not know. They were at a table near the fireplace, and as we passed on our way to a vacant table for two by the wide, mullioned windows, Martin called out, "Hey,

215

Walter! What's this I hear about ghosties and ghoulies next door to you?"

"You'd be surprised what we've got next door to us," Walter called back cheerfully, and they laughed, and we sat down. I saw Martin talking to the strangers and gesturing in our direction, and they looked at us and smiled, but the smiles were constrained and uneasy. Martin saw me looking at them and raised his glass in an affable, silent toast. That was to be the tack, then. Amusement, constraint, and polite incredulity.

A few days after that Walter came home later than usual and was silent and abstracted during dinner.

"Okay, what?" I said finally, when the silence had spun on into the evening. The television set beat futilely against it.

"Well, Charlie called me in just as I was leaving. He asked me what the hell was going on over here. He said he'd been hearing some pretty funny stuff about us thinking the house next door was . . . not quite right or something. I tried to gloss it over, but then he said old Winkler, he of the prison bed empire, had called him this afternoon and pulled his account. Said he didn't want his firm's impeccable old name connected with weirdo goings-on like that."

"Oh, Walter. Oh, dear God."

"Oh, it's no great loss. Charlie was laughing about it. The guy's been a royal pain in the ass ever since we got the account. It didn't amount to a hill of beans as far as billing went, and the creative department is going to rejoice mightily. Charlie said we probably ought to lie low on talking about it, though—meaning you and me. He said the guy had heard about it from somebody he didn't even know, at a Rotary meeting or something."

"Did you tell Charlie about it? About what we think, I mean?"

"No. I'm going to have to, though. I made a date for drinks with him Friday after work. You want to come along?"

"I guess I ought to. I'm the one that got you into all this."

"No need if you don't want to. I guess it would be

216

better if it was just me, at that. If anybody in the world will understand, Charlie will. I should have told him everything tonight, but I just didn't feel like talking about it."

"No. Of course you didn't."

Another card came from Kim Dougherty the next day. I read it up in my office, with Vivaldi splashing from the radio and my coffee pot bubbling, and Foster's grating, sleepy purr making a cosy counterpoint to both. Outside the late January wind prowled and fingered the shutters and ticked the bare, wet twigs of the big water oak against my windows, but inside it was warm and rosy-lit, womblike. I was spending a lot of time up there during those weeks, the still weeks of waiting again.

"Things are looking up," wrote Kim in his sprawling, flyaway hand. "I'm on staff now in restorations, in strictly a lackey's position. I have a room in the old section, in a funny, narrow old house that leans right out over the Arno. And I have met me one tough lady. I'll write more later. I just wanted you to know I'm alive."

Chapter Twenty-Two

FOR A time after that Walter and I lived very quietly in a shell of routine and household ritual and ordinariness. We were both strangely tired and went to bed early most evenings and slept heavily and dreamlessly. A kind of peace settled over us, the sort of narrow peace that I imagined pioneer families lived in during the bitter black winters, when dark fell early and lingered late, and snow piled silently against doors and windows, and commerce with the outside world was suspended until spring. Our normal winter world of work and shopping and errands and dinners on trays before the fire in the den expanded to envelop us totally, to absorb and swallow us.

We drew closer than ever to each other. It seemed then, for a space of time, that we were sufficient unto ourselves; we might have been strangers in a strange city, newly married, knowing no one and needing no one. There was about that time a timelessness. We dwelled little on the recent past, and not at all on the future, the spring and summer to come. Television and the radio, the newspapers and books became very important to us; we followed the local professional basketball and hockey teams with an attention that bordered on obsession, and watched programs on television that ordinarily would have left us limp with boredom or gasping with disbelieving laughter. We both read the papers from cover to cover as avidly as homesick exiles in a foreign country might devour the papers from home. I pulled out my cache of seldom-used cookbooks and experimented with exotic recipes for curries and Chinese dishes and elaborate, spiced stews and soups, spending long hours, after I had finished my day's work, in my bright, shuttered kitchen. We ate the dishes judiciously, lingering over them and rating their relative merits with the absorbed seriousness of gastronomes. Walter painted the woodwork in the dining room and kitchen, and we repapered the downstairs bathroom. We went to few of the small, informal dinner parties that flourish on our street in the cold months. It was not that we were not invited. Few were given. With the Guthries away, and the cold silence between Claire and me, the street seemed to draw in upon itself, as Walter and I had done, and lights glowed most evenings only from the backs of houses, where kitchens and dens were.

We saw nothing of the Greenes, or of Norman Greene, anyway. His shining, clifflike Lincoln left early on those mornings; I would hear it start in the driveway next door before it was light, while I was still showering or dressing in our bedroom. I did not pull aside the curtains to watch him drive away. I knew that Melissa was home from the hospital, for the time being, anyway. I saw Susan Greene from my office windows occasionally, carrying the bundled-up child to her car, and they would drive away, to return an hour or so later. I assumed they were going to the doctor. Susan did not look up toward my window to wave, as she had in the early days of their occupancy. She looked drawn and tired, and her small, square body under the smart, belted green coat she wore seemed diminished, shrunken somehow, as if she were losing weight. At the one ballet guild meeting I went to that winter, safe in the knowledge that Claire was not a member, Eloise Jennings told me that they were attempting to treat Melissa at home, but further hospitalization would be necessary if she did not improve soon.

"Well, at least she won't feel like she has to give another of those awful parties, with Melissa sick," Eloise went on, oblivious to the slanting look of fury Gwen Parsons shot her and the sudden small silence that fell in the room. Eyes turned toward her.

"Although even that would be better than sitting home all winter, like we've been doing," she continued. "Have you ever known things to be so dull around here? I guess, with Charles and Virginia gone and Colquitt and Claire not speaking . . . I don't know what you all are fighting about, Colquitt, but I wish you'd patch it up. You're ruining everybody else's social life. Oh, come on, we're among friends," she caroled when Gwen attempted to interrupt her. "Everybody knows they've had a tiff."

The eyes turned to me, embarrassed but veiled, with speculation and something else behind them. Eloise saw that she had the group's attention and, flown with her success, said in a coy singsong, "Could it possibly have anything to do with a certain haunted house, Colquitt? Now, *that's* the best thing I've heard all winter. I told Semmes the other night—"

"You talk too much, Eloise," I said, setting my cup and plate aside and getting up. "You're a regular one-woman transmitting station. Thanks for the refreshments, Marilyn. I'll bring those press releases by when I'm done with them." And I walked out of the room and got my coat from the closet in the foyer.

Behind me silence rang like a bell, and then a soft, murmuring surf of women's voices broke, and I could hear Eloise saying aggrievedly, "Well, I'm sure I never meant to *offend* her, but everybody's talking about what she and Walter told Susan and Norman Greene, and if she can't take a little kidding—"

"Oh, shut up, Eloise," I heard Gwen Parsons say, and I let myself out the front door. I did not go back to the ballet guild, and I did not tell Walter about the incident.

I knew that people probably were talking now, and not just on the street. But we saw few people that winter, and so I did not know, nor did I think much about, the extent of the speculation.

Toward the end of February the weather turned bitter cold, black-ice cold, and the temperature dropped to 12 degrees, then 10, then 8. An ice storm came hissing and slithering out of the north, silent and feral in the night, and in the morning there was desolation and ruin. Trees and power lines were down, streets were sheeted solid with pocked gray ice, lights and heat were gone from many homes and businesses in the city. Our neighborhood was not so badly hit as some, but it was two days before we had lights and heat. Walter could not get to work, and judging from the cars parked in driveways on our street, neither could anyone else.

We lost no trees, but a monster oak was down in the Guthries' garden, and a great limb had crashed through the roof of the Jenningses' house. Walter, returning from a skittering, windmilling foray up and down the street to assess the damage, said that the Jenningses had packed up and gone, probably to Eloise's parents' scanty little frame house on the south side of town, as the radio reported no vacancies in any of the hotels and motels around the metropolitan area. Semmes would hate that, I knew; he saw as little of his in-laws as decency allowed, and the children would whine and weep and overflow the little house, and would probably all catch sodden, nose-running colds. I was unashamedly delighted at the thought.

Walter reported that several other houses looked to be empty, but that both Claire and Roger's cars were parked in their driveway and smoke was coming from their chimney. Smoke plumed from the Greenes' chimneys, too, and flickering lights appeared in some windows and disappeared and reappeared in others. I thought the Greenes were making do, as we were, with candlelight and the fireplaces, and I knew that Susan's stove was gas. In any other time I would have gone over to see if they or the child needed anything we might have to offer, but of course I did not. If the child worsened, I knew that they would take her back to the hospital.

We closed off all our rooms but the kitchen and den and kept a fire roaring, and slept the first night on sofa cushions pulled up in front of the fireplace. My stove was gas too, and it generated enough heat, if we left the door open, to warm the kitchen and cook simple meals. In the manner of children, who love the novelty of natural disasters and the disruption of routine, we enjoyed the two days even while we listened guiltily to the litany of disaster and hardship and privation pouring in over the transistor radio. Nothing had to be thought of but warmth and survival; the enforced isolation gave a sort of sanction to our own self-imposed exile. We read aloud to each other by the light of an old kerosene lantern Walter had never gotten around to throwing away, and dozed fitfully in turn, one of us always awake to keep the fire going. We played Scrabble and chess and started a mind-boggling jigsaw puzzle of the Unicorn Tapestries at the Cloisters. Razz and Foster, fizzy-tailed and wild-eyed with the storm, prowled the shrunken perimeters of their winter kingdom and finally burrowed nests for themselves deep in the tumbled sofa afghan and slept.

At nine o'clock on the evening of the second day without lights someone hammered at the kitchen door, an urgent, insistent rattling against the frozen panes. I had tacked a blanket over the glass and we could not see out. Having heard radioed accounts of sporadic looting in the blackened ghetto neighborhoods, we hesitated for a moment, looking at each other, and then Claire's voice came, calling, "Colquitt! Walter! Are you there? Let me in!"

Her voice sounded strange and high. We scrambled for the door and pulled it open, and she stumbled into the kitchen, her hair wild around her face, dressed only in woolen slacks and a sweater and sneakers. I pulled her, stumbling, into the den, and pushed her down onto the cushions in front of the fire, and Walter dislodged the cats and draped the sofa afghan around her shoulders. She was shivering so hard that it was a moment before she could speak. Fire, I thought. Their house has caught fire, and their phone isn't working. But then I remembered that phones on our street were working; I had talked to Gwen Parsons that morning.

"What's the matter?" Walter said. "What's happened?"

"It's Duck," she gasped, breathless, beginning to cry. Her face was leached to an unearthly white in the leaping firelight and there were the frozen silver tracks of tears on it.

"It's Duck. He called, he just called—" She could not go on.

"What's the matter with Duck?" I said, my heart cold and still with dread. "Claire, is he sick? Has there been an accident? What—"

She drew a deep, shuddering breath and looked up at me. Her face was ravaged, wrecked, blasted, ruined. "Duck is married," she said, her voice trembling like a hurt child's. "Duck got married three days ago and has dropped out of Yale and isn't going back. They drove to Maryland and got married, and they're staying with her sister in Alexandria until he can get a job and they can find somewhere to live. He isn't coming home. He isn't even coming home! I don't even know where he is now, because he wouldn't tell us! Roger was going to go there, Roger was going to go get them and bring them home, but Duck said if he came they wouldn't be at the sister's, they'd go somewhere else and we wouldn't be able to find them! Oh, Colquitt, he's just . . . thrown it all away, all of it, everything . . ."

She was crying with the deep, tearing, uncontrollable sobs that do not allow even breath, and I held her and rocked her shoulders and murmured to her in distress and grief until the awful keening slid into soft, tired breathing. Walter went into the kitchen and brought back the brandy bottle and three glasses. In a little while she was able to sip some and to talk again.

"Tell me, Claire. Start from the beginning," I

coaxed. "Who did Duck marry? Do you know the girl? Was it Libby?"

"Oh, of course Libby," she said. "Who else? We knew they would one day, and that was fine, that was perfectly all right, but not like this—not just . . . throwing away his whole future, not running off in the night, dropping out of school. What kind of life can he possibly have now, with no education, with no money, with a baby—"

"A baby?"

"Oh, yes, a baby. She's pregnant. Why else would they—and besides, he told us she was. About three months' pregnant, and never said a word to Ford and Anne. Afraid to, I guess; you know how Ford has always been about her, how terribly strict. Roger's gone over there now to see what we can do about it, but Duck said they didn't know about the baby. Libby wouldn't let him call them. Libby told them she wanted to visit Dorothy—you know, the oldest Fleming girl, the one who works in Senator Gordon's office. And since it was finals week at Chase and she'd finished, they let her go, and she and Duck met in some terrible little town in Maryland and got a justice of the peace to marry them, and that's that. He asked us to tell the Flemings, so I guess Roger's done that by now."

Walter and I looked at each other. Claire's labored breathing was the only sound in the room for a time. Then I said, "Claire, I know it's an awful shock to you, but nowadays—I mean, kids just don't *have* to get married anymore—there are . . . other options."

"You mean abortion?" She grinned at me, a mirthless, awful death's-head grin. "Ford Fleming's daughter? She'd die first, she'd literally die. I think Duck would too. He says he wants this child; he says he's glad to be married. I said, well, why not let her, oh, go away and have the child and put it up for adoption, and I said we'd pay for it if Ford and Anne were opposed to that, but I know they wouldn't be in the long run. But he said absolutely not, he was going to go to work and support his family like any man would, and later, maybe, he'd go back and finish school. But, oh, Colquitt, he won't; they never do. And of course his scholarship's down the drain now, so we said we'd pay their living expenses if he'd just stay in school and finish, and pay for the baby and all, but he wouldn't hear of that either. Oh, my God, my baby, my good, bright boy—"

"You couldn't . . . stop it somehow? I mean, are they both eighteen?" Walter said.

"Yes. Both of them. Libby's birthday was right after Christmas. It's legal, it's perfectly legal, and there's not a thing in the world we can do about it! With any other kids, I'd say maybe, after things cooled down, they'd listen to reason, they'd come home and talk it out with us, they'd let us help, but she's so afraid of her father, and you know Duck. He does what he says he's going to do. He always did, from the time he was a little, little boy. He was always so . . . *honorable*."

I said nothing, because there was nothing to say. I did know Duck. Claire was right. Having done this thing, he would see it through. He would accept no help. He had never been a childish child; he was Roger to the core. I remembered a summer day when he was about ten and had been cleaning debris out of our creek, and had brought a slim, vivid green whip of a small snake, cradled carefully in his hands, to my back door.

"I found him in the creek, Mrs. Kennedy," he'd said, "and I thought I might take him home and see how he works. It's really neat the way all those little bone things fit together, like a zipper. See? But I wanted to ask you first, because he's your snake."

My eyes filled at the memory of the small boy and the little snake, and the gentle, cupped hands.

"Claire, dearest baby, I'm so terribly sorry," I said, and she looked up at me over the rim of the brandy glass.

"I know you are," she said. "I came to tell you you were right. You were right, and I was a stupid damned fool, and I'd give anything in the world if I'd listened to you, and now it's too late."

"Right about what?"

"About that house," she said, and the venom in her voice shocked me. It was pure, palpable, hissing hatred. "That damned evil, hovering, sneaking, crouching, monstrous killer of a house over there. You told me, you knew, you tried to tell me when Susan and Norman first moved in, and I thought you were *jealous* of me and Susan Greene, and all the time you *knew* . . . well. It's too late to apologize to you, because you should hate me for the things I've said about you, and it's too late to help Duck, but I can tell you right now that we're getting out of here before it touches Roger or one of the other boys. We're moving, just as soon as I·can find a house big enough, and I don't care where it is so long as it's as far away from this street and that house as I can get. I'm not going to stay here one minute longer than—"

"Claire, what in the name of God are you talking about?" I said.

"That's where it happened, of course," Claire said. "That night—you remember—the night of Gwen and Carey's party, around the first of December? Don't you remember—Libby was baby-sitting with Melissa, and I said to Susan, 'Well, don't think she's doing you a favor, because Duck will be over there before you're out the door,' or something? And Norman made those awful cracks about them? Well, Duck *was* over there. He went. And they . . . after Melissa was asleep, they . . . it was the first time, Colquitt. He told me it was, and I absolutely believe him. You know how Libby is—was. And Duck's funny; I'm not such a fool as to believe he's never—slept with a girl before, but he simply would not, not with Libby. He loves her. He really does. They've gone together since eighth grade. There never was a time they didn't plan to get married, someday—and he would not just casually—he *says* so. He says he just doesn't know what came over them; one minute they were watching TV and eating popcorn, and the next minute— But I know what came over them. You know, don't you? It's the same thing that came over Buddy Harralson and Lucas Abbott. And Anita Sheehan. And it happened to Virginia too, didn't it? Or something awful did, there in that house. I got too close to it, didn't I, Col? *Interfered* with it somehow. So it reached out for me, only not me but someone who means more to me than my own life. And I will *not* stay and wait for it to—to—get at Roger or Rog or Tommy. I don't *care* what Roger thinks, we're moving."

She stopped, breathless and blank-faced and wild-eyed, and Walter said, "What *does* Roger think about all this, Claire? About moving, I mean. Does he believe what you think about the house?"

"I don't know what he thinks, because I haven't talked to him about it yet, but I'm going to. He can think I'm just as crazy as you, Col—and God forgive me that—but we're going to move no matter what he thinks. And if he won't, I'll take the children and go without him."

"He wouldn't let you do that," I said.

"No," Claire said. "I don't think he would. Whatever he says, in the end we'll move. It may take a while, but we will. And if you had one ounce of sense, you'd go too—you, of all people, who caught on— but if you don't, that's your affair. Stay and warn people if you think that's the noble thing to do, but you'll regret it."

"Are you going to tell people, Claire?" I asked almost conversationally. We three might have made a scene from an eighteenth-century madhouse, sitting there in the primal firelight talking of unutterable things. A tableau out of Bedlam. I felt only bone-deep fatigue and a ghost of remembered grief and fear.

"No. I'm not going to tell anybody. We're just going to move and live our lives and not say another word *ever* about it to a living soul. I don't want to talk about it anymore. I don't want to see that house ever again. I don't *care* what happens to it or to anybody who lives there so long as my family is away from it. It's . . . insane, and crazy, and awful. Things like this don't happen; I don't have the equipment to deal with this. But I wanted to tell you—I wanted you to know that I—"

"I know. Don't say anything more about it. We won't talk about it anymore. I promise we won't ever mention it again. But, Claire, please don't just move out tomorrow. Think about it when you feel better."

"I'm not ever going to feel better about this," she said.

"What do you think we ought to do about the Greenes, then?" Walter asked.

"I don't care what you do about them. You warned them, didn't you? You saw how far that got you, didn't you? I care about her and the child, but not enough to have everybody in town talking about me and my family the way they are about you and Colquitt. And I know I'm responsible for that. Do you think that's not going to haunt me to my grave? I can never, never make that up to you, but it's *not* going to happen to us. Not to my children. If you ever tell anybody what I've told you tonight, either of you, I'll swear you're lying. I will. I'll swear you're lying and crazy and anything else in the world I have to swear. I know that makes me the lowest crud who ever walked the earth, but I'm going to salvage what's left of my family's *normalcy* while there still is some, and we're going to have a decent, sane life if it kills me. If you still want to be my friend on those terms, I'd be proud to have you, and I wouldn't deserve it. But those are the terms."

"I accept them," I said. "Any terms you want. No mention of the house ever again. No mention of any of it. I've never been so miserable in my life as I have these past few weeks when you were so . . . gone away from me. There isn't anything worth that."

She began to cry again and put her arms around me and hugged me. "So have I been," she said, weeping. "So have I. I love you, Colquitt. I couldn't stand it if anything happened to either of you. Please, God, listen to me and get out of here before something terrible happens to you. I can't lose you twice."

When she was quieter I bundled her into one of my coats and a scarf, and Walter got the flashlight and walked her back home. I went with them to the edge of the driveway. The clouds had parted and the moon sailed, high and white and dead, among the flying tatters. In the moonlight the ice-sheathed trees tossed and tinkled like great crystal hands fingering the sky, weaving and reweaving an incantation over the sweetly sleeping shape of the house next door.

Chapter Twenty-Three

CLAIRE DID not change her mind about moving, as I had thought she might after the initial pain and shock of Duck's marriage subsided. The next week she began looking for another house, poring over the Sunday real estate sections of the paper and driving through the neighborhoods she thought might be compatible, following the winding streets that had home-for-sale signs on the corners. She did not go to Margaret Matthieson, who handled most of the buyings and sellings in our set, or to any of the other brokers she knew. I did not ask her why, but I thought I knew: she wanted no explanations, no more talk.

There had been some talk, quiet ripplings of surprise and curiosity, when the news about Duck and Libby's marriage filtered through the neighborhood, but she had been publicly wry and resigned about it in her brisk, nose-crinkling manner, and even though people must have suspected it was a marriage of convenience, no one knew for sure, and would not for some time. So there were tentative congratulations too and no real surprise. Duck and Libby's eventual marriage had long been a foregone conclusion on the street. Claire said only, when asked what the children's plans were, that Duck was going to work a while in Washington and then they'd see where things went from there. Only Walter and I and the Flemings knew that he had taken a sort of clerk's job with the Postal Service and that they were living in a cramped and faded second-floor apartment out beyond Catholic University, on the northeastern fringes of the city. Claire and Roger had flown up to see them, and Ford Fleming had gone too, but they refused to come home. Claire talked little to me about Duck. I do not know how she persuaded Roger to make the move; we did not see much of him, and he did not speak of it when we did. I don't think anyone else on the street knew that they were looking for another house.

With the barriers gone between me and Claire, I had hoped we would be close again, close and easy and affectionate, as we had always been. We did spend a lot of time together at first, just after the night she had come to tell us about the marriage. I went with her on several of her house-hunting expeditions, and we would walk through this sprawling old house and that one, me trying to imagine my own things in the alien spaces, placing a sofa here, a secretary there, thinking what I would do with this breakfast room or that sun porch. It has always been a game to me, prowling through those houses whose families don't, for one reason or another, want them anymore. A rather poignant game, because there is about a waiting house a sort of mournful abandonment, a wistful air of "Why are you leaving me? What went wrong?" Even when the families are still in residence, their possessions still in place, their dishes still in cabinets, their clothes still in closets, there is a melancholy air of finish, a breath of ending.

It is a titillating game too, because it is exhilarating to me to imagine Walter and me living within new walls that do not know the shape of us yet, walking on earth and among trees that have not yet felt our fingers and spades or lent us their shade. But it is in the end only a game, because it is unimaginable to me, even now, that we should live anywhere other than where we do.

It was not a game to Claire. Armed with lists and pages of measurements and stern requirements, she would work her way through the houses, eyes measuring as coldly and precisely as a computer, making a note about peeling paint here, about small closets there, about an extra-generous dining room or kitchen in yet another. She would consult her lists and check off her requirements one by one.

Outside in the car, or when we had stopped for lunch, she would study her notes and discard this and that house and make a check mark on the ones she wanted to come back to. There were few of those, and in the end there were none. I said nothing, even when we had just been through a house that seemed to me altogether splendid, and perfect for the Swansons. Many of them were out of Walter's and my range entirely, but money was hardly an object for the Swansons. The simple fact was that, for all her clear-eyed efficiency and matter-of-fact demeanor, Claire loved her house and was bleeding inside at the thought of leaving it. But she did not say so, and so the search went on.

When we first picked up our mended friendship I had felt almost giddy with it, as I remember feeling in the early days of college, when I had left home for the first time in my life and everything and everybody was as new as I was, and anything was possible. The city seemed a totally new and provocative territory to me, misted in a kind of glamour, with promise and portent dancing around every corner, glancing with the sun off every soaring downtown tower. After the numbed days spent alone with Walter or the few clients I had seen, Claire's company was like that of a companion only recently met but with whom you know a sweet, strong alliance is going to develop. I felt absurdly young and gay and chattered and laughed with sheer silliness. Claire did too for a time, even when I knew the pain and unease were weighing heavily on her. We laughed at the people we saw in restaurants and joked cruelly about the owners of the houses we inspected, and once we spent an entire afternoon in a scarred and carved back booth in a drive-in that was the province of students from a local engineering college, drinking beer and talking about our own college days. I would come in from those afternoons flushed with the raw March cold and the unburdened closeness, and Walter would look at me and smile and say, "You look like a kid who's sneaked off from the sorority house and drunk a six-pack behind the stadium."

"I feel like it," I said to him once, early on. "I feel twenty years younger and have been making a perfect ass of myself."

"It's about time," he said, but his smile was guarded.

But you can't go back, not really, not at our ages, Claire's and mine. There was too much weight of living, too much history between the people we were now and the times we had struggled back to. We could not really reach those times, and we had nothing else of substance to talk about. Too much that was forbidden, taboo, lay between us. Our mutual histories were what we had had in common; what we had loved about each other was what we had become because of our histories, and we had agreed not to speak of the most recent portions of those. The house, the horror, the pain, the unbelievable that we both now believed lay between us like the carcass of a great, dead animal. It could not be spoken of, and it could not be gotten around. It canceled our mutual past, and it lay over any mutual future we might have like one of those black holes in space that had frightened me so unreasonably and awfully when Walter read about them to me from *Time*.

Finally we found ourselves lapsing into small silences, and casting about for something else to talk about, and meeting, then shying away from, each other's eyes. The aching void of loss I felt when I thought of Claire and Roger gone from the street would swim over me, and she, catching my thoughts, would snap back into the rigid grid of her steely efficiency and say, "Well there's time to look at one more. There's one over on Maidstone that sounds interesting. See if you can get the waiter while I run to the ladies'." And we would shrug back into our coats and our years and go out into the wind once more. I did not go out with her so often after the silences began, and she did not call so frequently.

Once, desperate to get her back, to rebuild what we had had, I broached the subject of Norman and Susan Greene. They were not strictly on the forbidden list, but we had not talked about them, I knew that she had not seen Susan Greene since the night at our house, and I thought that Susan must be hurt and bewildered by the defection. I thought that Melissa must be better, because I did not see Susan take her to the car so often these days for the trips to the doctor. But still, worry must hang heavy over her sandy head, and she would wonder why Claire did not come anymore.

"Have you seen anything of Susan Greene lately?" I asked over the last lunch we were to share together.

Claire frowned. "No," she said. "I've talked to her a couple of times, but I've been so busy with this house-hunting. I really ought to have her over, but she doesn't like to leave Melissa."

"Is she better?"

"Susan says she thinks so. They've got her on some kind of steroid and it seems to be doing the trick. Maybe there won't have to be an operation. I hope not." She might have been talking about an acquaintance, someone she hardly knew. I remembered their two faces together in my kitchen on the day I had met the Greenes. So alike. The leaping closeness, the back-and-forth flame of compatibility. The house had taken more from Claire than she knew, or perhaps she did know.

"I realize I said I'd never go back over there," Claire said suddenly, and I started at the words. Were we going to speak of it, then? Perhaps we should after all. Perhaps we must.

"I really meant that too, Col," she went on after a time. "I know Susan must be hurt to death and doesn't understand, but I simply can't go over there, and there's no way I can tell her why, not after the way he blew up when Walter went over there. I guess I just hoped I'd find the house I wanted right off the bat and we could move, and that would be that. Moving could be my excuse for not going. But it hasn't worked out that way, and now something's come up that I just don't know what to do about."

She paused, and scrabbled in her handbag for one of her rare cigarettes, and lit it, blowing smoke into the silence.

"What?" I said finally.

"Well, another party."

"Oh, God. Not really, with Melissa so sick, and after that other thing?"

"I know. But this is a different thing, I think. You know I told you I'd talked to her once or twice. Well, once she asked me to go to lunch and shopping with her, and I said I was busy, and then she called and asked me to come over and have coffee and just talk. I think she'd heard about Duck and wanted to help. Anyway, I couldn't think of anything to say, because she must know I've got time to run over there for a minute even if I couldn't go shopping with her. And I said I had the rug cleaners coming and would call her back—but I didn't. And I didn't even feel particularly bad about it.

"Well, she didn't call for a long time, and then she called day before yesterday and said that there was a visiting professor from Russia at City for a month or two, and Herr Professor wanted to have a reception for him, just a school thing, with only school people there. I gather he must be something of a big deal in Norman's circle, because she said he'd planned the menu already, down to the nth degree, and hired a bartender and a maid to serve and a cleaning crew to come in and do the whole house on the day of the party. Imagine how *that* must have made her feel. And he's ordered engraved invitations from Tiffany's again, and made her mail them last week, three weeks ahead of time, so everybody would be sure to get them. And then she said, 'We're not asking anybody from the neighborhood this time, but I would be very proud if you and Roger would come. I really need somebody who's on my side at this thing, because if I screw it up again I don't know what will happen to us.' She sounded so *defeated,* Col, so humble. And *proud* to have us, my God, after the way I've treated her!"

"You're going, aren't you," I said. It was not a question. The fear came flooding back and filled me, coldly.

"Yes, we're going. Just for a minute. With all those preparations, and those awful invitations, we just can't not go. This will be the last time, but we can't not."

"No," I said. "I guess you can't not. When is it?"

"Two weeks from Friday night. We'll just drop in and stay a half hour or so, and then maybe we'll come over and have a drink with you all. It's been ages since we've really gotten together."

"That would be fun," I said. "Oh, no, damn, Claire, we're leaving for New York that morning. Walter has a casting session for some commercials, and we thought we'd splurge and make a week of it. The St. Regis, three or four shows, at least one hideously expensive dinner somewhere fantastic, the whole bit. He can charge a lot of it off to the agency since we'll have some of the clients in tow part of the time—not my idea of paradise, but I'm not knocking it. I thought I told you."

"No, but lucky you. Oh, well, I'll call you when you get back and tell you about it."

New York was marvelous. It always is, to me. No matter how many times we go back, it's as though I come to it fresh and new as the first time I went there, in college. The skies were a cold stew of smog and sooty rain, and people on the streets were sharp-faced and jostling, and we did not dare walk in the theater district anymore, as we had done so often, and the cab drivers were more outrageous than usual, but I did not care. Even a sanitation strike, waxing yeastily into its second week, with frozen garbage piling up in the grimy vestiges of snow at the curbs, did not dampen my spirits. I become another person in New York, smarter, sleeker, springier of step, brisker of speech, longer of stride. I always dip into Bergdorf's or Bloomingdale's—I will *not* call it Bloomie's—on my first day there and buy myself some small, splendid and totally alien thing, and let myself be surprised by my own image in the glittering windows on Fifth Avenue—a long-legged, flying-haired New York woman—for a little while. I come back laughing at myself but liking myself better too. The spell lasts for weeks.

We have several friends there, and during the day, while Walter pored over skeletal, interesting young women and pretty young men, I shopped and lunched with my women friends, and drifted into Brentano's and Scribner's and Rizzoli's and the Strand, and walked through the small galleries on upper Madison Avenue which Walter flatly refuses to enter. He will suffer the Modern and the Guggenheim and the Frick with me, and loves the elephantine old Metropolitan and the Museum of Natural History, but he will not go into the small, pretentious ones.

We saw four shows, and did indeed dine late and

sumptuously at Lutèce and Le Cygne, and did indeed spend too much money. We dined early and hugely at the Russian Tea Room too, and went to hear Bobby Short at the Carlyle, and went to dinner at the home of friends in the Village, hard by NYU, and to a gloriously cluttered, tall brownstone on Eighty-third Street, which had, in its creaking, curly iron elevators and bulbous bayed windows and high, medallioned ceilings, that indefinable cachet about it that spells New York and no other place on earth. We met for drinks once at the Algonquin simply because I wanted to, and once at P. J. Clarke's simply because Walter wanted to. The clients were amiable and urbane men who walked easily in the city, and their wives were smart and very thin, and they were all good company. We had champagne for breakfast the last morning we were there, lying late in a tangle of silky St. Regis sheets and stretching limbs deeply and sweetly sated with each other. I bought boxes of Godiva chocolates to take home to my clients and Claire and Roger, and we left on a six-o'clock flight from La Guardia, scrubbed and scoured clean of fear and strangeness and inwardness, filled instead with the city we were leaving behind.

IT WAS late when we turned off onto our street, and raining, but the air was the softer air of approaching spring. Our tires whispered in the snake tracks left by other cars, and streetlights were haloed with opal mist. Few lights burned on the street. It was very quiet. As we paused to turn into our driveway I glanced at the Greenes' house. It rose, dark and stiff and unlighted, into the still-bare trees; no cars stood in the driveway. It looked, all of a sudden, blankly and ringingly and irrevocably empty. I knew that no one was there; I knew that no one lived there anymore, and did not know how I knew, and was afraid with a sharp and terrible fear. I put my hand on Walter's arm.

"Let's go by Claire and Roger's for a minute before we go home," I said. I could hardly breathe.

He looked at me. "All right."

He drove on down the street to their house. It was dark too. No cars were there. The front windows were shuttered, something I had never known Claire and Roger to do. There was a dim white oblong on the front lawn, and Walter pulled the car forward until the headlights picked it out. "For Sale by Owner," it said.

"Walter," I said. "Walter, they're gone. They aren't here anymore."

"Don't be silly, Colquitt," he said. "She's probably found something she liked and they've put the house on the market, but they wouldn't have moved away this soon. That takes weeks."

"Their cars aren't there."

"Well, good God, they've probably gone to a movie, and the boys have the other one out. We'll give them a call later on——"

"No," I said, and was out of the car before he stopped it, and running across the wet night lawn. I could not see through the shuttered windows, and the front door is solid, but I knew that the French windows from the den onto the back patio had shutters, and I ran around the house, stumbling down the little flight of brick stairs at the side and onto the patio. The shutters on the back windows weren't fastened. I pressed my face to the cold glass. The light from the Harpers' upstairs bedroom window next door filtered wanly through their drawn curtains, and after a moment I could see into Claire and Roger's house. There was nothing there. Claire's prized old random-oak boards, polished lovingly once a week and left bare, were empty of furniture and drifted with a fine skin of dust and balls of slut's wool. The walls were naked except for light, ghostly rectangles where pictures had hung. A roped bale of magazines stood in the middle of the emptiness. Nothing of Claire and Roger remained.

I met Walter in the driveway coming after me. I snatched his hand and pulled him back to the car.

"Get me home," I gasped. "Right now. They're gone, and the Greenes have gone, and something else has happened. I know it. I've got to find out where they are."

He said nothing. He drove back to our house, and I was into the kitchen and dialing information before he had wrestled the first suitcase into the house. I stood there in my coat and dialed. It seemed forever before the operator answered.

"A new listing for Roger Swanson," I said. There was a long silence, and then she was back.

"Would that be Roger Swanson on Marywood?"

"No. I don't know. They've just moved in the last week—it might be R. C. or maybe Roger C.—"

"This must be it," she said. "Roger C. Swanson, on Brittany Village Way. It's a condominium development."

I knew the place—shoddy, pretentious, cramped, and overpriced. It had been built a couple of years before when a great old estate on the fringes of our neighborhood was sold to a developer and carved into a ghastly, rococo parody of a Breton fishing village. We had all mourned when the great old hardwoods had come down and the red earth had bled through and the sterile, ridiculous town houses had begun to rise. Claire hated it so much that she found another, longer route to the shopping center.

"That can't be right," I said.

"It's the only Roger C. Swanson in new listings, ma'am."

I dialed the number she gave me. It rang and rang and then Claire answered.

"What in the name of God has happened to you?" I shouted without identifying myself, weeping without knowing that I wept.

"Colquitt," she said after a moment. Her voice sounded frail and thin. It was the way Claire would sound when she was very old.

She told me then, briefly and remotely; it was only later that I learned any details, and then mostly from the newspapers. She and Roger had gone over early on the night of Norman Greene's reception for the visiting Russian, and had waited with them in the living room, with the house glowing and immaculate around them, the child sleeping peacefully upstairs, the bartender busily polishing and repolishing his glasses, the uniformed maid shuffling primly behind the laden buffet table. They waited for the guests to arrive. They never came. The minutes stretched out and conversation died. Norman Greene's face had swelled, gone radiant and incandescent with rage. Susan Greene had brought drinks and passed nuts and chattered desperately and then had fallen silent. Norman Greene had gone to the telephone and made a call, and then another, and another, and had come back into the living room, his face wiped clean of anything but a pure, silver fury.

"They didn't get their invitations," he said. "The invitations never got there."

Stiffly he had wheeled and walked to the silly fantasy of an escritoire in the downstairs bedroom, and opened the drawer, and brought the double handfuls of creamy, stamped envelopes back into the living room. Susan had dropped her head and begun to cry silently.

"I thought I mailed them," she said. "As God is my witness, Norman, I thought I mailed them three weeks ago at the post office at the center. I was on my way to the doctor's with Melissa, and—"

"Melissa," he howled. "Melissa! It's always Melissa, isn't it, Susan? That dirty, stinking, *reeking,* whining little bastard, that little illegitimate bastard that I gave my *name* to, my *name,* when your own *family* had thrown you out, when your own *family* wouldn't have you and your bastard under their roof—"

"That was it all along, Colquitt," Claire said dully into the telephone. "That was why she put up with him all along. It was gratitude. She had a child out of wedlock, probably while she was in art school, and kept it—it must have been practically over her family's dead bodies—and he met her and married her and gave her illegitimate child his name, and she was grateful to him for it. On top of all her money she gave him her gratitude. Her own family threw her out, but he took her in, and she spent the rest of her life being grateful."

Norman Greene had started to scream then.

Claire and Roger had not stayed to soothe, to mediate. They had snatched their coats from the bedroom and fled, blindly, into the night.

They were almost to their own driveway when they heard the shots. Three of them—two close together, and then, in a moment, another. Flat, trivial poppings that might have been firecrackers but could not have been anything but what they were. They had stood still in the street until they heard the high, endless screaming begin, and then they had run back to the house and into the empty living room, where the hired maid was pressed against the wall, eyes closed, screaming as though she would never stop. They heard the bartender on the telephone.

They had run up the stairs to the bedrooms on the second level, but they were empty. They climbed the stairs to the child's room on the third floor. The room that hung cradled so gently in the enfolding trees. Pie Harralson's baby's room.

The Greenes were there. Norman Greene lay on his back, one arm dangling into the open toy chest that stood against the inside wall. Susan Greene lay on the bed, on her side, one arm flung across the child, who lay with her arms still reaching out toward her mother. Her eyes were open, as if in surprise.

The newspapers reconstructed it neatly the next day. After a domestic argument, Mrs. Susan Greene, of 1114 March Valley Road, N.W., had shot her husband and her eight-year-old child with her husband's service revolver and then had turned the gun on herself. All three were dead on arrival at Townsend Memorial Hospital.

Chapter Twenty-Four

I DON'T remember the rest of that night. To this day I cannot tell you precisely how we came to the decision we finally reached. I know we did not sleep. I do remember that when dawn came, soft and swollen with rain and the sense of unseen things budding in the woods, we took fresh cups of coffee and sat on the steps to the patio, breathing in the fragrant steam and sitting quietly for the first time since I had hung up the phone on Claire's listless monotone. We were both still in the clothes we had put on the morning before in that faraway green-and-cream room in the St. Regis.

We were not the same people we had been the night before. The long hours of anguish and horror had birthed an implacable new sense of resolution in us. We became a simple one-purposed organism. Time—our past, our future—ceased to exist for us that night; there was before us only a single, unending now. When Walter said, irrelevantly, pointing to my barren zinnia beds, "That should all be dug up and fertilized before we plant this spring," I looked at him as though he were discussing a rice paddy. Flowers and tennis and shopping and Colquitt and Walter, the appreciators, the enrichers, were gone. I did not mourn them then, and I don't think he did either. There was nothing left to mourn with. We have both had flashes of regret for those vanished, golden people since, but they've been only that—flashes, a gently aching nostalgia as for people known and loved long ago in a distant youth. It is not nearly so bad as I had feared it might be. You only grieve for roads not taken by choice, not for those you have passed by because only one is left to you.

I went first to Claire. The Breton fisherman's cottage was just as awful inside as out. Roger and the boys were out, and Claire was still in her flannel nightgown. Her hair was bent into spikes around her face from her pillow, and her face was dull and old. She looked at me for a moment as if she did not know me.

"Colquitt," she said. And finally, "Would you like to come in?"

She murmured something about coffee and disappeared into her kitchen. I looked around the living room. A few of her lovely old pieces stood about the walls, lined up as if they had been left where the movers set them down. They dwarfed the low-ceilinged little room. There were piles of newspapers and magazines on the sofa and coffee table, and overflowing ashtrays, and a pair of sneakers and a hockey stick on the credenza in the little foyer. The carpet was the raw, opaque green of unwashed emeralds. I could see down a narrow hall and through the kitchen out to a small walled patio. Rog and Tommy's bicycles leaned against the wall, and two plastic garbage cans sat in square cement holes, dug apparently for the purpose. A flash of wiry brindle whisked through my line of vision: Buzzy, a chain affixed to his collar and some out-of-sight tethering post.

Claire came back into the room in a pair of Levi's and a sweat shirt and rubber shower clogs, damp comb tracks in her subdued hair. She carried a silver tray with two mugs of coffee on it.

"Is instant all right?" she asked. "I can't find the percolator. Black for you, right?" She shoved a pile of magazines off the coffee table and set the tray down. We sat facing each other at opposite ends of the sofa.

"Well, what do you think of our new little nest?" she said.

"I—it's not bad at all."

"It's a goddamn horror, and you know it," she said. "But it will do until we can find something bigger."

"When did you move?" I said.

"We moved the next day," she said unemphatically. I did not have to ask her the day after what.

"It took some string-pulling on Roger's part," she said, "but he knows the developer, and he got a bank truck and some of the maintenance guys to move us. We were in by nine o'clock that night. I had the rest of the furniture stored."

We drank our coffee in silence, then she said, "This isn't a social call, is it, Colquitt?"

"No," I said. "It isn't a social call. I came to ask you if you would help us, Claire. It's time now."

"No. No, I won't help you, whatever it is you're planning to do. I told you that before. I'm not going to help you, I'm not going to talk about it, I'm not going to think about it. I guess you mean to try and warn people now, don't you?"

"Yes. We're going to see Chick Herren at the paper first, and then the radio and TV stations. I don't know who after that, but whoever it takes. But, Claire, we need your help, we need it desperately. You're the only ones who've been . . . touched . . . who are around to corroborate what we say. People might pooh-pooh Walter and me, but they couldn't ignore you and Roger too. It's not enough just to say the house is dangerous, unfit to live in; we'll have to tell why. We'll have to show how it happened."

"No."

"Claire, that house has *killed* now. It's done the worst thing; it's taken life. Do you think it will settle for anything less next time?"

Her face lit into fury. "Are you telling *me* it's killed? Do you think I'll ever forget what we saw in that bedroom for one minute as long as I live on this earth? Do you think I want to come in one day and find Roger and Tommy and Rog with . . . their heads splattered on the wall? Leave me alone, Colquitt! You do any damn thing you want to about that house, you say anything about it you want to! Rent a billboard, hire a sky writer, write your congressman! I don't care what you do. Just leave me and my family alone!" She began to cry. I moved to touch her shoulder, but she shrugged away.

"Claire, baby," I said, "you don't have to be afraid of it anymore. You're away from it. It can't hurt you if you don't go near it."

"You don't know that! You don't know *what* it can do! For all I know, there's some kind of . . . contagion that comes from it, some horrible kind of virus, some thing that spreads in the air. I could be carrying it right now; you certainly could be, as close as you are to it—"

She lifted her streaming eyes to me and they were not quite sane.

"At least," I said, "let me tell people what you believe, if you aren't willing to tell it yourself, Claire. What if it goes on the market again? What then? What if somebody buys it? What about *those* people?"

"I don't care about those people or any other people! Hear me well, Colquitt, because I'm not going to say it again. If you mention my name in connection with that house, I will swear on my mother's grave that you are lying and crazy and—and whatever else I have to

242

say. If I ever hear that you have said one word about me and my family, we will sue you. We will take you to court. I want you to leave now, and I don't want you to come here again. I don't want to see you again. I don't want you to call me. If we run into you anywhere, we will leave that moment, because you are too close to it, and if you stay there, you are both as good as dead, and I will not let it get at my family through you!"

"Claire," I said. "Claire—"

She jumped up from the sofa and balled her small hands into fists and began to scream. She started toward me, her fists raised, her eyes blind. I backed toward the door.

"Get out of my house," she shrieked. "Get out of my house! You're dead, Colquitt, you're a walking dead woman! Get out of my house!"

I turned and ran through the door and slammed it and stumbled down the little cobbled walkway to my car. Behind me I could hear her still screaming.

"You're dead, you're walking around dead, you're dead—"

I drove home, thinking only, mildly, "Claire is gone. I'm going to miss Claire."

That was on a Sunday morning. That afternoon Walter and I went up to the big Safeway in the shopping center that is open twenty-four hours a day, every day, and stocked up on groceries. We were out of nearly everything, since we'd been away a week. I had a list, and we went methodically up one aisle and down another, slowly filling the cart with the items I needed. The store had that damp, dingy, white Sunday look to it, and the people who were shopping were not the same people I ran into during the week. There were no tanned, hard-legged matrons in tennis clothes, no harried young mothers with small children in tow, no shoals of drifting blue-haired old ladies, no grave-faced chauffeurs with lists. The people were young, and many of the men were bearded, and all had the same damp, dingy white look the store wore.

"It's a whole different subculture," said Walter, looking around.

I caught sight of us in the mirror over the meat counter, two tall, slender, graceful people in well-cut slacks and heavy sweaters. I thought we looked like attractive strangers, people you see on the streets and in restaurants or passing cars whom you do not know but know instinctively are *of* you, one of your own. I thought too that Walter and I looked far more alike than I had ever realized. Perhaps it was true. Perhaps the single-minded unity that had sprung between us that night showed, somehow, on our faces.

In the gourmet department, where Walter was foraging for the almond-stuffed olives he favors for martinis, we ran into Eloise Jennings clutching a round wooden box of Brie. Semmes's touch, I knew. Eloise is Cheez-Whiz material.

"Colquitt! Have you heard about that perfectly *awful* thing with the Greenes?" Eloise was so full of the news that she did not even greet us. Her entire body twitched with it.

"Yes," I said. "Claire told me when we got back. It's horrible, isn't it?" I glanced desperately at Walter to see if he was through and we could escape, but he was studying a display of mustard pickles with his back to us, across the alcove. His back was rigid with interest and concentration on the pickles. He could not have failed to hear Eloise's piercing voice, and I could have shaken him.

"Oh, it's just dreadful, just unbelievable," shrilled Eloise. "She seemed so *normal,* but of course you can't judge a book by its cover, I always say—and the poor little girl! Had they been fighting, do you know? The paper said there was an argument—"

"Not that I know of," I said.

"Well, you're lucky you were gone, otherwise you might have been the ones to—I understand Claire and Roger found them. I wonder if there was a lot of, you know . . . mess?"

"I expect so, Eloise. I doubt if many shootings are very tidy," I snapped, close to tears for the first time since the night we had heard about it. Would she never shut up?

"Awful for Claire and Roger, of course. You said you'd talked to her—where on earth *are* they? They didn't tell a soul they'd moved. I guess she just couldn't stand living there, with that house to remind her every time she passed it."

"They've taken a town house nearby. They had a buyer for the house, a very good offer, and the people wanted to take immediate occupancy, so they got out as quickly as possible. The town house is just temporary," I lied.

"Well, you'd think she'd tell somebody. I never heard a word about it. Speaking of houses, will the Greenes' go back on the market, do you know? Gwen said his brother came down and moved their things and took the . . . remains . . . back to Boston or wherever it is. There wasn't an inquest, Gwen said; it was perfectly apparent what had happened. The gun was still in her hand. I suppose the house will go to the brother."

"I don't know about the house. I don't know a thing more than you do," I said. "Walter," I called, "hurry up. I want to get this frozen stuff home before it melts. Will you excuse us, Eloise?"

"Wait a minute, I want to tell you what the police said—'"

"Well, I don't want to hear it. You wallow in it, Eloise. It's your natural milieu." I turned and wheeled the cart toward the check-out counter, not waiting for Walter.

"What's the matter, Colquitt?" she shouted after me, her voice strident with outrage. "You think the ghosts are going to come over there and get you too?" Heads swiveled after me. I could feel the eyes in the small of my back.

"Damned harpy," Walter muttered in the car on the way home, but there was little heat in his voice. "We're probably going to get a lot more of that, you know. Is it going to bother you too much?"

"Not in the least," I said.

Chapter Twenty-Five

WE WENT together to Chick Herren. Walter called first, and Chick was waiting for us in his corner office in the newspaper building downtown, his feet propped up on the elderly rolltop desk he had salvaged from the old building. He grinned a friendly greeting, but there were questions behind his sharp blue eyes.

"What brings you two downtown on a school day?" he said when we had seated ourselves on the sagging couch across from his desk. "A scandal among the advertising fauna? A hot tip on a new lipstick?" Like most newsmen, Chick suffers advertising and public relations people with offhand indulgence.

"It's important, Chick," Walter said formally.

"It better be. I've got old man Thornton *and* his crazy sister waiting for me in the board room, probably all ready to sign over half their stock to that half-wit nephew."

"It is."

Carefully, clearly, logically, and coldly, Walter spelled it all out for Chick Herren. He began with the murdered animals, the scene in the Harralsons' bedroom, her father's death. He fitted in the withering of Kim's talent and his flight to Europe. He told of the Sheehans and their history before they came, of Anita's shock at seeing Duck Swanson, the television movie, the telephone call. He did not, of course, mention the incident with us and Kim Dougherty or the one with Buck and Virginia Guthrie, and I could see clearly, hearing it all so precisely and unemotionally like this for the first time, in sequence, what gaping holes in the fabric of slowly building terror the missing incidents left. But we had agreed.

He moved on to the Greenes and told of the child's

illness, the ludicrous mingling of pity, embarrassment, and horror of that first party. He finished with the unmailed invitations to the second one, and the final blind rage that had led to the shootings, though he did not mention what Claire had told us about Melissa's illegitimacy. We had agreed about that too.

He did not elaborate on Claire and Roger's trouble and their fears and their move, but he did say that something else pretty terrible had happened to neighbors who had had contact with the house, and that they had moved away and were unwilling to talk about it. I knew that Chick would know whom we meant.

Walter's even voice brought them all vividly before me again, the Harralsons and the Sheehans and the Greenes; they breathed and walked in the room, their quirks and vulnerabilities, their pains and weaknesses, the tools with which the house had destroyed them, so clear as to be almost palpable. We had rehearsed what we would say and how we would make our presentations, but I felt a wondering admiration at Walter's skill and clarity. I had never seen him make a new business presentation for the agency, but I understood then why Charlie Satterfield said he was the best in the business at it. The horror hung there in the air, whole and living.

"In short, Chick, we feel that it would be fatal for anyone else to occupy that house," he finished. "We're not sensation seekers; you know that, of course. But we cannot sit by and let anything else happen over there. If we could afford it, we'd buy it ourselves and tear it down. I'm trying to locate Greene's next-of-kin or whoever owns it now, and I plan to call them and tell them just what I've told you. I'll go there and talk to them if it's necessary. The house must not sell again.

"We don't pretend to understand *what* it is over there; we can't explain it. We think that it operates by isolating the . . . the most important things in people's lives, their vulnerabilities, and turning them around and using them to destroy. We think it needs that sort of primal vitality for sustenance. And it has killed now. It won't stop short of anything else next time. We feel that people *must* be warned. There doesn't seem to be anyone else to do it except us. We know the risks we're running; not a few people in town already think we're playing with half-full decks, to put it mildly. That's why we came to you. I can understand why we wouldn't be believed, but a public warning, printed as straight news coverage in a reputable medium—"

He stopped. Chick Herren was looking at us intently, without expression.

"That's it," said Walter. "That's all. I can't do it any better than that."

Chick swiveled his chair around and stared out the window, whistling tunelessly. He waited. He turned around again.

"Walter," he said. "Colquitt. I can't print that. The thing with the Greenes, that last thing, the shooting—yes. That's news, unsavory as it is. And we did carry it. The other things—they're explainable in a terrible kind of way, aren't they? Products of the weaknesses, the flaws in those people. I know they happened; I've no quarrel with that. I know you're not liars or sensation seekers; you know I know it. But they're not *news*. And what it all adds up to, what you think it adds up to—a *malignant* house, a haunted house, if you will—that's Hallowe'en stuff at best. It's a nasty story; the hair stood up on my neck listening to you. But it *is* a story; any of it, all of it could be put down to coincidence, grisly and one-in-a-million as it is. Don't you see that? It's too awful even to make a feature of. We *have* run features on haunted houses, but they're Robert Louis Stevenson stuff—a ghost in crinolines flapping around an old antebellum wreck, a place where somebody's crazy old great-great-grandpa stomps around scaring shit out of whoever sleeps in the Blue Room, or whatever. And we ran those practically over my dead body. This isn't funny. It's—unspeakable. I can understand how you might think what you do, living so closely with it, watching it all happen bit by bit—but I can't print it. We'd be laughed out of business." His face was seamed with concern and distress; his whole body was bent forward with it. Chick is a thoroughly nice man.

"What if something else happens over there?" I said. "What if it *does* go back on the market, and somebody does buy it, and they . . . *die?*"

"We could report the deaths. And that's all I could

do, or anybody else, I guess. I'm sorry, Colquitt. I really am. Even if I did run it, old Thornton would print a retraction the next day and fire my ass. I just can't help you."

"Do you believe us?" Walter asked.

"I—don't know. I believe *you* sincerely believe it. That must be all you can handle on your plates right now. My whole life is facts, Walter. It's what I live by, for better or worse. Sometimes I think we news people shut ourselves off from half there is to this existence —'there are more things in heaven and earth, Horatio' —but there it is. I don't know if what you say is true or not, but I do know that I simply cannot help you, and couldn't if I flat out knew it *was* true. I'm really sorry. It must have been a year of hell for both of you."

"What do you think we ought to do, then? We're not going to stop with you, you know," said Walter. "We're going to the television and radio stations next. And we'll find somewhere else to go if those fall through."

Chick sighed. "I wonder if you know what you're letting yourselves in for? What life is going to be like for you if you spread this stuff around?"

"We pretty well know," Walter said. "We're getting some of it already. Don't you see, Chick? It just can't matter. This could go on and on—we can't just sit over there and watch it keep killing and destroying."

"Have you thought about moving? If I felt the way you two do, I'd move in a minute. Like those neighbors of yours. Just get out."

"Who would there be to stop it then, Chick?" I said.

He took off his glasses and rubbed his eyes. "Who, indeed," he said. "Okay, I guess if I were you, I'd do the same thing you're doing. Go ahead and go to the stations. I don't think you'll get anywhere, but one of the whacko ones might give you some feature time. Talk to Ernest Lipschutz at KMO; I'd say he's your best bet. I really think the best thing to do is find whoever inherited it and see if you can convince him not to put it back on the market. That, or burn the damned thing down."

Walter laughed mirthlessly. "Don't think it hasn't occurred to us."

We rose to go, and he walked with us to the elevator. "Be careful, you two," he said abruptly as the doors began to close. He was still looking after us, his face troubled, when they slid shut and we started noiselessly down toward the street.

We got much the same reception from Howard Ogletree at the afternoon daily. Since both papers are owned by the same communications group, we might have guessed that we would.

We saw the general managers of two of the network television affiliates the next day. The first, a civic legend with more awards and plaques and public-service trophies than Bob Hope, fidgeted unhappily in his bescrolled office and slid sheering glances at his telephone, obviously hoping he could reach it and summon aid should we become totally irrational.

"I don't think it would be in the public's best interest to disclose this—this theory of yours, Walter," he said carefully. "This station's reputation has been painstakingly built, over the years, on the foundation of service to the community—"

"Morris," Walter said tiredly, "that's what we're trying to do."

But it was no use, and we went away, leaving him regarding his citadel as though the walls had turned to some sort of extraterrestrial jelly and betrayed him.

Clark Massengale, the manager of the CBS affiliate, was more sympathetic and blunter. "I can't touch it," he said when we had gone through our paces once again. "Morris Leonard called me a while ago, right after you left his office, and I thought he was going into cardiac arrest on the telephone."

"What could it hurt, Clark?" I asked. "If it's really so unbelievable, then what's the harm in it? And if even a few people did believe it, we'd be that much to the good."

"For starters, it could hurt the station pretty badly," he said. "Our credibility would be zilch overnight."

He did not seem to disbelieve us or think we had some sensational axe to grind or even seem to suspect that we were mildly demented. I suppose most newsmen are beyond surprise. He simply wasn't going to help us.

We almost did not go to talk with Ernest Lipschutz at KMO. He is a newcomer to the city, a pale, finger-snapping, ferret-minded man brought in to shore up the station's sagging ratings. He speaks in terms of packaging images, marketing news, audience awareness. The unhappy news teams wear wire-rimmed glasses and station blazers and chortle vibrantly over transit strikes and consumer ripoffs and the weather. But in the end we did go, and he listened to us with rapt intensity and watched us with measuring eyes.

When we were finished he said, "Can you guarantee me an exclusive?"

"I don't follow you," Walter said mildly. I knew he did.

"Would you sign an agreement not to talk to any of the other media about it? It has possibilities—we could develop it pretty nicely, I think. Maybe the two of you out in front of it telling your story, some interviews with neighbors—you know the sort of thing. Maybe even a tour of the house if we could get permission—show where all those things happened, and so on. What about those first two families, the ones who lived in it before the Greenes? Could you put me in touch with them? We could afford a little something for everybody who'd agree to appear. Not much, but—"

"Shove it, Lipschutz," Walter said conversationally. The two telling white furrows bracketed his mouth. He rose and pushed back his chair.

Ernest Lipschutz leaned forward and smiled. "How much are you asking, Kennedy?" he said.

I pulled Walter out of the office before the chair he overturned hit the carpet.

THE SPRING came early; a hot, dry April brought the dogwood and azaleas flooding into full bloom and ebbing out again within a week, leaving shriveling brown lace against the new green. We dug up beds, set out bedding plants, mowed and raked and mulched and fertilized. Without the Swanson boys on weekends, the yard work expanded to fill most of our free time. We did it slowly and thoroughly and with absorbed relish. We did little else. With Claire and Roger gone, and the Guthries, the street seemed as silent and lifeless as though it lay under deep snow. In the soft, fruity air of April, under the tender new blue of the sky, it was as disturbing and out of context as a ghost street. Women did not seem to go often on their morning rounds to grocery stores and hairdressers and meetings, though I might not have noticed if they had.

I was spending a lot of time in my office, submerging myself in the swelling spring tide of promotions and projects. There was a new formality between my clients and me now; they did not come so often to my office. We met, then, in their offices, and business was done, and there was no lingering over coffee or five-o'clock drinks. I was not surprised. I knew the talk had reached them, but still not sufficiently so that they were forced to acknowledge it, at least to me. We saw few of our friends; that did not surprise me either. I did not think that they had dropped us yet. Rather, they would wait to see what we would do next. We might still be taken back into the circle if we remained quiet.

We went seldom to the club for lunch or tennis, preferring to work in the yard and garden. I honestly do not believe we felt constrained about encountering them, those pleasant people we had known for so many years. It was rather that reality lay then in the two of us and in our house and lawn and gardens. And in the new purpose that bound and dominated us even when it lay iceberglike beneath our surfaces. Like old ice, it did not chafe with the waiting. Everything else was as pale and bleached and faded as images in an old photograph.

The house next door stood silent and empty and beautiful in the green shadows of the awakening trees. Grass grew tall and rich. Birds sang enchantingly in the woods behind it. The creek sang and shouted between its ferns in the brief, hard rains.

In the middle of April Walter called Dr. Holderbein at City College and got the name of Norman Greene's brother in Boston and placed a long-distance call to him. I was in the den leafing through a hoarded pile of *Smithsonian* magazines, and listened detachedly as he worked with infinite patience once again through the story we had told so often during the last weeks. I thought once more how lucid, how beautifully constructed, how tightly knit and infinitely reasonable it sounded. I also thought, for the first time, that it did not sound sane. Walter talked for a long time, and then there was a brief silence, and he replaced the receiver carefully in its cradle and came into the den.

"What did he say?" I asked, knowing.

"He said I was a goddamned ghoul, and he threatened to sue me if he heard another word out of me, and he slammed down the phone."

"Is he going to put it back on the market?"

"I don't know," he said. "I didn't get a chance to ask him. Colquitt, have you ever thought we might be . . . mad? Just insane, and not know it? They say you never know it if you are."

"I've thought about it," I said. "I just now thought it when I heard you talking to him. I suppose we could be. It could be . . . the start of what it's going to do to us. But I don't think so, Walter, because that isn't what's best about us. I don't give a flip about my sanity, or lack of it, if it doesn't isolate me from you. No. We're not insane. Don't you see? That's too clumsy. It's cleverer than that; it doesn't misread people. That wouldn't separate us, destroy us."

"It could if we both ended up in the funny farm."

"No. That's not enough. It wouldn't stop with that, after the Greenes. It wouldn't . . . drop back."

"What do you think it will do to us, then?" Walter said, and for a blazing instant the bell jar lifted and I was aghast and terrified and utterly astounded once again at these words we were speaking to each other in this quiet, sunny room. But then the dome slipped back into place and the whirling void was gone.

"I don't know. Nothing, probably, if we can't succeed in doing anything to thwart it. If we leave it alone. If we don't—your guess is as good as mine. You know what it almost did once."

"Well, we're batting zero so far," he said. "What's next, do you think?"

"Wait," I said peacefully. "Wait and see. We've done all we can for now. It still isn't on the market.

Maybe it won't be. If it does go up again, then of course we'll have to do something else."

"Yes," he said. "There are other things. Listen, you want to go see the new Woody Allen movie?"

THE NEXT week Walter and Charlie and two or three of their young creative staff flew down to the South Carolina coast to make a new business presentation to a carefully rustic new resort that had sprung, full-blown, from the deep forest and scrub palm of that gentle, tawny shore. They had been invited to make the presentation, and I knew that hopes for it ran high at Kennedy and Satterfield. It would add in excess of a million dollars to the agency's billing. They had worked on it for months, and advance intelligence had it that they were a virtual shoo-in, that the presentation was a mere formality. They were to be gone two days.

When the phone rang at nine o'clock on the first evening he was gone, I was surprised to hear his voice.

"Where are you?" I said. "Aren't you supposed to be plying the brass with their own liquor tonight?"

"I'm at the cottage," he said.

"The cottage?"

"Our place, on St. Agnes. We wound up faster than we thought, and I thought a day or two down here would not be amiss, seeing as how we've all busted our asses on this thing for so long. I rented a car and drove down. Why don't you get the noon plane down tomorrow, and we'll fly back Sunday?"

"Walter . . ." Strangeness spun out over the wire from the island. "Did you get the account?"

"No. We didn't. Listen, I'll tell you about it when you get here. Come on down, Col. The weather's fantastic."

It was as hot as summer on the island, the sun blazing out of a vast blue sky, the surf booming in under a freshening wind. We did not talk about the resort account until we had stocked up on groceries in the shabby little village and I had made us tuna fish sandwiches and we had struck out up the empty April beach.

They had gotten through the presentation, Walter said, and had gone for drinks to the absurd little thatched restaurant on the beach. The official word

254

would not come until the next day, but everyone was full of high spirits and hearty mutual admiration. The development's president, a squat, fishlike man who had not been in the meeting, joined them. Midway through the first drink he turned to Walter and said, "Walter Kennedy. Walter Kennedy. I think I know someone who knows you."

"Who's that?" Walter said.

"Ernie Lipschutz," the man said neutrally, looking out over his beach to the slice of his sea that was visible through the overhanging thatch. "He was one of our first property owners, has the big contemporary on the beach on the other side of the inn. He was down last week with his family. They came by the house for drinks; his wife was in school with mine. A real go-getter, Ernie is. He mentioned you."

"Yes," Walter said. He knew then that the account was gone. Back in his room in the inn, he had called Charlie in and told him about our meeting with Ernest Lipschutz and what had led to it and what had happened in his office. So the brief phone call from the resort's marketing manager half an hour later had not taken Charlie by surprise. He had said only, "Why don't you go on down to the cottage and spend a few days? I'll tell the rest of the crew. We'll go on back first thing in the morning."

We talked no more about it except that Walter said, "If the house goes back on the market, Col, and we have to . . . do something more, I'm not sure I'll be able to stay with the agency."

"Charlie wouldn't expect you to leave," I said, honestly shocked.

"No. He wouldn't. He'd let every account we had go down the tube before he'd suggest breaking things off. That's why I think I'd pull out. There are thirty people who make their living at the agency. Would you mind so awfully?"

"No," I said, and tears started in my eyes. But they were tears of love.

We stayed the remaining three days, and loved each other in the still-chilled nights under the slightly ratty old thermal blankets and swam in the still-chilled water, and lay in the sun, and bought fat, fresh shrimp from the returning boats at the municipal pier at sundown and boiled them in beer and bay leaves. We took the Sailfish out once, but the wind was still petulant and fickle, running docilely across the water with dimpling fingers and then doubling back and lunging at our stern, so we brought it in. No terror dogged our memories, no portent lay over our days. That time was of and to itself, as whole and round and perfect as an egg. It was only at the weedy, sun-struck little airstrip, when we boarded the frail old DeHavilland that serves the island twice a day, that I had the piercing sense of an impending ending that would, this time, be a final ending.

When we got home, about three o'clock on Sunday afternoon, the lawn of the house next door had been newly mowed and a "For Sale" sign stood beside the mailbox at the edge of the street.

The next morning we called Jay Whitten at *People* Magazine.

Chapter Twenty-Six

WHEN THE story appeared a couple of weeks later the response was swift and ugly, uglier than we could have anticipated. As *People* stories go, it wasn't all that sensational; certainly it was not *National Enquirer* stuff. There was a large photograph of us in our patio chairs looking grave and rather ridiculously well-bred—we had dressed carefully for the photographer in conservative sports clothes, seeking to preserve every small shard of credibility we could salvage —and only a small photo of the exterior of the house next door. Even flattened into black and white banality, it looked full and vibrant and exquisitely dimensional, seeming, as Walter said, to preen for the camera.

The terrible, spiraling saga was all there, but it had not been distorted or personalized, and the only direct quote was one from Walter: "We are telling this story solely to warn the public. We consider this house extremely dangerous and unfit to live in. We have no explanation for what has happened there. Our theory is that there is some sort of voracious, malignant force operating in the house which requires for its sustenance the essence of each person who occupies it. We think it obtains its sustenance by preying on the weaknesses and inherent flaws in the characters of the people who live there. The fact that these incidents may then seem to be explainable in human terms, and the number and sequence of them merely coincidental, makes the house doubly dangerous, in our opinion. If you examine each instance of tragedy you can see that the things that each individual held dearest were taken and turned around and used for his destruction. We do not know what this force is, or how it works, or why. We deeply regret that we may have caused any persons embarrassment or harm in disclosing this story. We have done it in order to prevent far greater harm."

I thought it a formal and dignified statement. It might as well have been an open invitation from the Manson family to drop in for a tour of the commune.

The cars began arriving early that morning. Do people get up early on *People* day? Most of the cars slowed down in front of the house next door, paused for a while, slid on to pause before our house, and then drove away. But many of them stopped, and people got out and stood in silent knots at the edge of the lawn, staring solemnly up at the house. Most of the people I saw from my office window that morning were women, many with children by the hand or in backpacks or toting infants in plastic carriers. Some of the older children made elaborate, jeering forays down the driveway toward the house, and their mothers would call them back sharply.

The women wore polyester pants or shifts, and some had fat plastic curlers in their hair. They gazed impassively at the house, and looked with slanting suspicion over at our house and at the other houses on the street, as if knowing their paths would never lead them to streets and houses like this, and resenting it. Once or twice I saw two women murmuring to each other and then looking around at all our houses and laughing. I wondered if they were glad that trouble and sensation could strike here too, among the mailbox names that they had seen in society and financial pages of the newspapers. Some brought out Instamatics and took pictures.

Around midmorning I saw Gwen Parsons' car come down the street and pause, blocked by slow traffic and parked cars. She backed into the Swansons' still-empty driveway and turned around and drove off in the other direction, and the crowd on the lawn in front of the house jeered and cat-called. I grimaced in brief pain. I had not thought about the effect of the story on the others on the street. Shortly after that Eloise Jennings came out of her house with two of her children, saw the crowd, and went back in. I knew she would be on the telephone immediately. I wondered maliciously if her own mother and sisters were in the crowd, and then was ashamed at the thought. By afternoon the stream of cars had become a river, and passage was nearly impossible.

Three of my clients called that day and canceled their accounts. I had anticipated it and did not blame them. The severings were polite and unheated.

"You don't have to explain," I said to each. "I'd do the same thing under the circumstances. I can recommend two or three good free-lancers if you'd like to keep things on a small scale."

Walter called shortly after noon. "Is it bad?" he said.

"I guess so," I said. "At least it's pretty awful for everybody else on the street. The cars are lined up like Indianapolis; nobody can get through. But nobody's bothered me so far, no calls from anybody we know. Except that three clients have canceled."

"You want me to come home?"

"No. It doesn't bother me, except that I hate it for everybody here. How is it there?"

"Very polite. Very jolly. Everybody pretending they don't read *People* and nothing ever happened. It can't go on, though. Charlie has a call on his desk from the Fruitcake King. As soon as he comes in from lunch I'm going to tell him I'm taking a leave of absence until we see how things go so he can truthfully tell clients I'm not around anymore. Then I'll come home."

"Are you sorry?" I said.

"No, baby, except for the other people on the street, like you. It's not as if we didn't expect something like this."

"They're awful people, Walter. The ones who come and gawk, I mean. They're taking pictures."

"Well, they aren't the kind who buy," he said practically, "and that's what counts. See you in a little while."

"Come in the back way."

With nightfall the traffic abated and the phone calls began. The first was from the realtor who was handling the sale of the house, and I was glad that Walter was there to take it. I could hear the man shouting all the way into the den. He threatened to take us to court. The second was from Norman Greene's brother in Boston threatening the same thing. Walter was not upset by the realtor's call; he thought the publicity would net the man a good many serious inquiries among the cranks, and the threat would come to nothing. Norman Greene's brother bothered him deeply.

"It's not the possibility of a suit," he said, coming back into the den gray-faced. "As soon as all this dies down—and it will eventually—I don't think he'll want to expose his family to the publicity a suit would bring. He has kids. Even if he does go through with it, it will take a long time, and I don't know what will have happened by then. It was the pain. He was just . . . anguished. God, if we've done the wrong thing . . ."

"We haven't," I said, going to him and putting my arms around his waist from behind. His back was rigid. "I hate the pain too, but it's not as though we identified any of the people who lived there. Only the people who knew them well will know who we're talking about. If we've stopped it from selling, don't

259

you think it will have been worth it? Any amount of pain, what is that to more death?"

"There's a certain kind of person who'd love to live in that house," said Walter. "You know the kind; you saw some of them today. What if we've *lured* them there? What if it's working through us to get people? I couldn't live five minutes with that."

My heart froze; I had not thought of that. But then I thought of those sly, faded people, and I said, "Not one of those people could begin to afford that house. The people who could won't come near it after this. We have to believe we've done the right thing, darling. Otherwise nothing is worth anything. If anyone seems serious about it, we'll warn them—call them, or go see them, or whatever. And if somebody does buy it, they won't move in right away. We'll watch very carefully. I'll watch every day. If the sign comes down, there'll still be time."

He twisted around in my arms to look at me intently. "Time for what, Colquitt?"

"Time to go over there during the night and burn it down," I said. I had not thought of it before consciously, but it had been there in my mind, whole and polished and inevitable.

"Colquitt, we will absolutely and surely go to jail if we do that," he said.

"I don't think so. I think if we do that we won't be alive long enough to go to jail."

"Won't be alive?"

"Walter, if you can believe the rest of it, surely you must believe, you must know, that if we destroy it, it will destroy us in turn."

"Kill us somehow, you mean."

"Yes. What else would matter enough to us except to—to die, and not have each other anymore?"

"You don't think it might just separate us somehow for the rest of our lives?"

"No, because we'd still have what we'd been to each other. Even if one of us died, the other would still have that; it would have to kill us, Walter. It's already shown us that it could. Don't you remember?"

"Yes," he said.

It was perhaps a measure of how far we'd traveled

down that road we'd taken the night we returned from New York to find the Greenes dead and Claire and Roger gone that we could stand in our bright den, with April throbbing and singing around us outside, and Razz and Foster noisily glomming their dinners in the yellow kitchen, and speak so mildly of arson and death. Perhaps we *were* mad, had been mad for a long time. Somehow I know that we were not, and are not. No, we are as sane as one can rightfully expect to be in one's lifetime. We were, that night, simply pared down to one essential inevitability. The madness lay next door.

"If it doesn't sell, then of course we won't have to worry about that," Walter said thoughtfully. "What then?"

"Then, if we're absolutely sure it won't sell—if the brother will agree not to sell it ever, or the city condemns it, or it gets struck by lightning or something —I'd kind of like to sell our house and see if Charlie will let us buy his half of the beach house, and go live there, on the island. I'm not sure we'd be safe here even if we stayed completely away from it. But we have to stay until we know for sure one way or another."

"Yes," he said. "I see that. The island—that would be nice, wouldn't it?"

"It would be wonderful," I said peacefully.

The phone rang again; it was a man who said he'd been a Catholic priest but had left the Church to practice white witchcraft and could, for a nominal fee, exorcise the house for us. Walter explained that we did not own it; when the man began to intone thin incantations over the telephone he hung up.

The next caller was a woman who was sure that what was possessing the house was the shade of her departed husband. "He hung around here till I got married again," she said. "And then I lost him for a while. I'm sure that's him, though. I'd know the sonofabitch anywhere."

The next was children, giggling. After that Walter took the phone off the hook.

The slow, frozen ooze of cars did not stop the next day, or the next. Over the weekend, traffic became so congested that the angry realtor brought in an off-duty policeman, and he kept the cars in motion, at least. The lookers, thwarted, jeered and cursed him, and many, wise to the logistics of sensation-watching, parked their cars on other streets and walked to the house. Beer and soft-drink cans and Big Mac boxes littered the mown lawn and drifted over into ours. Kodak boxes and wrappers bloomed like a field of golden poppies; cellophane crackled underfoot like January ice. A large banner was affixed to the "For Sale" sign: "By Appointment Only." Neither the new sign nor the policeman could stem the tide of older children and the scattering of dull-eyed women who came up through the woods behind the house to peer into the blank windows and break off pieces of shrubbery, to pocket pea gravel from around the plantings at the base of the deck. One fat woman lifted up her children, three in turn, to crane thin necks into a side window; she gave each a methodical whack on the buttocks when she set it down again. Our doorbell rang often, and there were frequent rappings at the front and back doors. Once, going to draw the curtains in the den, I heard a hoarse woman's voice shout, "There she is! I see her! They're in there!" This was followed by a veritable fusillade of knocks on the glass of the French door of the kitchen. I fled up the stairs to the bedroom, where Walter was watching a baseball game on the little Sony.

"If you can't stand the heat, stay out of the kitchen," he said laconically, and, insanely, I laughed. We opened the doors to no one.

We did not stop answering the telephone for two or three more days, though. There was always a chance that some serious buyer might attempt to contact us, and we wished to talk to these people. But none of the calls were from serious buyers, and the ones we took became dimmer and eerier and sicker and slyer, especially during the nights. Finally we stopped answering, and on the fifth day after the story appeared, Walter, red-eyed and haggard, called the telephone company and got an unlisted number. During the entire week no one that we knew came to our house, and only Eloise Jennings called.

"I hope you're happy," she shrieked. "I hope you're proud of yourselves." And she hung up.

For a while, in the nights, there would be the sudden sweep of headlights in our driveway, and horns would blare, and people would shout and beat on the sides of cars, and then back crazily out of the driveway. One morning we awoke to find our trees painstakingly laced and webbed with toilet paper. After a horrifyingly loud, heart-stopping three A.M. report that I took to be a shotgun blast but Walter said was a firecracker, Foster Grant came streaking up the bedroom stairs, eyes wild, tail blooming, ears back, fur singed, and from then on we kept the cats shut into the house. A predawn tinkle of glass was the window into the basement at the back of the house. After a couple of windows were broken in the house next door, patrol cars made regular, silent sorties up and down the street, and the nighttime cacophony gradually dwindled to an occasional squall of tires and horns. Our mailbox had been painted with orange obscenities the first night, but we went out to collect the mail only after nightfall, so it did not matter so much. Most of the mail was the type you throw away, face flaming, after reading a sentence or two. We did not go out until the household supplies were depleted, and then we found a twenty-four-hour Colonial many miles away in a scanty, alien shopping center and stocked up as for a siege.

We did not call the police. We hardly even spoke of the daytime invasions and nighttime terrors. We both felt, obscurely, that we must take our medicine—tough it out, endure it. We had known, after all, that there would be reaction. It was the sheer, malevolent gaiety of those faceless invaders that left us weak and sickened behind our closed doors and curtained windows. We had expected alarm and indignation and, certainly, derision. We had not expected primal, hunting joy.

A few likely-looking prospects did come to see the house, marching erect and expressionless through the fluid crowd at the street, the agent nipping at their heels like a sheepdog. The crowds howled and crooned; none of the likely-looking ones came back.

I was glad. These were the people whom, had they returned, I would have felt compelled to seek out and warn. I had meant to do just that with everyone who came to see the house, everyone who called. But except for those few, there could have been no ken between me and the people who came. Ashamedly, I realized that I had never in all my life really known that those others existed. I could not imagine their lives. We could not have spoken.

As in the winter, after Walter had gone to talk to Norman and Susan Greene and Claire had broken off our friendship, we drew into each other again. We slept long in the hot days, not knowing precisely what time it was when we awoke, because of the shrouding curtains. In the nights we sat on the darkened patio. Television and magazines and the newspapers drowned us once again; crossword and jigsaw puzzles and books from the central library downtown, which stayed open until nine in the evenings, opened arms to us. We talked a great deal, but I do not remember much of what we talked about. The island, and New York, and our courtship and the early days of our marriage. Things far enough in the past for safety. Nothing ahead. We laughed a lot, and it did not seem strange to us that we did. I wrote cards with our new telephone number to a few people—my remaining clients and the Parsons and a handful of out-of-town relatives and friends. Walter called and gave the number to Charlie. No one called. No one we knew wrote. Every night when we walked down the driveway to the mailbox we checked to see if the "For Sale" sign still stood beside the mailbox of the house next door. It did, grass growing taller around it. The lawn, where it was not flattened by the feet of the pilgrims, grew spiky and weedy in the slowly creeping heat of late spring. The lawn service employed by the realty firm did not come so often now. Cans and wrappers and boxes lingered for two or three days before someone came to pick them up.

Everything ends of course, and with the closing of school and the coming of the real heat the cars thinned and the night noises faded, the letters dwindled, and the hungry-faced people found fresher sustenance and moved elsewhere. We began to go out again during the daylight hours, to the market and the drugstore and the dry cleaner's, though in other neighborhoods. Once or twice we went to lunch, in little places out near the river or in the heart of downtown, where we had not been before. We talked a lot, and drank a good bit, but we did not get drunk. I remember that we had a very good time at those lunches and at the movies we went to.

Once we drove to a new singles bar that I had read about in the newspaper, and we drank and danced until almost three in the morning, and laughed giddily in the car all the way home, and laughed in a nearly forgotten kind of simple, unencumbered joy in our lovemaking that night, like pagan children beside a warm ocean. If the physical boundaries of our lives were narrowed and straitened, the pleasures of us, one to another, stretched to infinite new horizons. There was joy and contentment and a rich enoughness to the things we said, and ate, and read, and watched, and did. I do not remember it as a bad time at all. I am very grateful—glad—for those days of proving.

A letter came from the president of the club, formal and symmetrical and freighted with genuine regret. The executive committee felt it was in the best interests of the club that we resign. Walter wrote back doing so. He was on the phone a good deal with Charlie in those days of early summer; negotiations for the sale of his half of the business were under way and could be handled by mail or phone. As Walter had expected, Charlie's offer was more than generous. We shall have enough. Charlie offered to come by with the final papers when they were ready, but we did not want to see anyone from that other time, the time before, and they arranged to meet in the office of Charlie's lawyer.

We saw Eloise and Semmes at the farmers' market one Sunday afternoon staggering under baskets of snap beans and squash. Eloise cans endlessly. They turned away. I saw Gwen Parsons coming out of the dentist's parking lot as I was driving in. I waved and she did too, and we both smiled, but she did not slow her car alongside mine as she would have done once, and I could not see her eyes behind the dark glasses she wore.

My last two clients called and canceled their accounts. The summer drew in around us and snapped shut. No one called, no one wrote, no one came. We lived. We watched the sign on the lawn of the house next door. By the middle of June it had not sold.

Still, we watched.

ON A Friday evening in the third week in June there was a strangely familiar knock on the glass of the French door in the kitchen—two slow, three fast, two slow. I was upstairs zipping myself into shorts. In midstride down the stairs I realized that it was Kim's knock, and stopped, my heart squeezed with joy and dread. Joy won, and I ran to meet him. Walter was in the basement foraging for the power drill. I could hear his feet hurrying up the basement stairs. He knew too.

I flung the kitchen door open and had my arms around Kim before I noticed the tall girl who stood beside and a little behind him. I stared insanely at her over Kim's shoulder, the shoulder of the arm that had not moved to embrace me back. She gave me a small, uncertain smile. I released Kim, who stood still, and I stepped back and looked at the girl and at Kim.

"You've come home," I said stupidly. "I knew you would."

Walter came into the kitchen and stopped, saying nothing, looking at silent Kim Dougherty and the pretty, embarrassed girl beside him. He reached out to me and put an arm across my shoulders.

"Come in," he said to them and stood aside so that they could enter. Kim hesitated, then came into the kitchen, pushing the girl lightly ahead of him. Still he said nothing. Then he said, "I brought Hope to meet you. We—I'm going to marry her."

In the flurry of congratulations and the small business of shepherding them into the den and the bringing out of ice and drinks, the dreamlike, one-celled calm in which I had moved for so long split, and unreality rang high and chimelike around me. I did not know where I was. Frames of reference were gone; I moved around my kitchen by rote, assembling cheese and

266

crackers on a tray without knowing where I had gotten them. The den looked strange, not mine. Walter, passing drinks, was a stranger in a strange room.

"How handsome he is," I thought.

Kim looked fine, tanned and hard-muscled, his red beard neatly trimmed, his gray eyes unshadowed. But there was distance in them. The girl was tall and slender and auburn-haired, like Kim; a dusting of coppery freckles lay across her straight nose and high, pure cheekbones. Her face was strong and almost masculine, but it was the grave, delicate masculinity of a very young page boy or a medieval saint. When she smiled, as she did often, hesitantly and sweetly, it softened into a hoydenish preadolescence. She looked a lot like Kim. "Beautiful children," I thought. "They will have beautiful children, tall and coppery, like good colts."

We sat in the late-afternoon sunlight. Ice tinkled.

"How long have you been back?" Walter asked.

"Two or three days," Kim said, rubbing Razz gently with the toe of his shoe. Razz crouched at his feet roaring an anthem to renewed friendship.

"We've been up with the family for a day or two, and to see Hope's folks," Kim said. "They're old friends of my folks, it turns out. We came back here Tuesday. I'd have come by sooner, but I've been in the office with Frank most of the time. I did try to call you, but your number's not listed."

His voice was level, and he did not look at us. I was sure he must know about the *People* article; his partner would have told him. I did not think he would know yet about the general reaction. I felt no way at all, except a waiting.

"You're going back into the partnership, then," Walter said. It was not a question.

"Yes." He looked up. The specter of his old white grin flickered, was gone. "You were right about one thing, Walter. It came back. All of it, sometime during the winter. Just . . . pouring back. I'm designing faster than I can get it down on paper almost, and it's good, it's some of the best stuff I've ever done. I've got three or four ready to go right now, and Frank's got the clients for them. I don't know if it was Italy, or Hope, or just getting away for a while—I suspect all three. But I think it's really this lady here. You know, she lived about thirty miles from me all my life, and then I have to find her in a damp, smelly sub-basement of a museum in Italy, with spiderwebs in her hair and rose madder on her nose."

He smiled at the girl, and she smiled back, and there was such an envelope of rightness and youngness and joy around them that pure terror stopped my breath.

"How did you come to end up in the basement of the Uffizi?" Walter said politely to the girl.

"I took part of my senior year abroad in Florence," she said. "The usual spoiled rich-kid trip, as Kim never ceases to point out to me. And it just got to me; I couldn't leave. I was a fine arts major at school, and I talked my way into the most menial staff position they had, for no pay, and here was this grim-faced, hollow-eyed lout tramping around day after day with a sketch pad and huge big feet threatening two thousand years of priceless treasures, and one thing led to another—and here I am."

"Well, Kim is just shot through with luck, and I hope he deserves it," I smiled at her around the choking terror. "Will you be staying a while, or going back East, or what? I don't imagine you've had time to find a place to live yet; maybe I could help. You'll be married at home, I suppose, but you'll want a place to come back to. Until Kim can design your dream house for you, of course." I managed another smile. "There'd be plenty of time for me to scout around for you, if you'd like."

There was another silence, and then Kim said, "We have a place. I closed on it this morning."

"Oh, well, then—where?"

"I bought the house next door, Colquitt. The Harralson place. *My* house."

"No!" I screamed. "No, no, no, no—" Redness broke around me, and then darkness that whirled and shrieked with wind and endlessness. I could hear my voice weaving in and out of it. When I came back to myself Walter was shaking me by the shoulders, and Kim was on his feet, his face whitened under the tan with fury and a sort of child's grief. The girl still sat on the sofa, her face stiff with embarrassment.

I stopped, silent, and looked up at Kim Dougherty. "Why?" I said, but only my lips made the word. No sound came from them.

"Because I read that goddamned crazy, malign bitchery of an article you all cooked up—oh, yes, we get *People* in Italy—and I could not *stand* what you had done to my house! How could you *do* that? You of all people, Colquitt—you *loved* it, you *understood* it, right from the beginning—you were my friends, you understood what I was trying to do, what the house was saying. And you—you *killed* it! It was made for people to live in gracefully and comfortably, good people who'd appreciate what it stood for, and you've driven them all away now. Who would want it after all that stinking shit about hauntings, and forces, and— Goddamn, I couldn't *stand* it. It's still the best thing I've ever done; it always will be. And by God, Hope and I are going to live in it and love it and show the world what malicious, crazy, *warped* people you are."

He stopped and took a deep, ragged, tearing breath and did not go on.

"Kim," Walter said very slowly and distinctly. "Listen to me, Kim. Those things—they happened. Other things did too that we aren't at liberty to talk about. One of them happened to you, don't you remember? Do you think we would ever in this world have taken such a drastic step if we were not absolutely certain we were right? You know about some of it, you were here the whole time the Harralsons—you saw it all, that night. You lost your own juices because of it. And you can't have forgotten that night that you and Colquitt and I— Please, let us tell you everything we—"

"No!" he roared. "Goddamn it, no! No way am I going to listen to any more of that shit! If—if awful things happened to people over there, it was because they were awful people to begin with! People who didn't understand it, who didn't deserve to live there. *There is nothing wrong with that house!* You are both crazy, and there is nothing wrong with my house!"

"Kim," I said, and my voice sounded cracked and high and silly in my ears. "You said it yourself. You said it before any of us really caught on. Don't you remember? You said it was a greedy house, that it didn't bring out the best of everyone who lived there, it *took* the best."

He looked at me in real astonishment. "I never said that," he said. "I wouldn't have; I couldn't have. I never thought that. Nothing's gone; I'm going better than ever—I just needed the change. Everybody dries up now and then. You told me that yourself, both of you did. I just don't understand what's *happened* to you—" The anger had drained out of his voice; a child's profound hurt and bewilderment remained.

"You don't remember," I said dully. "Of course you don't. That's how it's going to get at you. That's what it's wanted all along, *you*—that's why all that other stuff, all those other things, things bad enough so that we had to make it public, public enough to reach you in Italy and get you back. Because nothing else would have, would it? You wouldn't have come back here after what happened to you. But you don't remember, and that's how it's going to get you. And that's how it will get us. By knowing that we were the ones who—brought you back to it. That's it. That has to be it."

"Colquitt . . ." There was fear and sorrow and wariness in his voice. Kim thought we were mad. Dullness and lassitude turned my lips to stone; I could hardly push the words past them. It was as if I were very drunk or had been given novocaine.

"If you live in that house," I said with my stiff lips, "it will take everything that you have. It will take your talent again, like it did before. It will take your wife. It will take the best there is in you, the essence of you, and in the end it will take your life. It will not wait long to do it either. It will be very quick this time. I will not let you do this."

"You can hardly stop me, can you, Colquitt?" he said coldly and formally. He held out his hand to the girl, and, silently, her face averted, she took it, and he pulled her to her feet.

"I can stop you," I said, but Walter cut my words off.

"When do you plan to move in, then?" he said as

calmly as if he were asking about the time or the weather.

"We're being married tomorrow, at City Hall, at two o'clock. Frank and his girl will be witnesses. We plan to move in early next week. We bought some furniture in Italy, and it's in Boston now. We won't need much at first."

"That's all right, then," Walter said, as if to himself, and Kim looked at him oddly, but he didn't say anything else. At the kitchen door he stopped and looked back.

"I'm sorry," he said briefly. "I'd hoped there was some kind of mistake. I thought there must have been."

"I'm sorry too," Walter said, and the girl murmured something, and they walked around the patio and out of sight. I said nothing.

We sat for a while in the den, numbly, watching twilight fall on the house next door.

"The realtor's sign didn't come down," I said. "I thought there would be more time. I thought we'd know."

"It wouldn't have yet, if they just closed this afternoon." Walter said.

"Tonight, then," I said.

"Yes. It will have to be very late. We can't take a chance on somebody seeing it before it gets going good."

"You don't think we could change his mind if we talked to him again . . . ?"

"No. I don't think we could change his mind."

We sat very still, not talking, and I know that I thought about nothing at all. I don't think Walter did either.

At about nine o'clock, with the last flush of the sunset fading over the trees, Kim Dougherty came back. He was alone. I watched Walter as he got up from the sofa and walked into the kitchen. His steps were stiff and small and shuffling. He will walk that way when he is very old, I thought, and then I thought, I will probably never have to see him walk that way. I'm glad. I knew that the knock on the door was Kim's knock even though he did not rap out his old signal.

It could have been no one else. A small ghost of hope brushed wings across my heart and then was gone.

Walter came back into the den, and Kim followed him, large-handed and bumbling and quiet. Remembered dearness limned him in my dry, staring eyes.

"Could you spare a drink?" Kim said. His voice was chastened and small, a boy's voice. Walter went to get the drinks. Kim sat down on the hassock by the dead fireplace and studied his shoes. Razz and Foster stretched out of sleep on the sofa and went to eel around his ankles, and he scratched under their chins absorbedly. Walter brought vodka and tonics for all of us.

Kim swirled his drink around in his glass, watching the bubbles surge and break and reform, and then he lifted his face and looked at us, first at Walter and then at me.

"I just couldn't leave it like it was," he said miserably. "I'm sorry I yelled at you. I didn't mean to do that. I didn't come to do it. I want to try to understand all this. I—we can't just live next door to you with this hanging between us. I love you. I love you both. Hope would love you—I have to understand. You must have been going through seven kinds of hell."

Tears I thought were seared forever out of me prickled in my nose and started through my lashes. The remembered dearness bloomed into life, hurting unbearably. Perhaps there was still a way . . .

Walter began to talk. He talked for a long time. I listened; Kim Dougherty listened, attentively and gravely, looking into Walter's face. Every muscle and cord and fiber in his long body strained toward understanding. Only when Walter finished did I dare to look at Kim. I looked away again. He did not believe us. There was a long silence.

"Okay," he said finally. "I don't think you're crazy and I don't believe what you believe either. But I know that you do, and I can see what it's cost you to believe it. I can respect that. I don't give a shit about the *People* thing anymore. That's over; you've said it's pretty much died down. It shouldn't have gotten to me that way. The best thing now is for you all to watch us live in it. See how happy we're going to be.

See what a *good* life the right people can have there. It *will* be a good life. And when you've watched us long enough, when there are kids running all over the place, and—oh, I don't know—parties, and dogs and cats loping around, and good vibes to chase out the bad ones—then you won't have to live with this godawful fear anymore, this sick waiting. You were brave to stay. Anybody else would have pulled out if they'd thought what you did. I know why you stayed. You're good people. You're my good friends. Let me show you now. Let me fix things for you."

I said, tiredly, infinitely tired, without hope, for the last time, "Take it off the market. Never sell it to anyone else. Pull it down. Don't live in it. Don't do that. After all, it's only your first house. There'll be others; you'll build a thousand others—"

I broke off. I heard his voice in my ears, but he wasn't speaking. It was a younger Kim's voice, and it was saying something about other buildings, buildings that weren't finished. So long, it seemed so long ago . . . I remembered then, and something began to coil into my head like smoke, something white, something that could blind.

"Kim," I said, "once, a long time ago, when we'd just met you, you said something about having had two other projects while you were in school, but that they weren't finished. What happened to them?"

Walter glanced at me and then leaned forward toward Kim, bright interest radiating from him.

Kim looked at both of us, helpless distress and puzzlement lifting the bristling red eyebrows. "They were just two projects that never got off the ground," he said. "Why?"

"No reason," Walter said chattily. "Just curious."

"Well, one was a design competition, a fancy international thing with a fat cash prize," Kim said. "A winter sports arena outside Gstaad. The winning design was to be built. My faculty adviser—God, he was absolutely convinced my design would win. I think it would have too. He'd never had a winner; he was walking on air. He wanted that prize more than anything—" He stopped and looked at Walter.

"What happened?" Walter said.

"He had a heart attack and died the day I turned it in to him. We—I didn't submit it. It was more his than mine, really; it didn't seem right—"

"And the other one?" Walter said gently. They might have just met, been exchanging small, personal histories over drinks. I listened, the white thing swelling in my head.

"A studio for a photographer. I was in school then too, but it wasn't a school project. He was a *Life* photographer, a real hotshot. Friend of the old man's. He'd always liked my work."

The question burned vividly in Walter's eyes; they were leaping with a sort of life I had not seen for a long time. A sort of social merriness, inviting comradeship and confidences. But he did not say anything.

Kim answered the eyes slowly. "There was an accident on the site while we were pouring the foundation. A freaky, one-in-a-million kind of thing. He was—he was blinded. It wasn't finished; a blind photographer doesn't need a studio."

I could not tell if the last words were bitter or an attempt at bravado. There was another silence, during which the blinding white thing in my head burst soundlessly and rang in my ears. In the ringing white silence I heard Kim say in an astoundingly normal voice, "Both things were accidents of course. Awful, but you can't afford to let things like that slow you down. Every architect gets one or two like that. Thank God, I've gotten my quota over with early." He grimaced with distaste.

"I think we all need another drink," I said and got up from the sofa and went into the kitchen. I got out ice and rattled it in the ice bucket. I heard the conversation begin again, Walter and Kim's voices mingling in low, pleasant tones, and the stereo needle scratching abruptly onto a record. The overture from *Company* swam out into the kitchen.

"Walter," I called, "can you give me a hand in here for a minute?"

We stood together in the kitchen. I looked at him. The preternatural life still burned in his eyes.

"It's not just in the house," I said, "it's in him first. In Kim. That's where it starts. It was born in him. He's a carrier, some kind of terrible carrier, and he doesn't even know it. It will be in everything he ever builds for as long as he lives, and he'll never know it."

Walter looked at me mildly. His words were brisk and reasonable and senseless.

"Don't be silly, Colquitt," he said. "He's no goddamned vampire carrying the family curse down through the generations. We know all about his family; they're good people, substantial people, wealthy—celebrities even, in a minor way. If there was anything like that in his family, don't you think somebody would know about it?"

"They're not his family," I said. "Don't you remember? He's adopted. He doesn't know who his parents are."

We stared at each other. I watched as the life wavered and ebbed out of his eyes. He nodded finally. When he spoke, his voice and his eyes and words were perfectly, endlessly flat, as flat as the misted place where a hot summer sea meets the sky.

"Okay," he said. "Call him in here. Just give me a minute."

Chapter Twenty-Seven

IT IS very late. From the position of the moon, I'd say it was past midnight at least. We have been sitting on the patio for quite a long time; I do not know how long. We sit in the two white wrought-iron chairs that we sat in the day the *People* photographer came. Our hands are clasped between the two chairs; occasionally one of us will swing our joined hands and the other will give back a small squeeze. It is very quiet, except for the song of the katydids in the trees and the liquid trill of the diminished creek where it goes over the small waterfall in its bed next door. Hot summer sounds, both.

We have said very little while we sit here. Once Walter said, "I think you were the prettiest thing I ever saw when I first met you. You had on a white dress made out of some thin kind of stuff, and about a million crinolines. You had a gardenia in your hair, of all goddamned corny things. Do you still have that dress?"

"Of course not," I said. "I gave it to Goodwill a thousand years ago. You idiot. What would I be doing with a white voile dress and all those crinolines?"

There are only a few lights on the street now. Since it is a weekend night, they will burn later than usual. I am uneasy about that. But it cannot be helped. We must wait until they all go out, and then wait at least another hour after that. The fire must get that much start anyway. I wonder who will see it first? With the Guthries gone, it will probably be the Jenningses, across the street and down a little way. That will be all right. Their bedrooms are in the back of the house, and it will be a while before they notice.

I hope we have not waited too long. Already it is reaching out across the rhododendron hedge. Already it has fingered here, and searched, and found. The bodies of Razz and Foster lie in the basement of the house next door; we found them on the deck, unmarked, looking at us open-eyed and waiting as they did in life, when we took Kim's body there earlier, and carried it between us down the basement stairs. We did not have to break a window after all. I remembered that I still had the spare key that Anita Sheehan had given me.

They are all three there now in the basement, at the foot of the stairs, beside the pile of newspapers and kindling, and the yellowed drifts of desiccated old sheer curtains I found in our attic, and the cans of lawn-mower gasoline that Walter took there earlier. We carried the cats down last. We made several trips; in the dark, being very quiet, it took us a long time. It is there, in the basement, that the fire will start, though not yet.

But we cannot wait much longer. It will not wait. I hope there will be time.

The last of the lights are going out now. The

Jenningses'; one by one, darkness climbing the stairs. They are going to bed. Only the Parsonses' lights are left. Walter holds my hand. The stars are clean and old. The creek chuckles a thousand soft secrets. The air is still; tomorrow will be hot.

I wonder how it will happen.

Epilogue

LIGHT FROM a hanging copper lamp spilled down onto a round oak table, and the girl pushed back a cup and saucer to make room for the drawings unrolled there amid the clutter of a small dinner party.

"Get that edge over there, will you, Peter?" she said to her husband. The young man reached over and pinned a curling edge of tracing paper down with his flattened hand. The paper was rather brittle; flecks powdered the tabletop. The other couple leaned over the girl's shoulder to look. The female guest gasped, a small, soft, involuntary sound of pure pleasure, and the girl lifted her face to her friends and smiled radiantly. The last of November's leaves scratched and rattled at the window of the dining ell in the small apartment.

"Isn't it *super?*" said the girl. "It's just exactly what I've always wanted, right down to the ground. I didn't even *know* exactly what I wanted until I saw it, and then that was just it. Even with all the looking we've done, we'd never have thought of building a house if these plans hadn't just fallen into our hands. We got them from this young architect Peter knows; his partner did them, oh, some time ago, I guess, when he was in Europe. I don't know who he is—or was; Peter's friend said he died not long ago. Isn't that awful? The guy didn't say how, and since it was so recent, we didn't want to ask.

"Anyway, this Frank somebody, Peter's friend, said when he heard Peter talking about the house we've been looking for, he remembered these plans, and he dug them out of the files. I don't know if the guy had ever done another house or not, but he would have been a dynamite architect if he'd lived. Just look at it. It looks like it's growing right up out of the ground, doesn't it?

"It looks like it's alive."

Bestsellers from BALLANTINE